I0593830

Finding Virtue
Book 1 of Rangers in the Void Saga

John Kent

Loyalist Publishing

BATH, ONTARIO

John Kent/Loyalist Publishing
9675 Hwy 33
Bath, Ontario, Canada, K0K1G0
www.loyalistpublishing.com

Publisher's Note: This is a work of fiction. Names, characters, places, and incidents are a product of the author's imagination. Locales and public names are sometimes used for atmospheric purposes. Any resemblance to actual people, living or dead, or to businesses, companies, events, institutions, or locales is completely coincidental.

Finding Virtue/ John Kent. -- 1st ed.
ISBN 978-0-9937285-3-2

Dedication

To my family as we start our own journey to the stars.

Few men have the virtue to withstand the highest bidder.

—GEORGE WASHINGTON

CONTENTS

Losing Optimism 1

Losing Spirit 27

Losing Dignity 43

Losing Grace 59

Losing Peacefulness 69

Losing Temperance 89

Finding Integrity 103

Finding Fortitude 123

Finding Charity 137

Finding Hope 147

Finding Temperance 161

Finding Reason 191

Finding Prudence 205

Finding Honour 225

Finding Grace 243

Finding Benevolence 259

Finding Loyalty 279

Chapter 1

Losing Optimism

"What can you do, Gideon?" Theo Stinson asked as he stumbled into the engine room, the old engineer on his heels, the alarms blaring through the rest of the ship drowned out by the two chugging engines set on either side of the large room.

Theo's ship wasn't the gem of any fleet. She had three decks, the living quarters one hundred feet wide and five times that distance in length. The walls were their original steel gray and the paint curled at the corners and around door frames as the cold of space seeped into her bones. For the most part, however, it got them where Theo wanted to go. She wasn't fast, but he'd never missed a deadline or destination. Granted she broke down, but that's what Gideon lived for. The old man, his metal-braced knees bowed and knuckles gnarled, would likely die if his old ship couldn't fly anymore. Theo almost felt sorry for the man, knowing that this was likely their last trip. *Maybe you can convert her to one of those floating homes I heard about.*

Though Theo had intended to give his crew this news, the opportunity hadn't presented itself and the day was proving troublesome. *I'll get to it as soon as we land,* he thought. His crew was a little busy at the moment and calling them together for a meeting wouldn't be prudent. In truth, he'd made his decision the moment he'd accompanied his engineer into the engine compartment and watched the three grease-covered techs scrambling to keep the engines sputtering along; one man had singe marks on his sleeves.

This last load of cargo would earn enough for Theo to retire the ship. *Enough for everyone to retire,* Theo thought. His ship, the *Galena,* deserved better, however. He couldn't just let the ship drift into retirement, her engines going quiet. *It just doesn't feel right,* he thought as he glanced up to the vaulted ceiling where two overhead gangways ran the length of the room for access to the engines from above.

The day Theo had taken possession of the ship, he'd stood on that gangway to look out over what he'd done. He'd sat down with his wife to eat the picnic lunch she'd prepared, and they'd made plans for their eventual retirement. *It's time, Galena.* He wasn't sure whether he spoke to his wife or the ship, her namesake.

Gideon sighed and frowned, making his bushy eyebrows bristle. Had they been in any other situation, Theo would have been tempted to laugh, but instead he only noticed the stress radiating from his friend's eyes. *You haven't slept.* Gideon's hands shook violently from barely controlled excitement as he tried to tear the scorched shielding off the massive starboard engine that filled half the room.

Gideon glanced at Theodore. "Lad, I don't even know what's wrong with her. This morning when I came in, she was purring like a kitten, but now she's knocking like nothing I've ever heard. I don't even know if it was something that happened when we were attacked. It could just as easily be the temperamental bitch trying to get back at me for thinking of another woman last night. I don't think I pushed her too hard."

Theo closed his eyes. He inhaled the acrid smell of burnt Bakelite. *So hot, to burn?* Flames had burned the coating from some of the wires that ran back and forth along the ceiling and walls. *There's more,* Theo thought as he tried to sense what the old man was getting at.

Theo stood for almost a minute, striving to understand what the motors were trying to tell him, before he heard the intermittent knock the old man had mentioned. "One, two, three—knock; one, two—knock; one, two, three—knock."

"That's it, lad. Something's out of whack back there, but I can't tell what. I'm just glad it's only the one." Gideon stood with his own eyes closed, counting the knocks, though Theo could see he was counting far more knocks than he had. *What else aren't you telling me, Gideon?* he thought as the old man wrung his grease-covered hands. Two of the technicians raced by, carrying a large box filled with what Theo assumed were spare parts.

Theo pulled back and sighed. So close to Earth; all they had to do was stop. A small knock shouldn't make that impossible. After a minute of near silence, he took a deep breath and said, "Listen, Gideon. I don't feel like dying today. I am going home to Galena tonight, to whisk her off her feet and tell her that I love her."

Mention of his wife made Theo smile. He envisioned her thick, curly black hair, falling down over her face again, but he didn't need to see her luminous green eyes to know they were smiling at him. Involuntarily he let his mental gaze caress her body, following the voluptuous curve of her breasts and down to her hips. That was when she took her fists off her hips and punched him in the chin for taking the ship out again when he should have sent it in for a retrofit. *Ah, love,* he thought.

Theo shook his head and focused on the old man as Gideon said, "Ha! Lad, I would have thought you'd given that wish up about five hours ago, when those pirates hit us."

The day had dawned like any other, Theo waking to the chime signalling messages waiting for him from the crew, his wife, and a dozen companies either on Earth or Mars, all looking for him to transport their goods. The pirates had been a wrench he'd neither expected nor cared to deal with. Theo had been dealing with real and figurative fires ever since.

But pirates couldn't make Theo forget the fire he had for his wife. Taking a deep breath, he said, "Never, Gideon, never. You know her as well as I do. Now, tell me what I can do."

Over the years he'd spent enough time with Gideon to know the old man loved to complain almost as much as he loved to fix the ship. Theo had also learned to ignore the old man when he was doing both. When Gideon needed something, he would place it in front of Theo and let him know it was time to act. Until then, the engineer and his people would continue to race to and from, repairing or replacing as necessary until they couldn't anymore. *We'll be fine.*

Gideon shook his head. "Pray, lad. Go back up to your bridge and pray. I'll call when I figure out what's wrong down here. And for God's sake, don't ask for more power."

Theo and his crew had come through many close calls with the *Galena.* The ship had seen a lot of damage in her day. There were more welded repairs than original connections on the hydraulic and pneumatic systems, and he expected they could likely make duct tape a general expense, the way Gideon used it.

"Listen, lad—" Gideon ducked as something crackled in the rear of the compartment, sending one of the techs scrambling from behind the engine to investigate "—I've got this. Get up there and make the crew happy. It's what you do best."

Theo turned and made his way back through the engine room, his mind on the engines as they roared like warring gods, one baritone, the other an octave higher. As Theo moved, he saw the great engines for what they were: a bloated collection of years of repair. More than a dozen colours reflected the various ships they'd stripped to cobble her together. Dings marred the surface of the engines, some from ballistics weapons fire, others from Gideon in the strange love-hate relationship he had with his Frankenstein-like creation.

Hundreds of cables lined the walls and ceiling, many no longer connected to actual power conduits, as they were reserved for specific terrible events like plasma fires in either the starboard or port thrusters. Gideon even had one cable running the length of the ship labelled in writing Theo couldn't decipher. *And he likely wouldn't answer if I asked anyway. But then*, Theo thought as he reached the hatch between the engine room and the corridor that ran the length of his transport ship, *at least you're prepared*. Theo had met more than a few useless engineers in his time. He'd trade every other engineer he'd employed for an hour of Gideon's time. The old man had a symbiotic relationship with the ship and knew even the slightest change in the sounds she made. If anyone could get them home safe, it was Gideon.

Theo turned the wheel to open the hatch and slipped out over the bulkhead into the dark hall, jumping into the air to float gently while he swung wide to pull the hatch closed. With the power reserves sinking after the pirate attack, Theo had ordered nonessential systems cut, and that meant gravity. *Who needs it, anyway?* he thought as he smirked and rolled his eyes. *Gideon,* he silently added with one last glance back at the hatch, as though he could see through it. The old engineer was lost if he didn't have his feet planted firmly on the deck.

Turning the gravity off wasn't just flipping a switch however. The graviton particles coursing through the plasma conduits embedded in the floor panels were only stable when the energy output was consistent. Cutting the gravity likely saved their lives. *That'd be just what we needed. Death by black hole when the graviton's went into unstable deceleration.*

With practised ease, Theo dragged himself along the narrow corridor, grabbing the hooks welded to the ceiling at five-foot intervals. He made his way through the old ship towards the bridge, and ducking his head under massive overhead pipes, their faded paint beginning to peel. No footfalls echoed on the grated steel floor aloft. *I miss that sound.* He preferred the screeching of the engines, even if it meant something was wrong.

Another closed hatch waited at the end of the hall. *Finally,* he thought as he rubbed his hands against the pock marks in the steel.

The idea of having the air purged from the ship because someone forgot to seal a hatch wasn't Theo's idea of fun. He'd been half tempted to run a drill and vent the oxygen just to see the crew's reaction. *Fix everything up good and proper then.*

Theo paused before entering the bridge. He closed his eyes and leaned his forehead against the ceiling, the chill of the steel radiating over his skin. *You've gotten us home every time, girl. You can do it. I have faith.* The ship was almost four decades old, having flown thousands of AUs, but the last few trips to Jupiter Station had been hard on her. She was tired and needed a complete overhaul. *Just one more trip, love,* he thought, envisioning his return home to his wife.

Theo was sure his ship would have been fine, weathering the re-entry into Earth's atmosphere with ease, except for the pirate attack hours earlier. *Thankfully, we repelled them.* He winced and dropped his hand to the bandage on his thigh. He opened his eyes again to count the dark smudges on the wall where the pirates had nicked the hydraulic lines with their weapons.

Theo entered the bridge to find his crew strapped to their seats, shivering, their breath visible as they spoke. His first officer, Mykaela, sat in the centre of the room frowning as she listened to their constant reports.

Though Theo loved Galena, whom he'd married over two decades earlier, he did understand Mykaela's irresistible allure. Her deep brown eyes were like chocolate, seductive and sweet. He'd even caught Galena looking once or twice, caressing the woman with her eyes.

Mykaela took a deep breath before asking, "What news do you have, Theodore?" The words curled off her tongue like music.

Theo shook his head. "He's trying to… Gideon… He'll come up with something. He always does." He wiped the droplet of perspiration from his brow. *Just a small situation to deal with. Nothing special.* They'd been in some awful places and every time, Gideon had coaxed a little more life from his ship.

He noticed the furtive glances between Mykaela and the command staff, and raised his voice to say, "Listen to me, people. This is not the first time we've been this close. Do you remember the time the engines cut out and we skimmed the surface of the Moon? Yeah, that was closer than this one. The *Galena* still has scars from that encounter."

The name of Theo's ship had caused a few misunderstandings in his time, but he didn't have the heart to change the name he'd given her when he'd taken her over. *Doesn't feel right,* he thought. *Gideon wouldn't like it.*

Zak, the navigation officer, cleared his throat. "Hey, I still hear about that one when we go to the Moon base. 'Oh yeah,' they say, 'there was once a ship that almost grazed the dome.' I can't help but laugh."

Theo silently thanked the rotund man and earmarked him for a reward for this timely remark. "That's right Zak, we only had minutes to light the fires, but we did. Gideon lit them." Theo punched the air with his fist to accentuate his point. Several officers wore forced smiles. *Come on, people, work with me.* Before he lost his momentum, he said, "And some of you might remember the time we ran out of fuel just before we got to Mars? Yeah, that one wasn't fun at all, but we're all still alive. I have never lost a ship, ever."

Theo had to admit there had been more to the last story, but it was so long ago that most of the crew wouldn't remember it well. Of course, they'd survived, the ship coming away with little or no damage, but only after they'd converted their cargo to fuel. If offered the choice again, he would do the same thing. His people came first and he could absorb the loss of the cargo if he had to. *But only if I have to.* The cargo they carried now was more than lucrative, almost invaluable.

Theo took another deep breath. *That's right, Kat, nod a bit more. Ah, and you too, Frankie boy.* "You know Gideon is the best at what he does. He knows this ship even better than I do. He even sleeps here when we're docked. He'll make it work." Gideon didn't live on the ship, but it worked for effect as the communications and internal systems officers both smiled as if reliving their triumphs. *That's it. Come on over to my side of it.*

Theo closed the hatch and pushed off the wall to float toward the centre of the bridge. The room doubled as a communications room, with the short- and long-range officers sitting near the back of the room, where dozens of screens flashed with information. Like the rest of the ship, the room was square and functional. Every square foot was built to earn a profit.

Theo reached out, catching Mykaela's outstretched hand, and pulled himself to his seat, a leather-clad cushion that folded down from a recessed nook beside the first officer. As he landed, he shifted his gaze to the rest of his crew. "We're going to make it, people. I promise you that, just like Gideon promised me." *Well, he would have if I'd asked him, I'm sure of it.*

Theo took the time to meet each officer's gaze, locking long enough to offer a private nod of thanks and a whispered word of encouragement. *It's alright. We'll get through this. I promise.* When he was finished, he turned back to his first officer and asked, "What can you tell me?"

"We've got communications back online. There are several ships within distance, but they won't be able to do anything until we slow down."

That's encouraging, at least. We must be closer to Earth than I expected.

Mykaela went silent for a few moments before leaning closer to speak quietly enough that only Theo could hear. "I understand you want to be here, Theodore, but perhaps you should speak to Petr. I can do this."

Theo closed his eyes as the woman mentioned his son's name. He'd been trying unsuccessfully for the last hour to figure out what he should do with his son. It wasn't the first time he'd accepted Petr's insistence on accompanying him to Mars, but Theo hadn't expected the pirate attack earlier that morning. The pirates had wreaked havoc on the ship, storming through like conquering barbarians, stealing anything not welded to the deck. Theo was sure Petr would have been taken too, if he hadn't been secreted away in one of the more discreet holds.

Theo pursed his lips and asked, "Where is he?"

The woman shook her head and shrugged before saying, "I would guess in the centre."

Of course, Theo thought. He'd hoped Petr had been sedated as he'd requested, but someone, most likely Mykaela herself, had contravened his order. The exotic woman doted on Petr like he was her own and rarely let Theo put him into deep sleep as they re-entered the atmosphere. She didn't understand the pressure Petr felt when they returned to the proper gravity of Earth, a pain a spacer couldn't understand. *And you won't tell her for fear she will look at you differently, will you, bud?*

Theo dropped the belt buckle he was about to lock. He didn't waste any time explaining himself to his officers as he bunched he legs and pushed himself from his chair. "I'll be back in a minute. Keep an eye on Gideon."

As Theo came to the hatch, he placed his hand on the frame and turned back to his bridge crew. "We'll get through this, people. I promise." He smiled as the words washed over him like the light of the sun, slowly warming everything it touched.

Pulling himself past several closed hatches along the corridor, Theo finally floated toward a black metal door that stood in stark contrast to the slate grey of the wall. He tried the latch once and sighed as it refused to give, merely clicking as he pulled on it. *Come on, Petr,* he thought as he pounded on the door with his fist, *we don't have time for this, buddy. You gotta let me in.*

Theo wasn't sure how long he floated in the hall, pounding on the door, before the latch clicked and the metal door swung inward to expose a pitch-black interior. *Not a big fan of this,* Theo thought as he pulled himself through the hatch and latched it behind him. *I hope no one needs us.* He shuddered as the last vestige of light was stolen with the closing door.

Theo floated without speaking until the only thing he could hear over the ringing in his ears was his son's raspy breathing. After a minute of the deafening silence he pushed off the wall and gently floated inward until he hit his son and Petr let out a muted grunt.

He opened his mouth to speak several times, falling silent until he felt Petr shudder once, and then again only seconds later. *I'm sorry, bud,* Theo thought as he wrapped his arms around his son and pulled him into an embrace. "It's going to be okay, Petr."

Theo wasn't sure how long he held his son, but after a time, Petr's sniffles quieted enough to say, "I-I—Gideon said the ship was going to . . ." Unable to finish, he buried his face into Theo's shoulder.

"Hush, child," Theo said, frustrated that he couldn't see Petr's face to wipe the tears away. *Damn darkness.* "Gideon didn't mean that. He's just sad that he can't fix everything quickly this time."

"But . . ." Petr started, but then fell silent.

Theo hated the room where they floated. If light could ever shine within the room it would have illuminated a space five paces cubed. Pressurized, it was an archaic medical apparatus designed to calm the wayward soul suffering from any number of mental and several physical maladies. It didn't work for Theo, though, as every time he entered, he felt as if he were swimming outside the ship, his lungs about to be sucked into the vacuum. Every second was an eternity as he railed at the walls of his silent prison, the gravity pulling him in every direction at once. They were held perfectly in the centre of the room without straying in any direction.

Theo kissed the back of his son's head and said, "Gideon is the best, Petr, but sometimes he needs help. Maybe you and I can give him a hand, then we'll make it back to Earth for sure. Do you want to do that? You're way smarter than I am. You'll know what do to."

It was no lie. Petr's aptitude for the ship was far greater than Theo's. He'd been taking the ship's systems apart since he was barely old enough to walk. When he was permitted to accompany Theo on his weekly trips, he'd started solving some of the issues even Gideon had found trying.

"I don't wanna help him. I hate him," Petr said softly as he wiped his nose on Theo's shoulder.

"Sure, buddy. We can both do it. You can tell me what to do and Gideon will be impressed with what we accomplish. I'll even give you part of my cut."

Petr didn't care for the money, but he would understand Theo's need for it and absolute distaste for giving up a penny, even if it was to his son. Theo was sure that Petr would be moved by the gesture. On cue, Petr pulled away, saying, "Do you promise not to yell at me again?"

Theo silently thanked any god that was listening that Petr couldn't see the pain he knew was painted on his face. *Yell?* He licked his parched lips as his stomach churned. "Petr. Buddy, I didn't mean to yell at you. I just…I just meant for you to be safe. I didn't want those bad people to get you."

"But you told the doctor to put me to sleep. I hate being asleep."

So young? Theo was surprised with how old his son sounded. Petr spoke with more clarity than most of his crew and understood the complexities of science that Theo would never grasp. Theo secretly wished Petr would learn to hate the ship so he would someday go to university and become one of the scientists the government was always talking about needing. Petr the Great would one day solve the resource shortage on Earth and would never have to travel between planets where the terrible monsters of Theo's nightmares lived. *Space pirates.*

Theo took a deep breath, catching the soft scent of his son's hair. For a second, he was taken back to when his son had fallen off his bicycle and sat on their porch, crying. Theo had held him then as he did now, whispering to him that everything would be fine. *It was raining that night,* Theo thought. *So different on Earth. It's almost safe there.*

When Theo spoke, his voice was low, still lost in those memories. "I know, buddy, but it was the safest place for you at the time. You know I hate this room. It isn't safe for you if the power gets cut. I would never know you were in here because knocking on the door is the only way to talk to anyone in here."

Theo rolled gently around, preparing to swim back to the hatch, then silently cursed the room when he was unable to move. That was the other reason he hated it. Without gravity, it was impossible to move within it. *Hate doesn't even come close to what I think of this godforsaken hole.*

When Theo had been forced to use the room after he'd first taken possession of the *Galena,* it had almost driven him mad. Unable to speak to those beyond the sealed hatch, Theo had lived in silence, devoid of smell and touch for almost a week. *I have to get out of here.*

"Hey buddy, if I push you toward the wall, can you make it?"

Though he couldn't see Petr's face, Theo recognized the condescension in his son's voice as Petr said, "You aren't supposed to come in here without the propellant, Father."

Theo rolled his eyes. *Propellant. Of course. Why didn't I think of that?* He had to laugh to himself—he was discussing the finer points of propulsion in zero gravity when the ship around them was hurtling toward Earth, the engines out of sync and about to turn to dust. With a sly sense of irony, he couldn't tell which was more important, spending time with his son in his last moments or actually going out to help Gideon fix the ship.

Theo shook his head. "No. It's been a rough day, buddy. I didn't bring a propellant, but I think you can help me with that."

"What do you mean, father—oh, I understand. You're going to throw me and then use the back pressure to hit the back wall. That's a good idea. You should take my propellant, then."

"You got 'er, buddy," Theo said with a smile, though Petr wouldn't see it. *I knew you'd have one, bud. Just have to get you across first.*

Just as Petr had surmised, Theo put his arms on Petr's shoulder and pushed him toward the hatch. End over end, Petr spun away as Theo was pushed toward the back wall. They slammed into their respective walls almost simultaneously. *Let's get the hell out of here,* Theo thought as he fidgeted with the can of propellant he'd pilfered from Petr's belt as he'd pushed.

He bunched his legs and pushed off the wall, flying toward where he assumed the hatch was with one arm outstretched before him, the other aiming the can of air behind him. *Damnit,* he thought, realizing too late that Petr hadn't moved from his path. Theo tried to roll away, but too late; he hit Petr, pinning him against the door. Petr released the hatch and they burst out into the corridor, Theo sprawling on the floor, his can of air sputtering away out of control. It spun around for several seconds until the pressure released. *There's gravity,* he thought as he pushed himself to his feet. He cocked his head to the side. "There's gravity," he said aloud.

Turning to his father, Petr lifted his hand to wipe his eye before matter-of-factly saying, "Of course there's gravity. The black room is the only one that doesn't have it." He licked the blood from his lip and held his arm tight to his body, as if he'd burned it.

How long were you in there? Theo wondered. Petr must have been in the room for hours, since before Theo had ordered the power cut to the gravity. *At least you were in there during the last explosion.* Theo bent to collect his son in his arms, sighing as he momentarily rested his head on the boy's shoulder.

With gravity, Theo's feet were on the deck. *Now we're talking,* he thought as he closed his eyes, the sound of the ship embracing him like a lover. As he listened, Theo hitched his son up farther. "Come on, bud." Having the gravity back wasn't a casual event to be laughed at however. The energy required to establish the graviton flow was as close to astronomical as Theo understood and Gideon wouldn't have started the plasma matrix without reason. Especially when *it's not smooth,* Theo thought as he felt his weight fluctuate with every step. Theo had visions of tiny black holes perforating the floor as the gravitons flitted in and out of quantum space.

The echo of Theo's footfalls were a lover's caress as he quickly moved away from the terrible room Mykaela called the centre. *Anywhere but there.* Theo marched down the hall, ducking as he came to the pneumatic pipes so Petr wouldn't hit his head. When he reached the engine room, Theo found the hatch hanging open. He set his son down and stepped over the bulkhead, swearing as he knocked his shin against the steel. Tears welled instantly as he reached down to rub his legs. *Ouch, ouch, ouch,* he thought as he looked around the large room.

"What are you back for, lad?" Gideon said as he passed them, his legs creaking. The knock in the engines was more pronounced and accompanied by a squeal that sounded like the rotors were dragging and metal was scraping on metal.

Theo smiled and glanced down at Petr. "Petr and I came to help you." *Obviously, you need it,* he added silently.

Theo could see the emotions warring silently on Gideon's weathered face as the old man tried to determine the best response. *That's right, leave the crass comments at the door. We're here for Petr,* Theo thought as he dropped his hand to his son's shoulder.

After a time, Gideon's shoulders fell and he exhaled as he said, "I still don't know what I'm looking at and now it's screaming like a banshee. That girl that…uh, anyway, I…never mind. It's loud."

Theo glanced back to the corridor. "And the gravity?"

"There was a spike. I had to divert the energy somewhere," Gideon explained as he limped away from Theo and Petr. Spikes in energy output were bad in general and disastrous when they were already travelling too fast. *At least we could turn the heat up,* Theo thought as he shivered. Normally he was used to the cold of space, but his officers would appreciate a little more heat up in the bridge. *Heat would be a little safer than playing havoc with the gravity matrix too.*

Theo followed Gideon around the shadow of the large power generator on the starboard side of the room, saying, "What's your theory?"

"Do you think we'd be in this mess if I had a theory? I'd be fixing the damn thing so we could—"

A thunderous rumble erupted from the back of the room and a ball of bluish flame exploded forward. Theo watched in horror as the flames hungrily licked toward them, the liquid fire boiling over the engine in slow motion to run toward them like lava. Theo could feel the heat rising as he slowly turned back to where he'd left his son, a scream dying on his lips.

Theo felt the flames envelop his back as he scuttled around the generator. In one last lunge, he wrapped his son in an embrace to shield Petr from the explosion, just as they were both thrown toward the corridor hatch.

Theo cried out as the hair on his arms and head burned away. The heat coursed up his body as the flames danced around him, scorching every exposed surface on his body. His outer shirt and pants were gone in an instant. He curled himself around his son, refusing to let the flames touch the boy.

When Theo was able to open his eyes again, he lifted his head from his chest to survey the damage. *Thank God for thermosuits,* he thought with a sigh. Even so, the skin on the back of his head and neck cracked audibly as he moved and his arms still throbbed from the heat. *But I'm alive,* he thought, wincing as he shifted to let Petr stand. *I am alive.*

Theo's breathing was shallow. The oxygen in the room had burned away. When he was able to speak, he said, "Gid...Gideon." He tried again, louder. He had to yell several times before the old man crawled out from around the generator. He'd fared better, with only limited burns to his skin. His temple was bleeding and he squinted and blinked as if he couldn't focus on Theo.

Tears streamed down Gideon's face as he caressed the frame of the generator. "I can't fix it. I just can't do it. We're all going to burn." Gideon bit his tongue as he glanced at Petr.

Petr stared at the old man, his mouth hanging open. Cocooned in Theo's embrace, he'd weathered the fire storm without injury, but the words Gideon uttered left him speechless as he shifted his gaze between the two men. He shuddered violently and fell to his knees, the tears starting and running freely. "I want to see Mom. Father, please, can you…?"

Aw hell, what am I going to do now? Theo looked around the room. *Whatever it is, I'm going to need a stim to keep me awake.*

Though the end of the room where Theo and Petr stood was relatively unscathed, the far end was blackened by the explosion and fires still spouted from several ports on the engines. Theo wrinkled his nose at the acrid odour of burnt plastic from the destroyed consoles mounted on the walls. *At least the engine's stopped,* Theo thought as the room fell silent, but for the occasional groan from the generators.

"We have to get out of here," he said as he looked back to the hatch. *Airlocked,* he thought. Thanks to the fires raging through the engine room, he wasn't able to open the hatch and leave at all. *We're stuck.*

Theo glanced at his son, his own pain washed away as the last conversation he'd had with his wife coursed through his mind. It had been simple, with him denying any chance that pirates would attack. He'd flown hundreds of times without incident, compared to the few bow shots they'd received. The *Galena* was large enough that few pirates thought her weak enough to attack. Regardless, his wife had made him promise that he wouldn't let their son come to harm. *No one will cause him pain,* he thought. But Theo couldn't take Petr back to the black room and just leave him to wonder when the end was coming. *We'll come up with something. We have to.*

They needed to discover a way out, or they would suffocate. Already his breathing had become shallower. Theo calculated the air left at only a few minutes. He sighed and quietly whispered, "And quickly."

He made eye contact with his son and beckoned him closer. "Come here, Petr."

He could see Petr's breathing was laboured as he stepped closer. *Please don't make me do this. We have to find a way.* He couldn't let it end this way, his son gulping for air or burned from another explosion. Theo reached out for his son and stifled a moan as a portion of his shirt tore from his charred flesh and made him swoon, the room spinning around him. As he held his son's head gently between his hands, Theo heard the rumbling of another explosion about to spew flames in their direction. *Forgive me,* he thought as he brushed his fingers through his son's hair.

Another growl emanated from the back of the room. Theo hiccupped and held his son tighter. *Please no,* he thought and shuddered, tensing in expectation of the next explosion. "Close your eyes, Petr," he whispered and lifted his hand to cover Petr's mouth. *Forgive me.*

Petr gulped for air and said, "Fa—Father, why doesn't Gideon just do what we did in the black room?"

Theo closed his eyes, realizing Petr was oblivious to his plan. Petr was still trying to solve the mystery of their propulsion system. "What, buddy? What do you mean?"

"We're moving too fast, right?" Petr asked as he wiped more tears from his face. "Well, why don't we just dump the transport section and use it to stop us? Equal and opposite reaction, right?"

"Because buddy, we –"

Gideon limped closer and began to laugh, silencing Theo. His guffaws continued for almost a minute until he managed to say through gulps of air, "Ha! Petr's right. He's bloody right. We've been so focused on keeping the cargo with us that we missed our opportunity. Think, lad. We're trying to find a way to slow us down and control our attitude for re-entry. We don't have to. To hell with the cargo, I say, and the trajectory. We're close enough to Earth. All we need to do is stop."

"What are you suggesting?" Theo asked. His arms shook from being clenched around his son for so long. *Is there a way?* Any chance was worth exploring, but detaching the cargo hold required him to be on the other side of the door. Assuming the pirates didn't return, he could easily arrange for another ship to reacquire the hold. He would still be able to salvage the operation. *Though Gideon's likely going to lose his new house,* he thought.

"What do you need, Gideon?"

"Cut the umbilical," Gideon said flatly as he turned and started limping back toward the engines. The rumbling got louder.

Slowly shaking his head, Theo said, "Stay here, Petr. I'll be right back." He'd been the one to lock the system. *I'm sure I can undo it.* If he'd set the system to lock in an emergency, there had to be a way to unlock it.

Theo couldn't look his son in the eyes. Petr didn't know his end had been seconds away at Theo's hands; that his father had almost killed him. If that had happened, Theo wouldn't have waited to finish himself off. He wouldn't have been able to do anything else, too overwhelmed by the thoughts of killing his son. But now, he almost felt as if he'd already done the deed, and he stood in front of Petr's ghost, trying to explain why. He had no excuses, however; he stood naked, bereft of a shield to protect himself from Petr's insinuating stare. *I'm so sorry.*

Theo took off towards the hatch, unconsciously pulling on the handle before he realized it was magnetically locked. *Of course. That's why I came, isn't it?* Something must have hit him over the head, scrambling his brain, and he continued to flounder. He sighed and shifted away from the door to look at the scorched terminal beside it. He could hear Gideon's metal legs screeching as the old man disappeared behind the generator. *Find them, Gideon,* he thought, wondering if the techs had found refuge.

As Theo stared at the wall he felt what was left of his pant leg being pulled. Before Theo could even react, Petr opened a small sliding panel to the side of the hatch and adjusted wires and fuses. When he was finished, Petr stood back on his heels and smiled at his father before saying, "Well, open it."

Theo's attention was still on the fires burning farther down the compartment. His first thought was that he needed to keep the flames from reaching the other compartments, that the crew could vent the oxygen in the room, at least. *But that won't save them,* he thought as he reached out and pulled the handle. Everyone had a job on his ship. He had to do this. As though waiting for his command all along, the hatch capitulated, hissing open and violently crashing against the wall. *Oh Petr, you are a genius.* Only a genius could have circumvented his measures.

Theo jumped through the bulkhead, this time missing the knee-knocker, and started down the hall toward the bridge. With every limping step he took, the world shrank to the pain in his back that lanced down his legs. It was accentuated when gravity periodically let go and then returned, throwing him into the air only long enough to force him back down in a violent shuddering motion.

When he reached the end of the hall, Theo turned back toward the black room, then after ten steps he slipped around another corner. He stopped at the latch that would release the cargo. *This'll work. Only thing left will be to collect it later.* The gravity gave out again. Unsure whether it was by choice or accident, Theo floated into the air until he was standing on the ceiling, chest heaving. Sweat beaded on his forehead and his breathing was hoarse as he swallowed the bile in his mouth. *I can do this. It's nothing.*

Theo bunched his legs and pulled hard on the handle until it gave way. He had to reset his grip three times until the pressure let go, rubbing the flesh on his hands raw. "Damn," he said and then hurled, the mess floating outward like a cloud.

When Theo recognized his son floating in the air, gaping at him, he said, "It's okay, buddy. We're going to be okay. Why don't we go find—"

As Petr opened his mouth to reply, another voice interjected: "Captain, we need you on the bridge."

Theo shook his head as he looked at the officer floating beyond his son. *Sonya?* Why did his communications officer make her way from the bridge when she could have just called on his radio? *Comms are down.* The woman must have been designated a runner as soon as they'd felt the engine explode.

Taking a deep breath, Theo asked, "What do you want, Sonya?"

"Sir," the woman said breathlessly, as though she'd been swimming through the hallways for some time. She was smiling. Her body trembled with ill-contained energy. "There's a ship close enough."

Finally! Theo raised his eyebrow. "A ship?" *A ship. Freedom.*

"Yes sir. You have to come," the woman blurted, motioning for them to follow.

Theo raised his hand to cover his mouth as he began to cough. When he was finished, he gulped for air before saying, "Go with her, Petr. I'll be right behind you." *I need a stim.*

Petr nodded, his eyes lingering on his father for several seconds before he turned to follow the woman through the narrow corridors, dragging himself on the hooks welded to the ceiling.

As soon as they'd turned away from him, Theo swallowed hard, a grimace contorting his face. He rolled his head around several times as he tried to force the pain from his mind. *I can do this. Everything is going to be fine.*

When he reached the bridge, it was abuzz with activity. When he'd left, the officers were sullenly looking at the computer consoles, unwilling to meet his gaze. When he entered, they were rhyming off information for Mykaela. Latched to her seat, his executive officer was absorbing each report before ordering the officer on to the next task. When she saw Theo enter, she asked his escort, "Did you find Gideon, Sonya?"

The officers all fell silent, their gazes locked on Theo. "It's fine. Just a scratch." They must have known what he was doing, as the screen at the front of the room showed the transport section of his ship pulling away from the bridge. The gap was widening as the thrusters sputtered and the cargo hold spiralled off into the distance. Thankfully space offered something Earth lacked: room. *This is going to work,* he thought.

"What...what happened?" Mykaela asked breathlessly as she unlatched her belt and floated to his side. She cast a look at an officer on the far side of the bridge, silently calling for the medical kit.

As the woman approached with the kit and set about wrapping his hands, Theo asked, "What's our situation?" The instant the soothing salve touched his skin, Theo sighed. It numbed all feeling in his hands. *Better than stims,* he thought.

Sonya had already returned to her post. "We have two ships coming our way," she said. "They're both coming as fast as they can. It looks like the smaller one is going to win." She sighed as she finished, as if they'd already been saved and not just awaiting the prospect.

"Who are they?" Theo asked, wincing as Mykaela tended the burns on his neck.

"You don't want to know," Mykaela replied quietly so the rest of the officers couldn't hear.

Theo narrowed his eyes. "Who is it, Kae?"

"The small ship is an Earth-Moon shuttle," she said, her smile firm, her lips drained of colour.

Theo immediately understood it was the second ship she was afraid of as she turned away, unable to meet his gaze. "Who is the second ship, Mykaela?" He didn't need her to respond to know the answer. *Pirates.*

"Pirates," she whispered, echoing his thoughts. "I don't think they know yet." She nodded toward the officers diligently working at their stations.

Theo had to close his eyes to work through the throbbing pain. As it subsided, he breathlessly said, "Get me the shuttle captain."

"You aren't in any –"

"I am the captain, Mykaela; please let me do my job." As he spoke Theo pushed off and floated toward his chair as the salve that Mykaela had applied began to tingle along his neck. Theo glanced around to make sure his son was nestled in the cubicle built for him. He nodded to Petr's smile. *We're going home, buddy. This day is going to end soon.*

"Sir, I have the shuttle, Captain Kai," the communication officer announced.

Theo glanced to the screen. "Let me speak to him."

"Her, sir," the woman replied before adjusting the screen to show a woman's face.

Smiling, the woman immediately said, "Hello, Captain. I am not sure what we'll be able to do for you." She didn't notice until she was finished speaking how injured Theo was. When he began to speak, the woman's smile faded and her eyes narrowed. He could see her swallow.

"Captain Kai," Theo began. He imagined that his voice was calm as he spoke. "Do you have the technology to latch onto our transport section?"

Nodding, the woman said, "Yes, of course, Captain, but I understand you need assistance with your ship. Your lives are more important than your cargo. Perhaps the larger ship trailing you would be more suited to tractor the transport."

No time like the present, Theo thought as he chewed his lip. "Captain Kai, I don't want to alarm you, but that ship isn't going to offer any assistance. In fact, if I were you I would understand if you didn't want to help us for fear of crossing them."

The smile etched on Kai's face was practiced as she said, "I understand your predicament. What would you have me do?" She barely looked at her own people as she spoke.

"Come alongside our docking clamp," Theo said immediately. "We evacuate first and then we'll try for the transport." *With luck they'll still try to board.*

"Will they ignore us if they have your ship?" Captain Kai asked smoothly as she made several hand signals to her crew.

"I don't know," Theo admitted. "I think so." Pirates salvaged ships as often as they stole cargo. Theo had seen entire ships stripped to the frame.

"Well, at least there's something to look forward to," Kai said whimsically just before the screen went black. She understood the code and felt no qualms with the gift he planned to leave them.

"Okay, people, get the hell down to that hatch. Sound the alarm and move," Theo ordered.

On a typical trip, Theo's ship usually had fifteen crew members. His ship wasn't automated and required as many officers to fix her as it did to fly her. The recent attack by the pirates had injured two crew members and he still wasn't sure about the techs from the engine room. He hoped the alarms would warn the others of their intentions, calling them to the emergency hatch where Kai was going to dock.

The last to leave, Theo turned to look back through the bridge. Sighing and shaking his head, he whispered, "Goodbye, friend." That's what it felt like. He wasn't just leaving his dearest friend, but leaving her to nothingness. Those pirates were going to strip her down and rape her, leaving nothing but a broken body bereft of life. *Take her,* he said. *And remember me when she bites back.*

Theo waited for a few seconds, hoping the ship would whisper back, but when she didn't answer, he swung the hatch closed and turned away, tears welling in his eyes. The ship had treated him well for twenty years. She deserved more than to be abandoned.

"Why are you crying, Father?" Petr's question startled Theo. He seemed genuinely curious as the crew swam down the hall toward the airlock.

"It's okay, buddy," Theo said. "I'm just going to miss her, that's all."

Petr reached for Theo's hand. "So, will I, Father. She was good to you. Mother might appreciate the loss, though. She really didn't like her that much."

Theo suddenly felt a cool wave wash over his body and he smiled at his son. He ruffled Petr's hair, saying, "Buddy, I think you may be right. Your mother will have a party when we get home, won't she?"

Petr nodded and turned away, pulling himself along the long bar running along the corridor. Theo watched him turn the corner, just before his vision blurred again. Careful to find undamaged skin on his wrist, Theo lifted it to wipe the tears from his eyes.

When he reached the airlock, Theo counted eleven souls including his son. Sighing, he said, "Where's Gideon? And Zak?"

Mykaela floated forward. "Gideon's coming. Zak went to get him."

Theo let out the breath he'd been holding. Blinking several times to fight the tears, he said, "Have they come abreast yet?"

"Yes, but they're having difficulty—"

"Aye, but they better get their arses in gear," a well-charred Gideon yelled. His clothing was in tatters, though he'd found shelter from the explosion. "We've got about ten minutes."

"Where's Zak? I thought he was with you." Theo looked around the engineer to see if Zak followed.

"Hold yer horses, Captain," Zak said, appearing behind the older man towing two black bags. Theo's stomach lurched and threatened to upset. He patted the man on the shoulder as he passed by with the dead officers. *No man left behind,* Theo thought. Dead or alive, he owed it to the crew to take them home.

They waited another two minutes before the outer hatch started to melt, the steel heated into a molten trickle that ran down the hatch and pooled along the bottom. When the circular cut reached its beginning, someone yelled, "Out of the way," and kicked the door from the side. Tumbling end over end, the metal slab floated away until it clanged against the far wall.

"Hurry," Captain Kai yelled through the breach.

"Watch the slag, people," Theo said as he waited for them to filter through the hatch. The rumbling he'd heard from the engines had returned, reverberating through the bones of the ship. *At least you get to fight back,* he thought, wondering how long it would take the pirates to board.

"Captain, we have to go," Mykaela called softly as Theo sensed his ship falter.

Waving his hand, he said, "Yeah." Then with all the energy he had remaining, Theo Stinson pulled himself through the hatch into the shuttle, sliding out of the way as the hatch was swung shut with a resounding clang. He floated freely, as the shuttle had no gravity and all the safety belts were occupied.

The small hand that suddenly gripped his made it okay, though, and Petr's smile went from ear to ear as he said, "We're going home now, Father."

Theo lifted his other hand to rest on his son's dark curly hair. "You're right, buddy. We're going home."

Home? Theo thought as he stared out the hatch window at his retreating ship.

Chapter 2

Losing Spirit

Theo stepped through the door to his house and dropped his bag into the corner. He glanced around and took a deep breath. *Home,* he thought. The house wasn't his ship, but it felt right. It was where he and Galena had raised their two children, creating memories as old as the ship, and where he spent his time between runs exercising so he didn't lose muscle tone.

Theo craned his neck to look up the stairs. "Uh, where are the kids?" he asked as Galena left him by the door. It had taken him weeks to be able to look at his son, let alone speak to him. Now, as he walked through the door, he was refreshed and healed, the scars from his burns all but gone, the acrid smell of burnt flesh only fleeting.

Galena, having spent days at his side, uncharacteristically calm, without yelling at him or even speaking tersely. She didn't answer, just disappeared around the corner, only to return carrying a hammer and a broom. She smiled as she glanced between the two tools. "Choose your weapon, lover. You have about four hundred and sixteen hours."

Before Theo could respond, Galena said, "Oh, this is going to be wonderful. Wait, have you actually ever stayed home this long?"

Of course, Theo thought as he rocked back on his heels. He was exhausted from their walk through the grime-encrusted city to their small house in what was once considered the suburbs, now swallowed by the city as it overflowed the valley in its ever-expanding growth.

Theo sighed and said, "I'm not sure, love. Maybe back in eighty-nine."

Theo was the captain of a space ship, his body adapted to the differences in lighter gravity and air that was processed through mechanical scrubbers, stale, but clean. When he was earthbound, Theo was restless, finding no respite in the daily workings of humanity. In the days after he'd abandoned the *Galena*, he became even more so, the longing to be out in the void calling to him like a Siren, telling him he was destined for greater things, promising adventures of epic proportions. The irony of being dashed against the rocks like the ancient mariners wasn't lost on him as he dreamt of returning to space.

In the hospital, he'd been forced to lie on his stomach, quickly becoming acquainted with the nurses, doctors, and the white walls of the hospital room. Most of the staff were cordial enough, but after the third day he knew everyone by the sound of their step and the smell of their perfume. He knew that the chief resident was sleeping with two of the nurses and those nurses were in turn sleeping with two other men that he could never identify, but was sure had to be related. *Or the same person*, he thought absently. Theo was sure that the staff all wore genuine smiles as they wished him off that morning.

During his stay in the hospital, Theo had had nothing but time to think. He couldn't get his mind around what had happened and what he'd almost done. It wasn't even that he'd taken Petr with him to Mars—he and Galena had discussed it at length before he'd gone on his weekly run to Mars and then to one of the Kuiper Belt asteroids. He knew she could see it in his face, the sickening feeling that he'd done something terribly wrong.

Galena had assuaged his feelings, propping him up against the pillows so he could listen to her read from a magazine. She'd stopped in mid-reading to tell him it was okay. Her voice had been calm, no hint of anger or deceit as she told him he shouldn't be so hard on himself. She hadn't let him speak or even look away as she informed him he'd done the right thing.

It's not that easy, Theo thought as he stared at his wife, the tools held loosely in her hand as if she were about to drop them. Galena hadn't been forced to make that decision, even though she promised she would have done the same thing, lauding him as a hero. Slowly, however, as the skin that the doctors grafted in the lab was laid over his body, he came to see her point, almost sharing it. While he was still a little raw when he saw Petr, he was eventually able to look him in the eye and speak to him without breaking down into tears. Theo knew it was the right decision with the information that he'd had. *But, Petr changed that.* With Petr's help, he'd been able to change everything. They'd won.

Resigned to his new lot, Theo chose the mop. He didn't realize how much work it entailed to clean the floors, but with a smile on her face, Galena was quick to point out his shortcomings. After the first three days, he grew bored of the exercise and found himself tripping over his family as they went about their own duties. *Only 365 more hours to go,* he thought, mentally ticking off another hour from the accumulated time his wife had spent in the hospital, hovering over his bed to make sure he was still alive and didn't want for anything.

Not for the first time, Theo wondered whether he should offer her more hours than she'd given him. Galena's fire blazed every day in the hospital and yet every day she sat in peace, smiling down at him, laughing at his terrible jokes, making those jokes worthwhile. *I owe you everything, love.*

"Father," Petr said in exasperation as Theo was cleaning the kitchen. "You can't clean that while we're trying to eat."

Theo glanced up and opened his mouth to speak, but caught himself and bit his tongue. "Oh, that's not good, is it, buddy?"

"You have to go to another –"

"Let him work, Petr," his sister Grace said as she appeared in the doorway from the basement.

Where Petr followed after his mother, his hair dark and body moderately overweight, Grace took after Theo. Grace was tall and wore her blond hair shoulder length. She always smiled, whether she was working or lounging around the house. She'd always been a happy and giving child, even with her younger brother. *Can't say I was that nice to my brothers.*

As Theo watched, the young woman strolled into the room like Theo himself and grabbed an apple sitting in a basket filled with pseudo-fruit on the counter. She smiled at her father before rushing back toward the door, her bare feet slapping on the hardwood floor. "At least if he does the cleaning, you don't have to." She winked at Theo before disappearing through the doorway, whistling.

Theo was surprised how well he got along with his daughter. She'd recently turned eighteen and rather than rail and scream at her parents like most of her generation, she was content, accepting their rules, even coming to them for advice. He suspected that much of their good relationship was due to his frequent trips to Mars, leaving her to her own machinations. Rather than sulk, Grace had rejoiced when Petr had been permitted to join Theo on his trips.

Theo pursed his lips. "Hey, now. I—"

Petr nodded and cut his father short. "Oh, I guess you're right, Grace." With that, Petr turned away and followed his sister.

Wondering if they got along as well when he wasn't home, Theo happily went back to work. It was short-lived, however, as soon he found himself wondering what it would be like to have the house designed like his ship. *No more loose utensils,* he thought. On Earth he couldn't clean everything with a pressure washer or magnet, drawing everything back to the diode in seconds. *I should build that,* he thought, wondering what it would take to set up an electromagnet strong enough to pull the utensils to the kitchen without frying the electronics.

The house wasn't large, but compared to his neighbours, Theo considered it a mansion. He'd worked hard enough on his ship, travelling back and forth to Mars, to pay for the house situated in one of the few remaining greenscapes on Earth.

Finished inside, Theo moved to the siding on the house. He set his air purifier on his nose and slipped out to the garage, where he found the pressure washer still in the packaging. After two hours of preparation, he'd put the washer together enough to use it without scalding himself with the hot water.

In the years since he'd started transporting goods, Theo had noticed a difference in the weather. This far outside the city core, the weather was unpredictable, with hail able to cut through the vinyl, leaving dents and tears in his siding. *I guess I have the time to fix it now,* he thought as he glanced around at the pristine condition in which his neighbours kept their own homes.

After days of cleaning and replacing siding, Theo's thoughts wandered back to his crew. He wondered if they were adjusting to their Earthbound existence. In a strange way, he had to thank the pirates for their timely attack. He didn't wish any harm to his crew, but at least they understood he couldn't return to shipping. He had no ship to return to. *Maybe I can work for one of the recycling crews,* he thought. The job would be close to home and he could return to Earth every night. *Just to keep busy.*

Far above the planet, recycled steel was being smelted for the fleet of ships being built that would transport the population of Earth spaceward toward the stations of Jupiter and the colony on Alpha Centauri. Some people would refuse to take the trip, unwilling to board sleeper ships, holding to the idea that Earth would recover. Theo half hoped it would. The Earth was a beautiful sight from orbit, the oceans and continents locked in a millennia-long embrace.

When the Earth died, the supplies that Theo had once transported from Mars would no longer be needed as they failed to reverse the terrible destruction already meted out to the Earth. Whether it was one generation, ten, or a hundred, the day would come. What mattered was how they lived until then. All of Theo's trips from Earth to Mars and back had been to make it better until that end. *And make enough for Petr and Grace to buy passage,* he corrected himself.

Theo realized then that it was Galena he'd failed the most. He'd spent so much time trying to supply her with the finer things in life that he'd forgotten to live it with her. Her smile was so wide now because he was sharing something with her that he hadn't for any extended period in many years: his time. It was a strange feeling, not having had a fight in so many weeks. At first, he'd thought it was because of his injuries, but then he'd recognized the bounce in her step. She was as happy on Earth with him nearby as he was in space. He wished that she'd accompanied him on his trips. He could have shown her why he did it.

When Theo finished the siding, he moved on to the roof, where he decided the life of a ship's captain wasn't that bad. At least on his ship he wasn't tripping over people. Granted the halls were narrow on the ship, but at least he didn't see his neighbours or hear them through the walls. The sounds on Earth weren't as beautiful as those his grandfather had told stories about. Birdsong had died decades earlier as the great trees went extinct, only to be replaced with howling wind and honking cars.

It was the stars that made him miss space the most. As night fell he sat on his roof, looking skyward, hoping to enjoy its spray of glittering diamonds, but the light pollution thrown off by the great cities was too bright for them to pierce. *Such loss,* he thought. Those stars had called him up when he was a boy, telling him of great things he would do as a ship's captain.

When Theo finished the roof, Galena had him start working on their lawn. One would think it was a moot point considering how little they had, but flowers and trees were Galena's passion, the true reason she hadn't accompanied him on his trips. Neglected, the flowers in her garden would have died in the time a trip to Mars took. The garden was where she spent her days when he was gone, creating a colourful landscape the neighbours envied—dozens of different species, hundreds of different colours, all different heights and an array of scents to seduce passersby. Galena planned her gardens to appeal to every sense, and even for philosophical meaning.

Theo was sure he'd far exceeded the four hundred-plus hours when he found his wife and daughter sitting on their back deck, staring out into those flowers. Theo pulled his respirator from his nose and waited for several seconds as he adjusted to the heavy air. "And what are my two beautiful ladies doing today?" He ran his fingers along the top of a tall lavender plant, then raised them to his nose. *Your favourite*, he thought, gazing at his wife.

Grace looked up. "Nothing, Daddy. I'm just waiting for Sean. We're going to a show."

Grace had spent her entire life on Earth, where her body was fully accustomed to the polluted air that enveloped the planet. She was able to run down the street without the respirator he carried with him. *Strange that I'm the one who needs this,* he thought. He was stronger and healthier, but the filthy air felt thick in his lungs, as if he were trying to breathe through a pillow placed over his mouth.

"And who is Sean?" Theo asked. He forced a smile to his lips. One thing he'd regretted during his travels was that, unlike Petr, Grace disliked the confines of his ship and refused to accompany him. Now she was a young woman.

After several silent seconds, Galena said, "I told you about him the other night, Theo, but obviously you weren't listening." She cocked her head to the side and arched her brow as if to say, *Don't ask.* Theo was sure he'd be informed of this mistake later, but that didn't change the fact that his daughter was traipsing off with a boy he'd never met.

Grace smiled at her father and jumped down from the steps to skip closer to him. She reached up and kissed him on the cheek before saying, "It's okay, Daddy. He's just a friend. I'm just saying goodbye."

Goodbye? Theo could see his daughter was fighting tears so he bowed his head, then looked away. "I thought perhaps we could catch a show later."

"Oh Daddy, can I have the—"

"Go ahead, Grace," Galena said as she knelt to pull a weed from her garden.

As though they'd somehow reached agreement in the past few hours, Grace nodded and turned to enter the house. She was gone in seconds, leaving Theo and his wife in silence.

Before he could speak, Galena said, "Leave it."

Theo sighed and silently set to work beside his wife. After a couple minutes, her scowl faded and she said, "There was a man here today when you were at the store. He'd like to see you in the anteroom."

Theo lifted a brow in query and waited for her to say, "I don't know."

Galena's nose twitched and she refused to meet his gaze. She knew the man's identity, but for some reason needed to keep the information secret. *Is it for your sake or mine?* he wondered. Who would he refuse to speak to, if he knew their identity? *And someone she wouldn't dismiss on her own. I'll know shortly.* He nodded, accepting her cryptic response, and dusted off his legs before following her into the house.

Slipping out of his shoes, Theo made his way to the anteroom, his curiosity gnawing at him. *Who would even call? Everyone knows the ship was destroyed.* He shook his head. He'd owned the cargo from his last trip and nothing remained of his ship. *A salesman?* Few would dare. Theo had been good, but his customers had already found new transporters. He couldn't afford to buy a new ship.

As soon as Theo entered the cubicle the family called the anteroom, the lights dimmed and a holographic image appeared in a shimmer of light on the far side of the room. The head and shoulders of a man dressed in a suit gazed back at him, smiling like a salesman, which instantly put Theo on edge. His smile told Theo to turn away before his silver tongue eventually left Theo bankrupt. His eyes were too narrow and he glanced furtively around the room as if searching for something to use to connect with Theo. *I don't have time for this,* Theo thought. His skin prickled with annoyance and he turned to leave.

"Ah good, I've been waiting for a couple hours," the man said softly, his voice almost squeaky.

I bet he's short, Theo thought absently. He could hear the rumbling of machinery in the background. *A ship salesman? Do you think I'm a fool?* Seven shipyards had called in the past week alone. He'd made sure to tell Galena he didn't care to speak to them. *Why didn't you screen this one, love?*

The man fidgeted with a small, shiny stone figure for a second before setting it down on the table beside him. *It's a knight. He's been playing chess? Waiting, eh?* Theo understood the game, even relished playing with Galena or Petr. He didn't, however, like the attitude the salesman projected as he set the piece down. *I am no pawn to move around your board, boy. At least Galena made you wait.* Aloud, Theo demanded, "Do I know you?"

"Oh—my apologies, Mr. Stinson. My name is Oliver Sando. I work for Lovett Technologies."

. Theo felt a chill run down his spine. Lovett Technologies wasn't a simple ship manufacturer or ship retailer. They operated one of the largest space transport operations in the system. They were the proverbial Joneses when it came to the rags to riches family stories. They'd taken a single ship operation and created an intergalactic shipping lane. Theo was sure they were the only company to be contracted to take supplies to the new colony in the Alpha Centauri system, and he'd heard rumours that they intended to send expeditions to three other extra-solar planets that had been discovered.

Theo sighed. *Two minutes.* "And what exactly do you need from me, Mr. Sando?"

The man's cheeks softened a little as he said, "Please, call me Oliver."

Theo took a deep breath, wondering how he could dismiss the man without making a scene. The suit and the smile slowly creeping back onto the man's face did not impress. "What would you like, Mr. Sando?"

"Lovett Technologies has an opportunity that we would like to discuss with you. Would we be available to meet?"

The last thing Theo needed was a salesman speaking in familiar terms and inviting himself to the house to meet in person. *You don't need to know where I live, thank you.* Digital mail was bad enough. Theo paid a great deal of money to have a relay bounce any communications so no one could find him, and he didn't want to lose that advantage.

The man kept glancing to the side. as if someone else was speaking to him off camera. It made Theo feel like the salesman wasn't actually speaking to him, but orating to an audience. *Is this just a training exercise? Sell to the man who's lost his ship?* It was a little depressing at first. All Theo wanted to do was disappear into anonymity, not jump back into another ship. He owed it to his wife and family. They didn't need the money. *Explain that to a salesman,* he thought. To a salesman, everyone wanted their wares.

"Mr. Sando, I'm actually quite busy these days. I have been cleaning my house up from the last storm."

The man was nodding as if he understood Theo's plight, though he likely lived on the fifty-seventh floor of an apartment building in the great city, and didn't know what grass or trees felt like. *I'd like to see what you'd do outside of the concrete.* Theo resisted the urge to shake his head.

Sando cleared his throat and said, "Mr. Stinson, I understand your issues, but I'm positive that listening to this proposition will be worth your time."

"Listen, I've tried to be cordial, Mr. Sando, but enough's enough. Please, if you don't get to the point right now, I will have to go."

The man sighed, his eyes dancing to both sides of the camera. His nostrils flared as he said, "Fine. Mr. Lovett would like to offer you a chance to leave Earth."

Theo rolled his eyes. Even if leaving Earth was an option, he wasn't going to change his mind less than a month after he'd promised his wife he'd be staying. He wasn't about to buy another ship to replace the *Galena*. He wasn't a ship's captain any longer. "Good day, sir. I wish you luck with your sales. I just don't think you'll fill your quota today."

"Mr. Stinson," a new voice suddenly said as the image blurred and refocused on another suited man. This one was older and well accustomed to his attire. He sported a bushy white beard and eyebrows almost as bushy. The man leaned forward, hands gleaming with half a dozen bejewelled rings splayed out in front of him. "Sir, I think you may know me."

Theo narrowed his eyes, realizing he was actually looking at Edward Lovett himself, a massively rich and aloof man, more concerned with his anonymity than Theo himself. For him to appear like this, the conversation was about more than selling a small transport ship. "What can I do for you, Mr. Lovett?" Theo asked. He heard the door at the back of the house close as Galena came to listen.

Edward Lovett took a deep breath before saying, "I want to first give you my regards. I know what it's like to lose a ship."

"Thank you, sir," Theo said. He suspected the man had felt far worse when he lost a ship. Edward Lovett was a material man and while Theo had lost his ship, it was the people he mourned.

"Now," Edward said as he shifted closer to the camera, making his face fill the whole room, "as my grandson was having difficulty explaining to you, I have a business proposition."

Theo sighed. The old man was going to embarrass himself by trying to sell him the same thing Theo had just declined. He wished they'd listened the first time. It would have been easier. "Sir, I—"

"Theodore, please listen," the old man pleaded. His face contorted and he had to look away from the screen for several seconds. When he looked back, the man's eyes were glistening. "I... Okay, Mr. Stinson. Here's the deal. I want you to take charge of a fleet of my ships going to Alpha Centauri."

The colony? Who would want to go there? It was barely established and the trip would take decades. Any hope of returning was a dream. Galena would have his head if he even contemplated the idea, which he wouldn't. The prospect of being stuck on a ship away from his family for years on end wasn't inviting. He wasn't even sure if he could live with himself on a ship for that long. It wasn't like his trips to Mars once a week.

The old man on the screen scratched his beard for several seconds before saying, "Wait, good sir. Before you decide, you must hear my proposition."

Theo shook his head for several seconds. He didn't want to hear the proposition. He wanted to go back outside and find something to do. But his mouth said, "Please continue."

"You may have heard that I have won the contract for transporting supplies to the Alpha Centauri system. I need someone I can trust to head my fleet."

"I would have expected you to have sent several fleets already," Theo said after a brief pause. "And then wait until the folding engines are perfected." Folding engines were decades away from perfection, but could still beat a fleet as it poked along in normal space.

The old man frowned suddenly. He glanced away again, unwilling to show his emotions. His gaze wavered as he said, "I have sent several fleets and two of them have actually made it past Jupiter Station. As for the engines, they are a dream for commercial use, Mr.

Stinson." He said the last breathlessly, as if it left a foul taste in his mouth, and so quickly, Theo barely heard.

Maybe you already have the engines, Theo thought. Perhaps, like the cure for cancer, the solution had already been created, but some darker power prevented Lovett from commercially using them. The engines would solve many of Lovett's issues. But then Theo realized, *They would create many of their own.* With enough money, anyone could join the transportation market. If Theo had never had to worry about pirates and could pop out at destination within minutes, his life would be far different. *But if the engines exist, why send the fleet at all?*

Edward Lovett didn't call up a small operator like Theo and offer an opportunity like this offhand. *There has to be an ulterior reason.* Theo was good, he'd been in the business for decades, building a reputation with his customers before losing only one ship, the *Galena.* Did Lovett think Theo's reputation could do the same for him?

Theo shook his head to clear his thoughts. Edward Lovett was becoming emotional for a reason. "And the rest of the fleets?"

The old man fell silent, face turned away. When he spoke again, tears coursed down his cheeks. "I have lost seven fleets so far."

Seven? Was he so determined? That dropped the success rate down to only twenty percent. *But then,* Theo thought with a mental shrug, *he was likely compensated for the losses.* Lovett would have been paid in advance. *Would I be compensated, if I lost another fleet?*

Theo was positive that he and his family would survive an encounter, but would he be compensated if the pirates who'd dogged him from Mars on his last trip somehow found him, out in the darkness of space? The *Galena* had been a tired ship. If Theo had a newer, faster ship, he could do anything. Theo knew the answer to his question already, but he asked it anyway. "And you think I can do better?"

The old man shook his head. "Perhaps, but more importantly, you have something that I do not—or rather, I would say, I have something that you do not."

Why wouldn't the man just wait for the engines? With the money he'd spent on ships and men, he could have funded the engine research himself, kept it secret, sold it for a bazillion dollars.

Then he put things together. "You have enemies that I do not."

"Oh, you don't," the old man said. "I have been quite thorough in my investigation. And yes, I do know of your decision never to fly in a spaceship again. And yes, I know you made that decision before the pirates damaged your ship."

How? Theo had spoken to very few people about his decision and he couldn't imagine any of them telling someone. Could the man have tracked down Mykaela or Gideon? The old man would have been a little bitter over Theo's decision, but not enough to speak to others of it. Unless someone got him drunk.

Edward Lovett continued. "You understand the need for these supplies to get to the colonies, don't you? Those colonies were established long before space pirates existed. They need the supplies."

The old man had the nerve to appeal to his better side? Lovett had to know that Theo was no patriot. He'd done all that he'd done for his wife and his family, not from some overblown sense of pride or need to benefit the greater good. Granted, he accepted that someone had to do it and yes, he was as qualified as anyone else, but why would the old man think that would make him accept? Perhaps he was so much the patriot that he expected Theo to do the same.

As if reading his mind, Lovett said, "You see, Mr. Stinson, I am not asking you out of hope you will become a martyr and jump at the chance of doing a great deed. I am asking you because then you won't be stuck on Earth as she slowly bleeds to death. Your cargo will pave the way for the great migration of Earth's people to the primary colony."

Theo knew it would eventually happen. He'd been working to send his family there. *But in their lifetime, not mine,* he thought. *A new home, where you can walk around without a respirator.* Alpha Centuari was pristine, with no smog, and trees growing in forests as opposed to little gardens like Galena's. Alpha Centauri had real animals that could fly and prance around because the air was clear.

"Wait—you said primary colony. What do you mean?"

Lovett drew a slow, deliberate breath as he stared into the screen. The corners of his mouth curled slightly as he said, "There are two colonies in the Alpha Centauri system. The primary colony is slightly larger than the available land on Earth and will easily accommodate the colonists that are expected to make the trip." He paused for several seconds, his gaze locked on Theo's face.

Colonists? Theo thought. *Have they built so many ships already?* Theo looked up, as though he could see through the roof of his house to the shipyards above Earth.

"And the second colony is slightly smaller," Lovett continued. "Very few people know of its existence. Once you deliver the cargo, you have my blessing and any amount of power that I wield, to make your way to the second colony to settle down."

Second colony? That prospect, while meaning little to Theo's current living arrangements, was fascinating. He was sure that Petr, if no one else, would be drawn to her shores. A completely fresh start with no neighbours living on his doorstep...

As with any new discovery, no one truly knew what difficulties and dangers the planet presented. It was entirely possible that it was worse than Earth. It could have storms far in excess of those that pounded on his roof and tore the siding from the house. It could be so cold during the winters that everything froze solid—assuming, of course, that it had winter at all. *No, they've already vetted that. The second colony is for a select few.*

Regardless, the addition of another colony, small or not, would be welcome when it came to relocating Earth's people. The prospect of moving from one overcrowded home to another wasn't something Theo wanted to think about—and *he* was used to the close confines of a spaceship. That said, at least the people would enjoy a new home devoid of the damages industry had caused. *But would you all go?* Theo wondered as he glanced around for his wife.

As Theo moved, he breathed in the elusive floral-pine aroma of lavender that told him his wife was near just as he felt her hand settle on his shoulder. She bent down to whisper in his ear, "You need to do this, Theo. It feels right."

You've already accepted, Theo realized as he thought about all the work he'd been doing around the house. He grabbed his wife's hand and squeezed it as he said, "I think we should meet, Mr. Lovett. We have much to discuss.

Chapter 3

Losing Dignity

Galena Stinson walked through the cold metal hallway, her arms filled with boxes full of food. "Kiss me, if you insist I go."

Theo laughed as he looked up from his handheld computer to his wife. Feeling frazzled that morning, she'd let her curly black hair fall as it wished and now it had fallen over her face, as it had in his vision the day he'd lost her namesake, the *Galena,* and was preparing to meet his death high in the skies over Earth. He reached out deliberately to brush back her hair and hook it over her ears, revealing her vibrant green eyes.

Theo knew his wife would rather be tending her flowers on Earth. As the time drew closer to their departure, she'd started telling him she could wait for him to return, rather than traipse across the cosmos, pretending to like space travel.

But then, this was your decision, wasn't it? Like Gideon, the woman tended to complain as a way of working through her issues. *It'll be perfect. You'll see.*

Aloud he said, "Ah, my love. If you were to stay behind, you would have grown old by the time I returned. Your beautiful hair would be a dull grey, and your skin no longer olive, but the colour of this floor. I would step from my ship almost as young as you see me now, and you would be bent and broken. I wouldn't recognize you."

"Is that what happened to your first wife?" she snapped back.

Galena was a whip in her responses. If she meant the words, he would have been concerned, but he knew this was just her way of accepting that this was goodbye, that Earth would be no more than a memory by morning.

"Oh love, you know you're the only one for me," he said with another laugh.

As they spoke, Petr strolled by, playing with his own handheld computer. He looked up and winked at his father before reaching up to adjust his glasses. "Mother, you should know that as we approach the speed of light, the mechanics of the universe don't act the same," he said. "Time actually slows relative to that outside of our awareness, so everything else speeds along away from us."

Galena bent low enough to look over her pile of food. "Thank you, Petr. Now run along."

Petr frowned at her. "You never listen, Mother. Everyone should know how to fly the ship, and the consequences of doing so. Someday we will have ships that fold space. Then you will have to understand the physics calculations and what the jump will do to the human consciousness."

Theo cocked his eyebrow at his wife. "That will be all, Petr. Perhaps you could go help your sister tie down your room."

"Oh yeah," Petr said as he looked up at his father, eyes glowing. "I have to show her something I found."

Theo bowed low, dragging his hand on the floor as he said, "Good. I'll talk to you later, okay? Before we disembark."

Petr snapped his heels together and saluted as he said, "Aye, Captain." When he left, he made sure to stomp on the grating that ran the length of the centre's corridor. Theo recognized the grating for what it was: venting for heat, and quick access to the artificial gravity and other piping conduits. Petr, however, used the grating to make as much noise as he could while moving from one room to the next.

Petr was smarter than Theo had been at his age, easily understanding the concepts of quantum physics that Theo still couldn't grasp. Petr was always ready for their flights. Had they been staying on Earth, Theo was sure his son would one day have his own fleet of transport ships. Theo had even made Petr an ensign on their last flight, just so he wouldn't climb through the network of hidden chambers surrounding the engines.

That was before the pirates had attacked, however. After that, Petr had fallen into a dark mood, unwilling to even glance at his father. It took some time for Theo to realize that it wasn't his decision to save Petr from further pain that angered the boy, but the fact that they'd left the ship to die alone. If Petr had had his way, he would have returned to repair her, salvaging what he could. Try as he might, Theo couldn't explain that the pirates had already stripped the ship, leaving nothing to fix. *Assuming they lived through Gideon's gift, of course,* Theo thought.

Looking back to his wife, Theo said, "I have something to show you."

Narrowing her eyes, Galena slowly said, "Where?"

"Come with me." He pirouetted like his daughter doing one of her dance moves and set off around a corner, hurrying down the hall to stop before a large sliding door. He pressed the button on the wall beside it and watched as it slid open, absently rubbing one shin against the back of his other leg, sure he had permanent damage from his close encounters with gangways on the *Galena.*

Though his new ship offered far more amenities than his last, Theo was careful not to look at it as his home. This was a means to an end, a corridor between Earth and Alpha Centauri. When they finished travelling through that corridor, they would dismantle their ships and use the metal for building real homes.

On the planet in the Alpha Centauri system they wouldn't be living in a house barely large enough for two, let alone four. When they stepped from their front deck they wouldn't be assaulted by the sounds of traffic or industry. Galena's garden wouldn't be the only one for ten miles. The air won't be scrubbed and they wouldn't need respirators. But for now...

Theo followed his wife through the door into a room in sharp contrast to the rest of the cold, metallic ship. A massive field of vibrant greenery covered much of the floor. Theo knew most of the plants, but couldn't call them by name. He hadn't crafted the room for himself, but for the woman he loved. He'd envisioned making love to her here in the field, among the grains and flowers. *It's your home inside mine,* he thought as he grasped his wife's hand. It was the only gift he could give her.

He watched the smile grow on Galena's face as she reached out to caress a two-toned dahlia, the sweet scent wafting in the air. A tear formed as she tried to speak, forced silent for almost a minute before she said, "It's...it's so beautiful."

The room was almost as big as their entire home on earth, spanning half the width of the ship. Though the area was meant to help scrub the carbon dioxide from the air and provide sustenance, Theo had brought in large crates of flowers and dirt. One day when his wife was finished, it would burgeon with flowers and greenery right to the walls. *And beyond, if I know you at all,* Theo added. Galena wouldn't let the steel walls stop her from adding colour to every hold in the ship.

Theo pointed toward the ceiling, knowing the most impressive was yet to come. "Look up, love. Look up."

Galena craned her neck to stare through the massive domed window overlooking the bay of the large station, where their ship was docked in a line with nine replicas, small shuttles buzzing around them like flies around bloated worms, filling cargo holds and fuel tanks.

Theo let her stare for a minute before he cleared his throat and said, "There is a metal shutter that closes on all the windows.

Artificial lighting will illuminate the room to make sure your plants grow."

Thinking he'd finally made her speechless, Theo added, "They're better than my old ship. That thing was a heap of rust and burnt plastic. She couldn't handle another trip through the water ring." Theo was disappointed with how drab this ship looked, though. The *Galena* had been so colourful, with her inventory of borrowed parts.

"But...how?" Galena asked as she stepped into a patch of grain. Bending low, she took a great whiff of the plants.

"All we have to do is one trip. Think about it. Mars, Jupiter Station, Alpha Centauri. We take supplies to Mars, food to Jupiter Station, and the rest of the food and ore to Alpha Centauri. This is one of those magical times when the planets are close enough to align Mars and Jupiter, and when we get to Alpha Centauri we settle down. It's simple."

"Simple?" Galena asked, raising an eyebrow. She knew the plan, had known it from the beginning, but that didn't mean they had to do anything out of the ordinary. They just had to prove to everyone how it would work.

Edward Lovett had asked for little when he'd handed the ownerships for the fleet over to Theo, but he been adamant that Theo would be performing for those who would invariably infiltrate his ship. Theo had to prove to them that *he* would make it all work, that *he* had been the architect of his plan, and that Lovett Industries was nothing more than manufacturer.

Theo took a deep breath and looked at his wife. *She's more beautiful every day,* he thought as he looked beyond the superficial worry lines on her face to her smile lines and the curve of her chin as she spoke. *You won't regret this, love. I promise.* Aloud, he said, "Exactly. When we get to Alpha Centauri, we sell the metal from the other ships for a property and use the metal from this one to build a house. They'll have laid the groundwork by the time we arrive."

"And…" Galena fell silent as she looked around the hold. "It's— how long will it take us to get there?"

Theo blinked several times. "It'll take us forty years, but we'll only feel ten." He said it matter-of-factly, knowing it wouldn't matter how much time he spent trying to explain it again.

Theo had charted the course a dozen times to make sure they travelled the fastest path through the shipyards at Jupiter Station. He knew it would take almost a month to transition their cargo before they headed off. Even with zero gravity, it wasn't going to be easy to move the cumbersome load. Then they would start the ramjet engines and take two trips around Jupiter itself to build momentum enough to slingshot out of the system. If they didn't get the timing right, they would have to wait two more years for the right opportunity.

"But, why us?" Galena asked.

"Why not?" Theo sighed. "There are a hundred stations orbiting Earth, half that many around Mars, and at least three dozen around Jupiter. The human race needs a real planet to call home. The scientists on Alpha Centauri have already done the basic tests and assure us that everything is in order. They're already working on a viable ecology. It'll be perfect. And by the time we get there, Petr and Grace will have lots of children to play with."

Galena's face contorted as she looked at Theo. "When was the last time you saw Grace play?"

"You know what I mean," Theo replied. "There are more families on the other ships. I made sure to choose the best crews."

A smile touched Galena's lips again as she pulled away and began to twirl around like a child playing in the fields of Earth. After a time, she bent low to grab a dahlia deftly in her hand.

"I knew you'd love it, Lena. No more travelling from Earth to Mars for us," Theo said happily as he joined her.

Until Theo had requested the flowers, the room had been functional, stocked with plants designed to maximize the food production and carbon dioxide scrubbing. The excess heat was then circulated through the corridors to counteract the cold seeping in from the cargo holds. His meagre addition had produced blooming flowers in a few weeks, blooms that sent up a heady perfume to mingle with the pungent aroma of damp earth while adding bright splashes of colour to compensate for the drab interior of the rest of the ship.

Giggling, Galena removed her shoes and walked through the dirt in her bare feet, letting the moist soil squeeze between her toes. "It's perfect," she said as she closed her eyes.

"Yes," Theo said as he watched his wife dance. "It's a vision."

After a time, Theo shivered and looked down at the young man who cleared his throat at his elbow. *Already?* Theo thought as he slid to a stop. He waited several seconds before nodding.

The young man was new to his crew, though he came well recommended from a friend Theo had met years ago. Captain Hendrickson had been adamant the young man would prove his weight in gold, so Theo had hired him. Theo didn't care that Hendrickson had fallen into trouble with the pirates more often than not in his travels. The man had done right by Theo when they were younger, and that was enough for Theo to trust his word. *But, what is your name?* Theo wondered as he looked at the young man, running through a list of names in his mind. Remembering how he'd logged the man's name, he blurted, "Ah, a ladder." The young man shook his head in confusion, but Theo said, "Yes, Jacob?"

Jacob was always clean-shaven, his clothing pressed, and Theo was sure he could smell a hint of cologne. *Someone to impress?* Regardless, Jacob was polite; he waited for Galena to acknowledge him before he said, "Mykaela wants to speak with you, sir." His face went a shade darker as he blurted out the exotic woman's name.

A frown grew on Galena's face as she split her attention between Theo and the newcomer. She chewed on the inside of her cheek for several seconds before saying, "You go, Theo. I have better things to do."

Theo smiled and reached out to touch her arm. With a quick glance at the windows above, he said, "She's not on this ship, Lena. She's on one of the others."

"Ah," Galena said as her shoulders relaxed. She'd returned to her shoes when she said, "Go, Theo. You have much to do, I'm sure. And apparently we'll have a lot of time later."

Theo smiled as he watched his wife meander off through the grain to the door. As soon as she left, he turned back to Jacob, his smile fading. "Lead the way, Jacob."

"This way, sir."

Theo followed the young man through the large plant-hold and out into a long corridor. The air was cooler outside, though some of the scents followed Theo from the room. On either side of this corridor were a dozen or more sliding doors that led into what he assumed were cargo holds. The air smelled of newly minted plastic and the awful stench of welding slag and paint. *Maybe you can fix that, love,* Theo thought as he glanced back to the plant-hold.

Theo's last ship had been a much simpler design, running straight on one level with the engines, bridge, and crew quarters in one section, the cargo holds in another. His new ship was far more complex, towering in three levels, the capacity of at least five of the cargo holds three times that of the entire hold of the *Galena*. The engines on his new ship, though centralized for power distribution, were far more powerful and more efficient, able to scoop energy from multiple sources. He'd almost fallen asleep when the architects had begun to explain their design.

"Sir, the bridge is this way," Jacob said as he waited, fists clenched. "Sir? The bridge…"

Theo looked up. "Oh, what? Which way?"

"This way, sir," Jacob replied.

Brow furrowed, Theo asked, "What? Why? Isn't it at the bow?" Bridges were always at the bow; it just felt right. Why would they situate the brain of the ship so deep within the cargo hold? It wasn't logical. The ship was a labyrinth compared to the *Galena.*

"I think it has something to do with pirates," Jacob offered. "Down here it's more difficult to get in. It keeps us safer."

How can you know so much? Theo thought. Perhaps he was as good as Captain Hendrickson had promised. Which was a good thing. With his first mate flying one of the other ships, Theo needed all the skillful hands he could get. "Pirates, eh? I'll tell you a story sometime that will get your heart racing."

Jacob glanced away, as though he already knew the story. "That's what Mykaela said."

Theo marched the rest of the way in silence, staring through the doors into darkened cargo holds only half filled with medical and other supplies for Mars. *Fewer chances of pirates if you don't have anything for them,* he thought. As a rule, any ship had to have a manifest of its cargo ready to relay to any passing police. Theo half wondered whether the pirates could read the digital manifest like a grocery list.

When Theo reached the door to the bridge he found a large piece of paper stuck to the frame by a sticky substance. The paper read *Bridge: Galena 2. Petr,* Theo thought, vowing to come up with a better name. Though an honour, it was still confusing for his wife to have the ship her namesake. It had been Gideon's choice with his last ship. *But not this one,* Theo promised as he looked around. *Huh, I never noticed. No pipes.*

Theo strolled through the door onto the bridge, where a dozen officers pored over various computer terminals. When they noticed him, they came to rigid attention and saluted, waiting until he acknowledged them to relax. Many had been military officers and still followed regimental protocol.

"Sir," a rotund man said as he waddled towards Theo, Petr trailing behind him.

"Hey Zak, where's Mykaela?" Theo asked as he looked around the room.

Zak nodded toward a far terminal. "Down on the end. It's a secure line."

"Since when did we need secure lines?" Theo asked, trying not to scowl. He'd never needed the security on his previous ship. *It must be Lovett.*

"Since ye bought a fleet of ships that can accommodate it," Zak replied with his usual dry wit as he turned back to the other officers.

Rolling his eyes, Theo moved to the terminal and said, "Thank you, Jacob. You can return to your duties now." He glanced back to make sure the young man wasn't looking over his shoulder to steal a glimpse of Mykaela before pressing the button to activate the screen.

The dark-skinned woman was instantly smiling back at him. "What are you thinking about, Theodore?" Mykaela always used full names. She was from a Scandinavian county that had gone bankrupt years ago and fallen to the pressures of the corporations. It was a rare place, where greenscapes were larger than the thirty square feet Theo had recently vacated.

Shaking his head, Theo said, "Nothing, Mykaela. What did you want?"

"Ever to business," the exotic woman purred.

Shrugging, Theo said, "You called me, remember?" As much as he knew the woman wanted nothing to do with him, he'd promised himself he wouldn't fawn over her and alienate his wife in the process. He knew he had to set the boundaries early, as Mykaela casually flirted with every human she ever met. It had come in handy on more than one occasion with the dock hands or the police, the former serious business, the latter a joke.

The police, a galactic joke in every way station, were dirtier than the pirates they were sworn to apprehend. Theo hadn't found an officer that didn't expect a bribe when they'd stopped him. He was sure at least one of the pirate vessels was connected to, if not crewed by, those same police officers.

Smiling, Mykaela said, "I just wanted to let you know that the rest of the ships have been prepped. We're ready to go whenever you are."

Narrowing his eyes, Theo said, "And what's that supposed to mean, Mykaela?"

"Ha," the woman said, as if she were speaking to a forlorn lover, "it means exactly what I said. We are all ready when you are, Theodore."

"Are you speaking for the fleet now?" Theo asked, shifting in his seat.

It had actually taken more effort to cajole his former crew into returning to space than he'd expected. Mykaela, the last to agree, had come with one condition—she wanted one of the ships when they were done. Theo didn't know if she wished to return to the Sol system or not, only that she wouldn't set foot on another planet. Her return to Earth must not have been a pleasant one.

Mykaela shook her head. "I wouldn't presume, Theodore. I only relay the information available on your screens."

"Ever my first mate, Kae, ever my first mate. I'm not sure I would want to make this trip without you."

"Don't tell that to Galena," she said with another laugh as she turned away. "Be careful, Theodore."

"Aren't I always?" Theo countered as he pushed away from the screen.

The woman offered a slight smile, something Theo didn't remember her ever doing before. Her glances were always rife with seductive grace, not genuine happiness or, in this case, perhaps fear. "I am serious, Theodore. Be careful. Pirates aren't forgiving. It's getting worse."

Was that a warning? Did she know something she couldn't repeat? Or was it just a reference to their last trip? In either case, Theo had developed a small case of paranoia since meeting Edward Lovett and agreeing to execute the man's machinations. He knew he was only a captain of a small fleet and not its owner, even if the paperwork said otherwise. This was a Lovett Industries expedition and that meant there were people wanting them to fail. Theo shook his head to clear the fears. He had more important things to worry about. "Don't worry. I've paid for an army of security officers. They'll protect you."

Mykaela sighed and looked away before whispering, "It's not me I'm worried about."

With that she cut the connection, leaving Theo staring at a dark screen. He sat for several seconds staring at his reflection as officers swooped by behind him. Though he recognized the face staring back at him, he was surprised to find several new lines around his eyes; tired eyes, his mother would say, sunken and ringed with shadows. His dark beard was beginning to show again in sharp contrast to his light hair. Perhaps the woman *had* heard something. *No,* he thought vehemently. Nothing would stop them. Any pirate attack would have to come from a fleet. *And they never band together. No one's going to attack us.*

Theo looked around the bridge, wondering at his new situation. Ten months earlier he'd been cruising back and forth from Mars, hauling cargo which at the time was of little or no consequence. Food for the rich hiding deep in the rainforests on Earth wasn't his idea of great accomplishments, but it paid well.

Theo shook his head and closed his eyes. *I'm doing the right thing. For Galena, the kids, even the crew.* It was the right path to take. As he'd told Mykaela, he'd hired enough security to protect them if pirates boarded. The ships were built to withstand plasma storms, converting the storm's energy into propulsion to send them to their destination. They were staggering their formation so if one ship fell out it wouldn't impede one of the others. *But brand-new ships won't break down,* he added.

With a deep sigh, Theo stood and strolled around to look at his bridge crew. They were younger than the people he was used to commanding. *This isn't their first rodeo, though,* he reminded himself. *And they're not the only crew.* He hadn't crewed one ship, but ten.

As soon as Theo came abreast of Zak, his new XO said, "What are yer orders, Captain?"

Theo had to school his expression as he looked to the rotund Zak. He liked the man, having crewed with him for almost a decade, but that didn't make him feel any more comfortable with the man compared to Mykaela. He knew Zak would perform his duties admirably; he'd done a great job as second mate. But he didn't respond with Mykaela's speed and accuracy. *I'll get you there. Don't you worry.* But it was going to take some time, pushing the man to perform beyond his comfort level.

"Sir?" Zak asked as if Theo had spoken out loud.

Blinking rapidly to clear his thoughts, Theo said, "Is everything ready?"

"Aye, Captain," Zak said with a nod, shuffling to a seat on the far side of the bridge. "I was up front earlier. I think it'll be a good show from there, if Petr wants to see the view."

Theo smiled and looked around for Petr, but didn't see him. "I suspect he's already found it, but we should make sure—"

"Captain," a woman said from the starboard side of the bridge, "I have Gideon on the comm. He says to tell you Petr is just fine where he is, and to stop worrying about him." As soon as she repeated the words, her eyes went wide and she covered her mouth with her hand, no doubt wondering if she should apologize or hide. She blushed and opened her mouth to speak a few times, but remained silent and lowered her eyes to her console, unable to meet Theo's gaze.

Theo rolled his eyes. "Gideon should know he's supposed to be keeping an eye on the engines instead of listening to the conversations on the bridge."

The communications officer huffed as the man on the other end said something Theo couldn't hear. Suspecting it had something to do with the woman's off-duty activities, Theo said, "Perhaps we should sound the general quarters and shove off? And can someone put up a picture of Earth over there?" He pointed to the large screen on the far side of the bridge.

The live feed from one of the station's external cameras flashed an image onto the screen. Theo recognized the dark clouds and broken satellites orbiting the planet. He was surprised to feel a sudden pang of regret as he visualized what the planet used to be like. Even before he'd started transporting supplies, Earth wasn't so far gone as it was now. *It was beautiful,* he thought, knowing his decision had been right. The next time he looked down on a blue world, he would have a few more grey hairs, but at least he would know it was home and not a planet riddled with centuries-old decay and destruction.

He looked around at his crew. "This isn't going to be easy. I know you all know that, but I wanted to thank you for choosing to come with us. We're all going to be seeing a lot of each other for a while, so I want to start off right."

The crewed sighed as Theo fell silent. He knew they weren't looking for a long-winded speech. This was no maiden voyage of terrified mariners, but experienced men and women he could trust, all focused on the same goal. *A new life, and in the meantime, a bit of work.*

Theo let a smile touch his lips. "And one last thing. As soon as we reach our destination, every last one of you is going to be filthy rich."

Instantly the crew erupted into laughter and cheers. Theo wondered if they were celebrating as vigorously down in the engine rooms. *Likely*, he thought. Gideon probably had several bottles of moonshine going around to the engineering crew. One last dip, he would say.

Theo didn't care that the definition of stinking rich was going to be different for them than it was for Edward Lovett. They were gaining a new life. Lovett was getting enough money to build a hundred more ships just like the one they flew. *I hope it's worth it,* Theo thought. Five people knew the truth about their expedition. Lovett and his grandson had made the offer while Theo and Galena had accepted.

Theo had told only Mykaela the details and that, only to convince her to join them. No one else had to know about the sham. They only had to know that he, Theodore Stinson, had purchased ten identical ships and was going to fly them to Alpha Centauri, taking much-need supplies to the colonies. *It's perfect.*

It took several seconds before the bridge crew quieted and Zak gave the order to decouple. Theo stared at the image of Earth on the screen for several minutes, the last few minutes before the ship went into full burn toward Mars, and beyond.

Chapter 4

Losing Grace

Theo looked out over a massive hold half-filled with cargo containers as a dozen crewmen tried to shove a large container back to the top of one stack. There were several hundred stacks, four containers high, arranged in rows within the hold. *Forty feet tall. They're bigger than I thought,* he mused as he calculated the length of the hold and the ship beyond.

The logistics crew wasn't concerned with how large his ship was as they tried to swim above the deck in zero gravity. *I thought they'd be more prepared.* Most had indicated they could work without gravity, welding and lifting as necessary.

"And you say it's better this way?" Theo asked Gideon as the older man shuffled closer. The balcony they stood on still retained gravity though it was light, giving them a false sense of being grounded whenever they shifted a foot. *Baby steps,* he thought as Gideon bounded closer, his thick coat crinkling almost as loudly as the metal framework of his legs creaked.

Gideon was as gruff as they came, having grown up on Mars during the colony's infancy. He knew what it was like to be living on the last of your oxygen and having to make do with what you were born with. Thankfully he'd been born with a genuine knack for all things mechanical. He could build a machine from a slew of junk to extract oxygen from a lump of coal. Even though it was a brand-new ship, the leather-faced old man had been particular about bringing duct tape. Theo was sure Gideon had a closet somewhere on the ship stacked floor to ceiling with the stuff.

As far as Theo was concerned, Gideon was the only reason his old ship had flown. He knew of a dozen pipes that had been held together by wire and duct tape that wouldn't pass grade, and he couldn't count the number of times the engines magically reignited at the old man's touch. If Edward Lovett had been serious about building the folding engines, all they had to do was let Gideon play with their designs. They would be ready in weeks.

Theo wondered if Gideon had pieced himself together in the same way he'd kept the ship functional. Gideon couldn't walk without his exo-skeletal legs and Theo had noticed on more than one occasion that computers reacted to the man without his direct touch. *I'm sure you have a hearing aid and new eyes, too.*

"Hey lad, what d'ye say?" the old man asked as he shifted his gaze from the workers.

"I asked," Theo yelled, "if you were sure that it was better this way instead of stopping to use the tractors." Their breath misted as they spoke and both men shivered.

Gideon sniffed. "Those monkeys couldn't tie down a chair already welded to the floor. You think they can get the tractors running in time for us to make our mark?" He shook his head. "Nah, lad. This is the best way. They're being paid well enough to learn as they go. I—just a second."

The old man shuffled over to the railing, cupped his hands to his mouth, and yelled, "*Hey! Pull that up evenly, you rotten fools. Don't do that! Right. Do it. Lift! Now!*"

In response, the twenty-foot steel container dipped a little as the crew tried to shift their position. Before the container rolled off the edge, the group corrected their attitude and, with their legs braced against the lower containers, they pushed up, lifting the heavy container and the supplies within until they could slide it onto the stack.

"We can call the marines. They're trained in zero gravity," Theo said as he cupped his hands together to blow into them. *Damn, it's cold.*

Gideon shook his head. "Nah, I don't trust 'em."

Taken aback, Theo asked, "Why not?"

Gideon's face went still for several seconds, as if he were offering a prayer to some invisible deity. He shook his head after a while and said, "I don't trust a man carrying a gun who was never a true officer."

Theo furrowed his brows. "Gideon, you know how bad it gets out here."

Shaking his head, Gideon interjected. "You could've gotten a better crew, lad. I could have recruited you a better crew." He fell silent, eyes glistening, and turned away, his body shuddering.

Within the hold, the last of the straps were tightened and the logistics crew raucously congratulated themselves as if they'd accomplished a great feat. Theo noted two officers from his previous crew, recognizing that they didn't react with as much animation. *You two know what it's like to accomplish something.* When they floated back toward the balcony where Theo and his engineer stood, Gideon yelled, "You lot better get it together. If that container had fallen while we were docking and gravity was rising, someone would be dead." He slapped his hands together to accentuate his point.

Gideon turned to Theo. "We aren't here to be their friend. Being friends gets you killed. It's as simple as that."

"Thanks for the pep talk," Theo said as he motioned for the older man to precede him from the hold.

"It's true," Gideon said as he stepped out, legs creaking.

"Not to change the subject, Gideon, but when are you going to grease those?" Theo asked as he pulled his coat off and slid it onto the wall hook outside the airlock. In a flash the coat was pulled into a recess in the wall, ready for the next time someone needed to enter the hold.

"Lad," the old man said, "I ain't gonna make it to Centauri. My legs won't carry me in heavy gravity. The creaking reminds me that I'm alive. Especially since there ain't nothing to do here 'cept yell at the kids when they're fixing their messes."

Theo had to admit the man had a point. The old engineer had little to fix and the trained monkeys, as he called them, were doing well at the regular maintenance. *But then again*, Theo mused, *this is year one*. They had a long time to travel before reaching their destination. Theo was sure he could cheer the old man up with a bit of work.

The two men walked for several minutes in relative silence before passing the galley, where Theo saw Grace speaking to Jacob at one of the tables, their heads together as if they were trading secrets. *One week and now they're best friends?* Theo wondered how long it would last before he had to separate them; shipboard relationships never lasted. *Maybe Mykaela has someone I can trade for.*

Theo watched his daughter for a moment, then reached out to Gideon, motioning for the old man to change direction. The old man nodded, and Theo strolled into the galley and meandered through the long tables.

Before they arrived at Grace's, Gideon cleared his throat and said, "You know, lad, I have to get going. But just the same, there was a time when you and Galena—"

"Not a word, Gideon," Theo said, clearing his mind of the memories Gideon conjured. How Theo had met his wife was nothing like how Grace was acting with young Jacob.

This ship's galley was much cleaner than *Galena*'s, owing mostly to the two officers furiously working behind the long counter. They'd collected all the trays and utensils left on the tables by the engineers and scrubbed the grease stains from the benches where they'd sat.

Pasta? Theo thought as he sniffed the air. *Lasagna,* he decided, and nodded to himself as he glanced at one of the abandoned plates.

The chef was a much better cook than Theo was used to, and made good use of the plant-hold that Galena tended.

When Theo arrived, Jacob jumped to his feet to salute, sparing a glance toward Grace before saying, "Sir."

"Hello, Jacob. Do you mind if I speak with my daughter for a minute?" Theo asked as he looked down at Grace.

Though he wasn't impressed that the girl had gravitated to the young officer, Theo knew that yelling at her or forbidding her from seeing him wasn't the answer. They were going to be on the ship for years, not weeks. If something soured between the boy and his daughter, it would have lasting effects. *Can't really drop him at the next station after we pass Jupiter.* Better to leave him on Mars than wait until their only option was to eject him into space. Though Theo would do anything for his daughter, the boy would have to do something far worse than break her heart to warrant being spaced.

Theo watched the boy leave, then cleared his throat. "Hello, Gracie."

Grace smiled at Theo and shifted over so he could sit. He could see she was still in good spirits, though he had to admit surprise—she'd never liked to travel with him when he was trucking supplies. On the few occasions that she'd accompanied him, Grace had complained about the lack of amenities. *But then, this ship has more amenities than our house did.* Theo still refused to call the ship by the name his son had chosen. It was bad luck to name a ship with a previous moniker.

"How are you doing, hon?" Theo asked as he slid onto the bench.

Grace had her hair pulled back into a ponytail. Thinking back to the days he'd spent on Earth, Theo supposed she was having a lazy day; otherwise she would have curled it. She was particular about her hair, saying it was a good way to judge a person. It took some time for Theo to understand the philosophy, but now with his daughter, at least it made sense. If she took the time to deal with it, then it followed that she was ready to deal with the day. "Hi Daddy," she said.

Theo watched Jacob leave.

"I just wanted to make sure everything was okay," he said softly to her. She was the only person for whom he lowered his voice. His son loved his exuberant tone, and his wife would slay him if he deferred to her.

Grace nodded. "I am…adjusting." She forced a smile.

"Have you gone out to the plant-hold?" Theo asked as he reached over to pluck what appeared to be a potato fry from her unfinished plate.

Grace lifted an eyebrow. "You don't really think I'd go there and get stuck helping her?"

Theo sighed, reminded of the tenuous relationship Grace had with Galena. *Mind you, this ship has more places where you can hide,* he thought, wondering how much time the girl actually spent with her mother. "Well, she isn't always there," Theo offered, though he knew it was likely untrue.

Grace rolled her eyes and prepared to rise from the table, but Theo reached out to gently grab her hand. As she looked at him, he said, "I know you may not agree with our choice to leave Earth, hon. I just want you to understand we are doing this for you and Petr."

Grace forced a thin smile. "That doesn't help much now. I don't know what I'm going to do for the next ten years or whatever. You may as well have put me to sleep and stored me in the lower cargo hold."

She was referring to the animals being held in stasis until the day they landed on Alpha Centauri. Grace had obviously grown courageous enough to explore the halls of large cylinders that Petr had found the first day and constantly asked to visit again.

Theo took a deep breath and said, "I'm not going to truss you up like a pig, Grace. You are a human being."

The young woman's cheeks twitched from contained tears. "Am I, Father?"

Theo sighed. "Yes, Gracie. You are."

"And you couldn't just let me stay? By the time you get there I could jump in one of those folding ships Petr keeps talking about, and arrive at the same time."

Theo couldn't help himself; he snorted. Obviously, the girl didn't remember the terrible side effects that Petr had quoted. Folding matter like metal and elemental components was possible on a small scale, but organic material didn't translate well. It would be decades before they could move complete objects, let alone living beings. Even if they built the engines, it would be too long before they arrived. She would be almost as old as Theo by that time.

"Fine, if that's what you think." Grace pulled her hand free and strode from the room, her steps even, her body poised. *Ever the dancer*, Theo observed, remembering the competitions he and Galena had been dragged to when Grace was younger.

After a moment spent suppressing his guilt over uprooting his family, Theo pushed away from the table and strode from the galley himself. He knew where he'd find his wife: tending her new garden.

He slowed as he entered, awestruck by what Galena had created in such a short time. It wasn't a plant-hold but a work of art, with every flower and plant placed for perfect effect. Pulling his shirtsleeves up in the warmer room, Theo noticed his son trailing one of Gideon's engineers around at the far end, talking to her as she tried to do some maintenance on a conduit. Petr bounced from one foot to another, incessantly questioning, impeding the woman as she tried to do her job. It was almost entertaining, Theo thought, watching the woman trying to ignore his son.

"Come to help?" Galena asked as she looked up from the vegetables she was planting. Her hands were encrusted with dirt and more than a little had migrated to her cheeks and nose, smudges on her sweat-sheened face.

"Should I be here to order you back to our quarters?"

"Ah, those are your quarters," she replied, wiping her brow with the back of her wrist. "These are mine."

"I'm not sure the cooks would entirely agree with you," Theo shot back as he helped her to her feet.

"Oh, I don't know. Shamus and I have a good working relationship. He's tickled pink that I have planted more vegetables."

"And where did the seeds come from?" Theo asked.

"Oh, I had them stowed for when we arrived at...at our destination." Galena still couldn't get her head around the fact that one day she would stand on a planet other than Earth, looking up at a sun that would look like Sol, but have a twin on the opposite horizon. "So, what are you doing here, lover?" she asked, again wiping her brow, managing only to smear more dirt.

"I had some time off this afternoon before we docked at the station orbiting Mars," Theo said. "I thought we could spend some time together."

Galena smiled mischievously as she bent to retrieve a garden claw from her pail. She straightened and handed it to him. "Then, here you go."

Sighing, Theo wondered if it was worth the fight to get her out of the room. *No,* he decided. As Grace had said, their trip was going to take a long time; long enough to get her out of her comfort zone some other time. Thoughts of his daughter reminded him of the young man she'd been speaking to when he found her in the galley. "Lena, I'm concerned about Grace's budding relationship."

Glancing up from her work, Galena said, "I know. It shows every time you look at him."

"It has nothing to do with Jacob. On a trip this long, it can't end with anything other than heartache," he said in a low voice. *You'll understand some day, Gracie. I just can't have you make that mistake.*

"That could be said about us too, you know," Galena countered almost instantly, refusing to lower her voice.

As she spoke, Theo knelt and tried to shift one of her plants aside to sow the seeds he held, but his clumsy actions snapped the plant at its base.

Galena stared at him for several seconds before grabbing the plant. She cradled it long enough to realize it couldn't be saved, then chucked it into a pile of failures. "Perhaps you should leave her for a time. She'll come around. Did you say you needed to do something before we docked at the station?"

Theo frowned, pursing his lips as he realized he'd been dismissed much as he'd gotten rid of Jacob earlier. *We may not have to deal with it, but you and I both know it won't lead anywhere healthy,* he thought as he stood and dusted off his pants. Though it was possible that he didn't know his daughter well, he'd been on a ship for three-quarters of his life, and knew how shipboard romances went. Jacob was looking for trouble if he thought Theo was just going to roll over and let him strut with his daughter. *Maybe I should put Jacob into a cryochamber.*

Theo turned to leave and found Grace staring at him from the doorway. She was red-faced, and her nostrils flared as she split her attention between Theo and her mother. Then she threw up her hands and spun to stomp away, her gate uncharacteristically awkward and ungraceful, her hand outstretched to guide her along the wall. Her shoulders shook as sobs wracked her body.

"Perhaps we can talk about this later," he said.

Unaware of her daughter's arrival and subsequent angry departure, Galena waved her hand above her head and returned to her work. She didn't look up as Theo stepped onto the path, nor did she move when he tripped over her tools near the door and chased himself from the room, swearing.

Chapter 5

Losing Peacefulness

T heo woke with a start and looked around the room without recognition. Remembering where he was, he shook his head and looked over at his sleeping wife, nestled against her sleep pillow so she didn't dig her knees into his legs. He had bruises on his legs from several nights earlier.

Just a dream, he thought as he dug his palms into his eyes, then pulled his feet out from under the elastic sheets of their tiny bed. He looked around their room, large by a ship's standards, but smaller than his bedroom in their house on Earth, measuring less than ten feet in either direction and housing their bed and a small kitchenette where they could prepare food. The latter was an addition Theo had come up with, hoping they could spend more time as a family, since his son's room was next door and Grace's not much farther away.

Theo's movements were tentative, the fading images of peg-legged pirates with eye patches still haunting him. He pulled himself along the pipe welded to the ceiling for several feet until he crossed the line into the section with gravity and his feet touched the floor. He reached for the clothing he'd set out the night before, just far enough away that the garments didn't float off when the gravity was cut in the other half of their room. The sleeping quarters on the *Galena* weren't designed with gravity, but the Lovett's engineers had found a way to incorporate the plasma gravity matrix inside the most of decks of new fleet without endangering the crew as they slept. Even so, in quarters so compact, everything had to be in place. Searching through the drawers under the bed was impossible in the dark. It made more sense to set it out before he crawled into bed so his clothing didn't float away when he opened the drawers.

Though he didn't mind the grey jumpsuit embroidered with his name, Theo wasn't surprised his crew had opted to make their own a little more colourful. Most had simply dyed them wild colours in hopes of adding life to the ship's subdued colour scheme; the more ambitious had sewn a patchwork of symbols to the chests and backs. Theo was sure they meant something, but didn't much care as long as it made the crew happier and more hard-working.

Clothed, Theo stepped up to the tiny cubicle in the wall and pulled out the latrine. As soon as he sat, a mirror extended from a slot in the cubicle wall and he lifted the electric razor dangling beside it and quickly shaved his face.

When he was finished with his daily routine, Theo moved to the door and appreciated the lack of lower bulkhead as he pressed the button to slide the portal open. No cracking his shins on *this* ship. *The best money can buy,* he thought smugly.

The silence that he'd enjoyed for the first ten minutes of his morning vanished as soon as the door opened. Lights flashed and sirens blared as officers raced along the corridor. Theo clenched his teeth. *Pirates,* he thought. The ships were too new to have any other problems. *Didn't anybody think to call the captain?* He reached for the communicator on his hip. "What's happening?"

Zak's voice came through clearly. "Nothing we can't fix, sir." The first officer was trying to sound calm, but couldn't mask his agitation nearly as well as Mykaela.

"And the reason why the terrible racket isn't blaring in my room to wake me up?" Theo asked as he started for the bridge.

"It should have been," Zak said slowly. "And besides, I sent Jacob to get you."

"And where is he now?" Theo asked as he rounded the corner and passed by the long corridor that led to the cargo bays. *He better not have stopped by Grace's room.*

But there he was, whispering something in Grace's ear. Theo frowned as Jacob glanced his way, and the young man saluted rigidly and rushed off as if Theo had dismissed him. *I hope you were just asking where I was, Jacob.*

Jacob and Grace had become inseparable since Grace had overheard Theo speaking to Galena in the garden before their first stop at Mars. Grace ignored her parents' requests for dinner and Jacob was frequently late for his shift. *And now he screws this up?* Theo had to admit the young man could have been looking for him, whispering in the girl's ear not because he was shirking his duties, but because of the blaring sirens. *That must be the reason,* Theo decided, though he vowed to ascertain that before it was too late to leave the young man behind. It wasn't that he was spending more time with Grace than Theo wanted, but that he wasn't spending enough time doing his work.

His thoughts returned to the alarm. *At least we made it past the first leg before testing the sirens.* He passed several doors, all sporting their own handmade signs from his son; like the *Captain's Quarters* on his door, these bore *First Mate's Quarters, Secondary Galley, Infirmary.*

Docking at the station orbiting Mars had been effortless, the supplies off-loaded quickly and food stores loaded almost as fast. The robots that hooked up the lines for fuel were the slowest part, only because the technicians on the station weren't entirely sure how to adjust their lines for the newer ships. *I could have made my money back three times over with this ship.* He had more capacity and faster tractors moving the supplies in both the full- and zero-gravity holds.

They sped toward Jupiter now, a zone so dangerous that more ships were left in pieces than arrived at destination. He'd been dreaming every night for the last week about pirates, most ending with him floating in space or bleeding out on the floor. If they were waylaid here, his trip would quickly run aground. No, *we'll get there fine. This isn't pirates. It could be a fire, which can easily be dealt with.*

Theo strolled onto the bridge like nothing was amiss, motioning for Zak to join him at the large imaging table showing the star system and all the stations therein.

Zak was drenched in sweat as he joined him. "Sir, I don't know how to say it, but we've got an incoming armada."

"You've got to be kidding," Theo said. *Pirates?* They were running dark so no one could read their signature and hot so they could close the gap to Jupiter in record time. *I guess it's time to test those marines.*

"There are two large ships and at least a dozen smaller vessels," Zak continued. "They're about an hour away."

"Can we bypass them?" Theo asked as he looked down at the glass-topped table, five feet long and three wide. Ten flashing blips depicted his ships, with several more to starboard, approaching quickly on an intercept course. The display was devoid of anything else. *We don't even have an asteroid field to hide in.*

Several seconds passed as Zak slowly shook his head, dripping sweat onto the table. He'd obviously been looking into his options long before Theo left his quarters. *How long was I out? Why wasn't I notified?*

Zak reached out and motioned over the table to draw several circles on the surface. When he pulled back, the screen zoomed in to show both fleets and a line between them, numbers counting down above the line.

They're closing in fast. "Are we sure they're pirates?" Theo asked. It could be a waylaid fleet of transporters.

Zak shrugged. "Well, they don't have a skull and crossbones painted on their hulls, but we're still pretty certain. They aren't transmitting on standard frequencies, and then there's the part where they're coming straight at us in the void of space, like they know exactly where we are."

Exhaling, Theo said, "So we can't get around them?"

"No. We're still accelerating. To change trajectory would mean adjusting our fuel calculations. Gideon doesn't think we'll make it." The screen shifted to show Theo's fleet alone as two dotted lines tracked off at different angles. After a few seconds, the new line terminated at a red X and the numbers flashing above the line flashed twice before going dark.

"What if we keep moving? Can we get through them?" Theo asked. It was always an option to just keep going, but more often than not, pirates left a minefield to blow a ship's hull. At the distance they flew, it was likely the pirates would have enough time to disperse a field. At least one of their ships would go down. *Not acceptable.*

"How big are they? What are our chances if we fight?" Theo was loath to ask the question. He was paying several hundred ex-marines and other onetime thugs to forget their dastardly days and fight on his side. He wasn't worried about their loyalty, but he did wonder if they had the men and arms to fight off a concerted effort by the pirates. He'd seen the worst that a pirate could offer and didn't want to inflict that on anyone, especially his family.

Across the table, Zak was going through a list on a small computer tablet. After a time, he frowned and pushed his finger along the tablet. He shifted his gaze from the tablet to the table, where the screen had adjusted again. Lips thinly pursed, he shook his head. "From what we can see, they've mounted a couple large guns to the front of the larger vessels, and the small ones are loaded. They'll tear us to shreds before they board us."

"What if we stop? Can the others make it?" Theo pressed as he stared at the guns mounted to the pirate ships. The ships themselves were dilapidated, their hulls dented and scorched from previous skirmishes.

Zak bent over the table and, using both hands, pushed the circles representing the rest of Theo's fleet out and around Theo's own ship, adjusting the trajectory only slightly. After several seconds he stood back, frowning, then lifted two fingers.

"How long do we have?" Theo asked as he moved toward the communications officer. His other ships could accommodate his crew. He could abandon the ship and catch a ride with one of the others, keeping everyone safe. One ship was an acceptable sacrifice if his people remained safe.

Without waiting for Zak to reply, Theo told the communications officer, "Send this to Mykaela: Pirates approaching. She is to stop with us and the others are to speed by. Once the pirates commit, she and her crew are to abandon ship. We will meet up with the rest of the fleet at Jupiter Station." They could easily get back on their path at Jupiter. They would still make it to Alpha Centauri. *This isn't going to change our plans.*

As the communications officer turned away and began speaking into her mike, Theo turned to the others and said, "Okay, people, here's the deal. First of all, cut that damned siren off. Second, I want shipwide."

The communications officer pointed to the station beside her as she continued to relay his message to the rest of the fleet. By her red face and minced replies, he knew someone was giving her a hard time. *Mykaela. Are you refusing to stop your own ship, or trying to make us not stop this one?*

Losing the *Galena* had taught Theo a lesson in timing. He wasn't going spend his time waiting for the pirates, watching as his son and daughter cried in the corner or his wife screamed at him to find a solution. He wasn't going to wait so long that the pirates stole every chance of escape from him. *Not again.*

Clearing his throat, Theo waited a few seconds before saying, "This is your captain speaking. I will make this simple. We are being tracked by a fleet of pirate vessels. We are not going to push the envelope on this. Prepare yourselves to abandon ship. We will meet up with the others at Jupiter Station. We expected something like this, people. We *are* prepared. Now move quickly. You know the drill. *Go!*"

The room fell silent, the only voice the communications officer's as she continued to relay information from the other ships and argue with several officers until she too fell silent. *We can do this,* Theo thought. They were prepared, with several speedy vessels on the cargo decks with enough room for everyone, ready to take them the rest of the way to Jupiter. *Once burned, twice shy.*

Theo knew they wouldn't be the same pirates. These ships appeared much larger and were obviously designed for deeper space flight. But they were still pirates, bent on killing and pillaging. *Maybe they've heard the fleet was Lovett's.* Theo had almost forgotten his connection to Lovett and the great game the old man played.

Aloud, Theo asked, "How much time do we have before we know if Mykaela and the other ships are complying?"

Zak glanced down at his table. "Not much before we meet the other fleet."

Gideon had been right about their fuel situation. It would take the better part of an hour to calculate the vector they needed to bypass the pirates, and the speed they were travelling would put them dangerously close before changing their trajectory. *We have to assume this will work. Two ships should keep them occupied.*

"Sir," the communications officer said as she pressed the receiver in her ear with a trembling hand. Her face had drained of colour. She looked furtively at Theo. "S-s-sir, they've already boarded us."

Theo's stomach lurched. *Already boarded?* Were their engines, their instruments so poorly crafted that the enemy could have reached them already, undetected? *No*, he thought. The ship they travelled in was new, built for interstellar travel, dependable, accurate. *There's something else happening.* Pirates could only board a ship if it slowed enough. It usually came down to a game of chicken as the pirates placed their own ships in the path of the transports, or the minefields they planted ruining the transport's engines, often blowing the crew into space in the process.

"H-how?" he said as the rest of the officers erupted with questions.

"I—security says that we have a dozen black-clad unknowns running around the ship, playing havoc with the systems. Gideon just sent a message about locking the place down and—"

Shaking his head, Theo interrupted. "New plan. We evacuate now. Close down this room and get in that shuttle. I want everyone gone in less than a minute. *Move*, people."

Theo knew his plan wasn't going to be executed well. He wasn't going to join them—he planned to find his family first. *Galena's still in bed,* he thought as he realized it had been less than ten minutes since he'd left her sleeping. He had two options: run now, or wait it out, hoping everything would be fine and that the reports from his frightened officers were mistaken. *No one can board us at this speed.* The only place they could have taken on boarders was Mars. *Someone knows.* A member of his crew was working with them.

Without waiting to see how his crew reacted, Theo ran toward the door. "Zak, close the door behind me and find out where my family is." As an afterthought he said, "Be careful what you say on an open frequency."

"Aye sir," the large man said, shuffling to the door as Theo left. Theo heard the heavy bolt slide across the door, locking the bridge down like a vault.

Theo rested his head against the door for a minute until the sirens stopped, throwing a silent pall over the whole ship. *I have to move,* he thought, then looked down the hall, first toward the room he shared with his wife, then toward the cargo holds. *Which way first?* Grace had been near their quarters when he'd seen her last. *I have to start there,* he thought, wiping the sweat from his face.

Theo didn't have to worry about where his son was. Petr spent most of his days infuriating the engineering staff with questions about the meaning of life and how it was processed through the plasma engines. Gideon would have locked his crew into the engine compartments by now. *Petr's as safe as he can be.*

Theo set off down the hall to his quarters. Galena had been up late, working in her garden, still not grasping the fact that they'd be on the ship for years. She worked incessantly, spending more time in the garden than she did at home. She wouldn't have stirred yet, if the sirens hadn't intruded on her sleep. *But why is that?* Theo wondered again. They should have woken them long before he left the room. Whoever had let the pirates aboard must have played around with the alarm system.

Theo paused at the first corner he came to, leaning around slowly for fear the pirates were lying in wait, their guns poised to blast him to bits. *Where the hell are those soldiers?* he wondered of the marines.

With neither a soldier nor a pirate in sight, Theo stepped around the corner and retraced his steps to where he'd last seen Grace and Jacob. *How the hell am I to know pirate from soldier?* he thought. He hadn't been on the ship long enough to meet the entire crew, and could easily mistake one for the other without proper identification. *They've been checked, though. It's not a crewmember.*

Theo jogged forward, his racing heart pounding in his ears. *She should be right here,* he thought as he reached the corner Grace had been leaning on.

He barely had enough time to react as a soldier coming from the other direction whipped around the corner, slamming right into him. They fell swearing to the floor in a jumble of limbs. As soon as Theo scrambled back to his feet, he recognized the other man. "Where have you been, Rick?"

"Looking for you," The clean-shaven ex-marine said in a low, controlled voice. "Zak said you were out here. Why the hell did you leave the bridge?"

Theo ignored the question, moving to peek around the corner. "Do you know where my son is?"

"Down with Gideon," the man replied as he climbed to his feet. He towered over Theo and easily outweighed him by a hundred pounds. "We're missing seven crew, your wife, daughter, and seventeen other family members. I have my team searching for them."

"And the...who the hell boarded us?" Theo asked. He could feel the sweat dripping down the sides of his face. *You should be taking care of that.*

Rick stared at Theo for a second before saying, "I don't know." Sweat beaded down his face as he looked away.

Are you even prepared for it? Theo had hoped the man responsible for the ship's security would be prepared for any attack. He looked up and down the corridor. "My wife is in our quarters and I saw my daughter speaking to Jacob about ten minutes ago, right where we're standing."

"Damn," Rick said, and shook his head. "I heard he was missing too."

"What is that kid's deal?" Theo asked involuntarily. Jacob should have known the protocol. If he'd circled back around to speak to Grace after Theo left, then they should be on an escape pod. "Well, it doesn't matter right now. Come on. You go down to my daughter's quarters and look for her. I'll get my wife."

"Sir," Rick said, grabbing Theo's shoulder. "Gideon said we should head toward the captain's yacht. He's going to wait as long as possible, but he won't be staying until they cut through the door."

"Fine. Tell him I want him to confer with Zak to ram that ship. I will check for Grace when I get my wife. Whatever you tell him, do not let him know that Grace and Galena are both missing." Theo squeezed Rick's shoulder until the man nodded in acknowledgement. *The last thing I need is Gideon playing hero, like he did in the old days.*

When Theo arrived at the next corner, he stopped to peer around it, pulling back quickly when he spied three armed men with their backs to him. *Of all the damned places,* he thought as he glanced around again. They were standing not ten feet from the door to his quarters. If his wife strolled out as he had, she would be riddled with bullets and left to die. *I have to get in there.*

Theo stared at the door for several seconds as he thought. *I can do this.* He was in good shape, almost athletic. He could take two bounding steps and slide into the inset door frame without the enemy noticing. He'd be in and have the door closed before any of them reacted.

One, two, go! Theo stepped around the corner and jumped to the side of the hall where the floor was plated, avoiding the noisy grating that Petr had a penchant for stomping over.

Chest heaving with anxiety, he waited, willing the armed men to remain where they stood, ignoring his chambers. When they did nothing, he reached up and pressed the button to open the door, his eyes on the intruders.

Nothing. *Open, damn you.* He pressed the button again and the door opened slowly, as if to mock him.

Theo felt his world collapse. *How—*

A man stood inside, hands planted on his hips, a rifle slung over his shoulder as he spoke to Galena. The man held himself erect, and from Theo's angle he appeared almost freakishly tall; he would have towered over Rick by several feet. "You will accompany me now," the man was saying. His voice was strangely baritone for one so thin, with an Earther accent. European? It wasn't what Theo would expect from a man on the edge of occupied space.

"Like hell I will," Galena said. She was still in the cubicle where their bed was nestled. The man stood in her line of sight so she couldn't see Theo as he'd collapsed into the room. If she floated even an inch one way or the other she would see Theo. *I have to move before she notices.*

"I don't think you understand me," the tall man said, staring down at her. "You will come with me now. I will offer you one opportunity to clothe yourself."

"Why don't you go swim outside," Galena snapped, reaching up to slap the man's face.

No, Galena, don't.

Deftly catching her hand, the man cuffed her twice in response, leaving a trace of blood on her lips. Several droplets floated toward the ceiling. Galena screamed as the man squeezed her wrist tight enough that the bone snapped with an audible crack. *God no, please no.*

As the man turned to drag Galena into the part of the room with gravity, Theo leapt to his feet and lunged, throwing all of his energy into one punch aimed at the man's abdomen. The movement threw all three of them to the floor in a jumble of pounding fists and kicking feet, until Galena was pushed back out of the gravity.

Theo was the first to detach himself and stand, his chest heaving. He glanced first to his wife to make sure she was free of the scrum, then set to the man as if his fists were bludgeoning weapons. *God damn you—* Blow after blow landed on the man's chest and stomach and then on his head, Theo's fists moving so fast that the man couldn't deflect the blows. *God damn you. You aren't welcome. Leave my family alone.*

Theo would have continued indefinitely, but Galena's good hand on his shoulder brought him back to the room. He pushed away as the man's head rolled back and hit the floor with a dull thunk. Blood pooled on the floor and floated in blobs into the air as it crossed the line into the rear of the compartment. Theo barely registered that the man was still breathing. *I should have killed you.*

He wasn't here to repel the invading force, however, only to abandon the ship. They had to leave.

With tears running freely down her face, Galena asked, "Where, Theo—where are the children?"

Theo looked away for a second, gulping for air. "Petr is with Gideon."

Galena's face contorted in pain. "And Grace? Where's Grace, Theo?"

Theo shook his head and turned to guide her away from her unconscious attacker. Stepping over the man, Theo walked to the door and flicked a small blue button on the wall beside a small screen. Instantly the screen came to life, showing an empty hall outside their room. *Good, they're gone.*

Bending close to his wife, Theo whispered, "Can you run?"

Galena nodded, tears still streaming down her cheeks. "I think so."

Theo knew the only thoughts on her mind concerned the fate of their daughter. She would live through having all her limbs broken, walking on shattered legs, if Grace or Petr were in trouble. This wouldn't slow her.

"When we open the door, we're going to turn left. At the end of the hall we have to start running. I want you to go straight to the bridge. Knock twice and call out for Zak. I told him to leave, but I know he hasn't yet. Do you understand, Lena?"

She nodded as she fumbled for her shoes. He knew she understood he wasn't going with her until he found Grace. He wouldn't stop until their family was safe.

They drew deep breaths in unison and then Theo pressed the button to open the door. As if a starting gun had gone off, they shot through the portal and down the hall, turning the first corner without incident. The trio of armed men had obviously gone off to some other purpose.

When they reached the point where Theo had left Rick earlier, where he'd last seen his daughter alive, Theo nodded to his wife and pointed in the direction she needed to travel.

Galena held tight to him with her good hand for a few seconds before kissing him lightly on the lips. Then she set off running. Her steps were slowing and she stifled a scream as she veered too close to the wall, brushing her broken wrist against the unrelenting steel. Theo had to force his gaze away as she limped around the corner.

As he turned away, the butt of an automatic weapon grazed his temple and dropped him to the floor. Recovering, Theo rolled away and kicked out at his attacker.

The enemy was well versed in close combat; Theo's foot only met the stock of the weapon. Before he had a chance to try again, something heavy hit the bridge of his nose and blood exploded all over his face.

"That's enough. Get him up," a rough voice called out.

"Yes sir," the owner of the weapon said.

Theo felt himself being lifted. All he could see was black leather boots; his left eye was already swelling shut. His right eye found the tall man he'd left in a heap in his room. *How the hell did you get up? Wait—why aren't you injured?*

"I see you've met my brother," the man said, and Theo understood. "I hope he didn't cause you much harm."

"He's dead," Theo lied. "I killed him and left him rotting in my room."

The man barely reacted to the news, only lifting a well-manicured brow as he looked Theo up and down. He nodded toward one of the pirates behind Theo. "You. Go find Damion."

The man set off at a run, back toward Theo's quarters, his footfalls echoing on the grated flooring.

"Now," Damion's brother said slowly. "I have a message for Mr. Lovett."

Lovett? This wasn't just random. The old man had been right when he'd admitted to having more enemies than he could count. So far out in the black of space, this man had tracked Theo and his ships, waylaid them, and now threatened them for being a part of Lovett's plans.

"Do you hear me, Mr. Stinson? I want you to give a message to Mr. Lovett. Tell your master that no one goes through here without a tithe. You could have avoided this whole process if you'd just answered my summons."

The man was speaking as if Theo should know him and the tithe he spoke of. "There was no . . . summons. What—?"

"I don't want to hear from you right now, Mr. Stinson." He looked behind Theo. "Bring him, and keep him quiet."

Theo was dragged for what seemed like an hour before they stopped before a sliding door. As soon as the door whisked open he felt a blast of moist heat and knew he'd been taken to his wife's garden. Within, he forced his head up so he could see. Another ten armed-men had corralled several of his people on the far side and tied them up within the plants, the greenery thrown aside like fodder. The room's beauty had been scarred, its life gone. Theo only smelled sweat and blood.

The tall man Theo assumed to be the leader looked away as his brother was helped into the room on the arms of two more armed men. "I see that you didn't kill Damion, but I must commend you on even putting him down. However, for that, I will take something from you."

"Go to hell," Theo said. He curled his lip and spat a gob of blood toward the man.

"Oh Mr. Stinson, you don't realize it yet, but I live there. But I digress." The man was well-spoken, Theo noted; educated. "Now, I realize you think I am terrible, almost evil, but I want you to understand I don't want everything. All I want is a stipend."

A stipend? Theo thought. The man was pretending to be civilized as he dragged every passenger out to watch Theo be humiliated.

Before Theo could respond, a commotion rose in the corridor leading to the bridge. "Get your hands off me, you no-good, rotten thief," a woman screeched.

Oh God, no. No Lena, please, no. You should be on the bridge. Please no. Tears welled as Theo forced his good eye to focus on the woman a man was yanking around by her hair, like a dog on a leash. Galena was throwing expletives at the man between yanks. Grinning, he chuckled to himself as he pulled harder, sending her into another screaming fit.

Bastard. Theo stared at the man, envisioning beating him as he had Damion. "Why don't you try doing that to me, you dog?" he said through gritted teeth.

Galena's captor snorted and then spit in Theo's face as he pushed Galena down at Theo's side. Galena grunted as she fell beside her husband, tears flowing down her face as she tried to protect her broken wrist. *Oh love, you shouldn't be here. Not you.*

Damion's brother cleared his throat, stealing Theo's attention as he took a step closer. "Mr. Stinson, my name is Deacon. Did you get that? Deacon. I want to impress upon you that I like this man."

In a flash, Deacon's face contorted as if possessed by some demon and his balled fist punched Galena's captor twice in the midsection. He kicked the man in the back when he fell to the floor. Deacon stood back on his heels, his face devoid of emotion. When he spoke he barely looked around the room. "And now he's curled up on the floor on the cusp of death because he disobeyed my orders. Please don't do the same thing."

Theo's face twitched slightly as he ground his teeth. He wanted nothing more than to tear the man to pieces, but he knew he wouldn't get the opportunity. He would be cut down before he took three steps and that would do his wife no good, not to mention his as-yet unfound daughter. *Be safe, Gracie.*

Deacon leaned in close enough now that Theo could smell his breath. It was surprisingly clean. Theo also noted that the man had shaved recently. *Why are you here?* The man was obviously educated and took care of himself. He would easily fit into any high society on Earth, far from any pirate's crew.

"This isn't going to work," Deacon said. "Someone get me a stim."

Theo heard a scuffle, then something was tossed to Deacon. When the man reached out, a small needle in his hand, Theo understood the implications. In a flash, the needle was pressed into Theo's neck and he felt the icy explosion of the stimulant as it coursed through his body, bringing him to promptly alert. Even Theo's left eye seemed to regress enough for him to see as he lifted his head to gaze around the room.

"Deacon, we've breached the bridge," one of the armed men announced. "It's deserted. We should be able to adjust the trajectory. We'll know in ten."

"What about the engine compartment?" Deacon asked.

"The old coot is good. He spent his time learning the systems better than I expected. He keeps turning on the steam vents as we approach so we can't cut through."

"Is he the only one in there?" Deacon asked. The man's cheek twitched slightly as he spoke and the arm he had resting on Galena's shoulder flexed involuntarily.

Radio man shrugged before replying, "He's turned off all the sensors. There could be a hundred people and we couldn't tell."

You are a genius, Gideon.

Deacon sighed and looked down at Galena. Without making eye contact with Theo, he said, "You are going to make Gideon open the door."

"Like hell I am," Galena said fiercely. "I'll do no such thing." The woman was stronger than any mariner Theo knew.

"Of course, you will, or I am going to make you lose something too." The man pointedly looked at Theo before continuing. "Now, I am going to give you my radio—"

As Deacon lifted his radio Galena swiped outward, sending the radio skipping across the open floor to finish under one of her plants. Before it could roll to a stop in the moist dirt, the man turned to Theo. Moving so fast Theo couldn't think to duck, he planted two solid punches on Theo's chin. Instantly light exploded in his vision and pain coursed through his mouth as several teeth were torn free to clatter over the floor. Finally, they dropped into one of the grates with a series of soft plinks. The stimulant did its job—Theo stayed alert. He spat another gob of blood into the dirt.

"Now," Deacon said slowly, "we have a choice. We can all sit here until this ship slams into mine, or you can help me and everyone lives."

"What do I care? My children—"

"Your son may be gone, but your daughter is certainly still on board. Now, before you make me abandon you and I leave on my shuttle, trust me when I say you, and only you, can keep her alive. Again, here is my radio. Call your man and have him stand down so I can save us. Go. Here." Deacon spoke in absolutes, leaving no room for dissent. He spoke softly, refusing to raise his voice even above the pumps operating in the rear of the room.

"God damn you. Why don't you just leave us alone?" Galena pleaded as tears traced down her face. She was trying to remain standing, but her legs were shaking violently, threatening to send her sprawling. Theo wasn't sure if he'd temporarily blacked out—he was sure she'd been kneeling at his side.

Turning to Theo, Deacon asked, "Is Mr. Lovett's cargo worth dying for?"

It wasn't, Theo knew. All he wanted was to get everyone out alive. He owed it to everyone in the hold and those still hiding in the engine room with Gideon. Exhaling loudly, he said, "I...I think I can do it."

"Good. Let his arm go." Deacon held out the radio. "Now, here is a radio. Don't screw it up and I'll let you all leave. I promise not to do—"

The rattle of weapons fire echoed within the hold like a church bell. Theo felt the two men holding onto his arms shudder as they were hit and then they slumped to the floor, pulling him with them. In the distance, Theo was sure he heard Rick calling for his people to stop firing. *That's right. Clear the room, but don't hit everyone.*

After a few seconds, Theo extricated himself from the mass of bodies. He pushed to his hands and knees and paused, hoping the room would stop spinning, before he crawled to his wife's side. Bullets flew overhead, ricocheting around the room. *Why are you using bullets?* Theo thought. Ballistic weapons were more accurate than energy weapons, but bullets ricocheted in every direction, not to mention the possibility of the bullets piercing a glass window or nicking a pneumatic servo and subsequently ejecting them all into space.

As if to prove his point, Deacon yelled, "You've killed us all, Theodore Stinson. Remember that when you get sucked into the void." Theo couldn't see the man, but by the sound of his voice he knew he was moving away from the hold. The bullets were still flying through the air, but less often as the combatants exchanged fire in short bursts. Theo could also see the flash of energy weapons as they were discharged.

Theo tried to speak, but nothing came out. When he tried again, his voice was hoarse. "Everybody stay low."

Turning back to his wife, Theo smiled. He felt his heart swelling as he draped his arms over her shoulders. "Everything's going to be okay, love." Though she didn't respond, Theo wasn't surprised. She was likely as terrified as he was and hitting the ground had probably knocked the wind from her.

"Who's there?" Theo called out as silence overtook the hold. The smell of burnt plastic had overwhelmed the scents of Galena's flowers until the room stank like one of the active cargo holds.

"Sir?" Rick called out. "My people are pushing them back now."

"Contact Gideon. If he can't stop us, we need to know."

"He can't, sir. We need to move. This way."

"Okay love, we need to move now," Theo said, looking back to his wife. He shifted, preparing to help her up, but she didn't push herself upward. Her eyes were open, but something wasn't right. It was as if she couldn't focus her eyes on him. *Lena?*

"Galena? Galena?" Theo shook his wife's shoulder. He moved again, and realized he was sitting in a growing pool of blood as it soaked into the dirt. He touched the warm, wet soil and lifted violently shaking hands to stare at the viscous red smears. *Oh God, no. Please, no.*

"Lena?" he whispered, shaking her again. Too late. It was too late. Galena was already gone.

Theo gulped for air, then the contents of his stomach erupted from his mouth. The world around him spun, the lights flickering like camera flashes. *Please, no.* Heart fluttering, he bent his head over Galena's still body.

"Sir, we have to go." Rick sounded muffled, as if he were speaking through a closed door.

Theo's vision had tunnelled; all he could see was his wife's body. All he wanted was to join her on the floor. *I...I'm so sorry, Lena.* He collapsed on top of her, not caring about the blood soaking his clothing or the distant zing of bullets echoing through the corridors.

"Sir, we have to move. Your family..."

Family? His family was gone. His wife was dead, his daughter gone. Deacon had insisted that he spoke the truth. Theo had to believe the man spoke the truth when he'd promised Galena that he had Grace. *Gone.* The girl was likely dead already. Theo had nothing left to look forward to. He didn't care about the mission or the other ships. His life was over.

He lay across his wife's body, her eyes staring through him. They weren't accusing him, though, only wishing him a silent goodbye as her flesh slowly cooled. She had no crass remarks. She had nothing.

Theo felt hands sliding under his arms to lift him to his feet, but by the time he registered that he was moving the world was beginning to shrink. His breathing was shallow and he couldn't keep his eyes open. *I can't breathe.* Without Galena, Theo didn't care anymore. He let the darkness overcome his senses, hoping he would join his Galena in the afterlife.

Chapter 6

Losing Temperance

Theo Stinson knew three things. First, his mouth tasted sour. It had something to do with the glass of clear liquid he was drinking, but he wasn't quite sure. Second, the room was no longer swimming, as it had been doing when he'd first started drinking the clear liquid. And third, his wife was dead. He didn't know how long ago that had happened, however, because of the clear liquid he'd been drinking since he'd arrived.

"More," he said, slurring only a little. He didn't care. The only person who could understand him was dead.

When he was drunk, Theo could still see her smile and sometimes hear her voice. She would throw snide remarks at him for throwing away his opportunity to set off again. He even longed for a punch or two, just for the contact it meant. *And your scent,* Theo thought. Whenever his wife slapped him in his dreams he caught the aroma of lavender. If he concentrated long enough, he could keep the smell for a whole minute before it flew away on the winds.

"Eat this." The words were accompanied by a bowl of slop that the barkeep kept promising him was safe to eat. As soon as the swelling in Theo's eye came down enough and he was able to see the gruel that he was being fed, he started chasing it with more of the clear liquid. *Ah, vodka.*

It wasn't a large bar, but it seemed to service a broad clientele. In the time he'd spent here, Theo had counted seventy-five regulars and ten thousand transients. Or so. He wasn't sure if it was an entirely accurate count, but he did know it was close, because after the second day he'd started marking the wooden bar with his nail to help him keep track. The barkeep—Bob, or Svend, or something like that—hadn't been impressed with the scratches, but after Theo had thrown his credit chip at the man, he'd fallen silent. An artifact from earth, the chip had enough money on it to pay for every person that came through the door for a year. The barkeep would likely replace the countertop when Theo marked it too much. *Maybe you've done that already,* Theo thought as he stared at the wood; it seemed harder, more difficult for his nails to mark.

As Theo forced the slop down his throat, the bald barkeep leaned forward to whisper, "You've got a visitor."

"I don' wannhim," Theo replied, lifting another glass of alcohol. His vision had been terrible since he'd been dragged from his ship, so he didn't bother turning to see his visitor.

"You don't pay me enough for that," the barkeep said.

"Take it," Theo replied with a shrug. He didn't need the money anymore.

The barkeep sighed and retraced his steps to the other end of the bar, where he leaned forward and spoke to someone Theo couldn't see. The only person he could remember was his wife, and she wouldn't be coming to visit him. *Looks invisible anyway. No one's there.* Theo chuckled to himself at his joke. *Think I'm crazy? You're the one talking to yourself.*

"Gimme a bottle. I'm going ter bed," Theo slurred. Instantly a bottle was pushed down the length of the dark oak bar. Leaning in close, he read the label aloud. "Grey Goose. Hmmm. It's gooooood."

Theo stepped back and waited for a second to make sure he wouldn't topple over, then shuffled away from the bar and down the length of empty tables to the door to the living quarters, always left ajar so Theo wouldn't end up falling into a heap, unable to stand for the alcohol, unwilling to try for his depression.

"'Scuse me," Theo said as he swallowed a burp and stepped around a ghost of his wife. She always seemed to be nearby. "I wish you were here, Lena. You'd like this place. I made sure to get a plant for you."

It wasn't much, but it was the thought that counted. Theo knew she would love the two plants he'd set by the faux window. They were real and he was sure the shorter one had grown at least an inch since he'd started watering them with the Grey Goose. Why not? It looked like water, but had more kick—it should work for the plants just as well as it did for him.

Theo looked at the bed as he entered his room. It had already been prepared for him, just as it was every night since shortly after he'd arrived. Unfortunately, it was made the way his wife used to make the bed, pulling the top corner down so he could slip into the side without ruffling the rest of the covers. Her side of the bed wasn't folded over, however, reminding Theo that she wouldn't be joining him. She wouldn't be running her fingers up his side or giggling when he tickled her in the morning.

As was his habit, Theo stopped just inside the small room to upend what remained of the bottle clenched in his hand. It tasted bitter and kicked back hard enough that he was forced to hold his breath. In the end, he couldn't finish it and was forced to pull away so he could cough. He discarded the bottle in the corner of the room; it hit the floor with a plunk. *I'll water the plants tomorrow.*

The bottles had piled up his first week, but when the bed started being made, the bottles disappeared, the few that had shattered being swept up as well. Now the bottles were taken away and the spilled alcohol washed from the floor. That was another thing he'd questioned in the beginning. He was sure the first bottles held more of the precious nectar. *It didn't take as many bottles to sleep before.*

"Shoulda just left 'em wit me. I coulda drank 'em in the morning," he whispered as he glanced back at the still open door. Theo waved his hand at it. *Fine then, stay open.* He didn't care if it stayed open. He didn't have anything to lose and the barkeep locked up both his alcohol and the front door at night. It hadn't taken long to learn that, after waking late at night with a hankering for more of the Goose.

Turning back, Theo noticed movement to his left. Ah, the mirror. "Oh, yeah. That." Belching, he stared at himself in the mirror. He remembered once looking at his image like this, a long time ago when his wife was still alive. The man staring back hadn't any prettier then, but at least he'd had all his teeth. The man now also had more lines around his eyes, bloodshot eyes that glistened. His long beard held trapped food particles and the vomit he'd spewed that morning when he'd awakened. His nose had grown bulbous and was a dull, throbbing red.

"You aren't worth it," he said to the man in the mirror before shuffling to his bed, his steps short, as if he were walking on ice and anything more than a few inches would upend him on the floor. He felt the alcohol sloshing in his stomach beginning to warm his core, like the gentle caress of a lady he would never feel again. It was a reminder that he was still alive. He wouldn't end it. He wasn't worth it. "Go to hell," he said before falling onto the bed.

As he hit, he felt his stomach jostling, then contracting like a rubber band. He felt his mouth open, ejecting alcohol onto the bed. When he was finished he fell asleep. The cleaners would fix it up in the morning; they always did. He was sure that was why the bed crinkled like the gravity beds on his ship.

When Theo woke again, he opened his eyes slowly, knowing the light would strike him like a sword. *I think it's the same room,* he thought as he looked around. He didn't care; it was a place to sleep.

Theo licked the dried alcohol and bile from his lips, wondering if today would be the day. Would his wife reach out to him and embrace him like she hadn't the day she died?

Need to make it go away. He pushed himself out of the sheets that smelled of alcohol and urine and shuffled to his small bathroom. When he was finished, he tried to pick the larger chunks from his beard, then jumped into the shower to clean himself as best he could. Then he jumped out and went back into the bedroom to put on his clothes. He would accommodate the barkeep by cleaning himself, but he'd be damned if he was going to dry himself.

When he stepped into the bedroom, Theo found his jeans and t-shirt nicely folded on the bed. *Damn,* he thought. He'd tried to shower fast enough that they couldn't switch his clothing, but he must be getting slower. *Maybe they're waiting outside the door.* He peered at the door, which had been closed, the red light indicating that it was locked flashing above it. "They must have been waiting," he mumbled to himself. He didn't care anymore. All he wanted to do was forget the memories that returned when he woke up.

Theo navigated unsteadily through the door and started down the hall, his bare feet slapping hard against the floor. Though he wasn't drunk, Theo still dragged his hand along the wall, counting every step he took as though that was all he could muster.

The regular patrons ignored Theo as he entered the bar and took his preferred seat, within sight of both doors, the one in case his wife arrived, the other so he could find his way home at night. *My new home,* he thought. His world had shrunk to a space fifty paces long with fifteen regular patrons in the morning and another sixty throughout the rest of the day. *I think it was fifteen. One, two, three.* Theo shifted his head in short bursts to stare at each of the patrons. *Seventeen.* Seventeen patrons plus his wife. She stood with her arms crossed and head cocked to the side as she stared at him.

Theo sat down, motioning to the barkeeper to pour him a drink. *It's eleven. That's late enough.* He needed the haze to make Galena's frown go away. When he was drunk she smiled at him without speaking much. *Ah, but your beautiful scent...* Theo closed his eyes as he took a deep breath.

Theo couldn't remember when he'd had to start drinking earlier, but at some point the barkeep had started to water down his drinks. He was sure the man was trying to punish him by keeping him sober.

"You shouldn't do this, Mr. Stinson," the bald barkeeper whispered, as if someone might overhear. Theo couldn't remember the man's name. It was something like Victor or Stewart. He'd been told half a dozen times, but each time was of little consequence. Every time the man spoke, Galena stood behind him with her arms crossed, a scowl on her face. Theo couldn't focus on the man's words when his wife was calling out to him.

"Pour it or I'll come over there and do it for you," Theo said, balling his hands into fists, but the barkeep was oblivious. The scars marring the man's face told Theo that nothing would intimidate him.

"I tell you what," the barkeeper said, again leaning in close enough to whisper. "You talk to the guy who came to see you this morning, and I'll pour you a drink."

No one comes to see me, Theo thought. His wife was dead, his daughter was dead or gone, and his son had disappeared with the rest of the crew from his ship. Even Rick, the last man Theo had seen from his crew, hadn't returned in weeks. No one would come see him. They could search through the stations orbiting Jupiter for years without finding him if he wanted to stay hidden.

Hidden from everyone except you, love, Theo thought as he grabbed the drink and downed it in one swig, then swore as he realized it was water—no burn, just the cool taste of scrubbed water. *You bastard,* he thought as he glared at the barkeep. I hate you, Svend.

It wasn't Svend staring back at him, but Galena, her lips pursed, her gaze steady. She was dressed in the same clothing she always wore when she was gardening—red shirt and brown pants. It would take a few more drinks to make her hazy enough to muffle her accusations. She never outright accused him, only reminded him daily of his decisions. Those were the thoughts he had to drown out and the

Grey Goose was the only solution; Grey Goose that Stewart wasn't offering.

Theo had loved the barkeep in the beginning—Svend had brought him the beautiful nectar that made everything go away. But now as he looked at the barkeeper, wondering who would care enough about him to visit, Theo realized the man was trying to dupe him. *Maybe my money ran out.*

He'd do anything to hasten the loss of his memories; if it meant talking to someone, why not? Theo spoke to his dead wife all day long. He wanted nothing more than to disappear into the void, chasing his heartache and the brewing headache away. *Fine.*

"He's outside," the barkeep said, jerking a thumb toward the door. He was fiddling with something under the counter as Theo turned away. *I hope yer getting my drink ready.*

Theo's world had shrunk since his wife's death and the loss of his ship. The crack over the head had given him a concussion lasting most of the trip to Jupiter Station, and when he awoke he couldn't remember much. He'd tried to find his family, but when Galena appeared he was forced to leave the primary station and go to one of the smaller ones. She'd haunted him through two more stations before he'd found the liquid solution. Theo wasn't sure whether Rick left before or after coming to the station, but one day the soldier was gone.

Fresh patrons were entering the bar when Theo pushed back from the oaken bar with its thousand tiny scars and slowly made his way to the door. In space, time meant nothing. Everything worked without rest, this far from Earth. No one scurried off to bed like children afraid of bedtime monsters. You worked and you slept, sometimes in that order, sometimes not. *Our monsters walk among us,* Theo thought. He was sure he'd seen a few pirates in his early days of running from his wife's ghost.

Theo didn't want to leave the bar; it was the only place permitted to have alcohol. He couldn't carry the Goose around with him when he ventured out into the drab old station. This early in the day, he still considered it a station. By midday he would remember it as a place in space that everyone passed through on their way to better places where he could never venture. And by evening, when his eyes were bloodshot and his eyelids drooping, it was hell in a cell, ten feet long by ten feet wide, where uncaring faces came and went through a door that led straight into the void of space.

This is just a door, Theo thought as he came abreast of the door, aware that he was still a little drunk from the night before—the walls moved as if they were part of a great lung, breathing in and out.

"Hello," a soft voice said as the door opened.

Theo glanced around several times before he realized the voice had come from below his line of sight. He looked down at a boy of perhaps eight or ten years. The boy's face was grimy and he wore a yellow jumper like those the regulars wore. He frequently pushed his glasses up further on his nose, looking away from Theo. *Ha, you look like Petr,* Theo thought, knowing it couldn't be true. Just like Galena's, Petr's face was painted onto every child he saw.

Theo cleared his throat and said, "Hello."

As soon as he spoke, the boy looked up, his eyes wide and hopeful. Unfortunately, the eyes that gazed up at Theo weren't those of a ten-year-old boy, but his long-dead wife, calling out to him to save her. *Please, no. I tried so hard. I...you...* He stepped back, slamming his head into the door; he swore.

"What's wrong?" the boy asked seriously, oblivious to the ghost residing in his body.

"Uh...uh, nothing." Theo didn't want to speak to the boy any longer, but as he stared down at the crooked glasses and oil-stained clothing, a memory tugged at his mind. Was this real? *It can't be. Petr died too. They all died. You DIED!* Theo pounded the door of the bar with his fist.

"I...I'm sorry," Theo offered, unsure of what else to say.

"Don't be sorry," Petr replied. "You didn't do anything."

"But I couldn't save her," Theo said. He didn't want to think about it anymore, but he had to make the boy understand that he'd done everything he could. He didn't want the boy to cry or think he'd done something wrong. *Maybe you were on the ship. Are you Zak's son?* Even thinking the name of his first mate made Theo reel as if he'd been shot.

"Things happen," the boy said simply. He was a strange boy, almost too serious. Theo thought he should have tears streaming down his face. Hell, Theo had felt that every time he'd even looked at an injured bar patron. He'd broken down into tears so many times, they'd started calling him Weepy.

Other than his rapidly blinking eyes, the boy wasn't displaying any emotion. It was like he had complete control. The image of his son wasn't fading, however, and suddenly Galena was standing beside him, her hand resting on the boy's shoulder.

"I don't know what you want me to say, Petr," Theo said. *No, I shouldn't call you by a name that isn't yours.* "I'm sorry." Perhaps the boy had been his page. He was awfully young to have been working on the station long. Perhaps he was a runaway, or left behind by one of the travellers. Theo looked up at the dull faces of those shuffling by, searching for the boy's parents. *Who would leave you alone?* It was almost as terrible as Theo's inability to save his wife.

The boy not named Petr was still staring at Theo as he reached out, his arms wide, to embrace him. He had a strained smile on his face. *Whoa, what the hell, boy? Oh, maybe you just need a hug.* Was it a game the barkeep had cooked up so he could change the countertop without Theo being present to protest?

Theo patted the boy's other shoulder so he didn't disturb his wife's hand. "There, there. Everything's going to be okay." What else could he say? He knew it was a lie. Whatever it was that brought the boy to his new doorstep wouldn't get better. Theo knew everything wasn't fine. The world was a hell Theo had created when he'd failed to save his wife. *And Gracie,* he added, lifting his hand as if it had been burned. The last thing he needed was his daughter's ghost manifested by his thoughts. *I need a drink.* The barkeep would surely have the Goose ready.

Theo patted the boy gently on the back and said, "It's okay, buddy. Uh, I have to go now, but why don't you come back again. Maybe we can have lunch or something." That would work. Theo would make the boy feel better by offering him a meal, something he likely hadn't eaten in weeks. He'd done his duty and now he could forget.

The boy pulled away to look up. He was crying, the tears streaming down his face. *It's not my problem,* Theo thought as he slipped back into the bar and shuffled back to his chair, where a drink waited for him. If he didn't start drinking soon, more of his memories would return.

Theo's first drink was warm and it burned as it went down, the tingling sensation coursing through his body. His second drink was a little cooler. Soon he lost count as he upended them into his mouth in quick succession. Theo wasn't a large man, but in the time since he'd arrived on the station, he'd built up a good tolerance to the alcohol. It took longer every day for Galena's dull stare to turn into a smile.

Theo's day was a blur once he started to drink. He was sure he'd had some food, but couldn't remember what it was. *Eggs,* he thought. He liked eggs and asked for them every day, knowing that what he was getting was only a protein supplement made to look and taste like the real thing. Thankfully they had no smell, or the other patrons would be appalled at the fool in the corner picking at his food with his hands, since he didn't have the coordination to use a fork. The regulars understood and he didn't care.

At the end of the night, Theo grabbed the last of the bottle that he was sure had been watered down and shuffled off to his bleak bed. Not quarters, just a room filled with a bed, a latrine, and a shower.

As the door slid open, Theo looked down at the floor. *Something's different,* he thought as he stared.

"Hey, baby," a voice whispered as he entered, startling him.

He shuddered and looked up. "Who're you?" he asked. He was unable to hold his head up long enough to look at the woman's eyes and instead found himself staring directly at her voluminous breasts. They were smooth and unblemished. She couldn't have been any more than twenty.

"I am your date for the night," the girl said. Theo glanced up, realizing she wore an inviting smile. Her eyes were a vibrant green. They reminded him of someone, but he couldn't capture the name. It was a woman with plump lips.

"I have a date," he suddenly said. "Galena is coming."

Oh, you look like my wife did when I met her, Theo thought as he stared at the woman's eyes. The girl standing in front of him, trying to pull him toward the bed, was beautiful. She didn't have the same colour hair, but then again, she was alive. *Did you colour your hair, love? You look younger.*

Theo could smell her perfume hanging in the air. It reminded him of a spring meadow, the scent of trees and flowers tickling his nose. She was almost as intoxicating as the Grey Goose coursing through his veins.

"Come down here and I'll show you a good time," she whispered as her hands roved over his body.

Theo shook his head. "Galena will be here soon." He finished the sentence with a hiccup. Galena had never been so present, touching him as she was now.

"Don't worry about Galena," the girl tried, but Theo instantly pulled back, his shoulders tensing. After that she said, "But don't you see me? I *am* Galena. Don't you recognize me?"

Theo couldn't remember much, only that his wife wasn't with him. She'd died in an accident on a ship with his son and daughter. He couldn't even remember how he'd survived, only that he now lived in the back room of a bar.

"Come and I will show you how to—"

You're alive, Theo thought as his vision clouded over. His brows furrowed and his cheeks twitched as he said, "No, she's dead." The woman didn't smell right. *Roses and lilies. That's not what Lena wore.* It wasn't that his wife wore perfume, but she loved the smell of lavender, using it in her bath and shower gel. The smell had permeated their home and their quarters on the ship she'd died on.

"Oh, Hun, I can make you forget anything," the girl whispered as she reached down to unbuckle his belt.

No, Galena would never do that. Tears streamed down his face. "I said my wife is dead," Theo repeated. The woman in front of him was trying to seduce him, make him forget his wife. Faster than he thought possible, Theo lifted his hands and pushed the girl over onto the bed. She let out a small scream, but it wasn't fearful. She was trying to make him feel like he was doing it right.

What are you? Theo's lips curled as he stared at the girl, no longer the image of his wife, but a petulant monster trying to lure him away. *A Siren,* he thought. Vibrating with anger, he lifted his hand and slapped her face, the blow landing with a resounding *snap. How dare you?* he thought as she instantly tumbled backward. When she looked up again, there were no tears and her face was relaxed, though an angry red outline of his hand marred her face. *You like this,* Theo thought. She was used to the treatment.

Theo fell to his knees as he broke into tears, his body wracked with sobs. *What have I done?* The girl had tried to seduce him, make him forget about his wife and the terrible things he'd done to his wife and family. Things that he knew were his fault, yet couldn't remember anymore.

Galena wasn't staring at him any longer, only a girl who could just as easily have been his daughter. *Gracie.* He leaned forward to push his forehead into the floor, then fell into the fetal position. "Leave me alone. Get out. *Get out!*"

Theo didn't know when or if the girl left the room, only that the room fell silent.

When he opened his eyes, he saw the girl sitting on his bed, not cringing, but expectantly waiting for another slap. She was tempting him to become the monster he knew he was. *But she...you deserve so much better.*

Theo fell asleep curled on the floor, repeating, "I'm so sorry. Please forgive me. I'm so sorry."

Chapter 7

Finding Integrity

T heo's dreams were filled with pirates with peg legs and eye patches stealing or blowing up transport ships. Through it all, every person he saw had his wife's eyes and spoke with his son's voice. "Why don't you come home?" they all said. When Theo attempted to respond, nothing came out and he realized his mouth was wired shut.

The pirates burned everything they touched: ships, stations, food, and even the people trying to stop them. In the end, Theo realized the only way to stop them was to swallow them whole.

When he woke, something was amiss. *It's too early*, he thought, still a little drunk. His stomach ached as if he'd been throwing up and he realized he was still curled on the cold floor. The pool of vomit had grown and he was sure he'd wet himself in the night; the acrid smell assaulted his nose.

When he opened his eyes, he found a girl on his bed, curled into a tight ball like a dog. "Who are you?"

Before Theo had met Galena, he would have taken any attractive woman to his bed, but since the day he'd met her, he'd never strayed. Even after her death, Theo considered himself married and refused to dally with anyone. *I...I don't remember, though.* He had to admit that he might have been too drunk the night before to remain in control of his faculties. He'd have to add another thing to the list that he couldn't forgive himself for, if he'd slept with the young woman.

Theo pushed himself to his feet and looked down at the young woman, noticing her petite body and smooth features. *So young.* A special place in hell would be reserved for him if he had touched the girl. *Did I touch you?* His memories were so foggy that all he could remember were the terrible dreams. *You know me, though,* he thought. She must have been invited to his room for some reason.

"Why are you still here?" Theo asked the girl, assuming she was a prostitute.

She shifted and said, "I can't leave."

"What do you mean?" Theo asked as he turned away. If she was in the room, she'd obviously known he was drunk when he'd arrived. *Were you waiting for me, or did I bring you here?* He couldn't remember ever seeing her before, but still his memories were as cloudy as his vision.

As the woman unfurled and stood, Theo saw the red mark across her face, as if someone had cuffed her. *Did I do that?* The cell in hell he'd envisioned shrank and somehow got warmer.

"I can't leave, because the deal is, if I don't leave with a thousand credits, then I will be beaten."

Maybe I didn't hit you. Knowing he wouldn't get anymore rest, Theo walked into the tiny bathroom, where he immediately knelt at the latrine and hurled. With every additional thought of the child in his bed, Theo hurled some more. *Did I do something in the bar? Did I solicit her?* He threw up again, dry heaving for several minutes.

Prostitution was a deplorable vocation, but he understood the need. Many captains refused to have mixed crews in transit, for fear of violence breaking out and destroying a vessel, so when they arrived at the stations around Jupiter, many of the crewmembers were restless, looking for whatever they could do to scratch their proverbial itch. Several prostitution businesses thrived throughout the stations, but Theo was sure he'd never even passed a whorehouse during his lucid stints. *I don't know her. I'm sure of it.* It was possible she'd arrived in his chamber before or after he'd retired and, failing to seduce him, she'd decided to separate him from his money.

When Theo could return to the bedroom without hurling, he walked in and pulled on his spare clothing without looking at the girl. He wasn't used to having someone in his room when he dressed, and shuddered when he realized she was watching him. *A little privacy would be nice.*

When he was clothed, Theo asked, "Why did you come into my room?" He wanted to believe the woman was good but, how could he? She sold her body, admitting she wanted a thousand credits for the deed—a sum of money that could buy you passage to any of the other stations in the Sol system.

"I was told to," the woman answered tentatively. "They point and I go." In the light Theo could see that her hair had been a wig. Her skin was smooth and bronze-coloured, save for the angry mark on her face. She was no taller than Galena, perhaps five and a half feet. Theo was loath to get close enough to see whether her green eyes were real, or techno irises.

They point and you go? "Every time?" Theo asked. *You deserve more.* Theo wasn't sure what he'd do if Grace had ever been forced into such servitude. For the first time, he was silently happy she wasn't around to be forced into such slavery.

The girl in Theo's bed frowned, then placed her head between her knees as she said, "Every time."

Theo's head was beginning to throb, the usual sign that he needed to return to the bar. He lifted his hands to his temples and squeezed his head as he closed his eyes. So early in the morning, it was the worst he'd felt since he could remember. *I need a drink.* The barkeep wouldn't serve Theo yet, though, so it wasn't worth returning to his seat for another five hours. He was stuck with the girl until he could convince her to leave. *Can I send her out to get hit like that again?* he wondered as he looked at her face.

Theo licked his lips, hoping he'd left a taste of vodka. "I'm not letting you go back to them." *Maybe there's some left in the bottle I took,* he thought as he searched the room with his eyes, seeking the bottle he was sure he'd brought with him.

The girl actually started to chuckle, her shoulders bouncing. When she spoke, Theo could see tears on her face. Her voice was hoarse as she said, "There's no way I can leave them. It doesn't work that way. They'd…they'd kill me."

Kill? Theo thought. Could the violence the cowardly pirates meted out taint the stations so much? Was no place safe? Theo knew the police weren't effective in the dead of space, but he had to believe they weren't all crooked. *They can't be. There must be someone to protect you.*

Theo shook his head to wash the thoughts away. All he wanted was to return to the oblivion that the clear nectar gave him. Even as he looked at the girl he could feel his memories returning, and he wanted nothing to do with them. At some point Galena had returned and stood with her arms crossed, splitting her attention between Theo and the girl. *Am I in the wrong, love?*

Theo looked away as tears welled. "Am I wrong, love?" Galena would be satiated when he'd attained oblivion, smiling at him instead of accusing him, reminding him of his failures. *I'm so sorry,* he thought as he spied the clear liquid-filled bottle in the corner of the room. Theo walked over and grabbed it. In one swift motion, he tore the lid from the bottle and upended its contents into his mouth, feeling the warm liquid coat his tongue like liquid fire.

He paused as he spotted the girl sobbing in his bed. *I'm not that man anymore. I'm not.* He stared at the girl for a second before sighing and dropping the bottle to the floor. "It's watered down anyway."

"What?" the girl asked as she looked up, wiping her eyes with her sleeve.

Theo shook his head. "Never mind." He realized she hadn't seen him fail, dragging the vodka to his lips like the addict he was. She hadn't seen him make the choice to make it all disappear. *The choice to run away.*

Theo had run once, leaving the memory of his wife and family on a ship he hadn't even named. *Grace and Petr.* Even thinking the name elicited a memory of the boy coming to him that morning. *Could it really have been real?* Theo had been sure it was just another cruel joke his mind played on him, showing him a world he'd lost. If this girl had found him, he had to admit his son could have just as easily. *What have I done?*

Theo's memories were a jumble, all fighting inside his mind, trying to be at the forefront. With every layer applied, he felt more tears. His legs shook violently until he fell to his knees. *I can't do this.* "I'm so sorry." He spoke to everyone he'd failed, a list that was still growing.

As if he was speaking only to her, the girl said, "Sorry for what?"

Theo froze. The girl's voice was timid, yet she'd genuinely asked him what he was sorry for. From her perspective, all he'd done was fall to the floor when she tried to seduce him. *No,* he thought as another image crossed his mind, one of slapping her. *I did that. I'm responsible.*

"What do you need to get away?" Theo asked smoothly. The thousand credits she looked for would be enough to take her anywhere she wanted. He may have been drunk when'd smacked her across the face, but it was the least he could do. If nothing else, he could get her on her way and then return to the oblivion he deserved.

The girl's reply was flippant. "A ticket off the station and ten thousand credits."

"Is that it?" Money was irrelevant to Theo. He'd only kept it to ensure a safe and quick transition when his ships left Jupiter Station, but when everything had gone to hell, he'd only spent money in the bar and for his lodging. He had more than enough to help the girl on her way. *Better that than in the pockets of the creeps who control you.*

The girl stared at him, shaking her head, obviously trying to determine if he was still drunk or being genuine. He wondered the same thing as his skin crawled as if bugs had dug under his skin and were trying to squirm through to freedom. He wiped the sweat beading on his forehead and closed his eyes so the image of his wife would disappear. *I can't have you here. I can't.*

It didn't matter that he closed his eyes; his wife chased him, her gaze still accusing. *I didn't do anything.* He'd done more to the girl weeping on the bed than he had to Galena. On the ship he'd sent her to safety as he went in search of his daughter. In the end, Galena returned, taken by the pirates as she flailed against the bridge hatch. She'd then been hit by a stray bullet as Theo's people mounted a rescue.

"I…I…" Theo hadn't done anything. Granted, his choices had set the stage, but he hadn't pulled the trigger. If he'd known what Deacon had wanted he would have cut it short, knowing he could have negotiated a peaceful solution. *I could have done it differently. I could have made it happen.*

Theo didn't know how long he'd been soaking up the vodka in the bar that had become his home, the ghosts hiding in his mind haunting him. Whether it was the concussion or just a mental breakdown, Theo hadn't been able to concentrate enough to achieve a coherent thought since he'd arrived.

"Who's Galena?" the girl asked, breaking his concentration. "I mean, you keep calling to her like she's here. I'm sorry; I don't want to intrude." She looked away as Theo's nostrils flared and he curled his lip into a snarl.

"My…my—it's my wife," Theo said when he could speak. "She's dead."

"I'm sorry," the girl replied. She was no longer trying to seduce him, but speaking meekly, more like his daughter would after she'd been caught doing something she shouldn't.

Theo forced a smile. "So am I." His wife was dead and gone, but the girl sitting on his bed wasn't. He couldn't save his wife. "But I can save you," he finished aloud, and moved to the small dresser beside his bed. He reached under it, making sure to look away from the girl as he knelt. Before his head exploded, Theo retrieved one of the small data chips he'd concealed when he'd arrived. It was supposed to have been a gift for his children, to purchase all the great things they would need for the rest of their trip, but they didn't need it anymore.

"What…what are you doing?" the girl asked as she followed him with her eyes.

Theo returned to the end of his bed and passed the small chip to the girl. As soon as she accepted the gift, he said, "There are fifteen thousand credits on that chip."

Eyes wide, the girl asked, "But why would you do this?"

"Because it's time to sober up," he replied, rubbing his temples again. "When you leave my quarters go to the barkeep and tell him you want to speak to Gideon. He will help you."

The girl stood, pulling her short skirt down as she moved to the door. She looked like a child, giddy from her first Christmas gift. "I don't know how to thank you. You're helping me and you don't even know my name."

"No," Theo said as he watched her. "I don't want to know your name. Just take the money and be safe."

The girl clutched the data chip to her chest and waited for several seconds before leaving. She tried to smile, but the angry welt on her cheek made it difficult. *Likely loosened some teeth.* He was certain he was the architect of the bruise that would be visible for days.

As soon as she left, Theo moved to the door and locked it. He wanted his privacy as he set about clearing his head. *Shower,* he thought. Nothing cleared his head like a shower, and he paid enough for real water, instead of the sonic cleansers that most ships and stations had.

As the water coursed over him, Theo contemplated the import of his memories. Those same memories he'd been trying to forget for what he assumed was a month were now attacking him with the same fervour the pirates had demonstrated when they'd destroyed his ship. He heaved again several times as he realized what he'd done while he was drunk, forgetting the world, ignoring his son, hitting the girl.

Theo turned up the heat to try burning away his guilt. He wasn't going to accept all of the blame, but certainly his portion. He had been the one to choose their path and as such he should have expected those pirates, even if the pirate Deacon was responsible. The tall man had blathered on about being civilized, but in the end, Theo knew it was Deacon's bullet that killed Galena. *What fool uses ballistic weapons anymore?*

Theo wanted to kill the man and leave him to float outside in space, his insides ejected as he hit the vacuum. Theo wanted to destroy the man's family. But it would do no good. It would take him years to find Deacon, and Deacon had an army to protect him. Theo would have no chance of meting out justice. He would end up like his wife and daughter. Though Petr might live, Theo had no false hope that Grace had escaped.

Theo had overcome all adversity he'd faced before, owning a ship to make himself rich enough to keep his family safe and happy. He'd kept his crew safe for years, skirting around the pirates and other dangers that space offered. *It must have been the concussion,* he thought. He didn't know how long he'd been unconscious, a gift from the butt end of a pirate's rifle. It had addled his brain then and had continued to affect him, turning him into something he didn't recognize. *It must have been the concussion.*

Theo would have flown to his son's side immediately, if he'd known he was alive. Theo had searched for him for weeks, but found no proof that his escape shuttle had survived. Everyone else that had survived could have fended for themselves, but his son deserved more. The concussion would have clouded Theo's thoughts, making it impossible to think properly. *I tried for so long, Petr.*

Theo's legs gave out, sending him crashing into the wall. Petr had accomplished what his father had not. He'd searched him out and now Theo had proven himself unworthy.

"*No!*" he said as he fell to his hands and knees in the water on the shower floor. He wasn't going to fall into that trap. Just like the girl who'd left his room minutes earlier, Theo was going to change things. *He* was going to make things better. It was what he did best.

Theo stepped from the shower and found his new clothing nicely adjusted on his bed. He glanced at the door, wondering if he'd locked it, and sighed as he recognized the red light above the door. *But then how...where did they come from?*

Dismissing it as some magician's parlour trick, Theo collected the clothing and pulled it on. As he moved, he glanced at the mirror beside his bed and sighed. *I guess it's time,* he thought as he returned to the tiny bathroom and grabbed the unused razor sitting on the corner of the sink. It was cathartic to see the ruff of hair slowly disappear from his face, each slice from the laser razor revealing more skin until he was left a caricature of the man he used to be. Staring at his sunken eyes and bulbous red nose, Theo knew it wasn't going to be easy to leave the room, let alone the bar.

"I'll make it right," he said not just to himself, but to his wife and to Gracie, his daughter whom the pirates would have killed on their way from his ship.

When he was ready, Theo grabbed what little he'd arrived with. He paused at the door to stare at the bottle he'd dropped on the floor. *Maybe I could just take a nip for courage.* He took a breath and shook his head, knowing it would lead down a path to nowhere.

His steps were steady as he left his room, the alcohol slowly leaving his system. He could see how filthy the hall was now as he looked beyond the tunnel the alcohol had crafted for him. When he stepped into bar, Theo was surprised to see several of the regulars look up. Before he could meet their gazes, they turned away. Instead of challenging them as he had in the beginning, Theo walked by the tables and then the bar. He held his fists tight and ground what few teeth he had left as the sweet smell of the Grey Goose vodka beckoned him.

No, he told himself silently as he shook his head. It was too easy to lose himself in her loving arms.

"What's your pleasure?" the barkeep asked as Theo reached his customary seat.

Theo stopped and looked at the man. *Victor. Your name is Victor.* He smiled as if he'd won a prize. He glanced at the clock ticking above the man's head, noticing Victor had started his shift early. "Water."

Victor cocked his head to the side, a silent smile growing on his lips as he reached under his bar to remove the credit chip Theo had given him when he'd arrived. "I guess you'll be needing this then, too."

Theo was tempted to leave the chip with the man, walking away from all it offered. *No, I will need it.* He accepted it and something else the man dropped into his hand. When Theo looked he found a little red pill. *Time to wake up,* he thought and downed the pill with the water the barkeep slid across the bar to him.

Up until that instant, Theo knew he was still feeling the effects of the alcohol, the buzz taking away the edge that reality was about to slap him with. Whether he was responsible or not was irrelevant, because as soon as he took the pill the rest of his memories of his lost wife and daughter returned.

Theo nodded to the man. "Thank you, Victor. How long will it last?"

The man shrugged and looked Theo up and down before saying, "A week, maybe ten days. It's not an exact science. And you're welcome." He smiled at Theo's use of his name, knowing it had been a struggle for Theo to do so. *I must have called you a thousand names until I got it right.*

Theo nodded. It was a short countdown to the day he had to worry about the cravings, but at least it gave him respite. *And sobriety,* he added silently as he headed for the door, passing the last image of his dead wife standing with her arms crossed, her brows furrowed as she said goodbye.

As soon as Theo left the bar he was surprised by the traffic. *A ship's come in.* A massive ship filled with frightened passengers making their way toward the lower quarters, all hoping to gain work in the mines on one of the moons. They didn't appear any stronger than Theo himself, hobbling away from their ship. *Likely has no gravity.* Though some looked longingly at the bar, none were steady enough to do so. They needed to stand in the gravity created by the spinning station for several more hours before they could stomach any alcohol.

"Excuse me, sir," a young man asked Theo as he started away from the bar. He was no older than the prostitute Theo had sent away that morning. The young man's flight suit was covered in grime and he sported several cuts on his cheeks.

"Can I help you?" Theo asked. He didn't want to ask, but he knew no one spoke to you on a station unless they were looking for you.

"Are you Theodore Stinson?" the young man asked. His eyes darted to every passenger as if fearing they were going to crash into him.

Theo hesitated. Had Gideon posted someone near the bar to spy him out? *It would make sense,* he supposed. The old man wouldn't want to lose him in the crowd if he got spooked. *But then you would send someone who would know what I looked like.* Theo scanned the area before nodding and saying, "Yes."

In a flash, the young man's face tightened. "There is a man on the second deck of the mezzanine who wants to speak to you. He said you would know what it was about if I gave you this." Reaching out, the young man dropped a tiny plastic tab into Theo's hand. It didn't take any time to recognize the name plate from the chip he'd given the prostitute so she could flee the station. *Damn it.*

With a sinking feeling of dread, Theo said, "How do I get there?"

The young man pointed to the long flight of stairs across the hall. "He's waiting. Don't be late."

Don't be late? Theo thought as he raised a brow. Were they hoping for him to happily walk into their trap? They must have found the girl before she could run. It was that or she'd immediately run back to the group, his credit chip in hand. *No, she must have been captured. She looked desperate.* Theo was sure it was the former. Otherwise it played into the terrible story that Jupiter and her stations had woven. It would be a travesty if the girl didn't take the opportunity he'd handed her.

Theo walked down the hall toward the stairs, weaving his way through the thinning crowd. The people meandering through the station were oblivious to him as he skirted around them, too weak to push through.

The station was a stark contrast to any ship Theo had flown, the floor fully rubberized steel plate, the walls full of colour, and the pipes absent overhead. Where ships were designed for short trips, stations were forever. They didn't just have a child or ten moving through the corridors painting walls or adding pictures, but an army of crewmembers hoping to keep their sanity. The walls were painted a soft yellow, the doors white. Paintings dotted the walls periodically, most depicting scenes from ancient Earth.

The gravity was a close approximation to Earth's so everyone could keep their strength for the mines snaking through the moons. If the shutters over the massive skylights weren't open above Theo's head, he could have imagined himself on Earth. The landscape of Jupiter spread from one end of the corridor to the next within the skylights, its iconic wind storm currently out of sight.

Theo's ears pounded as he found the metal stairs and raced down the steps. *Why would it matter?* he thought as he tightened his grasp on the chip. He could just disappear, letting the girl go to her own fate. *I can't do that.* He'd taken responsibility for her the second she'd left his room. *I can't abandon you now.*

In retrospect, Theo wondered whether he should have accepted the girl's name. If he'd done so then, his mind wouldn't be wandering to his daughter Grace, thinking that it could have just as easily been her. If Deacon had taken Theo's daughter off the ship instead of throwing her from the first airlock as he'd promised, then Grace could have spent the rest of her life an indentured prostitute, too weak and afraid to stand up and leave.

Theo slowed his steps as he came to the bottom of the stairs. *No need to announce my arrival,* he thought as he stepped onto the soft floor. The lowest deck on the station was the first any travellers would see when they disembarked from the ship, and as such it was the most colourful. Every door leading away from the cargo holds was painted a different colour, and someone had created a massive mural on the wall running the length of the corridor, a collage of hundreds of people walking on a planet, all laughing and jumping. Animals frolicked in the distance and trees dotted the landscape. Each face seemed to have been painted by a different hand, as though they were as real and different as the people streaming by in the corridor.

When Theo arrived, he didn't have to search for the nameless prostitute; she was talking excitedly to a short man sporting a long moustache, her arms flailing around as her voice peaked. The man was dressed in a fine suit, definitely out of place on the station crewed by miners. Three muscular men surrounded them, each wearing a suit similar to the short man's. *Businessmen?* It seemed strange to Theo, as if he were still on Earth, not hundreds of millions of kilometres away. Oblivious to his entrance, the men watched the girl pleading with them, tears streaming down her face, her makeup bleeding in the tracks, making her look haunted.

Theo used two passing crewmembers to shield him until he could step around the corner, where he was close enough to listen to their conversation.

"I-I'm so sorry," the girl was saying. Theo could see more bruises on her face and she stood with her weight on one leg, the knee of the other slightly bent, as if she was favouring that leg.

"Sorry, Giselle? I gave you the opportunity of a lifetime. You were supposed to get the man in bed, then take all his credit chips, not just one. And now you tell me he gave that one to you freely? What am I supposed to believe?" Moustache Man's baritone voice was quiet, as if he wasn't upset. His suited thugs stood around him with their arms crossed, staring outward, heads cocked, watching anyone who glanced their way.

"I-I don't—I'm so sorry," Giselle said as she fell to her knees, crying out as the knee she'd favoured hit the floor.

Doesn't anyone care? Theo wondered as two crewmembers passed by. *Am I wrong to think you're crew?* They were dressed in black slacks and had blue slashes running from shoulder to shoulder. Each man, robust and easily strong enough to make the four goons take notice, had a name plate on his left breast. Neither even glanced at Giselle, their gazes locked forward as if she didn't exist.

"Oh dear, don't be sorry," the man with the moustache said. Theo saw him ball the fist he held out of Giselle's sight. As soon as she closed her eyes, he hit her twice on the side of the head. "Don't be sorry, Giselle, just don't do it again."

Giselle let out a wailing scream, quickly stifled. "Please sir," the girl said as blood ran from a cut on her temple, "I didn't—"

The man wiped his hand on the shoulder of the girl's skimpy dress as he said, "Giselle, I own that bar. I own that bartender and every patron in it. I own you and I own the room you were in. I know you didn't sleep with the man. I know what he said to you this morning. Please give me some credit. In fact, give me a lot of credits." All four men laughed at his joke, their shoulders bouncing.

"I—I—" the woman sputtered.

"Now, because you didn't get his money, I have had to put another plan in motion." The man glanced at his wristwatch. "He should be joining us in about an hour. When that happens, I need you to be a good girl and wait right here for him."

You thought I'd be here later, Theo thought. They'd expected him to sit down for another drink at the bar before the boy found him. *Victor, too?* he thought. He liked the barkeeper, had hoped the man wouldn't be caught up in the machinations of the suited man, but if he was, then they likely knew that Theo was seeing visions of his dead wife and family. *No,* Theo thought. *You might own the bar, but I trust Victor.* Victor could have drained his credits himself, making the suited man's convoluted plans unnecessary. Moustache man may own the bar, but not the barkeeper.

Theo studied the man and his retinue. The muscled thugs had a hundred pounds or more on him. He wouldn't last a minute, suits or not. Giselle was grovelling to the man so much that Theo was sure she couldn't be persuaded to run. *But should I even try?* Theo wondered. Was he saving her if she didn't want to leave?

"Now Giselle," the man with the moustache said, "you are going to wait here until—"

The man paused and glanced around. As he turned, Theo saw a small radio nestled in his ear. He frowned and scanned the hall as a wave of people came through the cargo hold door behind him. Nodding to his guards, the man stepped back, a hand gripping the girl's shoulder. *He knows I'm close*, Theo thought, and pulled back a bit.

"You know what, dear? I don't think I need you anymore." As he spoke, Moustache Man reached into his pocket for something. *Damnit,* Theo thought as he saw the glint of steel. Theo couldn't let the girl die, even if the station crew were going to walk by without noticing.

Drawing a deep breath, Theo pushed away from the wall and turned the corner. His hands shook and sweat beaded on his forehead. *I can do this.* The question wasn't whether he could do it, however, but whether giving up his money would assure Giselle's survival.

"Mr. Stinson, I presume?" Moustache Man said as he turned away from Giselle, palming the blade. He lifted the other hand to twirl the end of his moustache.

Theo was no fighter. Of the few times he'd found himself compelled to trade blows, he'd always been on the receiving end. *Civilized men,* Theo sneered, first of the pirate Deacon and now the men in front of him. *Are you trying to fool us, or yourselves?*

Without waiting for Theo to respond, Moustache Man stepped forward and offered his hand for Theo to shake. "Mr. Stinson, I believe we have a transaction still unfinished."

Ignoring the man's hand, Theo said, "What do you want?"

"Oh, I heard you were quick to business. I like that," the man said with a slight smile.

Theo's cheeks twitched. "Get to the point," he said. "I don't have all day." The little red pill that he'd taken wasn't designed to relieve the symptoms of sobering up, only take away the cravings. With every second, he felt his stomach churn and the headache grow. The colours on the mural were beginning to bleed together with each painful throb inside Theo's head.

"Oh, where are my manners?" Moustache Man said, bowing, resting a hand on Giselle's shoulder so she couldn't run. "My name is Shamus Brett. When I was told you'd survived the pirate attack I was surprised, but still…glad."

What are you going on about? Theo thought. It wasn't coincidental that the man was acting like the bastard Deacon. *Can't you just leave me alone?* Theo had thought his tiny existence within the bar had gone unnoticed, but he was certain now he'd been watched, perhaps even set up. Deacon had wanted a stipend. Perhaps it was his twisted way of extracting what he thought was his due.

Theo balled his fist so hard, his fingernails dug into his palms, readying himself for a fight. If he was going to die, he was at least going to participate. Though Theo had promised himself it wasn't about his wife, Shamus Brett had made it so. *You want it, you come and get it.*

Theo lifted his arm to sucker-punch the thug on the right as the thug on the left stepped forward to grab for his arm. That thug was the faster; before Theo's punch could connect, he felt a hand on his shoulder and he was yanked aside blindingly fast. He was thrown against the wall, where he slid toward the floor, moaning, then doubled over in a coughing fit as two successive punches hammered into his midsection.

"Mr. Stinson, I want you to know this isn't personal. We just want the card your employer has given you."

Theo smiled and began to chuckle. Shamus Brett had just confirmed Theo's belief in the barkeeper. Victor had held the card for weeks without letting on he'd had possession of far more than he'd ever touched.

"What are you so happy about?" Shamus asked as he strolled over to stand over Theo. Shamus held his small blade ready to plunge into Theo's chest.

"You don't own everyone," Theo wheezed.

Before Theo could say anything else, Shamus Brett brought his fist down twice on his mouth, drawing blood. Stepping to the side, the man kicked Theo's chest and stomach in quick succession. "Oh, I do own everyone on this station, just like Deacon owns the sky."

The mention of the pirate's name made Theo's body tense. His wife appeared in the distance, walking along the hall, her hand trailing along the wall as if she were brushing the tops of tall grasses. Theo dropped his head. *You bastard, Deacon. You've already destroyed my life. Can't you leave me alone?*

Unable to lift his gaze from the floor, Theo tensed and stared at Shamus Brett's feet envisioning the blade sweeping toward his back.

I'm sorry, Petr. Theo wouldn't see his son again, wouldn't hold Petr in his arms and whisper to him that everything was going to be okay.

There was an audible gurgle, then one of the men fell to the floor, clutching his throat. Had the crowd finally reacted? Were they tearing into Shamus's goons?

Torn from his conversation with Theo, Shamus whirled toward the assailant, saying, "What the hell?" He swiped at the air with his blade as if protecting himself, then let out a *woof* as someone hit him in the chest.

"Why don't you all just run along and leave the gentleman and the lady alone?" The man's accent was Asian; Theo forced his head up and confirmed that the speaker was indeed Asian. He bowed slightly as if deferring to Shamus, swinging his chest-length hair and his own long moustache forward. He was dressed like the locals, in an orange jumper, with the name *Masajiro* embroidered on its breast.

As soon as Shamus had caught his breath, he retorted, "Why don't *you* just run along?" and brandished the blade first at Theo and then at Masajiro. Theo couldn't see if the newcomer carried a weapon. *You must,* he thought as the others edged away from him, their eyes darting toward potential exits.

Masajiro nodded. "Excellent. Now, send the young lady over and everyone will be happy."

"I doubt it," one of the other men said as he found the courage to circle around them. Giselle was still on her knees nearby, crying into her hands.

Theo put his hand on the rubberized floor and pushed to his feet, gaping as Masajiro, with dancer-like grace, slapped the blade from Shamus's hand, then flowed forward like water to kick the first thug's legs out from under him. He was on the other man in an instant, punching him in the throat to drop him to the floor.

Theo had learned to hate violence, but in Masajiro's case it was more like art. He watched Shamus and his henchmen retreat, their noses bloodied and egos bruised. *Where were you a month ago, good sir?*

Masajiro came to his side, quickly ascertained he was okay, then bounded over to Giselle. He reached out and swept her to her feet, where she stared at him in confusion. Without waiting for any response, the man urged the woman forward and yelled to Theo, "Run."

Theo didn't need another invitation—Shamus and his men were reaching for their real weapons. Masajiro may have disarmed them in close combat, but that wouldn't work in a gun fight. Theo took off after Masajiro and Giselle.

Chapter 8

Finding Fortitude

Rather than go through the door closest to the fracas, Masajiro took them back toward the staircase Theo had used. They quickly left the mural behind, entering a cold corridor, brightly lit but devoid of colour. It was wider than most, and a yellow dotted line ran its length. Theo caught the faint scent of petrol, and greasy smudges marked the walls every few paces.

"Where…where are we going?" Theo asked as they stopped to catch their breath. He leaned forward, placing his hands on his knees as he gulped air.

Turning back, Masajiro said, "I was hoping that perhaps you had the answer to that." He stood with his arm wrapped around Giselle, his chest barely moving as he spoke.

Theo snorted. When he left the bar, he was hoping to find his son, but now he wasn't sure that was the greatest idea. He couldn't risk his son or the officers looking after him. "I don't want—"

"We don't have that luxury," Masajiro interjected, looking back along the corridor. It was quiet except for a large robot shifting an antigravity pallet at the other end. The robot's servos snapped and whined as the pistons in its legs shifted it forward at a man's pace.

"Do you know of anywhere we can go?" Theo asked Giselle.

Wiping tears from her face, Giselle silently shook her head. Her eyes were shifting nervously and her chest heaved as she tried to catch her breath. Masajiro leaned her against the wall and turned to Theo. "I don't know what connection you have to that man and this girl," he said, "but you have to get us clear. Go. Now."

Theo stared at Masajiro, opening and closing his mouth for several seconds, lost for words. *I'd be able to help if I knew which station we were on.* "I-I've been in a bar for who knows how long. My head cleared long enough this morning to recognize my son from yesterday, a son I thought was dead with my wife and daughter. I know he's here somewhere, but I don't know where to start looking."

"Your son walks around here on his own?" Masajiro asked, not as an accusation, but more like Masajiro was trying to correct his opinion of Theo. He suddenly seemed forgiving, like he knew what it meant to have family. *Did they take someone from you, too?*

Theo's memory, from the point he'd found his wife dead until arriving at the station, was a blank. He was sure the memories would return as the effects of his drinking binge faded. In the meantime, he could barely stand for the pounding in his head and the beating he'd taken at Shamus's hands.

Whether he was with Gideon or someone else from his ship, Petr wasn't alone. And they were on this station, probably nearby—Petr wouldn't have been given free rein to wander through station corridors. Someone must have been around the corner while his son tried to communicate with him the morning before. They just didn't realize how much stress he carried, or the fact that he was dealing with a concussion. They would have come to his aid if they'd known he was compromised.

"You have an idea," Masajiro said sagely, watching him. He turned to check Giselle's injuries, his touch gentle as he prodded her cheeks and jaw. When he was finished, he stood and tied his hair into a ponytail.

Masajiro appeared as old as Theo, perhaps in his late forties or fifties. His eyes had dark rings around them, as if he hadn't found sleep in several days. His hands were like those of an artist, soft and supple, not those of a miner or station hand. *Medic, maybe?* Theo wondered.

Theo pushed those thoughts aside and nodded. "My son found me. He won't be alone."

"I don't want to sound rude, but we really don't have much time," Giselle said as she sniffled. She tilted her head as though hearing something in the distance. Until that moment she had been irrelevant, but now Theo stared at her as she stood, wondering if she was a willing participant in Shamus's plan. He glanced back down the hall where she was staring and asked, "What do you hear?"

As if attuned to the woman's thinking, Masajiro pointed back the way they'd come. "Our friends are coming." He paused for effect before pointing toward the end of the corridor where the robot was working. "And the police are coming from that direction."

Now they come? Theo thought, shaking his head. "That's good, then." They could tell their story and leave.

Both Masajiro and Giselle chuckled, the former shaking his head and the later cringing into the man's shoulder. She still trembled and both of her eyes were beginning to swell. If they waited much longer she wouldn't be able to see and they'd be forced to carry her.

It was obvious to Theo that his distrust of the police was justified and they wouldn't be getting any assistance. *I guess you were right, old man,* Theo thought as he remembered what Gideon had said about the police. Theo would give anything for him to be present, playing with his gadgets. Gideon wouldn't disembark from a ship, however, especially onto a station with the gravity turned up so high.

As his mind wandered toward the old man and his toys, Theo suddenly said, "Gadgets."

Turning to him with a look of confusion, Masajiro asked, "Gadgets for what?"

"My son wasn't on my shuttle and I haven't seen anyone else since I got here, so he has to be with Mykaela or Gideon. Either way, they would be in the shipyards. If it's Gideon, he's likely building more gadgets, and Mykaela would sell those gadgets from her ship to pay her people." *That's what they're waiting for. Me.* Mykaela or Gideon would both wait for Theo to come to them. They wouldn't have set off toward Alpha Centauri without him.

"The shipyards, then," Masajiro said with a nod. He bent to scoop Giselle into his arms as if she were a child, his muscles flexing beneath his tight-fitting clothing. *Could be a medic. Maybe an officer. They have nothing better to do.*

"I don't know which way to go," Theo said. He could hear the pounding footsteps of Shamus and his men. *They're trying to make noise.*

"That way," Masajiro said, pointing down the corridor toward the approaching robot. Theo had to catch up to him as the man rushed off, Giselle tucked neatly in his arms.

They ran for several minutes without seeing anyone in their path and for a time, the adrenaline masked the effects of his beating, but eventually Theo's steps slowed and his breathing became hoarse and laboured. "Are we far?" Theo asked as he rubbed his burning chest.

"Through the door at the end," Masajiro replied as he hiked the girl up in his arms.

They'd reached the massive robot and could barely hear each other. Behind them Theo could see Shamus had rounded the corner, but the man had refrained from pulling a weapon.

Several hundred yards down the hall, the yellow line on the floor that they followed brought them to a large double door. Nothing they did could force it open. First Masajiro pressed random buttons on the console to the right of the door, then Theo joined him. When that didn't work, Masajiro tried to pry it open. After a time, his attention on the approaching Shamus and a contingent of black-clad security officers following behind the thug, Theo pressed his head against the door in frustration.

"You there—stay where you are," one of the police officers commanded, her voice carrying down the hall, sounding like she was speaking right beside Theo.

Theo pushed away from the door and saw Shamus thrust his hand into his suit coat to grab a concealed weapon. Instinctively, Theo slapped his hip as if reaching for an invisible weapon. *Wait,* he thought. *Maybe I* am *wearing something that will help.* Pushing his hand into his pocket, he retrieved the credit chips Victor had returned to him. He weighed them in his hands for a second, then chose the one bearing his wife's name, written in black marker. Although no bigger than his thumb, it suddenly felt a thousand times heavier as he flipped if over, revealing the insignia of Lovett Industries emblazoned on the other side.

"It's a war," Theo whispered. Everything that had happened was because of Lovett's war. Deacon had boarded his ship to take from Lovett, and Shamus Brett wanted Lovett's card, the only proof Theo had that he'd ever dealt with the old man. The card wasn't just money, however, but access. Lifting it, he swiped it across the door panel, and sighed as he heard the chirp of acknowledgement. It was a war and Theo finally had a weapon to use.

Theo glanced down the corridor and ducked as a red arc of energy hit the wall beside him, the charge spreading out like a spiderweb over the metal. *Geez, close enough?* Theo wondered as he dropped to his hands and knees. Another energy arc followed before the door slid open far enough for the trio to slip through.

They were in another hall just as wide, but running farther into the distance than Theo could see, with doors on either side and a few dozen pedestrians walking its length, oblivious to the three newcomers. Masajiro reached out to depress the button that shut the door, the reflection of several more energy discharges making his face flash red as the police continued to fire on the door. *The fools. They could have hit an innocent bystander,* Theo thought as he peered through the tiny window inset in the door.

Masajiro turned away from the door to scan the hall, asking absently, "What did you say?"

Theo stared at him in confusion, unaware that he'd spoken aloud. "Oh—I said that it's war. All of this is happening to me—no, not to me. All of this is a war between Lovett Technologies and those pirates." Theo wondered how one man could create such animosity. Edward Lovett had made so many enemies that entire stations had banded together to fend off his agents. *Or supposed ones,* Theo amended, shaking his head.

"We need to lock the door," Masajiro said.

"You can't?" Theo asked. *Just a medic, then.* Theo stepped behind Masajiro and lifted Lovett's data chip. He was about to slide it into the port when he paused and switched it out for one of the others, placing the new one neatly in the lock. He pressed it hard, snapping it off inside the mechanism.

He turned and joined Masajiro in examining the new hall. Most of the pedestrians were officers clad in the typical orange jumpsuits and guiding small pallets of tools or supplies. Three robots shifted forward on their clunky feet with larger crates. They were loud enough to drown out the pounding on the door. *It must be the lower docks,* Theo decided, but admitted, "I don't know how to tell where they are."

For first time since they'd started running, Giselle spoke. "I can tell."

As soon as she opened her mouth Masajiro set her down on the floor. Though Theo was surprised, the man didn't interrogate the girl, but instantly set about checking her bruises again. He reached into his pocket and retrieved what Theo assumed was a stim, which he plunged into her neck. Theo remembered the affects of a stim. Minutes before the pirate Deacon had killed Galena, Theo had been given a stim so he wouldn't pass out from the pain. He'd been conscious to watch as his wife bled out on the field of flowers she'd crafted.

Unaware of Theo's internal struggle, Giselle said, "There is a list of every person that comes through the door."

Theo glanced to the door he'd pressed the card into. "Where is the next terminal?"

"This way," Masajiro said as he bent to heft Giselle into his arms again. The woman accepted the man's help as though she knew him. *Maybe a lover? A rich lover who wants to rescue his princess?* Theo wondered, but shook his head at the fanciful thought. Masajiro had fought off all four of their attackers. He was more than a simple medic.

Masajiro slipped around a shuffling robot and darted around three officers, stopping at a section of the wall that otherwise looked empty. He set Giselle down and tapped the wall several times, moving along in a line as if he were playing Chopsticks on a piano. After a second, he smiled and stepped aside as the wall split open like a book to reveal a computer terminal.

"How did you know that?" Theo asked, frowning. Was it possible there were other players in this war? If Masajiro had his own agenda, it would explain much. *A spy?*

Masajiro shrugged as he began pressing on the small screen. "Who are we looking for?"

"Gideon Santos," Theo said immediately.

Theo tried to concentrate on the screen as Masajiro searched on the computer, but a resounding crack as something hard hit the door they'd slipped through only a minute before made him turn. He glanced at the chip he'd broken off in the terminal. *Hope it holds long enough.* Three thunderous crashes echoed along the corridor and then a muffled voice yelled, "Let us in."

"Hey, what are you doing?" a woman passing by stopped to ask. She must have been a passenger from one of the ships, as she wasn't wearing any insignia, though she held herself as if expecting an immediate answer. Theo sighed and thought, *It would be a lot easier if you went on your way.* As if accepting his mental command, the woman shivered and stepped away.

"Another name," Masajiro barked as something hit the small window, cracking the glass.

Who has gone through the door? Theo thought. *Petr is the only one to come to see me.* "Try Petr Stinson."

Masajiro cocked his head as Theo said the name. After a few seconds, the man narrowed his eyes and said, "And that makes you Theodore Stinson."

Am I so famous? Theo thought. "How do you know my name?"

"There's a price on your head," Masajiro answered smoothly as he pressed his buttons. "You're a wanted man." He continued to glance back at Theo as if fearing he would disappear.

A price? Theo thought. What could he have done to deserve such a fate? He'd been transporting food and supplies to the colonies. What was so evil about that? He felt like he'd been transported to universe that prized corruption over virtue. It almost made him want to return to the alcohol. "At least there, no one bothered me," he whispered.

"What?" Masajiro asked, glancing back at Theo.

Theo shook his head and stepped away, crossing his arms as several people passed by. They were beginning to receive suspicious stares from those who heard the police pounding on the other side of the unyielding door. *They're going to come through,* Theo thought as he tried not to look at the door.

He was about to set off to search on his own when Masajiro suddenly turned away and motioned for Giselle and Theo to follow him. Minutes later, Theo heard a rough voice ask from somewhere ahead of Masajiro, "Now boy, what did you go and get yourself into now?" Masajiro stepped aside, to reveal Gideon arching his brow at Theo. As another resounding thud came from the sealed door, he shook his head and held up a hand. "I don't know what kind of trouble you've got yourselves into, but you'd better come with me. In about two minutes they're going to start cutting through that door. And there's someone coming from the other direction."

Masajiro looked from Gideon to Theo with a knowing smirk. "Gideon?"

Theo nodded. "Yes."

Gideon hadn't waited for them; he was several paces away, and Theo set off in pursuit. The old man only paused once, to fiddle with something he had in a voluminous pocket. When he was finished, the overhead lights faded and the gravity in the hall suddenly gave out, levitating all four of them slowly into the air. They scrambled for handholds. Only the flickering lights on the robots illuminated the corridor.

"We have to move down three more doors," Gideon said, sounding giddy, as if he'd been breathing pure oxygen. *You're happy.* Gideon was never happy; content, perhaps, but never happy. *I didn't think you'd be that glad to see me, old man,* Theo thought.

As others in the corridor loudly voiced their alarm, Theo and his group dragged themselves along the ceiling, using any handhold they could find. It's d*efinitely not designed for zero gee,* Theo thought, remembering the handholds welded to the ceiling of most ships as he pushed off in search of the next projection. He caught at a robot's head, surprised at its size, this close up. It dwarfed them all as it shifted forward by means of its independent power source.

Moving by the light of a flashlight he must have pulled from his pocket, Gideon paused at one of the doors. "I've shut the power off to most everything so it'll take 'em a couple minutes longer to get in, and the cameras won't be active to see which shuttle we've boarded. We should be able to get away in the dark."

Masajiro chuckled. "You aren't docked *here.*"

Gideon laughed, then said, "No, boy. It wasn't luck that you found us. We've got shuttles at all the exits, waiting for you. Mykaela's down three decks and Rick's on the other side of the station."

Mykaela and Rick? Had they all found each other? Had he been hiding so long, or was it easier for them? He'd hunted for weeks—he was sure it had been weeks. *How did I lose contact with Rick? I can't remember. It's like I've been drugged.* Of course, he'd been reeling from the loss of his wife, but he'd scoured the decks of three stations before giving up, and by that time Rick must have taken another job to pay the bills. Theo hadn't been able to contact him after that. That's when he he'd taken the first drink. *A drink at a bar fronted by a man connected to Deacon.* Was such a coincidence possible?

Theo had tried to keep an open mind. He told himself they would find him. All he had to do was send messages to the winds. He told everyone that came through the station, then later, through the bar. *Maybe it wasn't a coincidence.* Whether the thug Shamus was connected to all the bars or he'd been lured to the bar he'd found, Theo knew it was no coincidence.

Shamus knew he had Edward Lovett's card. The man was bent upon getting that card, not just for the cash it carried, but something else. Theo wasn't sure what. *But I will find out,* he thought as he looked at Giselle, wondering if the woman knew anything. *Not likely, but how far does it go?* Masajiro had intimated the police were connected.

"What's on your mind, lad?" Gideon said as he ushered the others into the shuttle, the light of the docking tunnel a stark contrast to the dark corridor.

Theo looked one last time along the corridor as the technicians at either end reset the lights. Someone had shut the robots down to stop them from careening into the passengers. *They'll have that door open shortly.* Theo shook his head. He'd have time later to think. For now, they had to survive. "Nothing," he said. "Let's get out of here. Where are the ships?"

Gideon shook his head as he locked the door. "No, lad, we sent the ships on to the colonies. We only have Mykaela's left."

"You sent them on?" Theo asked. *They survived. It was just my ship.* A smile crept onto his lips as he looked at Gideon. He could feel his heart racing as the knowledge that he'd won gave him strength. Galena's death hadn't been in vain. The other ships would go on to their destination and their crews would survive. The colonies would get their supplies and the pirates would have lost. *You've lost, Deacon.*

The shuttle was too small to have gravity and the seats were more like benches than chairs. Theo strapped himself in, not caring about the cramped space or the cold air. He was going to see his family. Galena was smiling now. He could see her leaning against the outer hull as if she had gravity. She was no longer in her work attire, but in her black sequined cocktail dress. It was the dress she wore when they went out dancing on Earth, or to take in a show—anything they could do to pretend the world outside hadn't been dirty and decrepit. Theo wiped the tears from his eyes, not bothering to hide them from the others before helping Giselle buckle herself into her seat.

"Call everyone to the ship," Theo said as if he hadn't spent any time away. "And tell the doctor we have injured." It was time to get back to work. He had a ship and a crew to care for. *And a son,* he thought. Petr hadn't died on the ship as he'd thought. He was alive and waiting for him. Theo had a reason to live.

Theo was thankful for the lack of gravity as the others took their seats, jostling him in the process. His chest was burning as he rubbed the lump on his side. *Definitely broken,* he thought, holding his breath. Giselle was also tentatively exploring her swollen eyes with trembling fingers. She whimpered and let her hands fall away.

Masajiro settled into a seat, looking bored as he glanced around the shuttle. *What's your deal?* Theo wondered. Masajiro had come to Theo and Giselle's aid as if it was nothing special. He'd beaten back Shamus and his thugs with ease and carried Giselle from the battle as if she weighed nothing, then assessed her wounds and administered quick first aid like a medic. Theo leaned forward. "You know about me and yet I barely know your name. What's your story?" he asked. It wasn't entirely true. Even with the headache trying to rearrange his thoughts, Theo had gleaned much from the man.

Masajiro either had a police or military background and possibly worked for them still. He knew too much of the inner workings of the station's computers not to be connected somehow. Theo could have believed he was linked to Shamus, except for the walloping he'd given the man and his thugs. *And you were surprised when I said my name. Are you surprised that I am alive, or have you heard something else about me?*

Though Masajiro hadn't spoken much, Theo had detected his accent. *Japanese. Earth.* His origins meant he was more likely to be a member of the military than the police. *Homeforce?* Theo wondered. The Homeforce, once a powerful organization on its own, had long since passed its peak some time after the uprising was quashed on Mars. Theo had heard of only a few of their massive ships patrolling space, hunting pirates when they could. *I bet you know Captain Kai,* Theo thought, remembering the shuttle captain that had saved his people near Earth.

It was possible those operating the few ships left in Homeforce had set their sights on a new target in the stations orbiting Jupiter. With a concerted effort they could rid the cosmos of the pirates that plagued ships like Theo's. *They'd need to get the stations to agree,* he thought. *And that's not likely.* The mining stations wouldn't appreciate the presence of one Homeforce ship, let alone a fleet. So far out in space, they'd more likely side with the pirates than the iron fist of Earth's small navy.

Masajiro's bored demeanour was a façade; he was watching the pilot and Theo at the same time. His arms flexed each time he looked at the hatch between the shuttle and the station, as if he was still looking for a fight. He had no response for Theo's attempts to engage the man in conversation.

"Masajiro, we are flying toward my ship. I don't want to be rude—I mean, I want you to understand that I fully appreciate and understand the gift that you have given me, but who are you?"

The man stared at him for several seconds, clearing his throat twice. Theo thought he was about to speak, but instead he reached up to pull a chain from around his neck. He passed it to Theo without speaking, and settled back into his seat.

Military for sure, Theo thought as he stared at the dog tags.

Masajiro had turned away when Theo looked back up, so he idly scanned the shuttle, recognizing it as one of the short distance shuttles from his fleet, designed to operate around the ships to assist in repairing the hull. Its designers had skimped on the gravity and internal systems, making it little more than a tin can with a steering rocket on either side.

The shuttle jostled and Gideon said, "Get up, we don't have much time."

Theo felt the tug of gravity and looked up to the window at the front of the shuttle. *We're here.* The ship couldn't have been far from the station, perhaps in a similar orbit. Rather than dock at one of the external ports, the shuttle pilot had taken them into the cargo bay, setting them down in one of the sections with gravity. Theo could see several other shuttles sitting nearby. Beyond them he saw massive containers stacked floor to ceiling. *We still have the cargo.* More importantly, they still had options: whether to stay or continue on to their destination.

Theo shivered as he disembarked from the shuttle, stepping onto the cargo bay floor. *It's not the same ship*, he thought, clenching his jaw. It wasn't the same ship that had killed his wife and daughter.

The heat from another shuttle landing nearby sent a blast of warm air through the group as crewmen jockeyed with the shuttles to drag them off to their docking bays. They were efficient, jumping to the commands of the senior officer barking orders from above.

"Hello, Captain." The words were accompanied by a gentle tap on Theo's shoulder.

Turning, Theo found Zak standing there wearing a wide smile, Petr sitting on his shoulder. Petr stared at Theo, his head cocked. *Are you afraid, or just confused?* Theo had done a good job of instilling both when Petr had come to the door of the bar. Petr should have expected Theo to open his arms in a wide hug, offering all the love he deserved, especially since it wasn't just Theo's wife that had died, but Petr's mother. *You deserve more.*

Theo nodded to Zak, motioning for him to lower his son to the floor. As soon as Petr was free, Theo knelt and opened his arms, saying, "Can I have a hug, Petr?"

Petr met his gaze, standing with his fists balled and his nostrils flaring for several seconds before he rushed forward into Theo's embrace. Theo waited for several minutes, until Petr stopped sniffling. He whispered so quietly that he wasn't even sure his son could hear him, "I'm sorry, Petr. I'm so sorry."

Chapter 9

Finding Charity

"**A**rgh!" Theo yelled as the doctor poked the flesh around his broken rib. "Do you call that your bedside manner?"

Theo had never visited the infirmary in the months he'd spent on his own ship. He was surprised it was so clean and bright, the medical machinery stored in cupboards overhead. The room smelled of rubbing alcohol, as if it had recently been cleaned. This infirmary had a dozen beds, twice the number of that in the *Galena. Galena*...the name didn't hurt anymore, Theo realized. Thinking of its namesake made Theo wonder if she would like the infirmary. It was much cleaner than the hospital he'd stayed in when they'd regrown his flesh after the fire. *Only a little smaller,* he thought as he looked around at the faces staring at him.

Petr sat beside Theo on a small stool, kicking his legs in concentric circles as if swimming. His smile was as wide as Theo had ever seen, his eyes sparkling an iridescent green as he said, "Father, where are we going?"

"Perhaps we can—"

"Lad, you know where we're goin'," Gideon said gruffly. "We're going to stop the bad people."

"What do you mean?" Theo asked. He looked from the old man to the others in the room. The proper course of action was to return to their previous path. Safety existed in the triple solar system of Alpha Centauri.

Though uninjured, Masajiro had accompanied them to the infirmary, quickly scooping up Giselle and carrying her down without comment, as if he'd become her permanent protector. He waited beyond earshot, or rather, what Theo assumed was out of earshot. Given the man's other qualities, Theo wouldn't have been surprised if he could hear through walls.

He could tell that Masajiro was curious about the ship and her crew, his eyes lingering on the officers as they passed, but he seemed unwilling to question them or Theo. *What do you know about me that fascinates you so?* The man waited with his arms crossed, wary, smiling when had to, but more often frowning to chase people away.

Masajiro stepped smoothly aside as Mykaela entered. The exotic woman barely acknowledged Theo's saviour as she marched into the room, her brows furrowed and jaw clenched. She pushed through the small group of officers surrounding Theo, her gaze locked on him. She lifted her hand slowly, as if she was going to hug him, but stopped abruptly and suddenly brought it down blindingly fast across his face. She stood silently then, staring at him until the tears glistening on her face dried. The room was absolutely silent. The others looked around for escape.

Theo knew he'd deserved the slap. He wouldn't make excuses, but he still had the nagging feeling that something had attacked him when he'd arrived on the station. He'd looked for days. He wouldn't have chosen the vodka if he'd known Petr had lived. Instead of responding to the woman, however, he decided on a different tactic. "What are you talking about, Gideon? Where are we going?"

"We've found them, Theo," the old man said. "We've found that bastard who...who killed Galena."

Theo shook his head and clenched his jaw as his heart fluttered. He didn't want to confront that demon so soon. He couldn't stand in a room with Deacon—not because he couldn't harm the man; nothing could stop that. No, he couldn't stand in the same room because he knew that if he killed the man, Galena's death would be senseless. Theo wrapped his arm around his son.

When he felt able to speak, Theo said, "No. We're going to Alpha Centauri."

"What do you mean?" Gideon sputtered.

Theo could see the others relax a little. Mykaela's shoulders softened as she leaned back against the other infirmary bed and Masajiro cocked his head to the side to listen. They were all intent on what Theo would command, some to assess his conviction, others to decide if he'd learned his lesson. *Deacon has taken his pound of flesh. His stipend.*

Theo winced as the doctor started to wrap the bandage around his chest, cinching it tight. *What the hell, man?* "You don't have to have so tight, do you?"

The medic grunted in acknowledgement, but refused to adjust the bandage. When the medic was finished, Theo stood and tested the bandage, taking several deep breaths before speaking. "I'm not going to have anyone else die for revenge. That's not why we came out here. We left Earth to start a new life. Our families deserve better."

"What do you mean?" a red-faced Gideon asked, spraying spittle in Theo's face.

"Just exactly that. We came out here on route to a better life, and now we're going to continue on that journey."

"No," Gideon said. "We are going to—"

"Gideon, my friend," Theo said as stepped off the exam platform and took another step to rest his hands on the old man's shoulders. He lifted his hand to cup the back of the old man's head, drawing him closer so he could whisper in his ear. "I know you miss your daughter. I miss her. Even now I can see her in the room. But that doesn't give us the right, nor the ability, to storm Deacon's palace. We have to trust."

"Trust what?" Gideon said as he shook his head. "Trust the police? Do you know what they did? They did nothing. They cordoned off the area so no one could enter and it remains closed to traffic. Pretty soon it'll be a forgotten relic, left in the hands of that damned monster."

Theo closed his eyes as welling tears blurred his vision. He wanted to follow the man's suggestion, storming Deacon's hideout in space so he could destroy the pirate's family. *But I'm not that man. I won't teach Petr to be that man.* It wouldn't gain him anything. Galena would still be dead. Grace would still be dead. Petr would likely be killed in the attempt.

"At…at least let us collect…her body," Gideon whispered, lifting his hand to wipe his eyes.

Theo thought for a few moments. He couldn't deny that he wanted to retrieve Galena's body. He'd tried to drag her with him as they'd abandoned the ship. Gideon's proposed mission would give him that opportunity.

It wasn't that Theo forgot that Gideon was family, more that he accepted Galena's wish never to speak about it. Theirs was a dark history, one best left buried. The only thing Theo could do now was open a new chapter and let the old man mourn.

Slowly nodding, Theo said, "Fine. We will return to the ship and retrieve their bodies." Then he added, "And then we will move on to Alpha Centauri. I don't want her death be in vain."

Everyone let out their held breaths as he spoke. Gideon nodded and reached out for Petr's hand. He gently pulled Petr away, to let Theo speak to Mykaela and Masajiro. Petr hesitated, holding fast to Theo's hand, until Gideon whispered something in his ear that Theo couldn't hear. In response, Petr's face lit up and he followed Gideon from the infirmary, a slight bounce in his step.

Theo let his gaze linger on his son for a minute before turning to Mykaela. "Kae, I want you to meet Masajiro. He saved me back on the station. Masajiro, this is the ship's captain, Mykaela."

Masajiro hesitated a moment before saying, "I thought that you were her captain."

Theo shook his head. He'd signed that right away a long time ago. "No," he said, "my ship was lost. This is Mykaela's. I am only a guest."

"And her owner," Mykaela said. Colour was beginning to return to her face and he could see her hands had relaxed. "Theodore, you have chosen wisely. Gideon has argued that we should go after them ever since we found you. He listens to the pleas of the waylaid every day and pleads for me to go out and stop them. He doesn't understand that we aren't prepared for battle. Rick's people..." She fell silent.

Clearing his throat, Masajiro said, "I thought when I saw you that you had honour. I thought that you were stepping in harm's way to keep the lady safe. Now, I know you have honour because you step away to keep us all safe."

Theo merely nodded in mute gratitude, then gestured for them to leave as the medic moved on to tend Giselle. What she'd most need afterward, he decided, was sleep.

Mykaela led them out of the infirmary and down the hall, past several doors labelled with Petr's scrawled signs. As she walked, she said, "Theodore, I have thought long on this. This is my ship, but I do not wish to take your place. You are captain—please, I beg of you, take back the position that is rightfully yours. And besides, per our agreement, she is not mine until we arrive at destination."

Theo had learned years earlier that fighting a determined Mykaela was almost as useless as fighting his Galena. He would spend hours arguing that he didn't want the job, only to have her go mute when the crew most needed her advice. She wasn't above using her spite against him. He sighed and nodded. "What would you suggest we do, then?" He knew his people well; Mykaela was happiest when she could suggest, not when she was forced to command.

"I said that I agreed with your command. Giving your family a proper burial is the most honourable end, and if we can help but one ship avoid the same fate as your own, then we have done a good deed."

A good deed, Theo thought. He was trying to do a good deed, something Galena would want. That's why she'd planted all her flowers; she'd called each one a good deed—for Earth, for the people, and for the plant itself.

It was the right thing to do and when it was done they would chart a new course, one that didn't mean their imminent destruction, though he had to admit that if the police and Shamus or one of his henchmen had anything to say about it, that was going to be difficult. For now, that wasn't something he wanted to say to the crew. He had too many questions.

As they travelled through the halls, Theo felt the pull of familiarity. He knew it wasn't the same ship, but corners and passages spoke to him, beckoning him toward the place his wife had called home, planting her flowers so everyone could enjoy them.

Down another hall, Theo suddenly blushed, realizing it was where he and his wife had made love as everyone else slept. He could still taste the salt of her lips and smell the flowers in her hair. It was a brief encounter, the memory lasting. They'd tried elsewhere, but this hall was the only one not frequented by the crew, empty of intruders. *Apparently, it's different on this ship.*

"Where are we going?" he asked as they approached this ship's plant-hold. His emotional wounds weren't healed. *Not there, please,* he silently pleaded as his steps slowed, his feet suddenly feeling leaden, like the gravity had been dialed up. He didn't need a reminder of the last memory he had of his ship. His mouth watered as it did before he took his first sip of Grey Goose, anticipating its sour, blessed taste. Even the pill he'd been given in the bar wouldn't be enough if he found himself in the plant-hold, reliving the memories of when his life had ended.

As they entered, Theo felt weak with relief. He shivered as the perspiration cooled on his forehead. While his wife had waged war on the hold's cold steel grating and hard lines, no one had done the same here. Instead of a vibrant garden, he found its dull shadow. Flowers didn't spread through the vegetables, and those that existed in regimented rows in square planters were pale replicas. It was mechanical and useful, nothing more.

"It isn't much," Mykaela said as she stopped in front of a small pile of dirt that hadn't been used.

Theo took a deep breath, inhaling the smell of moist dirt as he closed his eyes and envisioned his wife in the room. She knelt in the dirt, pressing seeds down with her thumbs. *You're smiling,* Theo thought as he imagined her working, sweat beading on her dirt-smeared forehead. Theo sighed and opened his eyes. *But that was a different ship.*

He could see by the myriad footprints indenting the dirt that perhaps a dozen officers had crossed it. The most frequent footprints were the smallest, and Theo knew he didn't have to look far to find the small imprint of his son's knee. *Trying to make it normal,* he thought. Petr had never been one to help his wife any more than what Galena had asked of him, but where Theo had used alcohol to make the pain go away, his son had found something more constructive. *There are flowers planted here.*

"It was Petr's idea," Mykaela offered. "He comes here every day, so the rest of us started to plant some seeds beside his."

Theo looked closer and saw green sprouts peeking through the moist dirt. It would never rival the perfect placement of his wife's garden, but it didn't matter. *You're trying,* he thought. It would take time, but eventually the garden would spread throughout the hold, a monument to his wife and the other crewmembers Theo had lost. Theo felt a tear trace down his face, but he didn't hide it. He felt proud of what Petr had done. It felt like the perfect homage. Where every blossom of Galena's creation had been perfectly placed, they would create something haphazard and dynamic; the same, but different.

"It's...it's going to be beautiful," Theo said at last.

"On Earth," Masajiro said slowly, "there are many gardens that go on as far as you can see, but none would be so honourable. You should be commended."

"Indeed," Theo said. "Petr has shown his virtue many times before, but it never stops him from trying for more."

"Captain," Masajiro said as he laid his hand on Theo's shoulder. It was firm, but Theo could see the man wasn't putting his full power behind it.

Nodding to the man, Theo said, "Yes?"

"I must apologize and offer you a bit of truth," Masajiro said seriously. He paused and looked at Theo as if loath to finish.

"You have already proven yourself to me, Masajiro. There is no need—"

"Perhaps you should wait until you hear what I have to say," he said. He was wringing his hands as if handling something to hot to bear.

You're nervous, Theo realized with surprise. *Are you going to give us some answers? Why now?* Theo half expected he would never get the truth, but he was being afforded the opportunity to ask his growing list of questions. How had Masajiro, so trained and knowledgeable, happened by at such a perfect time? Why was Theo wanted, with a bounty on his head?

Masajiro bowed low and spoke in a deliberate monotone. "I was not honest when I said there was a bounty on your head."

Could it be that easy? "Go on," Theo said with a quick nod. The pain in his chest was mounting and he was having difficulty breathing. He knew if he didn't stop soon he would likely pass out. That, or he would start chipping his teeth from clenching them.

Masajiro swallowed hard. "I didn't come upon you accidently. I had been watching Shamus for days. When I saw you, I realized I had to do something."

"So, what are you apologizing for?" Theo asked. "You made a choice to help me."

"No," Masajiro said. His shoulders slumped as he spoke and he glanced from Theo to Mykaela and back. "I didn't make that choice. My partner did."

"Your partner?" Theo asked. He raised an eyebrow. If the man had a partner, shouldn't he be here now? Or at least be helping them get off the station? As he processed Masajiro's admission, the answer suddenly came to mind. "Giselle," he blurted.

Masajiro sighed and nodded. "Yes."

Instantly everything fell into place. Giselle was no prostitute, hoping to grab a few credits from his purse. She hadn't run to Shamus hoping to ingratiate herself to the man so she could secure more favour. Giselle, if that was her name, was as much an undercover agent as Masajiro. She'd been snooping for information from Theo himself. Whether it was for Masajiro or Shamus, it didn't matter. Theo was the target.

You know, Theo thought. Masajiro knew Theo had slapped Giselle so hard that it had almost drawn blood, and that it had taken him every last effort to not hit her again. The woman likely had video surveillance, so Masajiro would have seen the look on Theo's face. *But then, you also knew I was drunk,* Theo thought. It was not an excuse, but it was an explanation.

If you weren't going to do anything then... This morning wasn't about me. Masajiro had stepped in to save Giselle, not Theo. Masajiro would have let Shamus kill him, except Giselle must have ordered him to help. At least she'd believed Theo's words were genuine.

"You would have left me there," Theo said softly as the other man nodded.

"I—I am truly sorry," Masajiro whispered and suddenly knelt. "I— you are more honourable than I thought possible. Please accept my apologies."

Reaching down, Theo pulled the man back to his feet. Theo had more questions, but his head was pounding. Whether from the lack of alcohol in his system or the realization that he'd barely escaped death, Theo was shaking. *Does it matter, your intentions?*

Theo bent forward to speak into the man's ear. "Nothing could make us even for the terrible deed I did to your friend, Masajiro. I could spend a thousand years trying to make excuses for my actions and then trying to make amends for the same. Know that. And please accept my invitation to stay. If you want, you may take one of the shuttles, but I would hope you both could join us."

Masajiro nodded. "For a time, we will stay."

"Good," Theo said. His world was shrinking and light was beginning to explode throughout his entire field of vision. He had to reach out to Masajiro just to stand. *I need some sleep.*

"Theodore," Mykaela said, rushing to his side. Her touch was warm as she slipped a shoulder under his arm.

Theo shook his head and said, "I'm fine. I just need some sleep." Theo needed more than sleep, but he had to work with what he got and regardless of where they were going, it was going to take a long time. He let Mykaela lead him from the hold, leaving Masajiro standing alone.

Chapter 10

Finding Hope

"Hello Father," Petr said as Theo entered the bridge.

Theo nodded to his son and smiled, forcing the idea away that he should go and hug Petr. *You won't like that will you, son?* It was refreshing, seeing Petr on the bridge rather than obsessing about the flowers in the plant-hold.

In the time Theo had been aboard the ship, he'd found his son toiling in the garden more often than Galena had when she was alive. Petr even forced the teacher to bring her small class of students out to the garden to learn about the flora he'd spread out across the floor. He'd almost taken over the class, teaching the younger children how to plant properly and where they could get the best food when the plants matured. While he thought it adorable at first, his teacher Aleem soon found it alarming, telling Theo on more than one occasion that Petr needed another outlet for his grief. *Wouldn't you just slap the man?* Theo thought to his dead wife.

Though Theo noticed time passing now, he found it far more constructive than drinking his days into oblivion. With the alcohol gone Galena didn't visit, smiling or not. Theo woke every morning to discover her missing before remembering the truth, and he was constantly stopping himself from asking aloud what she thought of his plans. He'd even had to return both hers and Grace's dinners to the galley after he'd collected enough for the entire family.

Theo's detox had gone much smoother than he'd expected, and his body was able to bounce back from the aching need for the alcohol that had clouded his vision and mind. *Never gone, though,* Theo thought as he remembered the few times he'd passed one of the holds where he knew crewmembers were distilling moonshine or other intoxicating liquids. He was drawn to the smell, veering away from his path until he forced himself back on track.

Theo couldn't tell his people the truth; couldn't let them see a weakness. He had to beat the addiction on his own, without the help or sympathy of his crew. *And besides, this way I prove it was a symptom rather than a choice.* Theo wouldn't have given up on his family if he'd known they were alive.

When Theo was with his son, whether in his quarters or in the plant-hold, he felt in control, managing to focus his thoughts on something other than the Siren call of the alcohol. Like the gentle caress of a dangerous lover, the alcohol only sent you to one place: *Hell.*

As Theo came abreast of his son, he asked, "What are you doing, Petr?"

Petr was standing on a plastic shipping crate so he could lean over the command table and control its contents. He was dressed in a baggy pair of officer's overalls like those Mykaela and Zak wore, as though he was determined to live up to the commission he'd been given so long ago, during Theo's short weekly trips from Earth to Mars.

Theo peered over the edge and watched as Petr forced the holographic figures to surround another at the centre. Petr had adjusted the screen to project the icons into three-dimensional space above the surface of the table. With every gentle swipe, his son shifted tiny flashing beacons around a much larger depiction of Theo's own ship, where Galena lay resting in the plant room she'd created.

Theo stared at his ship for a second before realizing something was amiss. *It's entwined with something,* he thought as he recognized a second ship protruding from the starboard side of the ship. It was a gruesome sight, the two ships embracing in death, tiny pieces of the hull floating around them where the two had collided. *How can anything have survived? The ship couldn't have an atmosphere left.*

Petr pushed the last small shuttle out from the larger ship, then straightened from the table and looked up as his father. "When we arrive at the ship, we first have to determine whether it is booby-trapped."

Theo nodded slowly. "You're right, buddy. We don't want to get on the ship—"

"No, Father," Petr interjected, "we have to make sure the area hasn't been mined. We won't be able to travel through the area without determining that first. We'd be cut down instantly."

Petr had always been a serious boy, but now he spoke like an adult, intent on his plan. *You've been stoked,* Theo thought as he looked around for Gideon. Petr's grandfather would have filled the boy's mind with thoughts of vengeance. A former naval officer, Gideon would have spent his time explaining the finer points of tactics, then Petr would have pressed on and within hours would have been the one drawing up the plans. *But you're right about the danger,* Theo thought with a sigh. Aloud, he said, "Show me." Theo had no intentions of meting out vengeance, but he still had to know what his son was thinking. Petr was smarter than most people three times his age.

"Well, first we have to deal with the mines, but I think Masajiro can help with that," Petr said.

"Oh?" Theo raised his brow. Petr was already operating the ship like he owned it, and he'd developed Theo's knack for understanding people. How else could he have delved into Masajiro's character so quickly?

Petr nodded. "Yes, he told me that he knew the frequency that the mines worked on. He could shut them off for a time, but he said they would likely be reactivated, so we would have to move the ship quickly."

"So, what do we do next, Petr?" Theo asked as he rested his elbows on the edge of the table and propped his head on his hands.

"We'll have to move the mines," Petr said matter-of-factly. It reminded Theo of the plan he'd crafted to get them all to the Alpha Centauri system; a plan, he reminded himself, that was his next step after giving their people a proper burial.

"How are we going to move the mines, buddy?" Theo asked as he noticed Mykaela enter the bridge.

"Well," Petr stepped up to the table again, "it would be easier with a folding ship."

Theo sighed. "Yes buddy, it would be nice, but we don't have one. We have to come up with a solution that doesn't involve that."

Petr stared at his father for several seconds before saying, "I know that, Father. I just mean it would be nice if we had one." He regarded Theo for several seconds. His nostrils flared when he spoke again. "We'll have to use the shuttles. First, we'll all deploy before we shut the mines off. Then we'll collect them along a straight line. We'll move them all to within reach of each other so when they reactivate, they will cause each other to blow up."

Theo had to admit that, if Petr was correct about Masajiro's ability to shut the mines down, it made sense. Of course, that was assuming the mines existed. Theo was hoping the ship sat alone, Deacon having taken his stipend. He couldn't help but notice the contempt in Petr's voice. Whether it was due to Galena and Grace's deaths or Gideon's rhetoric, Theo didn't care. *We'll have to have words about that later, son.*

Their expedition would accomplish more than retrieving bodies; they needed the supplies and parts they could strip from the ship if they were going to go after the rest of his fleet. If Theo had learned anything, it was that new ships were good for a time, but they still needed to be fixed.

"Have you been looking at Petr's plan?"

The question tore Theo from his reverie. Looking up at Gideon, Theo forced a smile. He wouldn't accomplish anything by alienating the old man and his ideals. "It has merit, though we will have to see the field before we can make any decisions."

Gideon chuckled. "I think you've been playing with your sauce a little too long, boy. We know what the playing field is like. We can see it."

Theo's eyes narrowed and he heard himself draw a sharp breath. "What do you mean?"

"The secure line was never severed. We've been looking through her eyes for weeks."

Weeks? Theo had a sudden vision of his son trying to explain to his wife what travelling close to the speed of light would be like. To Theo everything was happening at the speed of light, yet it was grindingly slow to those around him. They were working with information he didn't have. *It would be a little easier if everyone let me know.* "I think it's time you told me everything," he said to Gideon.

Gideon nodded and motioned for him to follow. Theo followed him off the bridge, noticing the distinct lack of creaking from Gideon's braces. *He's been doing some maintenance. He's still ready for a fight.* Theo shook his head. "Speak."

"It's alright, boy," Gideon started with his customary condescension. He'd spoken down to Theo since the first day he'd met him. It took quite some time for Theo to understand it wasn't a personal affront. The old man called everyone some variation of "boy." But as soon as Gideon started to speak again, Theo realized how hurt he was. His words were clipped and the man refused to meet Theo's gaze.

"While you were in that bar trying to get drunk enough to forget the rest of us, we've been getting things ready. We've reinforced every section of the hull in case we get fired at, made it possible to seal unnecessary corridors in case we get boarded, and we've trained everyone on board to do the right thing the next time it happens. We are prepared for war."

"Gideon," Theo said quietly, "don't you understand? We can't afford a war with these people. They've been at it far longer. They don't care about whether we live or not. Hell, they don't care whether they live or die."

"Aye lad, I know that. That's why we brought more soldiers on board. Ones that I can trust."

"You still don't get it, Gideon. I don't want my son—your grandson—to grow up thinking it's okay to retaliate, not to mention the fact that we'll fail."

"We aren't gonna fail, boy. We're gonna –"

"Stop it, Gideon," Theo yelled, loud enough that several crewmembers walking farther down the hall turned to see what was happening.

"I ain't gonna stop until that bastard's guts are being sucked out in the void of space."

"That's it. That's it." Theo threw his hands into the air and spun around as if to leave.

As soon as his back was to Gideon, he heard the old man whisper, "You don't have the right to tell me what to do anymore, boy. You lost that when you sent Petr back here in tears."

Theo turned so fast it made his stomach lurch. When he could see the old man, he stepped forward with his arms outstretched and in one smooth motion pushed Gideon to the wall, his elbow pressed against the man's throat. He waited until the old man met his gaze—it took several seconds. "First of all, I didn't send Petr away. I was drugged and wasn't in my right mind. And second, don't make me remind you how you grieved for your lost wife, Gideon."

Gideon's brows arched and then his face went flat as memories of his own dark past returned. He huffed and slumped against the wall, so limp that Theo had to support him. Theo had never imagined he would need to remind Gideon that he'd tried to commit suicide after his own wife had been killed shortly after Theo met him. That was the reason Galena hated to fly so much.

After a pirate attack had been repelled, leaving his wife dead, Gideon had mounted a team of his naval comrades and set out for revenge. To a man they'd died—except Gideon, who had been sent back in pieces; hence the need for the braces. It was a messy affair and the reason why Theo had become captain of the *Galena*. It was also the reason why her namesake never spoke to Gideon again and why Petr didn't know the man was his grandfather.

Tears coursed down Gideon's weathered face as Theo stared him down, his own cheeks twitching. *I'm sorry, but I have to do this.* He knew if he didn't, Gideon would never give in.

"Now," Theo said as he let the pressure off of Gideon's throat, "I don't want Petr learning the lesson that Galena did when we were younger. I don't want that. What I will do is accept that the crew needs to grieve and bury our dead."

The old man snorted. "The crew?"

"Fine, Gideon—*I* need it. I need to be able to say goodbye…to both of them. But no more than that. When we're done I will put us back on track to continue on to Alpha Centauri, where we'll be safe."

Both men were silent for several seconds until Theo added, "Now, I will accept this mission, if you accept that it isn't a war. Will you?"

After another deafening silence, the old man nodded. "Fine. I won't go after them. But you know someone should. You can't deny that."

"*No*," Theo immediately said. "I can't and I won't deny it, but we aren't them. We aren't prepared for that fight. Now, will you tell me what's happened?"

Gideon hung his head and whispered so softly that Theo could barely hear him, "I…I heard what Galena said in her last minutes. The words haunt me every night. They tell me that I am not doing enough. A mother of two beautiful children stood up to the pirates. Why…why can't we?"

Before Theo could respond, he felt Gideon's strong hand on the back of his neck. The old man lifted his own gaze to lock on Theo's as he said, "My intentions aren't to put Petr in harm's way, Theodore. I had intended to leave him on that damned station. You were supposed to take him in with you so we could do what was necessary."

The man had an answer for everything. Trying to put Petr out of harm's way? Trying to blame Theo for not letting them take the fight back to Deacon? The old man hadn't seen the look on Deacon's face. *You don't know how evil that man is.*

"What makes you think you can do it—blowing them out of the sky?" Theo asked. A sharp pain raced through his broken teeth as he clenched his jaw.

The old man shook his head. "*No.* We think we can do something on Mars."

Eyes narrowed, Theo stared at Gideon. What could happen on Mars? Because of the elliptical orbits of the planets, pirates weren't usually known to frequent the shipping lanes until much closer to Jupiter. *And they own the stations anyway. They may as well sit outside, picking off ships as they please.*

Gideon must have been watching Theo's eyes shift, because the old man cleared his throat and said, "How did they get on *our* ship? They certainly didn't board us while we travelled at several thousand miles an hour."

Theo pulled away, chewing the inside of his lip. Gideon was right. He'd asked the same question when Deacon and his brother had been traipsing through his ship. *How did they get on?* Someone must have let them on. *But I trusted the crew.* He'd personally chosen them all, making sure every person that joined them wanted to go to the colonies. No one would want to stay. Theo suddenly qualified that statement. Grace had wanted to stay. He couldn't count the number of times he'd overheard the girl bemoaning that to her friend Jacob.

Theo swallowed the bile he tasted in his mouth. "Jacob."

"Hendrickson sold you out, son," Gideon said with a nod. "He sold you out to these rotten…" He shuddered as he covered his eyes, tears beginning anew.

Theo had hoped Hendrickson would have held himself to a higher moral standard. *What do they have on you?* Hendrickson had been a good man, coming to Theo's aid on several occasions when Theo had flown *Galena* to Mars. But he also understood the power of the pirates. He knew how easily Deacon could have infiltrated every facet of Earth's government to ensure he had someone ready. *He caught me on the station,* Theo admitted to himself.

"Jacob must have let them board before we left Mars," Theo mused aloud. "I am not even going to ask if Jacob is with you." They would have told him if Jacob had survived. Jacob must have gone with the pirates when they left.

Gideon shook his head, but Theo continued without letting the man speak. "The question, then, is whether they had targeted us specifically, or just found us because we were travelling beyond the belt. Hendrickson would have to be doing that to everyone. No, he would burn too many bridges then. Lovett was the target, not us. Deacon knew the relationship."

"You got it, boy." Gideon's head whipped up so fast that Theo heard the chink of his exoskeleton shifting.

"This is *all* because of Lovett. But what did he do?"

Deacon had said Lovett couldn't send his lackeys without stipend, and those people on the station had wanted Lovett's card. What could the shipping magnate have done that was so terrible that everyone wanted a piece of him? *Everything,* Theo thought. A man couldn't become that powerful without stepping on a few toes in the process. They likely didn't have to have a specific reason; Lovett himself had indicated he'd lost several ships destined for the same port. That was the entire reason why Theo had set out on the ill-fated journey. Lovett and Deacon fought a private war without caring about the collateral damage. *But could it be so secret? Is it that simple?*

Theo looked at Gideon. "What aren't you telling me?"

Gideon licked his lips and shifted away from Theo as he took a deep breath. His gaze was still locked on Theo as he said, "Deacon and his brother are Lovett's children."

Stars exploded inside Theo's mind. *Children?* A family feud? They were trying to get back at daddy? Could someone's hate be so consuming? *It can't be.* Even Galena's hatred for her father had faded. She'd blamed him for the loss of her mother, ensuring no one admitted the familial connection. *But she didn't send you away.*

"But why?" Theo asked.

"Because," a new voice suddenly said from down the short hall, "When they were sent out here to take control of the outer zone, they realized they liked the people here more than their father."

Theo turned. Masajiro and his partner Giselle were slowly walking toward them. The swelling in the woman's eyes had abated enough for Theo to realize her eyes were brown, not green, and her movements were slow, as though Shamus had done more damage to her body than anyone could see. Masajiro, for his part, was clean and well-kept; he'd taken the time to shave and procure a new set of clothes. His gaze drifted to his partner periodically as he spoke.

Theo nodded acknowledgement. "Why did Lovett send them out here?"

"Because Edward Lovett wanted to control the zone. He'd lost too many ships here and wanted someone he could trust. Deacon and Damion were sent here to take control. They both share the same lust for power that their father has, and he believed he could trust them. But they saw it as an exile—so they've built themselves an empire to match his."

"And now they're at war," Theo finished.

Masajiro nodded. "Yes."

Theo stepped back as he digested this new revelation. *Deacon must still be tied to Earth.* How else could they have known he'd made the deal with Lovett? But why did it matter? It was just a stipend.

At least now he knew who they were dealing with. Lovett's sons. His dangerous and masterful sons. Somehow that knowledge relieved him—it wasn't just anyone who had infiltrated his ship. The two Lovett boys would have had long resumes before turning to piracy, and going by how they were running Jupiter's shipping lanes, they likely thought they should be crowned as kings. They believed they were due a tithe and everyone should bow to their leadership because they knew how to bring prosperity to the people. *You don't think yourselves pirates.*

As the thought crossed his mind, Theo said, "They think they can do it alone. They think they are the good guys."

"What?" Gideon asked.

Masajiro nodded. "They do indeed. That is why it has been so difficult to depose them. The people of the system love them."

"Why are you here, Masajiro?" Theo asked. Masajiro was somehow tangled up in the web that had been spun between Theo and the Lovett family. "And who do you work for?"

"The United Terran Government," the man replied. "I will not lie to you, Theodore Stinson. I work for the UTG. And I thank you for choosing not to go after them. I would have been forced to intervene."

Theo nodded, vindicated. His assumption had been correct. *Homeforce. I knew it.*

"Why?" Gideon challenged. He stared at Masajiro, his eyes narrowed.

You don't like him, Theo observed. Gideon's military experience came from the navy, which had once been commanded by the Homeforce. Gideon would immediately see Masajiro as a threat, a secretive, conniving man bent on his own machinations.

"Because you are not authorized with the badge," Masajiro said, his voice flat and unemotional as he stared at Gideon.

You've already researched us. You know his background and you're not impressed. The thoughts rolled around in Theo's mind before he spoke. The Lovetts were committing murder and treason thinking they were doing the right thing. They'd likely convinced themselves that Galena's death was Theo's fault. What was more, the people crewing the stations and lunar mines idealized Deacon. The police rushing after them on the station orbiting Jupiter were proof. *They weren't shooting at Shamus,* Theo thought as he remembered the blaster fire arcing over his head.

Theo narrowed his eyes at Giselle. "What were you hoping to gain from me?"

Giselle looked fearlessly at Theo. "Only the card that Shamus was looking for. That's all."

"Moustache Man?" Theo lifted his hands to touch the fading bruises on his face. On earth, he would have had his ribs and bruises magically removed, but so far out in space, only time could offer that healing.

"Our cover was blown," Masajiro said. "I could see that in his face. You offered the safest route."

Theo nodded slowly. He'd exhausted their information. What little they had left wouldn't help him anyway. *Unless...* Unless they could give him access to his ship. "Do I have legal access to my ship?" he asked.

Masajiro smiled. "Yes, you do." He looked at his wristwatch for a second before adding, "For another six Terran months. That is why the field surrounding the ship is mined. They can't legally keep you from it, but they can make it impossible to board it."

"Why?" Gideon asked. "They could just strip it."

Theo sighed, letting his shoulders slump. *Even your death is a game to them,* Theo thought as tears ran down his face. He closed his eyes as he continued. "I—it's because of the game they play. It serves their purpose to let her sit. First, it's a reminder to everyone of what could happen to them if they defy Deacon. But beyond that, it casts them in a favourable light, one of doing the right thing. They've probably sent a request to the UTG for salvage rights. A show for the home office."

Masajiro nodded.

"Then he won't attack us if all we're doing is salvaging my own ship," Theo blurted. He felt a cool sensation wash over his body. He'd been afraid at first to attempt the salvage, but now he knew they could make the run without raising Deacon's ire. If it came to it, a stipend was a small price to pay to bury his wife and daughter. *And that's only if you're there, which would surprise me.*

Turning back to Gideon, Theo said, "Let's go. We have a ship to salvage and a family to bury."

Chapter 11

Finding Temperance

Theo stood on the bridge of his ship and watched the main video screen as fourteen shuttles navigated through the mine field, dragging the massive explosives from their path. From this perspective, Theo could see they weren't like the shuttle he'd escaped in from the station. These sleek shuttles couldn't have been designed for his ship. With a glance he asked his first officer the silent question of their origin.

Mykaela nodded in understanding. "Gideon found them in the wrecking yard off of Jupiter main. He cleaned them up and put new hulls over the original. It was faster than trying to strip them down."

So quickly? he thought. He knew that he'd been languishing in the bar for awhile, but how could Gideon be so fast? *How many people did you find on Jupiter?*

Theo vaguely remembered hearing about the wrecking yard where the partially salvaged ships were dragged to their final resting place, with the intention that the metal would be melted down into something usable. Theo was half temped to start a business smelting the hulls. *Deacon likely owns that port too, though,* he thought.

Gideon's shuttles were well crafted, the weld marks almost nonexistent. It was as if the metal were fused together. Theo could see no windows on the shuttles and assumed the old man had opted for video screens within. It was a stark contrast to the clunky shuttles

Theo was accustomed to. *Definitely not meant for long distance travel,* he thought. If they lost power, the shuttles would be tombs.

The mines they pulled were almost as large as the shuttles. At first glance, the black boxes were inert, but then as he focused on them, Theo made out the glint of video cameras. They were well-designed, with thousands of smaller explosives trapped within a soft outer shell. If a ship came within targeting distance, the magnetic mines would automatically drift toward the intruder and release its payload. The explosives hidden within could easily destroy one of the shuttles or tear a sizeable hole in the side of his transport ship and cripple her.

After a long, silent pause as the crew watched in awe, Theo said, "How are we doing?"

"They're almost finished," the communications officer said. It was the woman from Theo's own ship, enlisted when Mykaela brought the two crews together.

Theo could almost close his eyes and pretend he was on his own ship several months earlier, his wife sleeping in their quarters down the hall. *But it's not,* Theo thought. Theo's ship had sounded different, with children's laughter and the hydraulic whir and thud of robots strutting around with supplies. Here it was silent, the crew intent on their mission. The robots were still, waiting for the supplies to start arriving. Aside from the plant-hold, it smelled more metallic on Mykaela's ship, almost lifeless—like Theo's first ship, the *Galena.*

Theo nodded to the communications officer and smiled. "Make sure they clear two more routes as soon as they can." He was confident that Deacon wouldn't come after him, but he still wasn't going to box himself in. Space was a large place and he couldn't see in every direction at once.

"Captain," Zak said. It felt right, having the large man at the navigation console. Theo had to admit, the man had done admirably as a first officer, but there was no question of whether Mykaela would step aside. Everyone had a strength. Zak's was flying the ship.

"Yes, Zak?" Theo prompted.

"I have enough room to start moving through," the man offered. His fingers played with several buttons on his console as if he were playing a piano. *You feel at home too, don't you?*

Theo could see in the straight shoulders and alert expressions that the crew was ready to get to work, but whether it was the excitement of him returning to his ship or them just wanting to be done with the entire mission was yet to be seen. *Perhaps a bit of both*, he mused. With the crew from both ships and Gideon's hired security, the ship was almost overcrowded.

"Are Masajiro and Rick ready with their teams?" Theo asked, fingers tapping the armrest of his seat.

It hadn't taken much prodding for Masajiro and Giselle to join them in their salvage operation, with their own mission at stake. They were already aboard, and it gave them something else to think about as they waited for their orders. They'd accepted on the premise that Theo would deliver them to one of the larger stations orbiting Jupiter when they were finished. They could blend in with the locals and get on with their search.

"Masajiro says everything is ready on his team, and Rick is just waiting for Gideon," the communications officer announced.

"Good. Take us in, Zak."

The screen flicked to show their destination. From their angle it wasn't familiar, but then Theo realized they were looking at the back end of the pirate ship. When they'd evacuated Theo's ship, it was rocketing toward the pirates' vessel. Zak had adjusted the trajectory, so they should have collided with the energy of a nuclear explosion, pulverizing both ships.

Though an ugly collision, something wasn't right with how easily the two ships had nestled together. *How could they have staved off such destruction?* It was as if someone had stayed on board during the whole process to keep his ship from the worst damage as the pirate ship pierced through the cargo holds, missing the living quarters completely. Although better than he'd expected, Theo knew his ship was in terrible condition, with no atmosphere. The pirate ship must have collapsed half of the hallways and transport bays as they collided.

"Let the teams know they will need full environmental suits. Damn it, that looks ugly."

"Yes sir," Lieutenant Paul said as she turned to relay the order.

Theo smiled and took a deep breath. It felt good captaining the ship again, like he'd been trying to play a game of chess with only his left hand before. He knew how much pressure he had to apply to his people to energize them and elevate their efficiency. They were alert right now; no one glanced back to Theo to see whether he was going to crack. *Do any of you even know where I was?* Mykaela could have kept that from them, only trusting the news with a few.

Theo looked around at his people, finishing with his son as Petr pored over the command table, shifting several pieces within like he knew something the computer wasn't telling him. "What's up, buddy?" Theo asked as he walked over.

The smile faded from Petr's face as he stared intently at his little figures. He dropped down to his heels and sighed. "Something's wrong, Father. Every time I move the little men it gets reset."

"Well, son," Theo said, chuckling, "it's just a computer—"

"No Father, you don't understand. I have put in every possible variable...well, almost. There must be something we're missing."

It was still so odd to hear the thoughts of an adult uttered by a child. Petr should have been running through fields on Earth, or at least preparing to do so on Alpha Centauri, not preparing a plan for salvaging a ship. Especially one that served as a tomb for his mother and sister. It was a terrible reality that Theo wished he'd never have had to entertain.

"Father?" Petr was saying. "What I am doing now is supposed to be shutting off the mines, but it isn't."

Treating Petr like a child would accomplish nothing. Petr would get his back up just as quickly as his grandfather, and then dealing with him would be impossible. Instead, Theo took another tactic. "What would cause that, Lieutenant?" Theo asked, peering at the table. "And besides that, I thought most of the mines were moved. What are you trying shut off now?"

"That's what I mean," Petr said. He stared wide-eyed at his father. "When we first started we downloaded the programming from the mines so we could track them. Now, that programming is saying the mines are going to return to their original position."

As Petr spoke, Theo glanced up and gestured Mykaela over. She approached gracefully, her brows furrowed as she glanced frequently at the main screen at the front of the bridge. "What is wrong, Theodore?"

"Petr, can you tell Mykaela what you just told me?" Theo asked.

"Uh, hello Mykaela. Um, I just told Father that the programs in the mines are making them return to where they were when we started."

Narrowing her eyes, Mykaela asked, "How long will that take?"

"I don't know. Three hours I think," Petr said. He was beginning to blush and he looked down at the table, unable to meet the woman's gaze. On any other day, Theo would have had to stifle a chuckle. *Don't worry, kiddo. Everyone gets that way.*

Petr's news was devastating. It had taken two hours to move the mines in the first place. It wasn't viable to shift the mines back if they had to move them again to leave the salvage operation. And it would be disastrous if they had to move quickly. Theo looked at his first officer. "What are your thoughts?"

Mykaela leaned over the table, flashing a smile at Petr before mulling over the situation, chewing on her lower lip as she concentrated. Theo let her weigh their options, knowing she'd come to the same conclusion. Swallowing, he turned back to the communications officer. "Get me Rick and Masajiro."

"They're awaiting your orders, sir," Lieutenant Paul said.

"Tell them that as soon as we leave them on the ship, we have to move away," Theo began.

"What? *No*, Father! I want to join them." Petr jumped down from his box to step in front of Theo. "I want to go. I want to get something from the ship."

Theo knelt quickly in front of his son, lifting his hand to caress Petr's face. "Listen, buddy. You know the problem. I can't let you do that. I need you here, doing what you've been doing."

"No!" Petr crossed his arms, glowering.

"I'm sorry, buddy. I can't have you over there. They have to move quickly and I can't be watching over you. You don't want to be left behind, do you?"

"I am going," Petr said flatly and stomped his foot. "This was my idea. I am going."

"*No*, you are not, Petr. This isn't a discussion. I let you in the bridge to keep an eye on you. Please don't make me ground you."

Theo hoped his stern voice was enough. Galena had always been the one to discipline the children. *Oh, I wish you were here, Lena*, he thought. He knew if she were, they wouldn't be here, though. If Galena was still alive they would be months into their trek to Alpha Centauri, instead of salvaging the ship she'd died on.

Petr stood vibrating with anger, his fists clenched so tight that his knuckles had turned white. "Fine—if you don't want me here, I'm leaving," Petr said and threw up his hands before storming toward the door faster than Theo could grab him.

"Damn it," Theo muttered, taking a step toward the door. He couldn't follow Petr, however; he had other issues to deal with.

Turning back to Lieutenant Paul, he said, "Tell Rick and Masajiro that I want them to board the ship quickly, and then we are going to move away. Tell them to prep one of the shuttles on the other ship, if they are available. If there isn't one, we will send the shuttles to them to load, but we can't stay."

Sonya was already relaying the information into her microphone while simultaneously typing on her console. The lieutenant had joined Theo's crew after she'd retired from the military, and had been a member for almost a decade, first as a junior officer running lines for Gideon and then as the communications officer. She spoke half a dozen languages, which came in handy when Theo was negotiating with one of the mining stations scattered through the vast asteroid belt between Mars and Jupiter.

Turning back to Mykaela, Theo said, "Speak your thoughts, Kae."

"I think you are making the correct decision. I don't want to get locked behind those mines," she said loud enough for the others to hear. The bridge was larger than the *Galena*'s, but designed concentrically, so all of the officers had a view of the captain's chair. Only Zak's navigation chair was oriented toward the bow of the ship.

Having another route through the minefield would offer Theo security. Instead, they would have to circle outside of the mine field, far away from the wreckage, until Masajiro and Rick were ready with the supplies. *Maybe the smaller shuttles can get through the minefield*, Theo thought. The escape pods he and his crew had taken in their departure were designed for long-term flight, but some of the shuttles nestled in the cargo holds could have been spared from destruction.

Theo glanced around the room before asking, "Then what?" Though Mykaela still retained control of her own crew, Gideon would have had them traipsing across the system in hopes of destroying Deacon.

Mykaela was silent for several seconds before replying, her gaze focused down at the table. "You know I am not in concurrence with Gideon, Theodore. I have no interest in becoming a pin cushion for pirate blades."

Though he wasn't surprised with her sentiments, it gave Theo some hope to know that his most trusted ally was still on his side. They didn't always agree, far from it, but when they did, Theo had no doubt that he was doing the right thing.

"Sir," Zak said, interrupting their conversation.

"Yes, Zak?"

"We'll be docking in two minutes, if you want to let the crew know."

It wasn't the crew that Theo had to inform, but their family members, hiding in their quarters. *The few who haven't found an occupation on the ship yet, that is,* Theo corrected himself. Mykaela had done a great job of ensuring her people were employed on her ship. *I should have done that,* he thought, remembering how his ship had run. His had been a family, hers an occupation.

As the information was relayed to the officers and their families, Theo turned back to his first officer. "Get some of the transport shuttles prepped. We'll have to have them waiting outside the ship at the auxiliary ports. I doubt the primary ports are available." Almost as an afterthought, he said, "Make sure they have good pilots. They may have to sneak by the mines."

Mykaela nodded, then laughed. "They are standing by, Theodore. Don't worry."

"I just don't...I just don't want anything to go wrong," Theo said. His heart was already pounding in his ears, and every small beep or whisper was an echoing boom.

On cue, the internal environmental officer looked up. "Sir," she said, "I have a breach in one of the storage units for the environmental suits."

"What does that mean?" Theo asked, stepping closer.

"Sir, one of the suits has been taken."

Silence fell over the room as everyone registered the statement. Had they been infiltrated again? Was their salvage team in danger? Or perhaps with their soldiers gone, his ship was the one in danger.

"Do we have anyone...which storage unit?" Theo asked as he felt his stomach sink. The room was suddenly unbearably hot.

"Just down the hall outside the bridge here, sir," the woman replied. He didn't recognize her and assumed she was one of Mykaela's choices.

"Sir," Zak interrupted. "We have docked with—"

"Petr," Theo sighed. "Mykaela, take the ship out of the mine field. I can't let Petr just run wild over there." *God damn it, Petr.* He pounded the edge of the table with his fist before rushing toward the door, visions of his son's insides being sucked out through an improperly prepped suit haunting him.

Theo passed three crewmembers in the hall, two barely escaping being barrelled over as he raced past them. The third crewman wasn't as quick, dodging in the wrong direction as Theo called out to make way. They collided, sending them both flailing to the floor. Theo pushed himself to his feet, made his apologies, and set off again, rubbing his throbbing chest. *Have to get there.*

Theo found the door ajar when he arrived at the closet where they kept the environmental suits, the only thing that would keep someone safe in a vacuum. Several suits were strewn about the floor in various stages of assembly. "Come on, Petr, please have done it right."

Theo grabbed a full suit still hanging in the closet as he dashed off again. *I can put it on faster than Petr did,* he thought as he ran. Theo was certain Petr would gravitate to his grandfather's team, even though it was farther from the bridge than Masajiro's. Masajiro wouldn't let Petr tag along.

"Captain," Zak's voice called out over the speaker system when he was nearly at the gate.

Theo glanced, pausing to kick off his left boot. "Yes, Zak."

"We tried to get them to digitally lock the door after they went through, but it was too late. We have another entry through the gate Rick's team chose about thirty seconds ago." The man's voice was quiet, almost tentative, like he was afraid to speak.

Petr will be fine. I'll get there. "Petr's going to be fine." Theo flipped his other boot off; it hit the wall with a resounding thunk. "Can you have them turn around and find him?"

"Communications are spotty once you cross over, but Sonya is working on it," Zak explained.

I can't worry about that now, he thought as he raced to save his son.

His chest was burning as he stopped in front of the gate and hefted the upper suit over his head. He wriggled in, wincing as the chest plate slammed into place. Dropping to the floor, he pulled on the pants. In all his years in space, he'd seen few people able to pull the hard rubber pants on while standing. It made him wonder how Petr had managed the feat. "I thought we had a hard line still with the ship. Can't we use their internal sensors?" When no answer came, he looked at the closest speaker. "Zak? Can you tell if Petr's suit has been set properly?"

Silence.

"Hello?"

"Negative, sir. He hasn't switched anything on," Zak said.

Theo let out the breath he'd been holding. *Don't panic,* he told himself. *You can still wear the suit without turning on the electronics. Petr will still be able to breathe. He knows what to do. You know it, buddy.*

Reaching around to latch the tab on the back of the suit, Theo noticed an officer down the hall, watching him. He clambered to his feet and shuffled quickly toward her. "Did you see Petr come through here?" he asked.

The woman smiled mildly. "Yes, sir. He looked very cute, all bundled up."

"Was he latched properly?" Theo asked as he lifted his helmet.

Her eyebrows went up. "Latched? I don't know. I thought he was just playing."

Theo dropped the glass bowl over his head and left the woman with her mouth hanging open. His movements were more cumbersome with the suit, but he moved as quickly as he could back to the gate. *You know how it goes, buddy.*

He mashed his fist against the control panel to force the airlock to spin around. Though it acknowledged his command, the gate was grindingly slow. *Come* on, *open!* Theo counted to twenty before it was open far enough for him to slip through without tearing any of the hoses from his suit. He was barely past the threshold when he hit the corresponding button on the other side.

"Theodore," Mykaela's voice suddenly said as the suit lit up.

"Go ahead," Theo replied, watching the door iris closed.

"We have a problem," she said slowly.

What now? Swallowing the bile in his throat, he said, "What?"

"Sir, we're getting a distress call from a transport ship about fifty thousand kilometres from our position."

"And that's a problem?" Theo asked. It was terrible to think someone else might be about to lose their ship, but he'd rather get that news than news that Petr was dead.

"Sir, they need help. They know we're here."

How? "Damn," Theo said. In all likelihood, they would be dead or gone by the time his ship arrived.

"Sir. They're being attacked by pirates." *Of course, it's pirates. What else is there, out this far? At least we know we're safe from an alien invasion.* Deacon's pirates had enough firepower to mount a sizeable defence of the system.

"Sir?" Mykaela said.

"Can you see what kind of ship is attacking them?" Theo asked, hoping he hadn't said his thoughts aloud. Though he didn't want to send his own ship into a war zone. That wouldn't help anyone.

"There appear to be two smaller pirate vessels," Mykaela explained. "We think we can—"

"Do it, then," Theo said. He didn't have time to worry about what the ship could or couldn't do. It was her ship and if she wanted to go, he wasn't going to stop her.

Theo stepped onto the docking pad and peered down the long tunnel. Seeing no bodies, he sighed in relief. Petr must have latched his suit well enough that it didn't instantly suck out his air. The metal grating catwalk shielded by a clear plastic tube extended out to a similar gate on the *Galena*. From his perspective, Theo could see that several vicious gashes had been torn into the side of his ship as if by massive claws. *I wonder if they fired grappling hooks at her to stop her from hitting them.*

With his first step, Theo realized too late that there was no gravity in the docking tube. His foot never hit the floor and he started to flounder in the air. He fired the thrusters on his legs so he could do a swimmer's flip and place his feet against the hull of the ship. He had to quickly so Mykaela could leave. *One, two, three,* he counted and pushed off, rocketing toward the end of the tube. Miscalculating, he hit the other pad with a bone-jarring thud. *It's a good thing we don't pay that medic per injury.*

Theo heard his boots clamp to the floor of the opposite docking pad with a deep metallic click. He narrowed his eyes. "I heard that." Sound didn't travel through a vacuum. Oxygen on the docking pad meant a proper environment within the ship was likely. If there was no vacuum, it wouldn't matter if Petr's suit wasn't latched properly. *But why isn't there a vacuum?*

Theo pressed the button beside the airlock door, counting again as it spun around to allow him entrance. As soon as it was clear, he reached through to grab the bar set above the door, and dragged himself in.

"I'm through the gate," he announced. "Release the shuttles and do what you have to."

"Sir, the shuttles will be waiting at the exits," Mykaela replied.

"Good. Keep me posted." Theo didn't want to use the shuttles to limp home to the Jupiter stations, not to mention what the loss of another ship and her crew would mean.

When he passed through the airlock and looked down the hall, he knew something was amiss. the light strips running along the walls were on, and it was obvious by the metal and plastic strewn around the floor that gravity had been restored. He sighed, realizing that his son would be fine. Gravity couldn't be produced if the ship was still venting atmosphere. *What the hell is going on?*

Theo lifted his hand to his helmet, waiting a second before pulling the release. One breath, two breaths. It was one thing making the assumption, and another, breathing the air. And though he wouldn't call it fresh air, it wasn't stagnant. The power had been restored some time ago.

Had they been wrong about the salvage? Could someone be gutting his ship already? Or perhaps his assumptions were incorrect about the timing. It was possible that Gideon had already restored power. *Not that fast,* he thought, shaking his head. He started down the hall, his steps exaggerated in the heavy environmental suit. Gideon may have restored the power, but he didn't reset the oxygen. *Someone else has been here.*

Theo lifted his hand to press the button for the suit's internal radio. "Gideon?"

Without pause the old man replied, "Theo. What are you doing on the ship?"

"I came to find Petr."

"Petr?" A pause. "Theo, where is he?" Gideon asked.

"Do you think I'd be calling you if I knew?" Theo sighed. It was a pointless conversation. Gideon obviously didn't know where Petr was, and it sounded like he had his own issues.

"Where are you, then?" Gideon pressed. "I will send someone to you to help. You'll have to find him quickly and then meet us in the control room."

"Thank you," Theo said. "I'm still out at the airlock. I can only assume that Petr went to the…to the plant-hold. He came over to…to get something."

Silence. Then the old man said, "I will send someone to cut him off. Perhaps you should come directly here. Some sections of the ship still aren't safe yet."

"And you know this because?" Theo said. He had no intentions of deviating from his course. Petr was his primary concern.

"Because there are some things that I have to tell you," Gideon offered cryptically.

Things to tell me? What further secrets could the old man be hiding? Finding out that the man had almost led them down a disastrous trail to attack Deacon and his people was bad enough.

"I'll be there shortly," Theo countered. "I will collect Petr first."

"No," Gideon insisted. "You should come here first."

"Gideon, until this very second I thought that Petr may have been running around with a breached suit. I'm going to deal with my son first."

"Theo, we have him. You should come here," Gideon said.

Now you have him? What the hell is going on? Theo turned and headed for the control room, wondering what could possibly have set the old man off now. They'd come for salvage and to lay Galena and Grace to rest. They couldn't have discovered something so soon after boarding the ship. Masajiro would call him, not Gideon.

Theo chewed the inside of his cheek. Gideon must have known about whatever information they were acting on now before they boarded. That was probably why the old man had been so particular about choosing the teams. Theo had assumed it had something to do with expertise, but then when he saw the roster, he was sure that every man had more experience with combat than engineering. After that Theo had assumed the officers in the shuttles would be the ones to start stripping the ship down once it was cleared.

Theo rounded the corner and realized the first of his mistakes. Not ten feet away, two officers crouched with their rifles aimed at him, only dropping them when he waved his arms. They were still wearing their environmental suits and had their helmets hooked to their belt loops. Their eyes seemed to look everywhere at once, the barrels of their rifles tracking. *You're wearing the sound dampeners,* Theo thought as he passed them. While Theo's suit crinkled with every move, the officers' were as silent as cloth, not plastic suits.

Theo found the operations room filled with officers. At first, he couldn't see Gideon. Cocking his head, he said, "What's happening here?" The crowd shifted, revealing the old man bent over a small screen, Rick and Masajiro at his side. They were in the midst of a heated discussion. As they looked up, Rick instantly looked away, unwilling to meet Theo's gaze. He mumbled something that Theo couldn't hear. Theo hadn't seen much of Rick since he'd boarded the ship with Masajiro. He almost thought that the soldier was trying to avoid him. Masajiro, on the other hand, looked to Theo with a smile on his flushed face. He nodded and glanced quickly to Gideon as if trying to tell Theo something.

"What's going on here, Gideon? Where's Petr?" Theo asked as he joined them.

"We're getting our revenge now," Gideon said quietly as he stared at the screen.

Looking down at the screen, Theo watched as a fiendishly familiar face looked around one of the engine compartments of the ship. Lifting his arm, Deacon pointed to several of the people surrounding him and they scurried around at his command. *Deacon.*

Theo felt his face grow hot. He had to close his eyes to stop himself from grinding what little he had left of his teeth. "What in the nine hells is going on here? Rick, start talking."

The man took a deep breath before answering—so fast that Theo couldn't absorb it all. "I just found out, I promise. Gideon's known since the beginning. He knew they were still here, or at least that they would be back. He got us to come here so we could get Deacon."

Theo balled his fists as he turned scowling to the old engineer. "Are you trying to get us all killed, Gideon? And where is my son?"

"No," Gideon replied. "I have it all worked out. All we have to do is surround them. We have enough firepower now, and they aren't prepared to fight us off. Then we can get him back to the ship."

"There's no ship," Theo said, seething.

"What do you mean?" Gideon asked. "We just have to get on the shuttle and move through the mine field."

"No," Theo said slowly. "Because I expected that everything would be fine, I let them go deal with the distress call that came through. They likely won't be back for hours. So, you'd better have a good way off this ship, because we're leaving now. We'll radio them when we have the chance and then we'll hide."

Theo looked around the room at the faces of Gideon's recruits, all retired military officers he'd flown with before purchasing *Galena*. They had come to Gideon's call as if he were a king summoning his subjects.

It wasn't fear for himself that prompted Theo to act, but for his people. It was difficult to order his people to leave, knowing that his wife's murdered body was on the same deck as he was, but neither was it cowardice. He wanted nothing more than to march down and kill Deacon. He just knew better. The monster calling out orders to his people on the screen was a hardened killer only playing at being civilized. There was no humanity in his cold, dead stare.

"Sir, I see the boy," an officer said.

Theo instantly turned to stare. The man was looking down at another screen, which displayed an almost ridiculous image of his son marching toward the plant-hold. The environmental suit he wore was far too large for him to walk properly, with its pant legs bunched up above his boots. *You must have been lowered into them,* Theo thought as he remembered the woman near the airlock. Cute or not, the woman would be staying on Jupiter station if she didn't have a better excuse.

"Have you actually sent someone to collect him?" Theo asked as he turned toward the exit.

"Yes," Gideon answered, stepping forward to confront Theo. "You have to do this, Theo. It has to be done right now."

"Gideon. All you've done since I came back on board is lie. Why in the universe would I care about what you want?" Theo moved toward the door.

"Because, Theo, ever since I realized the link was still open, I have scoured the ship. I have searched every last inch of her by camera and I can say with no doubt in my mind that Grace is not on this ship."

"*What?*" Theo exclaimed as he swung back around.

"They have her, Theo," Gideon whispered.

Gracie, Theo thought. They had his daughter. They had his daughter and the old man standing in front of him had known for months.

Theo wasn't a violent man, but instinct took over as he reached out and punched Gideon in the jaw, dropping the old man in a heap to the deck. "Don't you think that might have been something I'd have wanted to know?" he grated, standing over him.

"I figured you'd leave her like you did your wife," Gideon replied coldly as he wiped the blood from his lips.

"That's once," Theo growled, towering over the old man. "You don't get a second chance. Do you understand?"

Gideon must have seen the fire in Theo's eyes, because he nodded, then shook off the assistance of several officers and pulled himself to his feet, where he stood as waiting for orders. When Theo said nothing, he stammered, "I—I'm sorry. I didn't think—"

"You got that right, old man. You didn't think. And now I have to think for you, damnit." He looked around. "Does anyone have any suggestions?"

Masajiro immediately stepped forward. "We need to determine the validity of the distress call."

"Why?" Theo immediately countered.

"It could be a diversion," Masajiro explained. "They could know we were coming."

That was what they'd been arguing over when Theo entered, he realized. Masajiro was the voice of reason, trying to dissuade them from their course of action. Rick, though acknowledging Theo's authority, was questionable. He'd obviously sided with Gideon's plan, even if it was after their arrival.

Drawing a deep breath, Theo said to the man watching the screen, "You there—is someone close to my son?" A nod. "Good, make sure they bring him back here."

"Sir, there's a military officer on board," the man offered casually.

"What?" Theo asked. "Who cares? We know they're dirty. Sorry, Masajiro."

"Wait," Masajiro said. "Your officer is right. For all their dirty play, you can force their hand long enough for us to leave."

"No," Gideon whimpered. "Please...please don't. We have to save Grace."

Theo swung around and stared at Gideon for several seconds in silence before saying, "You know what? You get proof, then I'll believe you. Until then, we're leaving. Masajiro, please continue."

"The officer isn't here for any untoward dealings. They are required for all salvage operations. All we have to do is prove your right to the ship."

"No," Theo said. "All we have to do is make them think we have it. I have no intentions of keeping this ship. I just want off of it."

"What is your plan?" Masajiro immediately asked.

"The shuttles should be waiting at the gate—"

"Sir, we have a problem," the officer sitting at the computer terminal said.

Theo realized the import of the man's words as he gazed at the screen. The camera that had shown his son walking toward the plant-hold where they'd left Galena was now showing a tall man in a black environmental suit. Neither the suit nor the man were from Theo's new ship.

His face contorted in pain, Theo looked to Gideon and said, "You've killed me." He turned away from the terminal and said loudly, "Masajiro, take your team down to the engine compartment.

Wait for me there. I need to take care of something first. And keep your helmets handy."

"What is your plan?" Masajiro asked as he moved to follow Theo's orders.

"I...I'm not sure yet," Theo admitted. "I'll let you know when I get there. I promise. I won't lose a soul. I won't lose a soul."

Turning back as Masajiro left, Theo said, "Can you contact Mykaela?"

"I think so, sir," the man said as he typed into the terminal. It was difficult for him to press the buttons with his gloves on, but eventually the screen changed to show the face of Mykaela with Zak behind her. Interference crossed the screen in several jagged lines, and white fuzz periodically replaced the image.

"What is happening, Theodore?" Mykaela asked.

"Have you reached them yet?" Theo asked immediately.

She shook her head. "We have at least another half-hour. It looks like one ship is mounting an attack on the other, but we won't know until we can get closer."

Theo sighed. Should he take the chance and assume it was a ruse? Could he let an innocent crew die for an assumption? *No,* he thought. He couldn't let them die. He couldn't take that chance.

"Mykaela, we believe that ship may be a plant. Be careful."

"Shall we turn around?" she asked, immediately putting the pieces together: everyone on the ship with Theo was in grave danger.

Theo shook his head. "No. Just be careful. Return as fast as you can. We'll take the shuttles and disappear into the dark. Tell the shuttle captains to wait for our signal."

"Sir, we're losing the signal," the terminal operator said as more snow began to cover the screen.

"The mines," Gideon offered. "We were having problems with the feed before. It was spotty until we boosted the signal. We haven't set that up from this end yet."

"Damnit," Theo said. "Fine, just contact the shuttles. Get them prepped to clear the way, but until then, I want them powered down. Deacon obviously has ships around here somewhere, and they'll be back."

"What can I do?" Gideon asked.

Swinging his head to look at the man, Theo said, "Nothing yet. I don't need that kind of help." He couldn't afford to have Gideon screw with his plan, but he still needed him. Gideon's expertise with the ship was going to help vent the atmosphere. His people were still suited up, but not all of Deacon's were.

Theo hated Gideon's lies and subterfuge, but at least he understood the reasoning. *Gracie.* And for now, the old man was the only one Theo could trust to operate the ship from the computer terminal. But he couldn't trust Gideon and his followers to realize his plan. Theo stomped out of the room, headed for the engine room, calling back, "Keep him here, Rick, and make sure we have a clear path to the airlock. I don't care how you do it."

Theo marched down the hall flexing his arms. Periodically he let his hand fall to the helmet as he formed his plan.

Theo's path through the ship was eerily familiar, but strangely dark. The lights flickered on and off as the power fluctuated. The debris lining the corridor was in stark contrast to the sister ship Theo had just left. He was moving through the same halls, but they were a disaster, the walls cracked and steam rising from severed hydraulic lines. Most of the central grating that Petr had bounced on to make noise was melted, as though the temperature had surged when the two ships collided.

It didn't take long to find Masajiro and his men.

The military officer nodded in acknowledgement as Theo made his way through the group. "What is your plan, Captain?"

Theo looked at Masajiro for a second, thinking, *Are you with me?* "Do you still hold a rank?"

Masajiro nodded slowly, offering a curt, "Yes."

"Then I need you to come with me. Will Deacon recognize you?" Theo asked. Masajiro shook his head. Theo looked around. "Does anyone have a knife? I don't want a large one." He couldn't conceal a large weapon, but a small knife would work to puncture the seal of an environmental suit.

One of the officers passed him a small blade. *I can do this.* He had to, to save Petr's life. *And find out if you're alive too, Gracie,* he added. He wanted to believe his daughter had lived, but he couldn't let himself get too excited. He had to be composed to ensure his success.

Theo and Masajiro entered the engine room together. Theo knew by the quick movements of Masajiro's head that he was doing a quick head count. He would know what to do if violence broke out.

"Hey, what are you doing here?" Theo bellowed as he came through the door.

"What?" a voice asked and the room erupted with movement. Those working with torches and tools were instantly on their feet, looking to the door, expecting more people to come through. Several of them held weapons, though it seemed most of those had known Theo was coming—their grips were light and their eyes alert.

"I asked, what you were doing on my ship," Theo said slowly, spying his son at the far end of the compartment.

Petr was still wearing his suit and he held tight to his helmet. *Good boy, Petr.* The boy's eyes darted from Deacon to Theo. Unfortunately, Deacon towered over Petr, and a police officer sat on a stool behind them. She sat with her back straight, as if she resented her mission, and still wore her stark white environmental suit as if about to depart the ship.

Deacon's movements were almost regal as he turned to look at Theo. "Ah, now I understand. To answer your question, we are salvaging this ship as per our court order."

"Then you will cease your operations," Theo said simply. "This is my ship and I will be salvaging it. I expect you will be kind enough to return what you have already stolen."

"Stolen?" Deacon said, his voice rising a decibel. "This is a legal operation."

"Is it?" Theo asked. He needed more time to make sure the path was cleared. If Masajiro was correct and this police officer was uncorrupted, then Deacon was trying to play the part so he wasn't revealed as the pirate who'd caused the damage in the first place.

"We have a warrant to strip the ship as per—"

Turning to the police officer, Theo said, "Did you contact the owner of the ship?"

"What? Of course, we did. The ship belongs to Lovett Industries. They had no recollection of the ship being this far and released it."

"Why don't you go over to that terminal and prove it?" Theo said. Could it be so easy? He had been adamant about keeping the Lovett Industry name off the manifest.

Theo held Deacon's gaze as he said, "Why don't you come over here, Petr?"

By her grudging movements, Theo could tell the police officer wasn't present by choice. She stayed several paces from Deacon and her eyes darted from one armed soldier to the next. She obviously knew of Deacon's reputation and wouldn't want to remain. *Where's your own ship?* Theo wondered, feeling a twinge of guilt that he would have to leave the woman on the ship. He wouldn't manage to convince her to follow him, and abduction wasn't an option. At least, still dressed in her own environmental suit, it was possible for her to leave the ship unscathed.

Glancing to Theo, the woman asked, "What is your name?"

"Theodore Stinson," Theo said as he waved Petr to his side.

Deacon had other ideas. His hand fell to Petr's shoulder and Theo saw Petr wince at the pressure the tall man was exerting. *I need to think of another way,* he thought. Nothing would work if Petr wasn't able to leave.

"Why don't you let my son come over here, Mr....?" Theo said tersely, leaving no room for negotiation. Deacon would either have to acquiesce or show his hand.

Deacon stepped aside for Petr to leave, but pirouetted quickly and grabbed the boy as soon as Petr took a step. With his arm draped over Petr's shoulder, he said, "Now, don't you think I am a *civilized* man?" He grinned as he spoke.

The image wasn't lost on Theo as he watched the man hold his son like he had Galena, just before she'd died. The man was trying to frighten him, but Theo knew he had to remain calm. He had to win this using Deacon's rules. *You fool. We're not even playing the same game.*

"Oh, I don't doubt you're civilized," Theo said as he took a step forward. "I just want to speak to my son. Now, let him go before you cause a scene." He spoke the last so quietly that he wasn't sure the man even heard.

His white-knuckled grasp loosened just as the woman police officer said, "Oh, I will need proof of ID, but I will have to concur. This isn't Lovett Industries' vessel." The woman smiled at Theo.

Theo's hope was short-lived, however. The pirate standing at her side swiped her with his rifle; she grunted and crumpled to the floor, blood oozing from the wound.

As the woman wilted, Theo lunged out, grabbed his son's arm, and yanked. He heard Petr whimper, but the sharp movement broke Deacon's grasp. Before the man could order his men to fire, Theo lashed out with the blade hidden in his gloved hand. He smiled as he heard Deacon's suit tear.

"Do the right thing," he said quietly as he took several steps away from the pirate leader.

"You don't think you'll get away now, do you?" Deacon asked. "She's already out cold and you'll—"

The radio on the policewoman's hip began to chirp, cutting him off. A frown crossed his face and he motioned for one of his men to pick it up. The man came forward, crouched, and tossed the radio to Deacon without even looking at the prone woman.

"Have somewhere to be?" Theo asked. Moving slowly so the man wouldn't notice, he squeezed his son's hand to grip his helmet tighter. He had to show Petr he needed to don the helmet before they left the engine compartment. *Come on, buddy. Get ready.*

Theo's heart pounded so hard he could hardly hear the man's reply, but when Deacon started to smile again, Theo knew something was amiss. He had to control his breathing so he could hear what the man was saying on the other end of the radio.

"—are you?" came from the radio.

"This is Deacon Lovett," the pirate said happily.

"Where is Officer Wilkins?" the radio challenged.

"Oh, she just stepped out. The air was starting to get a little stuffy. I will send one of my men to retrieve her," Deacon said slowly. "Is there a message?"

Could the man be so brazen? He was talking to them like he owned their ship, too.

"Uh…" the radio operator stammered. Did he own them all? "Tell Officer Wilkins we need her to return. We have detained a ship for piracy."

The radio operator's words were a slap in the face to Theo. The police cruiser couldn't have been that far away. That meant they must have responded to the same distress call that Mykaela had taken her ship to answer. They would likely return before Theo even departed from this ship.

"Oh, and what ship would that be?" Deacon asked. His smile was growing, as if he knew something Theo didn't.

"The ship belongs to Theodore Stinson, but he isn't on board."

"Oh?" Deacon asked. "Now, isn't that ironic, Mr. Stinson? Your ship has just been impounded."

His ship? *My ship?* The police had taken his ship for piracy? Theo felt the room beginning to close in on him. All his hopes of leaving the ship were beginning to slip away. Even if the woman lying on the floor wasn't with the pirates, her crew was.

"Now, how do you think you'll be leaving *my* ship, Mr. Stinson?" Deacon asked as he dropped the radio to the floor.

Theo felt a gentle touch against his back, then Masajiro whispered, "Not all is lost. Remember that."

Before Theo could turn to see what the man was doing, Masajiro stepped around Theo and punched one of the pirates in the mouth, clearly breaking the man's jaw. Twirling to his left, Masajiro kicked low enough to trip two more pirates, who flailed wildly backward and landed senseless on the deck.

As Masajiro danced around the room, Theo lifted his helmet to his head. He heard the hiss of air being drawn into the vent shaft as he pressed the helmet down. Gideon had done his part. Smiling, Theo latched his helmet quickly, then turned to see his son following suit.

Clamping his hand around Petr's elbow, Theo dragged his son with him as he ran, legs pumping as hard as he could to move the heavy suit while bearing the weight of his son. As soon as he was close enough, he launched his son through the door toward the waiting officers. In his suit radio, he heard Masajiro grunting as he continued to beat on the pirates.

"*You!*" Deacon yelled at someone. Theo glanced back to see that the pirate had put his own helmet on and was moving to intercept Masajiro.

Theo smashed his hand down on the buttons for the audio system. "*Wait!*" he yelled. Apparently, the volume was high enough to silence the room. Breathing heavily enough that his breath fogged up his visor, Theo peered around the room. *That's right, just listen,* he thought as he glanced at Masajiro before focusing on Deacon, who was lifting his rifle. "You know the room is venting," Theo said, pointing to the vent shafts above the generators. "Perhaps you should check the tear in your suit."

Deacon's rifle hesitated as he stared at Theo. Then the pirate dropped his hand to his body to feel around for a breach. *That's it. Did you hear me cut your suit? Maybe not.*

It was a small win, but as Deacon searched for his breach, Theo and Masajiro darted for the door. They were both through when Theo heard Deacon yelling first for his men to suit themselves and then for one of the engineers to reverse the venting air. *I guess you found it,* Theo thought, hoping the tear would be enough to keep the pirate occupied. Theo slapped the button to close the door and set off at a run, knowing his officers had already returned to Rick, Petr in tow. Only his heavy breathing broke the eerie silence of the corridor. It reminded him of the dark sensory deprivation room on the *Galena.*

When Theo arrived, the others were waiting, their helmets latched. One of the officers held tight to Petr as he squirmed to be released.

"Sir, there won't be an ounce of oxygen on the ship in less than a minute," Rick said as Theo reached them.

"Good. Let's go," Theo said.

They'd only turned the first corner before being confronted by three pirates, who started to fire their ballistic weapons. *Idiots,* Theo thought as the bullets ricocheted around the walls. They could easily nick a hydraulic line or puncture the hull. Deacon likely figured it was more civilized to use the archaic weapons instead of energy rifles. Rick's new army was quick to retaliate with their energy weapons, quickly laying down suppression fire before cutting the enemy down.

"Rick, you were supposed to keep this area clear," Theo said as he knelt to check Petr's suit and helmet latch in the flickering overhead lights.

"It was. These are new," Rick offered as he pulled the trigger on his rifle to send another pirate skittering around the corner.

Theo hadn't asked for this chaos. All he'd wanted was to say goodbye to his wife and daughter. Now, if he wasn't careful, he and his son would be saying hello to them in the afterlife. *No,* he thought suddenly. If he were to believe Gideon, Grace wasn't gone.

As if thinking of the man would invoke a conversation, Gideon said, "I can do something."

Though he didn't want to show the man that he needed him, Theo finally said, "What?"

"The gravity," Gideon said. "Turn it up."

"And how will we get through if the gravity is turned up in this section?" Theo countered. He needed a solution, not another problem. If they turned up the gravity, something dangerous for the compromised environmental system, they would weld themselves to the floor just as much as the enemy.

"Just let me deal with that," Gideon replied, his breathing even in the helmet he wore.

Of course, Theo thought. Dressed like the others in a suit, Gideon's metallic legs were hidden, but they would work through the heaviest of gravity. "How do we turn it up?" Theo asked.

"There," Gideon said and pointed to a terminal on the far wall. It seemed miles away as sparks flew off the grey metal where the bullets struck.

And now we know why they use ballistics, Theo thought, shaking his head. Energy weapons were visible in any light or environment, but ballistic weapons were silent in an airless environment and only sparked at the muzzle of the weapon and where they struck.

Theo stepped around his son. "Petr, stay with Masajiro. Understand?"

"Father, I can do it," Petr said as he found his voice.

"No Petr," Theo said. He felt tears trickling down his face. He wasn't going to let Petr sacrifice himself.

"Father, I can do it. I can fit under the terminal and I know how to operate it," Petr explained.

Theo shook his head. He'd just saved Petr from Deacon's ire. He refused to throw him into more danger. Theo had to go himself.

"Father, I won't get hit," Petr said matter-of-factly. "I can make it."

Theo focused his gaze on his son through the mask. "Petr, you can barely walk in that suit. How do you think you'll run across the hall to press the button?"

Petr sighed, peering up at his father through his helmet. "Throw me like you did in the engine room. It will be faster than running, so they won't be able to do anything about it."

"Sir," Rick said suddenly. "I…I can throw him."

Theo turned to stare at the soldier. What was the man thinking? Petr was a boy. He wasn't an officer. He wasn't strong. All he was…was determined. *And smarter than any adult I know.* It wasn't just the danger to his son, however; Theo couldn't shake the feeling that Rick, too, was keeping secrets from him. The unease he felt around the man was likely unfounded, but it made him double think a decision like letting him literally throw Petr into enemy fire.

Theo nodded. He felt like vomiting. If anyone could achieve the feat it was his son, but that didn't change the fact that Petr was a child, his child.

The decision made, Rick didn't waste any time. Gripping Petr so he would fly head first, Rick swung him back, then tossed Petr across the hall as the other officers shot off a barrage of covering fire.

Petr hit the floor and slid until he stopped within inches of the wall. He scrambled into the cubby, out of the path of the weapons fire zinging the wall. *There's no oxygen left to ignite, even,* Theo thought, watching. With nothing to show where the enemy bullets were hitting, Petr would never know where he was placing himself in harm's way. *Stay down, Petr.*

"He made it," someone whispered as Theo felt his stomach settle. He'd made it. *Of course, you made it.* Theo was shaking visibly as he watched his son turn back and lift his thumbs.

Moving deliberately, Petr reached above the ledge and pressed the terminal screen. To Petr, it would be a game to show the adults what he could do.

Forcing the air in his lungs to release, Theo found his voice to say, "Can you guide him from here, Gideon? So, he doesn't have to come out of the hole?"

Gideon shook his head. Theo's stomach lurched again in response.

"It's okay, Father. I can do this."

Petr was so calm. *How can you be so calm?* He should have been crying like a little child, not gently pressing buttons on a screen as if they were all playing.

Theo watched his son point toward the end of the hall, then jump out and press the buttons on the screen in sequence. Theo's world moved at a snail's pace as first one, and then half a dozen bullets hit the terminal Petr was using. It exploded in a burst of plastic and glass shards. Petr fell back, his hands still stretched out toward the terminal. He fell quickly to the floor as Theo wondered, *Did it work?* Without an environment in the corridor, Theo wasn't sure whether Petr had accomplished his goal before the terminal was destroyed. *I don't see anymore bullets,* Theo thought.

Oh crap. It was too late to adjust himself as the gravity pulled him to the floor. In an instant, Theo was drawn down, his body too weak to resist the pull.

Gideon soon passed in Theo's line of sight. He could hear the man grunting and wheezing through the radio, but nothing else. *I hope you died, you son of a bitch,* Theo silently screamed at Deacon, though he expected the man would likely have survived. A man didn't get as far as he had without a few bumps. *Likely killed one of his men and stole the suit.*

After an eternity, Theo said, "What's happening?" He rolled his head from side to side to see whether he could change his vantage, but the visor yielded nothing new.

After several seconds Gideon passed by in the other direction. The old man stopped at Petr's terminal and shook his head before setting off in search of another terminal.

As the pull against his body abated, Theo pushed himself up. When he regained his feet, he could see Gideon was adjusting the gravity in the rest of the ship, his hands moving so fast that Theo couldn't keep track.

"What did you do, Gideon?" Theo asked slowly. He didn't have to ask, though. By raising the gravity in the rest of the ship, Gideon would essentially lock the pirates up until the generators failed.

Theo took three steps to the terminal to see the results and sighed. He felt a small pang of guilt as he realized the old man hadn't increased the gravity, but reduced it. He had chosen not to leave the pirates for dead, but make it impossible for them to follow. Looking to the old man, Theo asked, "Why?"

Gideon stared at Theo, tears streaming down his weathered face as he said, "Grace."

Theo understood. The man was hoping Deacon would remember the last act. Deacon would know they could have left him for dead, but didn't. Deacon would know that Theo had let him live and still played by the rules of the game. It was a gentleman's game, using swords when they carried pistols. They had to determine whether Grace lived, and the only way they could do that was to keep playing Deacon's infernal game.

Theo motioned Petr and the others into the airlock. His shuttles were waiting. With his ship impounded, they would have a tediously long trip back to Jupiter.

Chapter 12

Finding Reason

Theo glanced sideways at Masajiro and asked, "Are you sure this will work?"

Masajiro smiled. "They have no grounds to hold them."

"And me?" Theo asked. Though he'd given the ship to Mykaela, his name was still on the registration. It was his ship the police had impounded. He was the only person able to bail his people out.

All Theo wanted to do was take his ship and disappear into the night. He didn't even yearn for the taste of alcohol. He couldn't take care of Petr then.

Petr removed his own helmet and let it float off into the rear of the shuttle as he looked around and counted their people. When he was finished, he said, "Where's Gideon?"

Shaking his head to clear his thoughts, Theo said, "He's on the other shuttle, buddy."

Thinking of the old man brought a barrage of emotions. Theo didn't want to think about Gideon and his actions. All Theo wanted was freedom. Gideon had led them into a trap, not even telling them his reasons. If he'd been open, explaining the true reason why he'd taken those actions, it would have been different. With the possibility of Grace being alive, Theo wouldn't have dug in his heels, refusing to take the fight to Deacon. Theo would have found Grace. He would have made it work. *You could have told me, Gideon. You should have told me.*

Realizing Masajiro was still speaking and he'd missed much of what the man said, Theo turned back to him and said, "I'm sorry, what did you say?"

Masajiro gulped for air, still trying to control his breathing. He must have been holding his breath for over two minutes while he beat the pirates down, breaking arms and flinging enemies away from him like kindling. He was a superman, fighting without stopping until he'd accomplished his goal.

Masajiro had already admitted to Theo that he'd been tasked with returning the system to order, but what could one man do? Especially a man trained more in the art of war than diplomacy? Masajiro couldn't beat every pirate into submission.

"The police were looking for you to cut you off from your ship that was being salvaged."

Theo rolled his eyes. "Those were police that were looking for me on the station. You can't pretend they—"

Masajiro continued to speak as though Theo hadn't interrupted. "All we have to do is prove that your people weren't there to board that other ship."

"How do you know what they were doing? We don't have any proof," Theo said. He threw up his hands before pulling himself down to the seat beside his son.

He felt Petr shaking heavily and saw tears on the boy's face and realized he was crying. Bending low, he asked, "What's wrong, buddy?"

Petr shook his head and buried his face in his arms. After a time, he looked up, tears streaming down his face. He tried to speak several times, but he couldn't force the words from his mouth. When he finally succeeded, it was so quiet that Theo barely heard him. "But where's Gideon?"

"I told you, son, Gideon is on the other shuttle."

"But…but Gideon promised he would find Grace," Petr blurted. He instantly buried his face again.

You knew. Petr had known about the old man's plan. Had everyone else? Had they all played the ruse to get Theo on the damned ship, using him as a pawn to lay claim? How could they all be so stupid? They didn't need to keep it secret.

Theo shook his head. The order he'd drawn from the growing chaos was slowly sinking back into the mire. Everything he thought he'd known was unravelling. How could he have not realized they were going into a trap?

"But Gideon wanted to attack them directly," he whispered softly. Gideon didn't want to salvage the ship. He'd wanted to go to Mars. But then, what was on Mars? What could be so important to Deacon and his brother on Mars? The answer had to be simple. Theo knew he must already have the answer, but it lay hidden in the recesses of his mind. He realized how much damage his short tryst with the Grey Goose had caused. Try as he might, he couldn't focus his mind.

"Masajiro, what is on Mars for Deacon and his brother?" he asked.

The man shook his head. "Nothing that I know of."

Turning, Theo stared at Rick for several seconds before asking, "Why were you going to Mars, Rick?"

The man took only a few seconds to answer, but Theo could still hear the hesitation in his voice. Whether it was out of guilt or honour, the man admitted, "It isn't what's on Mars, it's what's coming from there."

"Ships," Theo mused aloud. The only thing coming from Mars was ships—ships that Deacon was waylaying and then salvaging. "What is he looking for?"

Deacon had been tearing Theo's ship to threads, and not just for salvage. A salvage operation went for the most expensive pieces first, then returned for the less accessible parts. With the number of torches at Deacon's disposal, he'd been looking for something in particular. *Something in the engine room.* Whatever it was they had been looking for had required an atmosphere. Why else ensure the corridors were sealed? *And they restored gravity, albeit a low gravity, given the damage to the central hydro lines.* Deacon still wanted something on that ship.

"Some form of technology," Rick offered casually, obviously uncertain of Theo's line of questioning.

Theo nodded. "Some form of technology. What would a ship...what would my ship have for technology that another wouldn't?"

Masajiro looked up then and said, "Sometimes it isn't about what someone has that is desired, but what everyone thinks they have."

"Well then," Theo said, "what was it that Deacon and his brother think I had?"

Shifting suddenly, Rick said, "They didn't think it was your ship, sir. They think it is Lovett's."

Of course, they do, Theo thought. He was right, of course. Deacon had asked Theo to send his regards to Lovett. *To your father.* The pirates had thought it was Lovett's ship. So what else was it that Lovett had, or everyone thought he had, deep within the engine rooms?

As if reading his mind, Petr reverently said, "Folding engines. They want folding engines."

Theo wanted to scoff at his son for his idle fantasies, but he couldn't. On some level he knew Petr's assumption was correct. Deacon and his brother were looking for the holy grail of space travel, a myth so ornate that it stood along with teleporters and perpetual energy. Rather than seek it out, however, they were expecting the mythical technology to just appear in their midst. They ransacked ship after ship that Lovett Industries flew for the sole purpose of obtaining that engine.

"Why?" he mused aloud. The Lovett boys had created an empire in the outer reaches of the solar system. They had an ironclad grip on the people, the military, almost everything. Why would they care for a folding engine? It couldn't be for ransom. If the technology even existed, it could be duplicated.

Deacon was either planning to go in toward Earth or out toward a place like Alpha Centauri. In or out didn't matter; the question Theo had to answer was why. Why would the Lovett brothers want a ship that could be in one place in one instant and in another the next?

"They're building a fleet of ships," he said slowly before looking to Masajiro. The horror painted on the man's face was enough to confirm his assumption. Whether or not the two brothers succeeded in finding the mythical machine, they still had to have a navy. They would need a navy long before they could attack anyone.

Leaning close enough that only Masajiro could hear, Theo asked, "How many ships do they have?"

Masajiro looked away for a second before he replied. When he spoke, his lips trembled, as though the words were poison. "Hundreds, maybe more."

Hundreds. Without even being said aloud, the word echoed through the shuttle. Deacon and his brother had amassed hundreds of ships. They hadn't been salvaging those ships they'd waylaid for parts or scrap. They'd been taking the entire ships. They had likely retrofitted them with weapons and then crewed them with angry naval officers turned pirates. The civilized veneer and ballistics weren't just a game, but a guise to fool anyone looking close enough. They didn't want to be noticed. *The poor idiots who still use ballistic weapons really can't afford anything else,* Theo thought.

The shuttle spun around him as he traced down the paths of his imagination. War was coming, but for whom? Bored with their subsistence existence in the outer ring, were the Lovett brothers looking to attack Earth? Or were they looking to expand their grasp on human expansion by taking control of the colonies? Could they have enough ships to attack Earth? It was baffling to consider. The Homeforce might not have many ships beyond the orbit of Mars, but they had hundreds of battle cruisers orbiting Earth.

"That didn't help us when the pirates attacked us near Earth," someone said, breaking Theo's reverie. They were packed too tightly within the shuttle for him to shift far enough to see the speaker. It took several seconds for him to realize that he'd been speaking out loud. He frowned, wondering how much he'd said—but then, he realized, it didn't matter. His revelations weren't secret.

"No," he continued, "it didn't help then. But just because we came through on the dark side doesn't mean the ships aren't there. Er…that Captain…Kai—yeah, that was her name—Captain Kai was there with her shuttle. That meant a cruiser had to be close. I mean, even if Deacon has a thousand ships, they wouldn't be able to take on a battle cruiser. Unless," Theo said slowly as his gaze rested on Masajiro, "unless there is something happening on Earth. What's happening on Earth, Masajiro?"

"Not here," Masajiro murmured.

"Not here?" Theo asked. "Where else? These men are in the thick of it."

Masajiro shook his head. "I don't mean you. I mean they aren't going to Earth." The man was obviously keeping more information to himself than he was telling.

"The colonies?" Theo asked immediately. "I understand that's why they would need the engines, but why would they need the ships? There wouldn't be a hundred ships total that have gone to Alpha Centauri."

Masajiro shook his head. "No, there are many, many people there."

Theo frowned. More than a hundred ships? Lovett had said two of his fleets had made it through and then there was Theo's, but that would only be thirty ships, at best.

"The first colony ships were filled with cryo-containers, hundreds of thousands, perhaps millions of people," Masajiro explained.

"So many?" Theo asked. "I didn't think—"

"The colonies have been established for decades," Masajiro went on. "They've had enough time to grow. Both are very strong."

Both strong? More lies. He'd been dispatched to the colonies for no reason! His ships had been filled with supplies to start a colony, not add to an existing one. Unless there was another reason for sending those ships. *At least Lovett didn't lie about there being two colonies.* "So, what are they doing on the colonies now?" Theo asked.

"Preparing for the people of Earth to be transported," Masajiro said.

"All of them?" Rick asked. "There has to be at least ten billion people."

"They won't all be going," Masajiro said matter-of-factly. "They won't all qualify."

"Money?" Theo immediately asked.

"No," Masajiro said. "Health and age."

"Lovett wouldn't be able to go," Theo mused. "That would be why he would build the engines. He wants to jump the line."

"So why send us?" Rick asked.

Theo shrugged. "I don't know. He said that he wanted to make sure this shipment got through—it was important to get supplies. But then he would also know if he could go himself. Masajiro, why would they only allow the young and the healthy?"

Masajiro looked like he'd swallowed his tongue. His eyes went wide and his face turned red. When he spoke, his cheeks were twitching. "There is a radiation field outside of the Solar System. Every ship that leaves has to pass through it."

Theo shook his head. "We've known about the radiation field for years."

"Certainly, we have," Masajiro said, nodding. "But we didn't understand the nature of it. We weren't prepared. The ships had shielding, but not enough. "

"And every person is then exposed to the radiation," Theo said softly. The thought led him immediately to his own people. Though it was still years off, his people would pass through that radiation field. "Deadly levels?"

"For the weak, yes," Masajiro answered. "Especially the elderly."

Theo hadn't chosen young people for his crew, he'd chosen families. The older adults wouldn't last through the trip and some of the middle-aged officers could be so sick they wouldn't be able to work when they reached the triple star Centauri system. That meant that the children would stand on one of the planets orbiting the primary star, but their parents wouldn't be there.

"Does Edward Lovett know about the radiation?"

Masajiro shrugged. "I can only assume. His company would have been informed so they could mitigate the consequences."

The consequences? Theo thought. The consequences were death from radiation poisoning and cancer. The consequences were more than Theo would have visited on his people. He would have taken his chances on Earth.

So, the brothers were likely looking to pass through the radiation to get to the colonies. They were looking for a way to jump through the field without risking their own people. "If Deacon and his people are looking to bypass the radiation field, then they would need the folding engine. But if they were going to pass *through* the field, they would need shielding. Lovett must have shielded his ships. That was why he wanted me to go. He really did want me to test it out before he went. I just didn't realize what I was testing."

Rick leaned forward. "So, there isn't an engine on those ships?"

I dearly hope not, Theo thought as beads of sweat trickled down his forehead. He didn't want to entertain the prospect of a magical technology that could allow Deacon Lovett to be anywhere he wanted.

Petr was tugging on his arm. Theo looked down at his son. The boy was frowning. "Why do we assume there is no engine?" he asked.

Theo cocked his head, baffled that his son, a boy far beyond his age in maturity, was so keen on the mythical technology. But then, his son had always fantasized about teleporting across the universe. Holding Petr's gaze, Theo said, "Tell me what you're thinking, Petr."

Petr looked around the shuttle and took a breath. "That...that man wanted something in the engine room. He said Mr. Lovett had hidden the connection in all of his ships. He was sure the folding engine was there."

"Petr," Theo said with a sigh, "they just don't exist. Even if he was—"

Theo stopped as Masajiro dropped his hand onto his shoulder. "Petr may be correct," Masajiro said slowly. "In a way."

Theo's eyes narrowed. *Still more secrets? Or has everyone gone mad?* Folding space was impossible; the energy needed was astronomical.

Before Masajiro could continue, the shuttle pilot swore and yelled, "Hold on!"

Without gravity they were spared the worst, but as the pilot frantically pressed buttons on his console, the craft lurched to starboard and then to port as the pilot forced the shuttle between two of the mines. The video screen at the side of the pilot's seat showed two more mines sputtering after them. *They're tracking us,* Theo realized, instinctively gripping the edge of his seat as the shuttle shuddered through another extreme command from the pilot. The engines screamed for several minutes as they rocketed through the minefield. Finally, the pilot slumped back into his seat and sighed, pressing the last few buttons to put the craft on autopilot. The man was bathed in sweat.

He turned back to Theo and smiled as he wiped the sweat from his brow. "Jupiter isn't in the same position she was last time. We should be able to refuel at the spaceport Orion and maybe even catch a transport ship."

Theo slapped the man's shoulder. "Good job, Jayce. Take a rest."

The last time the pilot referred to had been much easier for Theo physically, as he'd been unconscious for most of the ride, but he was sure his people would appreciate more than dry rations and sleeping in their environmental suits.

Theo looked around the shuttle, his gaze stopping on Masajiro's calm face. "Sorry," he said, "what were you saying?"

"About ten years ago," Masajiro began, "a machine was built here and in the Alpha Centauri system. The machine is so big that your whole fleet could have fit in it at the same time."

Theo shook his head. Everything he thought he knew was unravelling. In the space of minutes, he'd gone from contemplating the death of his people due to radiation exposure to the possibility that they'd be spared that awful fate, and now that was all under suspicion again. If Deacon had been looking for the engine or the key to it, then he wouldn't care about the protection the ship offered. *No,* Theo thought. It didn't matter what Deacon was looking for; Edward Lovett would still have had the ships shielded for a deep space voyage. *My people are safe.*

Masajiro cleared his throat. "The machine on the other side isn't working properly. They still need supplies to finish it—particularly the ore you're carrying."

It was slowly coming together now. Part of his contracted cargo was going to finish the machine. When it was finished, humans could move between systems. *Even if it takes us years to get there. All the more time to finish transfer preparations.*

"And at this end?" Theo asked quietly.

"There is only one now, near Jupiter."

"Now?" Theo asked, frowning in confusion. "Only one?"

Masajiro nodded. "Yes, there were three altogether, but now only two."

Theo frowned. "Three?" Understanding suddenly slammed into him like a shock wave. "Deacon built his own machine."

"Yes," Masajiro said. "With materials appropriated from their raids, and other sources."

Whether the machine under the government's control had failed or been sabotaged, the government would still want a viable option. If the machine in the Alpha Centauri system was any gauge, it would take years to build a new machine. Much better to just take one that was already built. Theo took a breath before saying, "The government wants it back."

Masajiro nodded. "They will come soon."

Theo sighed, his nostrils flaring. "Unless you stop Deacon first."

Deacon wasn't trying to take over the colonies in the Alpha Centauri system. He was trying to flee the Sol system. He was waylaying the ships leaving so he could control the people on the other end. If you needed a machine to jump, then he could control the entire process from the other side.

Theo scratched his head. "It's going to take years for my ships to arrive. Deacon doesn't have that long."

"You are correct," Masajiro said with a nod. "It will. Except they didn't need *those* supplies."

Those supplies? What other supplies could they need? Theo wondered and then said, "Lovett had three convoys make it through. He didn't say how long ago that was, or how fast they were going."

"Oh," Petr said, "you're right, Father. We were going to take forty years because of our speed. If they used solar sails it would be possible, but they would have to be prepared on the other end to assist in deceleration. Or—well, I mean, they'd have to have something along the way to adjust the trajectory."

"Like each other," Theo said. "If it was a fleet, they could use one ship to adjust the others. They would lose ships along the way, but the end goal would be to build the machine. The people that were already there could then build it."

Masajiro nodded. "Yes, they were unmanned ships."

"So now we know how he did it," Theo said. "We know Deacon is trying to leave. How long do we have?"

Masajiro shrugged. "We don't know. A week? A month? We've lost contact with the other side."

"It must be soon, but then…that still doesn't explain why he attacked my ship. If he was trying to stop Lovett Sr.'s ships, then why not the others? Rick, what happened after I passed out? Why didn't he stop the other ships?"

Rick shrugged and shook his head. "He had his own issues, trying to get off the ship. And then his people had to evacuate. The other ships passed by without stopping, otherwise we would have caught up with them. They knew the deal, though. It was Mykaela who turned, like you asked her. She picked most of the pods up, and then found the rest of us on the stations."

Theo frowned in thought. "You're right. Deacon was after my ship. There was something about it that was different, but what?"

"It was the primary ship," Petr said matter-of-factly. "It had the key to the portal."

"No," Theo said, but then, "*No!*"

It was possible. They could have built the machine without knowing about the key needed for the ships. Deacon would pay dearly for that key. In the beginning he wouldn't have known which ship the key was on. That was why he was waylaying ships.

Our ship was meant to get there. The hull wasn't designed for the radiation alone, but the passage through the portal. *Stipend. A ten percent stipend. One ship would be enough.* One ship would be enough, but Theo had made his impossible to use.

Theo started to chuckle as he looked at those around him. He could see beleaguered officers, exhausted officers. They had gone through a harrowing exercise, first in a failed attempt to find Grace, and then in their exit from Theo's ship. They all looked at him as if he'd gone crazy, perhaps a lack of oxygen causing him to laugh uncontrollably. When he was able to speak, Theo said, "I—I didn't take the primary ship. Galena didn't want it. She said it was bad luck. She made me switch it out with Mykaela."

Silence fell over the shuttle, the only sound the crinkling of environmental suits as the officers looked at each other. *That's it, people, think it through. We still have the key.*

Rick was the first to speak. He shook his head for a second and then asked, "Will he know it?"

"Does it matter?" Theo released his belt and floated up to the ceiling, the others ducking out of his way as he moved forward. When he was finished he hovered over the pilot, who was looking up at him. "Tell the others to make their way to Orion station, and look for a fast ship to get us to Jupiter before she's out of reach."

Theo turned to lock gazes with Masajiro. "Masajiro, are you an assassin?" he asked. He didn't need the man to speak to know his answer. Instead, Theo asked, "Can you get them released?"

Masajiro immediately nodded. "Yes."

"If I get you to Deacon, can you stop him?" Theo pressed as a plan coalesced in his mind.

"I will," Masajiro answered. The man was cold now, as he discussed the prospect of killing Deacon. It wasn't like he was going to kill him accidentally, or stop him by trussing him up and sending him back to Earth. Deacon had to die, and his henchmen had to see it.

"I will get you in front of that man," Theo said.

The decision he was making wasn't just for him; he was making it for Gideon and Mykaela and his son. *And Grace*, he thought. If Grace wasn't already dead, then Deacon was going to make her wish she was. Deacon would use her against Theo when things didn't go his way—as a decoy, or as leverage. Theo remembered the last man to cross Deacon—one of his own. Deacon had destroyed the man for his insolence.

"Rick, when we reach Jupiter Station I want you to contact someone. His name is Captain Charles Hendrickson. He won't like it when you find him so make sure you're fast."

With that, Theo pulled himself back to his seat beside his son, thankful they were on the shuttle built for his ships and not those Gideon had cobbled together. He reached out and embraced Petr, silently crying into the boy's shoulder. Galena's smile wasn't haunting him now, but spurring him on. Galena knew what he had to do now.

She supported him now, just as she had when she'd accepted Lovett's offer. *I hate you, you old bastard. You did this to my family. You and your family's greed.*

Chapter 13

Finding Prudence

Though Jupiter was farther away on its arc, their trip didn't take as long as the first time Theo had abandoned his ship. Dozens of ships were available when they arrived at Orion Station. Theo wasted no time in securing passage, though he was forced to leave the shuttles behind.

The ship Theo secured wasn't large, but when he checked the manifest on the ship, he smiled and clapped his hands before admitting that he knew the captain. After a good night's rest, they boarded the ship clean and refreshed to step into the sleeper units, the doctor injecting them with an oily liquid to force them to sleep.

The ship was designed for speed and not luxury, but with only thirty spare pods, Theo was forced to choose those among his people who wouldn't enter the cryo-chambers. At first tempted to let his son sleep, he thought better of it in the end and let Petr stay awake, sending everyone but himself and Petr, Masajiro, and Gideon into the pods. Theo was certain he could trust the ship's captain, but he felt more comfortable staying awake during the flight, and spending time with Petr was a gift he couldn't pass up.

When the ship docked at Jupiter Station, Theo followed Masajiro to the station's administration level to set about collecting his crew. Like most things from Earth, the government was defined by its opulence. Where below decks they had metal flooring, the government level boasted red carpet. The walls were painted with massive murals depicting land battles fought and won by the sword or long rifle on Earth, generations before humanity even set foot on the Moon. The floors and walls were free of grease, and the corridor smelled of cloves and dried flowers. *Perfume,* Theo thought. *And not the good kind.* He punctuated the thought with a sneeze.

Everything was larger than it needed to be, almost wastefully so. The halls were wider than his small shuttles were long, allowing twenty men to walk abreast. The ceiling was almost high enough that they could have fashioned another deck, yet even the piping that was exposed everywhere else on the station was concealed here. It was laughable to think what would happen if they lost gravity. Everyone would be thrown so high into the air that they couldn't reach the doors.

The door they stopped at was ornately carved and huge, taking up half of the wall at the end of the hall. Masajiro pressed his finger to the small screen beside it, then bent forward to look into the eyepiece. The door opened before he could step back, sweeping outward so they were forced to move from its path. "Let me lead," Masajiro said.

Theo waved him forward. "Be my guest." Theo was good with people, but in the enemy's den he knew better than to test his skills. Behind the walls of the government and to the police, he would be no one. To them he was a pirate, bent upon their destruction; those who knew better understood he was the enemy that Deacon wanted alive. He could only trust in Masajiro's plan.

Over a hundred people sitting in white cells waited for Theo to arrive so they could see the light of day again. Otherwise, they would be the first and likely only people ever convicted of piracy in the outer solar system. *Oh, the irony.* His people were charged with a crime they didn't commit as they tried to save a ship from a man who would never be charged for all the crimes he did commit.

"Giselle will be prepared for us," Masajiro said quietly. "She will let them all know."

Theo followed him through the door into the large chamber beyond where the police had carved out their own tiny empire. He shivered at the prospect of just walking through the door. If he'd been on Earth it wouldn't have bothered him, but this far out in space, the rules changed. Though he trusted Masajiro, Theo couldn't guarantee that any other military officer was only on the government's payroll. The police had adapted to the reality that Deacon and his brother had crafted.

The room they entered was so bright that Theo had to squint as he looked around. For effect, he assumed, squinting at the white paint on the walls and the white furniture. The officer sitting behind the desk, however, was dressed in black from head to toe, as though to accentuate the stark contrast. If they'd been anywhere else, he might have appreciated the curve of her hips. Here, as his body trembled with contained energy, Theo only felt contempt for the woman, regardless of whether she was clean of Deacon's taint or not.

"May I help you?" the woman asked without looking up from her work.

"Stand to," Masajiro barked, and instantly the woman jumped to her feet. "Where is your lieutenant?"

"Uh...uh...I think he's—"

"I don't care what he's doing," Masajiro interjected. "Find him. *Now!*" Masajiro's body language had changed. His accent had disappeared and his shoulders were square. He might have been an assassin, but that wasn't his occupation, only his mission. He was a military officer and understood the use of discipline.

The woman dropped back into her chair and feverishly started typing at her console, periodically stealing a glance at Masajiro, as if fearing he would suddenly breathe fire on her. Theo could see she was also trying to look around Masajiro, but the man was doing an excellent job of blocking Theo from her vision.

"Fine," Masajiro replied. "If you can't find him, then why don't you call up the crew manifest for the transport ship that was just processed."

"Oh, we don't—"

"Don't waste my time, Seaman. Find your lieutenant or get me the list. Unless you want me to start an investigation?"

"My...my lieutenant isn't responding," she sputtered as she continued to press her buttons. "Um...um...no, I will get the list." Her breathing was sharp as she typed faster, Masajiro's threat of investigation sufficient to spur her on. Sweat glistened on her forehead.

The woman closed her eyes and sighed. "Sir, I-I-I found my lieutenant. He's coming." The relief in her voice was enough to confirm that Masajiro wasn't an unknown player in this game. *You've been here before.*

"Can I help you?" a voice said from beyond the woman's desk. A tall man stepped through a narrow door. He wore a uniform similar to that of the seaman, although the man seemed somehow more deserving of wearing it. Unlike the woman, the man immediately met Masajiro's gaze, smiling as he strode forward confidently.

For some reason, Theo felt sure he was looking at one of the few officers still respectful of Terran law. Though he spoke to Masajiro as an officer would to his superior, he was confident and comfortable. *Like you have nothing to hide,* Theo thought.

The lieutenant's uniform was newly pressed, his shoes shined. His bald head was almost as smooth as his face, making it hard to judge his age. *No more than forty,* Theo thought.

"Captain Kojami," the lieutenant said, snapping to attention as he recognized Masajiro.

This mystery is deepening, Theo thought. Masajiro was more embedded in the security of the outer system than he'd let on. The questions it raised were growing. Was his undercover operation known so widely? Or had he been here previously? Though unlikely,

Masajiro could have been able to keep his true identity from Deacon and his henchmen. *Unless Giselle is the undercover agent and you the handler.*

Before Theo could ponder further, Masajiro stepped aside, sweeping out his arm. "I present to you Captain Theodore Stinson."

The woman at the desk breathed in audibly, the clicking of her computer terminal trailing off. The lieutenant's expression barely shifted, but Theo could see the man had made the connection as well.

"Mr. Stinson. I am sorry for your loss." The lieutenant paused. "I believe we have your crew here. Would you like to explain their actions?"

Theo opened his mouth to speak, but the pressure of Masajiro's hand on his elbow was enough silence him.

"Lieutenant Hollingsworth, I believe that is a conversation for your office," Masajiro suggested with a quick glance to the seaman as she resumed her typing.

"I suppose that might be prudent," the lieutenant said with a nod, then turned quickly to lead Theo and Masajiro out of the white room and away from its occupant.

The room they entered was decorated by a different hand. The lieutenant had done his best to personalize the walls with pictures and paintings, though otherwise it was stark, painted the dull grey that most ships and stations started out with. The desk was made of wood, perhaps a mahogany or oak. The lieutenant's chair was cushioned leather while the two chairs before his desk were hard plastic and not built for comfort.

Theo took in the pictures quickly, gravitating to one of Masajiro standing beside the lieutenant after some award ceremony, though both officers were far younger.

"It has been a long time," Masajiro said.

"It has, sir." The lieutenant motioned for them to sit. "I have tried to keep your seat warm, but you know how that works out."

Masajiro wasn't just known, he'd been the Captain of Jupiter Station! *But how long ago? Before Deacon was sent by his father, for sure.*

"Sir, I have to ask…" Lieutenant Hollingsworth said slowly. Theo could see now that the man's eyes were sunken, and he had to stifle several yawns as he spoke.

"Lieutenant, we have other issues that we have to deal with first," Masajiro said flatly, resting his hands on the desk and leaning forward. "It is imperative that we retrieve our people and our ship."

Lieutenant Hollingsworth cocked his head and clicked his tongue. "You know I can't just do that, sir. I try to do everything by the book, especially when Deacon Lovett and his ilk are involved. I don't want to give them the impression that they can get away with anything."

"I appreciate that, Lieutenant, but understand that we are trying to stop Deacon Lovett right now. The only way we can accomplish our goal is to be on our way."

Whether the lieutenant knew he was ineffectual or not, he definitely thought he was doing the right thing. He was determined to make everyone go through the motions. *That's why the police woman was with Deacon on my ship,* Theo thought before offering the woman a prayer. Her ties to the legitimacy the lieutenant offered had also made her expendable, which in the end got her killed.

"Sir, I don't doubt that, but what would you have me do? If Deacon heard that I had released your people without following protocol, then the next time I rounded up any of his, he would expect the same. I would lose the tenuous hold that I do have."

You honestly think you have some control over the stations? Theo marvelled. The man thought the officers on the station followed him and not the cash that lined their pockets when they overlooked some of the misdeeds of Deacon's people. *You likely believe there aren't any prostitutes or a rampant drug problem, too.*

Leaning forward and lowering his head to conceal his lips, Theo whispered, "Do you trust him, Masajiro?"

The reply was immediate. "Without question."

"And the woman out front?" Theo prompted.

Lieutenant Hollingsworth smiled slightly as he said, "I wouldn't trust that woman with anything if you want to keep it secret." He shrugged and added, "But, we're a little far out for reinforcements. I make do with what I've got."

Theo looked at Masajiro and nodded. In response, the man reached into his pocket to retrieve a tiny data crystal. The hard part was done, if Lieutenant Hollingsworth was going to look at the information it held. Theo wouldn't have to convince him of anything.

Palming the crystal, Lieutenant Hollingsworth asked, "What's this?"

"All the explanation you will ever need," Masajiro replied as he leaned back in his chair and crossed his arms.

Lieutenant Hollingsworth chewed his lip, staring at the crystal for several seconds. *Hesitation now?* Theo thought. A secretive agent, who had once run the station they occupied, was sitting in the lieutenant's office explaining his presence, and the lieutenant waited. *Maybe we shouldn't have come.* It was possible that Masajiro was incorrect, but Theo had to believe the man knew what he was doing. *This will work.* They just had to wait for Lieutenant Hollingsworth to come to grips with what Masajiro offered. Would he throw away his fantasy and look at the information? Theo wasn't sure he would make the same choice if he didn't have to. Theo did it to save his people; Lieutenant Hollingsworth had nothing to gain and everything to lose.

Lieutenant Hollingsworth looked again at Masajiro, nodded, and retracted his hand to slide the crystal into the terminal on his desk. He didn't bother turning the screen, but Theo could hear the audio well enough that he didn't have to see the video.

"There are two men in this world that you need to fear, Captain Kojami," a gruff voice that Theo couldn't recognize said. "The first is Edward Lovett. The man is trying to build an empire in the colonies and one day he will succeed."

"And the other?" The second voice was Masajiro's.

"And the other is Lovett's son Deacon," the unknown man replied. "Between the two of them, the whole damned galaxy is being ripped apart."

The man went on to detail the terrible battle that had ensued between the two Lovetts, and how it was affecting the shipping lanes throughout this system and that of Alpha Centauri. Even the pirates operating closer to Earth were falling under Deacon's grip, banding together to fend off the small police presence that periodically arrested the officers of a pirate ship. Theo had to wonder if it was possible that the *Galena* had fallen to such a crew. *Civilized,* Theo thought, and shook his head.

The unidentified voice continued to explain that the space folding machine that had been built near Earth had been large enough to take the entire qualified Terran population without the fear of radiation poisoning. In but a few months, the human civilization could have been saved, teleported across the light-years. *It's real?* Hearing it from Masajiro was one thing, but this was the proof on which Masajiro had based his career.

The battle that raged between the two Lovetts had shattered any possibility of exodus for Earth when Deacon's pirates, operating more like a military fleet, attacked the machine and destroyed it, levelling a decade of fabrication.

The gruff voice of the unknown man whispered, "That was before we found the machine Deacon constructed near Jupiter. That's why he's taken control out there."

You probably didn't believe it either, Theo thought as he looked at Masajiro. Petr had been going on about a folding machine for years, albeit one that was attached to a ship, not anchored near a planet. It was an explanation from Petr's futuristic stories, not reality. Not believing it was possible was the prudent course, but having a superior tell you like that took more than a little faith.

"That machine must survive," the gruff man was saying as Theo strained to listen. "Its companion in the Centauri system is almost complete, so we will have to move quickly."

Both the live Masajiro and his onscreen version sighed audibly. "Why will that matter, sir? What is the time line?"

As soon as the explanation left the man's lips, Theo felt his stomach lurch. If he had anything to throw up, he would have. He could see Lieutenant Hollingsworth's reaction was no different; the man's face had paled.

Theo should have known. Masajiro had already told him the details. He just hadn't connected the dots.

The gruff officer cleared his throat and said, "It's not our time line we have to deal with, but Alpha Centauri's."

"Excuse me?" the recorded Masajiro said. Theo wasn't surprised to see the Masajiro sitting beside him mouthing the words as if he'd memorized the conversation. This conversation likely haunted Masajiro as much as Galena's death haunted Theo.

"There is a terrible radiation field between our two star-systems," the gruff man began. "We didn't realize for a long time so we kept sending ships. It was a full cycle and four years before we received word. Forty years to get there and then four more for their signal to return. And in that time, we sent a thousand more ships and a million more people."

Adults, Theo thought. A million more people to get sick.

"My God, so many?" Lieutenant Hollingsworth said. He lifted his hand to his mouth.

"They've continued to work," the gruff man said, his voice lowered. "They've done their best to secure a home for us, but if we don't get there soon, it won't matter. Everything will stop."

Everything wouldn't just stop. The agricultural land that the colonists had cultivated would go fallow as the natural flora took over. They wouldn't have enough food to support the remaining population, especially when Earth's people arrived. The infrastructure on the planet would turn to dust.

While Theo contemplated the long-term effects of travelling through the radiation field, the images of all those people dying horribly flashed through his mind. He knew it wouldn't actually be so sudden, but he couldn't get around so many bodies littering the streets. And then the children and those few who survived, either through fortitude or with what medicines they carried, would be left with nothing; a generation of teenagers with no protection.

Theo knew his son Petr was a capable boy. So too had Grace been, but to think of them all alone on a cold, dead world was more than he could handle. If only Lieutenant Hollingsworth could have the same empathy when Theo and Masajiro pressed him for help.

The video continued and Theo was suddenly torn from his thoughts as the gruff man said, "Your mission, Captain Kojami, is to secure the gate at Jupiter Station. We have limited time to secure the colonies. Remove Deacon and the threat he poses, and secure that gate. You won't have any resistance from his brother. We will have the fleet ready to move."

"And the fleet is prepared to take care of so many people?" Masajiro asked breathlessly. Theo could hear the care in the man's voice. It had bothered him to see so much destruction.

"Captain, it is beyond those people to survive. Our primary goal is to secure the colony. The colonists will be dealt with as swiftly as possible."

"Swiftly?" Masajiro asked slowly.

It wasn't necessary to see what remained of the conversation. Theo could hear in the gruff man's voice that he didn't care about the colonists. They would be rounded up and thanked for their dedication. It didn't matter whether it was a bullet or being placed on a shuttle and then shot into the sun. They were all going to die and no amount of medical treatments would change that.

"What is your plan, Masajiro?" Lieutenant Hollingsworth asked as he removed the data crystal. He handled the little device like it was going to burn him.

"Deacon wants to take the colonies. There are a million people that deserve better," Masajiro said. His calm demeanour surprised Theo. Could he defy his commanding officer so? The gruff voice had as much as said they'd dispose of the people on Alpha Centauri, assuming they were alive at all. What could Masajiro hope to accomplish?

"And that's where I come in?" Lieutenant Hollingsworth asked as he looked from Masajiro to Theo and back.

Theo leaned forward to stare at Lieutenant Hollingsworth. He had the haunted look of a man disgusted by death. Theo knew he wouldn't have to push much to get his plan to work.

"My guess is, by the expression on the woman out in the other room, that Deacon knows who you are now, Masajiro," Theo said. "And I suggest we use that to our advantage."

Lieutenant Hollingsworth narrowed his eyes. "How?"

Theo smiled. It was his to lose now. All he had to do was lay out the plan that would keep Deacon's attention from his real goal. It all hinged on Theo's faith in Masajiro. *I trust your honour, Masajiro,* Theo thought as he remembered the first time he'd met the *military officer.* Masajiro had saved Theo on too many occasions, almost dying in the process on Theo's ship. He could have easily suffocated in that engine room as he slapped Deacon's people around. But then, his goal had been Deacon himself. Theo may have simply been a means to an end. *But is that any different now?*

Taking a deep breath to steady his words, Theo said, "Here's the thing. Deacon's goal is to find a magic box. If we can keep his mind focused on it long enough for us to disappear then we can stop him."

Lieutenant Hollingsworth raised his brow. "Stop him? You mean end game? I'm not sure you—"

"I mean if we don't stop him soon, a lot of people are going to die," Theo said flatly. He stared at Lieutenant Hollingsworth. *Do it, man. Prove to me that you're a force for good.*

Lieutenant Hollingsworth split his attention between Theo and Masajiro. He shook his head and said, "What are you suggesting?"

"You've already said the woman out front couldn't be trusted. I suggest we let her know what we're looking for."

"And then?" Masajiro asked. The man played his part perfectly, adding the correct tone when Theo needed to nudge his audience.

"Then we take our ship and disappear. That box will keep him occupied long enough for us to get to Mars and then we'll set our trap."

"Mars?" Lieutenant Hollingsworth asked. "What's on Mars?"

Turning to him, both Theo and Masajiro said, "Ships."

"Ah," Lieutenant Hollingsworth said. "I think I understand."

"Good. Will you help us?"

Theo hadn't asked the man to commit treason, but he may as well have. Lieutenant Hollingsworth would have to set a group of suspected pirates free. *Come on, see it as Masajiro's mission. Take it on as your own,* Theo thought, hoping the man would bow to his will as he leaned farther forward in his chair.

Lieutenant Hollingsworth sat in silence for a minute, opening his mouth several times until he nodded and said, "What do you need me to do?"

"Actually," Theo began as his plan coalesced. Theo Stinson was a planner. You had to be when you owned your own transport ship. He took everything in, often changing a plan when he discovered new information. *And you've given me an idea,* Theo silently said to the lieutenant sitting across from him.

Before Theo could speak, Masajiro leaned forward to say, "Deputize them."

Theo cocked his eyebrow at Masajiro. *Deputize?* It wasn't an option he'd entertained, but it accomplished his goals and alleviated the barriers they were encountering. *You did say earlier that we couldn't go after Deacon because we weren't legally permitted to do so.* As deputies they could stroll off the station without worrying about the repercussions. They would be able to protect targetable ships without fear of being recaptured by the police. *It's perfect,* he thought as a smile touched his lips.

Lieutenant Hollingsworth sputtered for several seconds before his words began to make sense. "I—uh...uh—I...not—um...I'm not sure I can do that."

"Yes, you can—or rather, I can and you can witness it," Masajiro said, rising to brace his hands on the desk and lean forward over Hollingsworth. *Intimidation now?* Theo would accept any help the military assassin deigned to offer.

Lieutenant Hollingsworth chewed the corner of his lip and stared at the wall before returning his gaze to Masajiro. "How will that work?" he asked.

"I can deputize them with a witness," Masajiro said slowly. "You will be covered, so you can legally release us. In the meantime, she will do us a favour and tell Deacon where to go." He nodded toward the reception area.

Theo stifled a chuckle at the comment, then said, "Let us do this, Lieutenant. We'll get it done."

Lieutenant Hollingsworth sat breathing heavily for several seconds, as if he'd narrowly missed his own death. Then his shoulders slumped and he said, his voice was distant, "Do it."

Theo pushed away from the desk and stood so fast, the chair toppled backward. He walked quickly to the door and flung it open, then turned back as if with an afterthought. "Damn it, man, I need my crew and my ship to get back to my salvage operation," he growled loud enough for the woman to hear. "There is an important piece of cargo on that ship."

It took a few seconds for Lieutenant Hollingsworth to catch on, but he quickly followed Theo from his office. "I understand your situation, Mr. Stinson, but I just can't help you. I have to do everything appropriately and the means waiting for the captain's report on your crew's arrest. It will be at least a day before that comes in."

"A day? My ship will be stripped by then. Hell, it was almost stripped when I left it to come deal with my people." Theo threw up his arms and stomped around the room.

"I am sorry, sir," Lieutenant Hollingsworth said with just the right amount of bland concern.

Theo looked at the woman from the corner of his eye. She was trying not to be obvious, but she was clearly listening. She was no longer typing at her terminal and she'd cocked her head their way.

"Sorry?" Theo yelled, turning on the lieutenant. "My wife died on that ship and I haven't even been able to bury her. What should I tell my son?"

"Well sir, I think that—"

"Think?" Theo was only half acting; his emotions were taking over. "You *think?* That bastard has my daughter. I will never see her again. All I have left of her are my memories because I can't even get on my ship to collect my pictures. Please let me get the black box. I— I won't..."

Theo fell to his knees, tears streaming down his face. He didn't care if the woman took the bait. All he cared about was leaving. He wanted to disappear, but he knew he couldn't. He knew the better man would do the right thing and sacrifice himself to ensure the survival of those people. The better man wouldn't think about selfish exploits. *It's what Petr would do,* Theo thought. Petr would traipse across the universe to save his sister and then traipse in the other direction to save the people on Alpha Centauri.

"Sir," Lieutenant Hollingsworth said. Though Theo didn't care, he could hear the difference in the man's voice. Lieutenant Hollingsworth obviously understood Theo had broken down, and wasn't sure how to deal with it. He stammered for several seconds before saying, "Can you come back into my office?"

Theo sniffled, then wiped his nose on the back of his hand before he stood and followed the lieutenant into his office, pausing in the doorway to rest a hand against the frame and lower his head into the crook of his elbow. After a minute, composed again, he continued inward.

It felt good to let the tears flow. At one time Theo would have crafted a plan to collect Galena's body and then swoop in to save Grace before they zoomed off to save the people of Alpha Centauri. He would have dreamed about the adventure for weeks, until he had the perfect plan. That had all changed with Galena's death.

Theo needed to be that man again. He was a ship's captain, able to get through any difficulty. Wasting away in a bar was beneath him, not worth dwelling on. *I have to get my people free. You will help me,* he thought firmly, willing the lieutenant to comply. *You will help us.*

"Please sir," Lieutenant Hollingsworth said, breaking his reverie.

Theo shook his head and looked at the man as though he'd never seen him. "I...I'm sorry," he said, shuddering as he pushed the door slid shut behind him.

Lieutenant Hollingsworth lowered his eyes. "That's...uh...it's okay."

Theo wiped his eyes. "I-I'm okay. It's okay. It wasn't your fault."

"*No,*" the man said. He swallowed hard before continuing. "What happened to you shouldn't have. And you aren't the only one. If you can make this stop, then I will let you go, but you have to promise me you can do it."

About to answer, Theo realized the man was speaking to Masajiro. He watched as the military officer nodded to the lieutenant. *I will stop Deacon Lovett.*

"Then follow me." Hollingsworth motioned for Theo and Masajiro to follow him through a door in the back wall of his office. They entered a short corridor that ended at a narrow set of corrugated steel steps going down two flights. At the bottom stood a long line of cells filled with people.

As soon as he came abreast of the first cell, Theo heard a woman saying, "Here's the deal, people. As soon as they arrive we will have to move quickly. They will have us all go to the centre of the hall and bend down on one knee."

"And what is that for?" Theo asked as he strolled down the hall.

"Theodore?" Mykaela's voice exclaimed from the back of one cell. She pushed her way through the crowd until she could see Theo and the others.

"Miss me?" Theo asked happily as he forced a smile. It wasn't difficult to smile, as he felt genuinely happy, but the emotional floodgate that he'd opened was still ajar and he longed for his wife's touch.

"Theodore, if you weren't going to come soon, I was going to start murdering her," Mykaela said as she threw her thumb toward Masajiro's partner, Giselle.

"Well, isn't it fortuitous that I arrived?" he said.

Theo's people were jammed into the cells like rats, dozens of people in each small room. The women and children were separated, but the cells offered no privacy for the latrines. *Civilized,* Theo thought, and shook his head. His people had been in those cells for at least a month, ever since they'd arrived on Mykaela's ship.

Lieutenant Hollingsworth moved toward the back wall and swiped his identity card on a screen that depicted all of the cells. *No one else in there, eh?* Theo mused. The barred doors slid open. Tentatively at first, then faster as they realized it wasn't a joke, his people poured out of the cells.

Theo sidled through the growing crowd to Masajiro and asked, "How long have you been planning to deputize us?"

The man shook his head as he met Theo's gaze. "Not long. I've had to do it before, though not with as many people."

"And Giselle magically knew?" Theo asked. Theo knew the pair had a communication device, but it was good to have the man's nod as confirmation.

Theo nodded and waited for Masajiro to push through the crowd, then turned to face them. "Captain Theodore Stinson," he announced in a carrying voice, "I commandeer your ship and grant you the field title of police captain. I grant you the ability to bestow the position of police deputy on any and all of your registered crew."

"I observe and verify," Lieutenant Hollingsworth called out.

Then it was done. Theo had hoped it would feel different, but it didn't. He wanted to feel stronger, but instead his arms felt weak and he could barely stand. Looking around at the crowd, he wondered, *Do you feel any different?*

Though most of his crew understood the implications of what had just happened, some were just coming to the realization. *Petr will scream,* he thought. Petr would be infuriated that he wasn't deputized and would beg Masajiro for the honour as soon as they returned. He would be heartbroken to know there was no ceremony.

Taking a deep breath, Theo turned toward Lieutenant Hollingsworth and said, "How do we get to my ship, Lieutenant?"

Hollingsworth's smile vanished almost instantly. He shook his head several times then said, "It's down the hall. Captain Kojami knows the way."

The lieutenant's own mission was complicated by Deacon Lovett's presence in Jupiter's space. If Masajiro accomplished his goal, then Hollingsworth would have at least half a chance of keeping order. If Theo and Masajiro failed, then nothing would stop Deacon from plowing through the system and destroying the lieutenant's zone of influence. *We'll get this done.* Deacon would see justice.

Theo shuddered as he felt a hand on his shoulder. He turned to see Mykaela staring at him. "We're with you, Theodore. Know that," she said. "We understand the risk we take."

Do you? Theo wondered. Could the woman understand death the way he did? His wife Galena would never smile at him again or whisper to him at night. She would never see Petr grow up. *Or Grace,* he thought. Blinking away his tears, he said, "They have her, Mykaela. They have Gracie."

The woman's face went blank as she absorbed the news. Theo could see her going through the same calculations that he had, and when she spoke again, her voice cracked. "Just tell us what to do."

Theo licked his lips. "We need to work with what we have."

"And that is?" Zak asked, pushed several people out of his path to join them. The stay in captivity hadn't been easy on the man; he'd lost enough weight that his clothes looked several sizes too big.

Theo glanced from his navigation officer to the rest of his crew, realizing that no one had eaten much—most of them looked gaunt and exhausted. Theo could smell them now, here at the centre of the crowd. *You lot need a shower more than we did,* he thought.

As Theo scanned the crowd, Zak said, "We made sure there was enough for the kids. And no, they didn't keep them here, they let us keep them here. Lieutenant Hollingsworth did his best to accommodate us."

Theo raised a brow as he glanced back to the cells and their inch-thick steel bars. "I'm not sure I'd call it accommodations, Zak."

Zak shrugged and followed Theo as he followed Masajiro down the hall. "You were saying, Captain?"

Theo shook his head. "We have a ship and a crew. All we need to do is get Deacon, on our terms."

"And you think you could set him up?" Zak asked.

"I think we have what he needs," Theo replied. They were still on a station with ears around every corner. He couldn't afford to let every secret out just yet.

They reached the end of the hall and Masajiro began loading the bedraggled crew into a large transport train, one car after another. *I suppose they couldn't bring the riffraff through the front door,* Theo thought, watching.

Remaining with him to go with the last group, Mykaela asked, "And what does Deacon need?"

"The key to the machine that will let him travel to the Alpha Centauri star system," Theo answered. Though it still sounded ridiculous, saying it aloud made it real. "I'll explain later. Just believe me for now."

"I understand," Mykaela said, nodding toward Giselle.

Theo nodded his own acknowledgement to the military officer. Giselle had done most of the explaining for him before Theo showed up. All he had to do was reveal his plan. Taking a deep breath, Theo continued. "Rick is contacting a friend. When it's time, we'll go to Mars and set the trap."

"Will it work?" Zak asked.

Theo forced a smile. "Now Zak, what kind of question is that? Will it work?" Theo threw up his hands as he boarded the shuttle with the others.

Chapter 14

Finding Honour

Theo opened his eyes and glanced around the dark room. He knew it was familiar, but it didn't look right. It was sparse, and it felt like something was missing. *It's too quiet*, he thought as he rolled over to nuzzle his wife's neck.

When Theo found nothing in his bed he sighed, whispering, "I miss you, Lena."

"Papa?" a voice broke the silence. Petr stood in the doorway, a grimy stuffed animal clutched to his chest. Tears streamed down the boy's face.

Petr was haunted by the same terrible nightmares that had pushed Theo to drink. Theo knew most of them, but Petr still kept some as close as he clutched the stuffed bear he held. Petr had been reserved even during the months they'd spent together travelling to Jupiter in the transport ship. Theo had discovered most of Petr's nightmares as the boy cried out in his sleep.

When they were still earthbound, Galena had taken care of the children, diligently making sure Petr's nightmares didn't consume him. Theo remembered calling earth from his ship so Galena could woo Petr to sleep onboard. They were long nights, trying to comfort Petr. *No different than now.*

Theo pushed the covers aside and said, "It's okay, Petr. Come here."

The second Petr approached, Theo could smell the acrid stench of sweat and urine. Petr's dreams had been so terrifying that he'd released his bladder, likely what had awakened him.

"It's okay, bud," Theo said as he wrapped his arms around his son to draw him over the threshold of the gravity barrier.

"I...I..." Petr fell silent as he floated closer.

"Shh," Theo whispered. "It's okay. We'll be fine."

"I miss Mom," Petr said, sniffling into Theo's shoulder.

How the times have changed, Theo thought. Petr had been a serious boy, almost too serious. Theo couldn't remember Petr ever using that moniker for Galena. Instead, Petr had chosen to call his parents mother or father, at times even using their first names. Petr had no connection to his grandfather beyond that of one crewmember to another.

Burying his face in his son's neck, Theo said, "I know, buddy. I miss her too."

Petr sniffed for awhile before mustering the courage to say, "I had a bad dream."

"I know, buddy. I know. It's okay." Theo reached up to wipe the tears from Petr's face.

Theo wanted to make it all go away. He wanted to wrap his arms around his son and make Petr feel fine. He wanted his wife to walk through the door and laugh at the pair, and his daughter to join them. None of that would happen, Theo knew. Theo shook his head. *No, that's not true. I will find you, Gracie.*

Petr sniffed again and whispered, "It's because of what that man said."

Theo narrowed his eyes as he pulled away from Petr. "What do you mean, buddy? What did the man say?"

Petr took a deep breath. "He said he was going to do things to her."

Theo felt his ears burning as Petr explained what Deacon had said. *How could you, you bastard? How could you?* No good person would do the things Deacon had promised, nor would they tell those things to a ten-year-old boy. Deacon was more abhorrent than Theo had imagined.

"It's okay, buddy. We'll stop him before that happens," Theo whispered softly.

Theo had to find something else for Petr to think of as they approached their rendezvous with Captain Hendrickson. He couldn't leave Petr thinking about the disgusting acts Deacon had threatened.

Petr wiped his nose on Theo's shoulder. "There's more."

What could be worse than Deacon threatening to rape your sister? Theo didn't even want to think about it, but finally, he asked, "What…what did he say, buddy?"

"He…he said if you didn't give him the key, then he would make me wish I died with Mom," Peter blurted.

Theo swallowed hard. *How could you?* How could any man be so evil? Deacon revelled in destroying all that was good in Theo's life, all because he'd made a deal with Deacon's father, Edward Lovett. *A deal with the devil. Another devil,* Theo corrected himself. Theo hadn't met a Lovett that wasn't a devil.

Not about to let Deacon steal his son's sleep, Theo said, "Listen, buddy. Don't let him scare you. I'm going to make sure no one hurts you ever again. Okay?"

"Okay," Petr whispered. "I love you too, Fa—Dad."

Theo smiled. "I love you too, son." He pulled Petr into a tight embrace. *You win, Galena,* he thought, remembering the number of times his wife had asked him to be more fatherly.

As soon as Petr's breathing slowed, Theo laid him down on his bed under the sheets and shifted so he could pull himself out of the cubicle. He floated above, watching the rise and fall of Petr's chest for five minutes, until he was sure Petr was sleeping. Then he twisted around and pushed himself out into the common room, where he gently touched down, then startled. *Who? What—* "What are you—" Theo fell silent as he realized he was staring at Mykaela.

Mykaela had been a part of their family ever since Theo had met her, quickly becoming his first officer and now his most trusted advisor. In another life, Theo supposed he might have made a life with the exotic woman. She was beautiful, her scent intoxicating, and he knew without a doubt that if he made a pass, she wouldn't push him away, but let him sate his desires. *But not yours,* he thought. Like the vodka, sleeping with Mykaela would only be a crutch, not a solution.

You must have started watching him when I was gone, Theo thought as he stared at the woman in the darkness. "How long until we meet up with Hendrickson?" he asked.

"We're close enough to speak to him."

Theo nodded. *At least that's something.* He wanted the man to feel the heat when he pressed him for information. Theo could demand more of Hendrickson if the man felt threatened.

Mykaela stood and grabbed the clothing that Theo had laid out for the morning. She threw the bundle at him, saying, "Come with me, Theodore. I need your insight."

When they were safely away from Theo's quarters, Mykaela said, "What is your plan, Theodore? Everyone has been asking."

Theo glanced back to his quarters, the mirror of those he'd shared with Galena, though lacking in anything he would call theirs. It was cold and as lifeless as Theo felt when he was alone, devoid of the plants she'd brought home, or her scent. *It's just not home.*

He set off toward the bridge, his first officer in tow. "The first time Deacon found us was on Mars. He boarded us himself. He didn't leave it to anyone else. My plan is to replicate that. All we have to do is have Captain Hendrickson set it up again."

"That simple?" Mykaela asked as she matched his step. She was good at asking questions, making Theo rethink his plans when they weren't strong enough. He relied on her to put life into perspective, even though she was pulling her punches a little now because of what had happened to his family.

"That simple," Theo replied with a firm nod. Deacon wasn't looking at specific ships, only ships that bore the Lovett Industry stamp. The pirate believed his father had placed the jump engines on Theo's flagship, but Theo hadn't taken that ship. That ship he'd given to Mykaela.

"And you think it will be Deacon to board the ship?" she asked.

"There is no questioning that. He will come as quickly and with as much firepower as he can muster," Theo replied. "We just have to make him believe we've taken on a new mission to transport goods from Mars. We have to make him think we've given up hope of going to Alpha Centauri."

"Because he believes his key is on this ship," Mykaela mused.

"Whether it is or isn't is of little consequence," Theo said. He still wasn't sure if the key was on the ship. It was possible, but more likely it was on every ship that Lovett Sr. built. Would the magnate chance any of Theo's ships failing to make destination? *I wouldn't,* Theo thought and then said aloud, "What matters is that we make Deacon believe it."

Mykaela turned so she could place her delicate hand on Theo's shoulder. "I would believe you, Theodore. I know he will too."

Theo jerked a little as her hand pressed against his shoulder. He couldn't remember the last time he'd felt the touch of a real woman. *How long has it been, love?* he silently asked his dead wife. Pulling away, he asked, "What day is it?"

Mykaela frowned. "Excuse me?" Perhaps the woman *was* trying to seduce him, and only reacted this way in pain. *No,* Theo thought. She was only confused by his question.

"The day," Theo said as he stepped away. "What day is it?"

"September first," Mykaela said.

The words were like a gunshot through his chest. *Has it been so long?* He knew that travelling through space played havoc on a man's senses, not to mention the how long he'd been held in the embrace of the vodka, but it couldn't be that late in the year.

Reading his face, Mykaela said, "It's true. I do not jest."

True. It was the first of September, almost a year since his wife had been killed and his daughter taken. It didn't feel so long. It felt like a week, perhaps two, like the time he'd spent in the hospital bed after his first ship had gone down. "So long," he whispered as his gaze grew distant. "She's been gone so long."

"We'll get her back," Mykaela said, assuming he meant his daughter. To Mykaela, Galena was no longer Theo's wife. Grace was family. *And still alive.* Theo shook his head. He lowered his voice to say, "What do you suggest?"

"It isn't my suggestion," Mykaela said slowly as they reached the bridge.

Theo stared. "Whose suggestion is it?"

"It's mine, lad," Gideon said from just inside the bridge as the door slid aside.

Theo turned away, cursing under his breath. He didn't want to listen to Gideon's plan. Any plan the old man crafted was disastrous. *Don't you get it, Gideon? I can't trust you.* Theo would end up questioning everything the old man suggested.

"Wait lad," Gideon said. "I know what you're thinking."

"Everyone seems to," Theo said as he turned back. As much as he wanted to leave, Mykaela was blocking his path and he couldn't push past her without getting too close for his comfort. Sighing, he motioned for Gideon to lead the way back into the bridge. Theo didn't have the energy to fend off Gideon, or even question whether Mykaela had been part of his ploy or just his messenger.

Scanning the bridge, Theo noticed that Zak, seated at the navigation station, was wearing a better-fitting uniform. Masajiro was leaning against the holotable where Petr had laid out his plans for salvaging Theo's ship. He nodded to each in turn, wondering whether they'd been planning this coup long or if it was Gideon's plan alone. "What do you have to say, Gideon?"

The old man took a deep breath as he approached. "It's going to take another month before we reach Mars...and then who knows how long after that before Deacon arrives."

"Yes," Theo said. He knew that already. It was a fact they'd discussed many times. In the world of space travel, nothing happened fast.

"Well," Gideon said, "I've been talking to Masajiro and I think we've found the key."

Theo snorted. Of course, he should have made the connection earlier. They'd been back on the ship for over a month since leaving the military station orbiting Jupiter. Focused on his quest to find Deacon, the search for the key had waned. Gideon must have kept searching, however, and now he'd found the prize.

"So where was it?" Theo asked.

"It's not really like that," Gideon explained, his body quivering with excitement. "The ship itself is the key. There are components throughout the entire ship that, when combined, serve to operate the machine. In fact, if I'm right, we don't even need the machine."

"So, it is an engine," Theo said slowly.

The old engineer shook his head. Theo knew he was about to launch into a lecture that Theo wouldn't be able to understand.

"Okay, so the hull of the ship," the man lifted his arms to encompass the entire room and the ship beyond, "has certain points or nodes there are...well, I don't know what they are. What I do know is that when we operate the key, they make it possible to move matter from within the nodes to pretty much anywhere."

Theo leaned close and asked, "So what's the machine for?"

"The machine is for bigger things," Gideon explained. "It does what they say it does. When we get the ship closer we can operate it."

"How?" Theo asked immediately. "And why, if the ship can travel...right. Because then you could move more ships at once."

Just as Theo expected, all of the ships he'd acquired from Lovett Industries had been fashioned with the same key. He wasn't surprised the ship could operate entirely without the machine. Edward Lovett couldn't trust anyone to overthrow his son on Jupiter Station. Lovett would build every ship with the ability so they didn't have to change much to get him off the planet. *But why not just go?* Theo wondered. If the ship was operational, why not just go to Alpha Centauri, already?

Gideon shifted to the holographic table, his legs still working silently. When Gideon was finished manipulating the table, it changed to show a mock-up of a massive space station. It looked like a spider, its body at the far end and eight long legs pointing straight out behind. Several smaller ships floated around it. Theo estimated the scale to be large enough to encircle hundreds of his own ships side by side. It was almost terrifying to imagine the work that it took to build the machine.

Gideon cleared his throat. "The ship doesn't have the energy to open the gate. It has to capture energy from a different source and focus it through the gate." *That's why he can't just leave,* Theo thought. Edward Lovett didn't have a power source large enough to operate the engine.

Pressing on the table, Gideon said, "Okay, when the energy is focused on the machine, it opens a wormhole from one place to another. All of the matter is taken from one place and moved to another."

"Yes, yes, it's called folding," Theo said impatiently. Sometimes Gideon got so excited about his discoveries that he forgot how condescending he could sound, whether his students were knowledgeable or not.

"It isn't just folding, Theo. Folding takes matter. What we're talking about will transport everything—you and me and everyone here. We would arrive on the far side of the jump with the same thought we had going into it. Nothing would change."

Nothing? Theo thought. How could being moved from one place to another change nothing? It would change everything. They were flying around in a ship that could change everything.

"Gideon. I...I just—"

The old man's face went still, his smile fading. He opened his mouth several times and then spoke quickly enough to cut Theo short. "Don't believe me, Theo. Believe Lovett. It is here in his words."

"What?" Theo had a white-knuckled grip on the table. *Lovett sent us a message?*

"I found it only an hour ago," Gideon said defensively, throwing up his hands. "That's what led me to everything else."

"Found what?" Theo asked as he stared at the three-dimensional mock-up of the folding machine.

"The message," Gideon answered. His eyes locked on Theo's as he reached down and pressed the table again.

The computer accessed the information, flickering several times until Theo recognized the face of Edward Lovett, looking just as he had the day Theo had made his deal. In retrospect, the man looked tired, his face wan and thin. Theo thought of the decision that had brought him to his present situation. What would have happened if he hadn't made that choice? *It wouldn't be me making this choice now.* Galena would still live and Grace would still be with them. Theo sighed. *But you're not.* His wife wasn't coming back, but he had the chance to save Grace. *Not a chance,* he thought. *I will find you, Grace. We'll get you home soon.*

As the video began to play, Theo realized how feeble Edward Lovett looked. Lovett's eyes were sunken and his movements slow, his words slurred. "Hello, Theodore Stinson. I want to congratulate you on arriving at your destination. Now, as you can see, things aren't as pretty as we had originally thought. For that, I have to apologize. I needed someone I could trust because you now have two goals before I can let you continue on to your destination. The people on the planet below you need your help and the medical supplies in your hold. The second thing is for you to come back through the portal."

Before you will let me, continue to my destination? Theo rolled his eyes. The words Edward Lovett chose implied that he cared about the people on the colony, but his flippant attitude belied his true intentions. The old man wanted Theo to return through the portal, ensuring the passage was safe. *You don't know if the portal is completed on the other end,* Theo thought. *You need proof that it's ready.*

"I am hoping that more of you made it, but if you are the only ship, then you must prepare for our arrival. First you will clear the machine of debris and then you will come through to this side. Your ship will already have recorded the information we need and sending it through conventional means will take too long to get here. Now, don't worry about the details, everything is described in this file."

Theo shook his head and turned away from the video playing on the table. *There's no difference between you and your sons, Lovett. You both wreak havoc as you try to control everything around you. You don't care who you step on or who gets killed.* Someone could use the ship to create a new empire, flashing in and out of anywhere they wished.

The eyes of everyone else present remained glued on Lovett's image. Masajiro seemed enthralled with Lovett's revelation, his gaze distant as his thoughts carried him somewhere out in the cosmos. *What would you do with it, Masajiro? Would put the technology to work?*

Theo wasn't sure what to believe anymore. He'd been lied to so much by Edward Lovett, Deacon Lovett, even Gideon. Everything was suspect. *I wish you were here to clear the minefield,* Theo thought to his wife. Galena would have sorted through the junk and found the truth.

It had all made sense for Theo to take the ships to Alpha Centauri. He and his family would have a new start and Lovett Industries would add to their coffers as the mission was completed. When Theo learned that the radiation field between Earth and Alpha Centauri would have taken a terrible toll on the colonists, he could understand a mission to save them. He could even grasp the concept that Edward Lovett desperately wanted to travel to the colony and had crafted a massive machine to do it in an instant.

But why not just tell me? Theo wondered. Was it just because of Deacon? Could old man Lovett hate his son so much that he wouldn't trust the mission to the commander of the fleet? Perhaps it was another ruse, with another piece to the puzzle still missing. *That has to be it. There has to be more.*

Edward Lovett's image was explaining the need to travel back to Earth first so they could bring more officers through along with doctors, ground workers, farmers. They needed people to shore up the infrastructure. And no wonder—the radiation would have taken a much higher and more tragic toll than Deacon's stipend. "The radiation poisoning is deadlier than they thought," Theo said aloud, his voice sounding strange to his ears, like someone else was speaking.

"Pardon, Theodore?" Mykaela asked as the others glanced his way.

"I said, the radiation poisoning is deadlier than they thought. Think about it. Medical science has all but cured cancer on earth. If you have enough money, you can do anything. Edward Lovett is probably a hundred and fifty years old."

"What does that mean, lad?" Gideon asked as he reached down to pause the video.

"How long have they been sending ships to the colonies? In all that time, they couldn't send a machine or clad the hulls with something to protect them until now? No way. Lovett had me specifically choose families. Why?"

"Well…" Gideon began, then fell silent, with no answer for Theo's question.

"Families," Theo reiterated. "Whether it's radiation or something worse out there in the void, he didn't expect many adults to survive. Only children."

Theo let the realization sink in for a few seconds before he asked, "What other information is available on the computer?"

Gideon played with the tabletop screen for several seconds before he looked up at Theo. The colour had drained from his face as he said, "Everything. There's everything. From shining shoes to how to build a tent."

"The man doesn't know how to tell the truth," Theo said as he stepped back from the table again. Whatever was beyond the outer rim of the Solar System, Edward Lovett was afraid it would kill the adults, leaving only children to fly the ships. *Maybe there is no one at all on the colonies,* Theo thought. If they arrived to find nothing, then Earth's salvation was questionable. *Unless they bring everything through a portal.*

The flight would take years, leaving most, if not all, of the adults dead. Edward Lovett expected the children to finish the job and open the gate back home. Grace and Petr would have arrived to inherit a life of hard labour, not lounging on a beach.

Thinking of his son, Theo looked at his first officer and said, "Petr."

"What is it, Theodore?" Mykaela asked. Her brows were furrowed and she lifted her hand to his shoulder.

Theo said, "Can you check on Petr. He's…he's had an accident."

The woman's eyes softened as she smiled. She nodded and turned away without question, used to the job of wet nurse. She would march to Theo's quarters without comment and change Petr when Theo himself should have done the deal an hour earlier. *I did what I had to and now I ask the same of you,* Theo thought as he watched the woman leave. Petr would understand.

"Okay, Gideon, get to the point," Theo said.

Gideon took a deep breath before saying, "The way I see it, we have three problems."

Theo nodded. He'd been trying to figure out that issue since they'd left Jupiter.

Mirroring Theo's thoughts, Gideon said, "We have to find Grace, stop Deacon, and do something with the machine so no one can travel through to the other side."

They must be alive. Right? They could be rushing to save no one, or a hundred thousand people, all suffering from the effects of radiation poisoning. *A hundred thousand children,* he added. Even if there was a chance of only one child, he owed it to that child's parents to save him. *That's all I'd ask for Petr and Grace.* The universe would be a different place if someone had deposited Grace in his arms months ago.

Theo shook his head. It wasn't that simple. "We aren't going to stop someone from travelling through, Gideon. We have to be the first to go. If we aren't, either Deacon's people will go and kill them all, or the military will go and do the same."

Gideon smiled suddenly, as if he'd won. "But I just said *we* don't need to use the machine."

Why don't we need to use the machine? he wondered for a few seconds, before remembering what Gideon had said to begin the conversation earlier. If the ship worked as Gideon believed, they wouldn't need the machine to travel to the neighbouring star system. They could go right now. They could go anywhere.

Theo rocked back on his heels as a shiver coursed through his body. *We can go anywhere,* he thought as he stared at Gideon. When he was able to speak again, he said, "You want to jump to where Deacon is and destroy the machine."

Gideon nodded. "I do."

"As do I," Masajiro said, nodding.

It all made sense now. With the machine gone, Theo would control the only thing able to bounce back and forth between the systems. *We can control when and how we go to Alpha Centauri,* he thought.

Theo wasn't above jumping to destroy Deacon's machine. It would add to their chances of rescuing Grace from Deacon's slimy grasp. The evil pirate wouldn't be able to rely on his superior numbers. Theo would have the upper hand. All that remained was to make sure he wasn't jumping into a trap. "How will we see anything?"

"They took the bait…literally," Gideon said. Without waiting, he adjusted the table again.

The screen displayed a grid of various videos that Theo couldn't sort out, but slowly, as he watched, they began to flicker from one recognizable scene to another. In one, several spacesuited forms rigidly moved inside a room with large cylinders and in another they walked like robots down a massive hall, the lights attached to their shoulders illuminating the burn marks of weapons fire on the walls as debris floated around them. *This is…* The ship was a mirror to the one he now flew. He was watching Deacon's men mount another salvage operation.

"How long have you been receiving?" Theo asked.

"About an hour," Gideon said.

So, he'd done it all at the same time. Perhaps they hadn't crafted this plan too long ago. Gideon may not have had the chance to explain everything. It would explain the interest everyone displayed now. They were as curious as Theo. *But what are you keeping secret this time, Gideon?*

"Okay, tell me your plan, Gideon." Theo surprised himself with the request. He wanted to hate the old man for the decisions Gideon had made when they'd tried to stop the salvage. Theo had expected something simple, but found something far more complex. *And special,* he thought. If they were fast enough, they could jump in and destroy the machine long before Deacon noticed. Theo could save Grace and reunite his family without the bloodshed a frontal assault would require.

"Getting in won't be a problem," Gideon said. "I'm sure the ship is designed to jump to the machine automatically. I've already isolated the frequency they're using for the radios, so we can hear them when we jump. Our problem will be when we want to leave."

"Why?" Theo didn't want to end up with more problems than they already had.

"Power," Gideon grunted. "The power consumption for the jump is astronomical. We're going to use up all of our power getting there. I don't know how…"

We aren't just happily going to jump back out, Theo thought. They might be able to go through the back door when they arrived, but they would be forced to cut their way through on their exit. They were likely going to end up limping away from the battle. *We have to be fast.* Theo had to separate the monstrous man from his machine if he was going to survive, let alone win.

Theo had once trusted Gideon implicitly, following the man without question. *That was a long time ago,* Theo thought. After Deacon killed Galena, Gideon had become secretive and aggressive. *But I can't blame you,* Theo thought. Gideon was only doing what he thought best to save his granddaughter and avenge his daughter. *It didn't happen to me, did it? It happened to us.*

Theo shook his head as the memories flooded his mind. During the attack that had seen Galena's death, Theo had been injured, suffering a concussion so terrible that he didn't remember being removed from the ship. "Just Rick pulling me away."

"What's that, lad?" Gideon asked, cocking his head to hear better.

"I said, all that I remember was Rick pulling me away."

"So what, lad? I don't understand." Gideon looked to the others for explanation.

"Don't you remember what you told me, the last time we were putting a plan together?" Theo said as he turned to his father-in-law.

"Yeah lad, I do," Gideon sighed. "I said that, while you were in that bar trying to get drunk enough to forget the rest of us, we'd been getting things ready."

"Exactly," Theo said, punching his right hand into his left. "And I told you that I had been drugged. I remember leaving the shuttle and looking for you—for all of you—and yet finding me in a bar took you little enough time that you could clad the ship for war. Who found me?"

Gideon shrugged and looked around at the others. "I guess it was Rick."

"Rick," Theo said as a tear traced down his face. He hadn't lost himself in that bar, he'd been trapped. Rick had betrayed him, depositing him in the hands of Deacon's henchmen. Rick had known where he was the entire time. *It wasn't just Hendrickson on Deacon Lovett's payroll,* he thought.

Everything was beginning to make more sense as Theo explored Rick's deceit. Rick had shadowed him, taking him right to the place where Deacon could get a stranglehold on him. *But why?* Rick had had so many opportunities to do so much more harm. *You've helped us. You've killed his men. Did you kill his men?* Theo remembered watching Rick shoot at the pirates on his ship when they'd tried to recover it, but he couldn't be sure the man had hit any of them. *I trusted you with my son.*

"Masajiro, I have a request," Theo said. "Two, in fact."

Theo recognized the gleam in Masajiro's eyes. He knew the man understood what he was going to ask. *At least in part,* Theo thought. "I want Mykaela and Petr off my ship. Will Giselle do it?" Theo asked as he wiped his eyes so no one could see the emotion it betrayed.

"She will," Masajiro said with a curt nod. Theo could see that Masajiro loved the woman. Perhaps not the way he'd loved Galena, but Masajiro had a deep respect for his partner. It would serve Masajiro well for Giselle to keep Petr safe.

Theo nodded to the man. "Thank you." He looked away. "I want a shuttle prepped for those families still left on board. When this is finished we will return for them." The fact that the ship could bounce back in the blink of an eye made it a promise, not just wishful thought.

The smile faded from Theo's face as he looked back to Masajiro. "Please discover what Rick knows. Determine what he has told them too, please." *We can't afford to be compromised.* Theo knew he would never see Rick again. Their time was short and the methods Masajiro needed to use would leave the man close to death. If Rick survived, he would be carted off to jail when Theo and his crew accomplished their mission. *You wouldn't last long enough with me to give answers,* Theo thought fiercely.

He turned back to Gideon and asked, "How long until they know we're watching them?"

The old man frowned and licked his lips. "Not long. A couple hours, at best."

Taking a deep breath, Theo looked around at the bridge crew. "Then we have a couple hours, at best."

Masajiro left the bridge without ceremony. He knew his mission. Theo didn't need to announce it to the crew. The information Masajiro discovered was imperative for Theo's plan.

As soon as the door slid shut, Theo turned to Gideon. "Tell me your plan."

Gideon locked gazes with Theo for a minute, the silence falling over the room palpable until Zak huffed to break it. Gideon took a deep breath and said, "Two goals, two ships."

Gideon thumbed the screen. "She might look pretty, but that ship is going dark. There ain't much left after the last encounter. Definitely not enough to operate the machine."

That makes sense, Theo thought. The derelict ship couldn't muster the energy needed to jump let alone operate the machine. She would implode before she could open the gate. *They must have their ships close by if they want to activate the gate. They'll have to move fast if they operate the machine.* Aloud, he said, "So we jump to the machine."

"We jump to the machine," Gideon said in agreement as he nodded. "And then we blow it up."

"And Grace?" Theo said and frowned.

"Objective two," Gideon began, "is to find Grace. That, you will do. Here's the way I see it. Of all these scenes, we haven't seen

Deacon for more than a minute in the beginning. That means he's either on his way back to the fleet, or already there. We need him distracted."

"So, I'm bait?" Theo asked. Seeing the bastard that killed his wife again wasn't something he was looking forward to. He'd rather be done with the entire prospect. But at least if he came upon the pirate, Masajiro could complete his own mission. *And that's who's going to get grace,* Theo thought. Masajiro was covert enough to fly a second ship to where Grace was and extract her. The distraction of the machine exploding would keep the fleet at bay and Theo would keep the self crowned king from realising their true intent. *Messy, but worth the risk. Especially with Rick's intel.*

As if he was reading Theo's thoughts, Gideon nodded his head again and said, "Not just intel, lad. Rick's misinformation that we send back before we jump in. They'll never know what hit 'em."

Chapter 15

Finding Grace

Theo Stinson sat in silence beside seven soldiers, all dressed in military grade environmental suits, their helmets on but not latched. The officers sat like robots, their gazes locked on the opposite wall, their energy rifles gently resting on their laps. *In and out before they know we're here,* Theo thought as he turned his head to look at them.

It had taken some time for Masajiro to extract the truth from Rick, a deed Theo wasn't proud of, but knew had been necessary. They'd discovered another twelve officers on Theo's ship compromised by Deacon Lovett's tendrils. *That's the last of them,* Theo thought. Rick plus the twelve officers had all come on at the same time when Theo had been recruiting for his original trip to Alpha Centauri. *Wish I'd had more time to investigate them.*

Those thirteen officers were now languishing in a room Gideon had jury-rigged as a brig, something Theo had never required before. Pirates were either taken back by their comrades or dispatched. Forcibly confining any nefarious or rowdy officer was uncommon. *Not anymore, I guess,* Theo mused. Anyone heading toward Jupiter Station would have to be prepared to cross paths with Deacon Lovett.

Theo was now assured that he could trust the men he was taking to save his daughter and stop Deacon Lovett. Unsure whether Masajiro's ministrations were enough, Theo had spread his trusted officers throughout the ship to determine who was committed to saving his daughter. *And two star-systems,* Theo silently added. The galaxy would be a safer place with Deacon gone. The list of people Theo could trust was short. Those Theo couldn't decide on were released in a shuttle to head toward Mars, a trip that could take several weeks in the small vessels. Theo promised them safety when he was finished. *I need a lie detector.*

"Are we ready?" Theo asked, and watched the officers lift their thumbs in assent.

This will work, he thought. It was a simple plan, one that didn't need much adjusting after Masajiro returned with the intel gleaned from Rick. They would jump in, secure the ship that Grace was trapped on, and leave, relying on the element of surprise for their success.

Getting into Deacon's fortress wasn't going to be hard, but leaving was. The energy expended to operate the ship's jump engines would leave the ship crippled and defenceless. They would limp away from any battle they encountered. *Gideon will find a way.* Gideon was back in his element in the engine room, solving near disasters. In the engine room he wouldn't be planning a daring rescue plan, only finding a way to return the reserves to a point where they could leave without being destroyed. *Unless it works and then that won't matter,* Theo thought.

The ship was a transport shuttle, designed to take supplies to Alpha Centauri. Though it had been engineered with thickened bulkheads and energized to stave off the radiation of the universe, Gideon had made it battle ready, spending months preparing for the inevitable battle with Deacon. *She'll make it through,* Theo thought as he looked around the small shuttle. The ship was well built and militarized by a military officer into a breaching shuttle. She would survive the conflict long enough for Theo to find his daughter and stop Deacon.

Theo took a deep breath and slowly exhaled. The small sprig of lavender he'd placed on the inside of his helmet was like a breath of heaven. With every inhalation he was transported back in time to when he knelt in the dirt, planting flowers with his wife. *It's home,* Theo thought with another deep breath. The scent was intoxicating, not like the alcohol that he'd funnelled down his throat, but true ecstasy. Theo could feel every bone in his body aching for his wife, but it wasn't painful, only bliss.

"Okay, people, here's the deal," he said slowly as he closed his eyes, imagining Galena at his side. It seemed fitting that she would watch as he rescued Grace. "I don't know what's going to happen now, but I want you all to stay calm. It will happen quickly and—"

 The transition was far stranger than Theo had imagined it would be. He'd expected everything to stop, or at least his perceptions, like he was sleeping, and then waking to find everything just like before, only their ship would be in the middle of another fleet.

But as Theo spoke, trying to prepare his people in the shuttle and the ship at large, he felt his skin itch, as if he'd been rolling in poison oak. If he wasn't clothed in an environmental suit, he would have begun scratching at his arms and legs. *It's painful,* he thought as the sensation rose in intensity from an itch to a burning, his entire body engulfed in imaginary flames. *Thank God you aren't here, Petr,* he thought, knowing that his son would relish the pain, knowing they would be suddenly transported millions of miles.

Theo tried to force his eyes open, but the entire shuttle was filled with a blinding white light, so intense he could almost see it through his closed eyelids. He felt as if he were swimming as time slowed around him.

When the shift came it bore no resemblance to sleeping, but more like they'd suddenly stopped *being*. He didn't hold his breath. He didn't need to breathe. The irritation on his skin stopped, but then just as quickly he realized he couldn't feel his toes, nor his fingers. The scent of lavender vanished and unlike before failed to return, as though he no longer had the piece stuck in his helmet. *It's so peaceful,* he thought, and envisioned himself in the sensory deprivation chamber on his first ship. His thoughts were the last to go, flying away from him as if he'd died.

When the light returned, Theo's breathing was laboured and he found himself screaming as loud as the officers behind him. His voice stopped then, and he felt like he was breathing through water, unable to force enough air into his lungs. He closed his eyes, hoping it would help him focus his thoughts. *Where am I? What am I doing? Why am I in the shuttle?* He tried to shift enough to glance around the small breaching shuttle. Theo's hearing returned with his thoughts. Many voices spoke simultaneously to him, overwhelming him. *Slow down, people. I don't understand.*

The world snapped back into focus like an elastic as Theo took a deep breath to calm his mind and inhaled a sudden whiff of lavender. *Fields of flowers. Galena. Grace.* Like a whip, he was focused again. "Situation?" he barked.

A quick barrage of reports came through, none as bad as they could have been, so Theo pressed the button to mute their discussion. Theo had one mission and that was to save his daughter. They'd folded space, teleporting, so he could ensure his daughter's safety. He wasn't going to waste his time listening to reports.

Theo didn't need a computer screen to see the hundreds if not thousands of ships in the field they'd appeared in on the dark side of Jupiter. The ships varied in size, ranging from short distance shuttles like Theo's breaching shuttle to massive cruisers built to drag ore from the asteroid mines. Half of the ships looked in decent shape, but the rest looked as though they'd seen war, their hulls dented and scorched. *Have your people arrived, Masajiro? Or is this the damage Deacon inflicted when he took them?*

Theo had never seen so many ships in one place. The stations were efficient enough to have a ship's cargo unloaded and her crew back on board within hours. Here in Deacon's back yard, however, Theo had to admire what the man had done. In a different time, the pirate could have been considered a hero if he'd taken those ships to suppress a misguided government. *He could own the Solar System.*

Theo understood what the machine had become to Deacon. Masajiro's people were coming. The only way Deacon could keep his fleet in one piece was to move it, and the smaller shuttles couldn't travel quickly enough to just leave. *Are you trying to overthrow the government or just protect yourself?* Theo wondered.

Deacon wasn't trying to go to Alpha Centauri, he was leaving Sol. Deacon had no respect for anyone else and deserved no better from his enemies. *I suppose you see me that way,* Theo thought. To Deacon, Theo was the enemy, trying to thwart his plan. *Do you consider them your people or your slaves, though?*

Theo stared out the window at the armada of ships. *What the hell?* The ship Theo was heading toward wasn't at all what he'd expected. Rather than a transport ship, replete with cargo, the ship was a police cruiser—long, and at least as large as Theo's own ship, with little damage, her hull clear of scars from weapons fire. The ship looked as though she'd been assembled only recently. *Have they hijacked a police ship*? Theo thought as he counted the gun ports. *Are you so bold, Deacon?*

Deacon was bold, but to steal a police cruiser would be infamous. Deacon wouldn't have been able to keep that theft secret. The only thing worse and dastardlier than the pirates scourging the Solar System were the police bent upon dominating it themselves. *Sorry, Hollingsworth. No offence meant.* It had to be the police vessel that had been present when Theo defied Deacon during the failed salvage operation. Deacon had killed the ship's captain in that altercation and blamed it on Theo. *But then that ship had escorted Mykaela and the crew to the station,* Theo thought. It couldn't be the same ship.

Theo started calculating the adjustments he needed to make to his plan. *Protocol. I have to follow protocol.* He couldn't just storm the police ship, regardless of whether he had a right to protect his family.

He had to follow the rules, not just for the sake of the police crew, but also for Deacon's twisted game.

Deacon had a penchant for being in the middle of the action, partly for the exhilaration of watching his victims cringe and cower beneath him and partly so he could control his people. The pirate kept a tight grip on his people, cajoling, beating, or humiliating them into doing his bidding. As civilized as he purported himself to be, Deacon was as heathen as it came. If the pirate wasn't on the salvage job, Theo expected he would revel in lounging on the police cruiser. *You're here.*

"Okay, we have to move quickly," Theo said quietly, unsure anyone could hear, especially if their ears were pounding as much as his. He lifted his hand up to confirm his helmet was latched, the scent of lavender reminding him again of his mission. *I will get her back, Lena. I will find her.*

Theo checked his instruments, listening to the radio chatter, hoping none of the ships in the armada could see them, knowing that if any could, it would be the ship they flew toward. His hands shook as he made periodic adjustments to the shuttle's attitude. All was silent.

He took a deep breath. *I hope this works, Gideon,* he thought as he pressed the sequence of buttons to allow him to communicate with his ship. If Gideon had calculated properly, the ships surrounding them wouldn't hear what he was about to say. "Do we have access, or will we have to cut our way in?" He would rather find a place to dock his shuttle, but he wasn't going to waste his time looking, especially if they knew he was coming.

Theo waited, but there was no response from his ship. *No choice but to continue.*

He brought the shuttle up beside the cruiser and moved close to the docking hatch. Instantly, the radio chirped as the police cruiser demanded, "Unidentified shuttle zero seven niner niner, identify yourself."

Damn it. They must have proximity sensors. Wait, they're reading our signature. Only active police cruisers can do that. Was it possible this was a legitimate police cruiser, and they had already recovered Grace? Was it possible the military had already taken control of the great machine?

While Theo wondered whether he should offer his real name, the radio chirruped and a woman said, "You have permission to board, Theodore Stinson."

You know, Theo thought as he stared at the looming ship.

As Theo communicated with the police vessel he continued to search for contact from his own ship, but all he received was silence and static. *Gideon should be firing on the machine, but there's nothing.* Gideon's assumption that Deacon was out salvaging the ship must have been wrong. *Deacon has to be here. Deacon was ahead of us the whole time.* He must have towed Theo's ship here from the beginning and would obviously know their plan, or at least a part of it. The conversation with the station lieutenant had been irrelevant.

Theo shot back in his seat as the realization came to him. *This is an exchange.* They wanted him to exchange the ship for his daughter. Deacon was no idiot and would likely try to double-cross him, but that didn't matter. Gideon would perform one last feat and destroy it before Deacon could take possession.

Theo didn't have to fear that Gideon wouldn't come to the same conclusion. The old man hated Deacon and would ensure the pirate suffered for his actions. *Not a bad Plan B,* Theo thought with a wry grin. He would play the man's game. *For now.*

The officers flying with Theo fidgeted with their weapons as he pressed the sequence of buttons that would allow the police cruiser to take control and glide them in for docking.

When the door slid open, Theo's heart was pounding. Whether dead or alive, Grace was somewhere close by, alone and afraid. Gideon had said they had been talking of her for some time through the link. Theo didn't want to know where Gideon had discovered his information; he couldn't get wrapped up in the deeds that were necessary to garner the information. But Gideon had said the men had been less than flattering with their comments. *Please be a real police cruiser. Please let Deacon be captured already.* It would be a clean ending for Deacon to fall to the police and lose his control over the armada.

Theo swallowed hard. *Why* is *the police cruiser here? And why the hell didn't they attack?* Theo wasn't going to board the ship and rush through in search of Grace, nor would he wait in his shuttle in hopes that Masajiro would accomplish his own goal. *I can't even communicate with them.* The police would notice and likely decrypt any message before Theo's people could respond.

"Stay behind and follow in five minutes," Theo said as he dropped his helmet to the floor, abandoning the sweet smell of lavender with it.

He climbed through the airlock and took a dozen steps before he had an entourage. The three men that fell into step with him were bulky with muscle and towered over him, each carrying a long energy rifle in his hands and a pistol strapped to his hip. While none of the weapons was trained on Theo, he knew the men wouldn't care if they accidently shot him. Police shuttle or not, these men were hired guns. They were dressed in military fatigues, but lacked police or military insignia—and they smelled like they hadn't washed in days.

"Where are you taking me?" Theo asked as he looked around the hold. *They must have hijacked her. Why else would they send thugs to greet me?*

"How many people do you have with you?" the first officer asked.

"Two," Theo replied smoothly. They weren't going to believe him anyway.

The man lifted his hand to his ear and said something too quiet for Theo to hear. Afterward they led Theo through a maze of corridors. The ship wasn't like the opulent station Lieutenant Hollingsworth presided over. The corridors were low-ceilinged and narrow, the flooring corrugated plate steel. When they reached the third door in a long corridor lined with full-sized sliding doors, the lead officer stopped and pressed several buttons on the console beside the door. Theo heard a small click and the door silently slid aside to reveal a small captain's mess.

Deacon Lovett sat with his left ankle resting on his right knee as he tapped the table with his right index finger. "Hello, Mr. Stinson," the pirate said. "I am glad you accepted my invitation."

Theo narrowed his eyes. *Invitation?* What invitation could the man have been speaking about? There had been no conversation. Gideon had noticed Deacon was on the ship. *No, you knew then. You've been feeding Gideon misinformation.*

"What's wrong, Mr. Stinson?" Deacon said. "Come in. Sit down."

I have to control this conversation, Theo thought as he stepped through the door and took a seat, his suit crinkling as he shifted.

"Would you like something to drink?"

You taunt me now? Theo thought. Then, *You think I don't know I was drugged.* The thought set off another as a plan evolved in his mind. "What do you want Deacon?" he said.

The pirate raised his eyebrow in response.

"I said, what do you want? You know what I'm here for. What are you asking for?" Theo asked. He crossed his arms and waited for the pirate to respond.

"I love that about you, Mr. Stinson," Deacon said as he reached out to pluck a grape from a bowl resting on the oak table beside him. "You get right to work. I can understand why my father chose you." He sat back in his chair and put both feet to the floor so he could lean forward, his fingers steepled. "You know what I want, Mr. Stinson. I want the key. I have been through your ship and I know it's not there."

Theo narrowed his eyes. Had they convinced the man that only Mykaela's ship had the key? If that was the case, then Theo still had the upper hand. But if it wasn't and Deacon was playing a ruse, Theo had to be wary. *No, you have no clue,* he decided. "And you think I can just give it to you?" he asked.

"No," Deacon said as he shook his head. "I don't think so. I think I am going to have the captain of this ship arrest you and all of your people for breaking out of jail. I think you will be rounded up and then I will strip your ship and find the key."

Theo smiled. Deacon was oblivious. *You think you're smart, but you're not.* Deacon didn't know that Theo and his crew had all been deputized. Lifting his hand to tap an imaginary window, he said, "There is a problem with your plan."

Deacon leaned closer, "And that is?"

"The police have no authority over me or my crew," Theo said. He steepled his own fingers and leaned forward to match the pirate's posture.

Deacon sat back. "And why would that be?"

"Because, before we left the police station, Masajiro Kojami deputized me and all of my crew. As far as you're concerned, I am the police. The *real* police."

The pirate reacted as if he'd been slapped in the face. He rocked back in his chair, trying to grasp the import of Theo's words. If he killed one, he had to kill them all. He couldn't leave a man alive to tell the story. Theo now had the upper hand. *Where are your rules now, Deacon?*

Deacon was an animal at heart. He couldn't box him in, only herd him toward the gate. Theo cleared his throat and said, "Now, this is what I am proposing. You let my daughter go and you come with me. The rest of your people can disperse."

"Disperse?" Deacon asked. "You think I'll just stop? I don't have a problem killing all of you. You will all be dead and I will—"

"No, you won't," Theo interrupted as a smile played on his lips. "You won't because I will destroy the ship and the key with it and then in a week or a month or however long it takes, the naval fleet from Earth will roll in here and pick off your ships like bugs. Your only hope now is to run."

Deacon laughed, but Theo could hear the desperation in his voice. As the room rang with his guffaws, the pirate stood and started to circle around the table. His fists were balled, ready for a fight. *One I can't survive,* Theo realized. The man was much larger, and built for violence.

"Oh, by the way," Theo said. He had to waste more time while his people found Grace.

Deacon paused only long enough to ask, "What?"

Theo's heart was pounding so hard, he could barely hear the man through the thrumming in his ears. He had to speak loudly just to hear himself. "I wanted to thank you."

The man narrowed his eyes further. "For what?"

"You've brought me closer to my son than I thought possible," Theo began. He was about to add more, but the screen on the arm of his suit chirped quietly before he could continue. He glanced down before adding, "And one more thing. The door is about to open."

"I doubt it," Deacon said as he lunged forward. The man likely thought he could force Theo into relinquishing his hold on the ship.

As Deacon moved, Theo tried to stand, but the suit made it impossible to react quickly. Before he could duck, the larger man had an ironclad grasp around Theo's throat. In one smooth motion Deacon twisted Theo around until Theo was looking at the door when it opened.

Leaning closer, Deacon whispered, "You will be the first to die, Theodore Stinson, only because your daughter isn't in the room. Remember that."

Theo swallowed hard as he recognized Masajiro entering the room. *It's about time.* Masajiro had discarded his own suit somewhere in his travels and walked around comfortably in black fatigues. Theo wanted to call out to the man, but he had no voice to speak. It didn't matter, though, as another man entered the room right after him.

The grip on Theo's throat lessened as Deacon said, "*You!*"

Masajiro nodded in response.

Discovering Rick's subterfuge hadn't just cleared the crew of any turncoats, it had staved off the inevitable attack that Deacon intended to mount. Pretending to be Rick, Theo had sent misinformation to Deacon, telling him of Masajiro's plan to attack the machine when Rick delivered Theo to Deacon.

The second man that entered, however, made Theo react like Deacon. "Jacob," he hissed.

"I found him outside your daughter's cell," Masajiro said softly as he dragged the young man into the room and sat him down hard in the seat that Theo had been pulled from. Turning to Deacon, the assassin said, "Is the life of your son worth that of your prisoner?"

Your son? Theo peered at Jacob. The young man who'd dragged Grace off into space was the animal's son.

Deacon cleared his throat. Theo could feel the man shift, trying to position himself to lunge at Masajiro. "Perhaps we can make a deal," Deacon said softly. His breath was hot on Theo's ear.

"Good, then this is what I propose," Masajiro said as he straightened his back. "I suggest you let Mr. Stinson go and then as I leave, I will release your son."

"Oh, I thought you were going to negotiate for the girl," Deacon said as he began to chuckle. "Did my son have his way with her too much? Was she unrecoverable?"

Masajiro shook his head. "No, she's already disembarked from the cruiser. She won't be any concern of yours anymore."

"Oh, I doubt that," Deacon said. "I think her dreams will be filled with thoughts of my son and me. I know my dreams will be of her."

As he listened to the animal speak about his daughter, Theo clenched his jaw so tightly, his teeth ached. How could the man be so evil? Surely being sent to Jupiter Station wasn't enough to cause the transformation. Had Lovett Sr. tried to unload his son on the stations, hoping some pirate would kill him?

Lights sparkled in Theo's vision and the air managing to trickle down his throat became scarcer as Deacon tightened his grip. *I need...I need to get free.*

"I tell you what, Officer Kojami. Why don't I let you off with a warning and you go back to where you came from? Oh yes, I do recognize you. You were once a prominent officer on Jupiter Station. Do you remember the day you were sent away?"

Had Masajiro been so close without tasting blood? The assassin had his own secrets, but he was honest. He intended to end Deacon's reign because it was the right thing to do, not because of some personal vendetta. Even so close to his own end, Deacon was attempting to weave a web of lies.

He must be getting ready, Theo thought. He was seeding Theo's mind with uncertainty so when that release came, Theo wouldn't side with Masajiro. A second's hesitation would be enough for Deacon to set into Masajiro, leaving Jacob to turn on Theo. It was definitely coming soon.

It didn't matter, though. Grace was safe. She was on the shuttle. *Safe, Gracie. You're safe.* As elation washed over him, Theo suddenly saw his wife. He couldn't remember the last time he'd seen her, but she was as beautiful as ever. She was smiling at him, reassured that everything would be okay for her children.

Theo didn't care if Deacon killed him. In the ensuing battle, Masajiro would kill Deacon and the machine would end up in pieces. *I've beaten you, Deacon.* All that remained was to go to the Alpha Centauri system. A flight for someone else, though. Perhaps Petr, one day.

Deacon looked at Jacob. "Where is Damion?"

Theo remembered Deacon's hulking brother, a man eviler than Deacon himself. He'd been the one to first attack Galena on the ship. It was because of him that Galena had been in that hold and because of him that she had died.

Jacob was calm as he replied, "I don't know. I was in with Gracie when *he* came in."

Theo gritted his teeth. "How dare call her that?"

Deacon tugged at his throat, silencing him. But the man didn't stop pulling—he yanked Theo to the side and then sent him headlong into Masajiro and Jacob. He connected with Jacob and they both fell to the deck. Thankfully the suit Theo wore absorbed most of the concussion.

When Theo rolled back to his feet, Deacon had closed ranks with Masajiro and they were trading blows. Though larger, Deacon was doing little damage; Masajiro nimbly ducked his punches and, as Theo watched, sidestepped one outstretched arm to deliver two punches to the pirate's midsection. Deacon roared in pain. *He's got you,* Theo thought triumphantly.

As the two fighters backed off to their defensive positions, two meaty hands slammed down on Theo's shoulders, then literally tossed him through the air. He careened over the table and into the chairs on the far side, carrying them to the floor to shatter beneath him. *Damion,* Theo thought shakily as he pushed himself off the floor.

"Keep him occupied," Deacon bellowed to his brother as he darted toward the door. Was he leaving Damion to clean them both up? *You coward.*

In response, the large beast-man kicked out and connected with Masajiro's chin, sending the assassin crashing to the floor. Blood splattered across the wall.

Before Theo and Masajiro could regain their feet, Deacon fled from the room, so intent on his goal that he left his brother fighting and his son sprawled unconscious on the floor.

Theo took a deep breath and mumbled, "He's going after the ship." He pushed himself to his feet, coughing, and stood swaying a moment. Oblivious to the smaller man behind him, Damien stood over Masajiro, whose face was covered in blood. Forcing one foot in front of the other, Theo tottered around the table, moving as fast as the suit and his injuries would permit, picking up speed until he barrelled into

Damion. He felt an explosion in his head as Damion swung his fist and propelled him back over the table in one smooth motion. If Theo hadn't been wearing the suit he would have cracked his ribs again.

Groaning, Theo rolled over and pushed to his hands and knees, thinking, *I have to get out of this suit.* He looked up to see Masajiro regain his feet and close ranks with Damion. The large man was strong enough to toss Theo around like a child; Theo was sure he would do the same to Masajiro. But Masajiro locked his arms around Deacon's shoulders and yanked forward, then pushed Damion to the floor. He twisted the larger man's head up at an awkward angle and Theo heard a snap. Damion went limp, his neck snapped.

"Where were you a year ago?" Theo asked as he pushed himself back to his feet.

Masajiro stepped over Damion's body, his eyes on the door. "Follow me."

Theo was no warrior. He was barely able to stand after the exertion and wanted only to run back to his shuttle and return to his children. *Children.* Theo didn't want to follow the assassin as he finished his mission; he wanted nothing to do with the growing pile of bodies. But he knew he had to see it through to the end. Theo wasn't just saving his daughter, even if that was all he cared about. He'd joined a greater cause, one that required him to make sure Deacon was brought to justice.

But as he moved to the door, Masajiro stepped back to hover over Jacob. He reached down, about to mete out to the young man the same punishment he'd given his uncle. "Wait," Theo said. "No, no, no."

The assassin split his attention between Theo and his target for several seconds before he stood and walked out of the room. Theo shook his head as he watched the man leave, disturbed by what he'd just averted. He let his eyes linger on Jacob for several seconds. Jacob was nothing like his cousin on earth, the man who had stuttered when trying to convince Theo to take on the mission to Alpha Centauri. This boy was forceful and angry, yet had hidden his terrible side for months on Theo's ship. Jacob had convinced Grace that he was the picture of virtue and then helped steal her from Theo, participating in the piracy that had killed Galena. *Gracie. You called her Gracie.*

Unsure why, Theo reached down and pulled Jacob up to a sitting position before hefting the young man over his shoulder. *Damn, you're heavy,* Theo thought as he navigated back to the door to follow Masajiro. With every painful step he took, Theo replayed Masajiro's and Jacob's entrance into the room where he and Deacon had been negotiating. Jacob had been uncomfortable with Deacon's questions, calling Theo's daughter by her familiar name. The young man hadn't been able to meet his father's gaze and he'd reacted with fear when Deacon had intimated what they had done to Grace.

No, Theo thought. How could the young man partake in such a terrible act if he was a good person? *Because he hasn't been offered a choice.* Theo hitched Jacob further up on his shoulder as he silently added, *Until now.*

It would have been easier to leave Jacob, but Theo wasn't that man. He'd uprooted his family and flown out on a spaceship toward Alpha Centauri to create a better life. *Everyone deserves that chance,* he thought and continued down the corridor in search of Masajiro.

Chapter 16

Finding Benevolence

Theo found two bodies lying on the floor as he shuffled along the hallway, recognizing them as his honour guard when he'd boarded the police cruiser. They lay together, their necks broken, their rifles still clutched in their hands. The third thug had obviously slipped away from Masajiro.

"Where the hell did—" Theo fell silent as he heard weapons fire from the corridor opposite that leading to the shuttle. Smoke wafted down the hall, assaulting his eyes and nose. *That way,* he thought, and set off again. Jacob groaned on his shoulder and began to move as he came to. *That's right, boy; wake up so you can walk on your own.*

"What the hell are you doing, Gideon?" he whispered breathlessly. They should have felt the concussion of the machine exploding by now.

"Huh...what...?" Jacob mumbled before he slumped, again unconscious.

"Damn it kid, you're heavy," Theo grumbled. He hoped he'd made the right decision. He hoped that Jacob would prove his worth.

After several seconds Theo heard another barrage of bullets as they bounced around the halls. *Ballistics? Police definitely use energy weapons.*

"Keep him pinned down."

Deacon. He couldn't be too far.

"Sir," another voice said, then fell silent.

As Theo approached, he found Masajiro leaning against the wall, his shoulder oozing blood from an energy burn and pouring from a bullet wound on his leg. Grimacing, he was pulling his belt tight around his leg to staunch the bleeding. When he finished, he reached into the pack he carried over his shoulder and retrieved a suction bandage. Not waiting for assistance, he pulled the back off with his teeth and slapped the sealing material over his leg. He closed his eyes as it suctioned tight.

When Masajiro opened his eyes again, he frowned at the body slung over Theo's shoulder. He licked the corners of his lips and nodded before saying, "If you feel he has worth, I will accept your judgement."

"I do," Theo replied. *Finally, some humanity.* Theo was beginning to wonder if the "military officer" had been sent to kill indiscriminately. "How are we going to make it through?" he asked as he set Jacob down against the wall.

Masajiro shook his head. "I'm not sure we can."

"Do we have to?" Theo asked. "Aren't they police officers? Can we not just order them to turn on Deacon?"

Masajiro chewed on the inside of his cheek. After a pause, he said, "No, but we may be able to call for help."

"Who? Are the other officers still on the ship?" Theo asked. It was possible that Theo's people had remained, branching out to the other parts of the ship.

Theo felt his hopes falter as Masajiro said, "No, but we can call on this ship's officers to help."

This ship? Theo hadn't seen a real police officer since he'd arrived; he half-expected that Deacon had murdered them all when he'd taken over the ship. *Who could be left?* After an eternity, Theo said, "Then get to it."

Masajiro wiped his brow and pointed to a terminal on the far side of the hall. Theo was instantly taken back in time to the first time he'd reboarded his ship to salvage what remained and retrieve Galena's body. Upon their retreat, they'd sat staring at a terminal they couldn't touch until his son Petr had volunteered.

"How do you want to do it?" Theo asked.

Masajiro shook his head and limped over to look around the corner. In response, another barrage of bullets zapped down the hall. He pulled back instantly, clenching his jaw.

"Where is Deacon going?" Theo asked. He'd originally assumed that the pirate would go for a shuttle, but they were moving away from the ports.

"The bridge, I assume," Masajiro said. "The ship's captain will be there. They will try to force our hand and then attack your ship."

"Attack? Tell me that Grace is safe, Masajiro." The police cruiser had hundreds of guns that could fire on Theo's ship or the shuttle as it crossed through space.

Masajiro nodded as he leaned back against the wall and coughed. "What is your plan?"

"You know that something's gone wrong. We should have felt the explosion by now. Send a message to Zak. Tell him to leave as soon as she's on board."

The one thing that Theo liked most about Masajiro was his ability to think. It took no time for the assassin to grasp the rest of his plan. "We use the police cruiser to bring down the machine."

"Exactly," Theo said. The ship had enough firepower to destroy the machine, not to mention half of the fleet before navigating away from the pirate ships. The explosion from the machine would take care of what remained of Deacon's fleet.

Almost as if finishing Theo's thought, Masajiro said, "That is on the assumption that the officers on board are here by happenstance and not by choice."

"Which is it, then?" Theo asked. It had been a question he'd been asking himself since he'd boarded the ship. How much control did Deacon have over these people?

Though Deacon was a monster, he'd gained a massive following; thousands of people believed him their salvation, able to take them through the gate to the Alpha Centauri system, where they could start their lives anew. Deacon's power was so great that he'd been able to plant over a dozen people on Theo's ship, ready to sabotage Theo's plans.

As if to contradict Theo's assumptions, Jacob suddenly said, "The only control Deacon has is over the men in his presence."

Kneeling at Jacob's side, Theo asked, "What do you mean, Jacob?"

Jacob could have been lying, but Theo had to believe he wasn't. Jacob had to know the price for Theo bringing him so far.

Jacob rubbed the angry bruise growing on his forehead as he said, "I...I said that Deacon...that my father only has power over those in his presence. He thinks that everyone believes the facade he projects is the real him, but they don't. I hear them whispering in the mess. They know something's wrong."

It made sense. Theo had experienced that persona on more than one occasion. Deacon tried to show that he was the saviour of the outer system, playing by civilized rules. To do that he had to create the persona of a martyr. He couldn't let the people see the beast hiding within.

"How many people actually know what he's like?" Theo asked, ducking as red lightning coursed around the wall as Deacon's people opened fire.

Jacob shook his head. "Most of the others out there are just people. They all think the pirates are someone else, but the people on our ship know it."

"Because he doesn't leave any survivors," Theo said. Galena's death was no accident. It was no stray bullet that killed his wife, but one aimed at her heart. *Rick was on the ship still, trying to find out about the engines.*

Deacon wasn't all that much different from Theo. They both inspired the people around them. They both saw their situation and wanted more for their families. Theo wasn't sure what he'd do if his father had banished him to the outer planets before he'd met Galena. *No,* Theo thought, *I wouldn't have become you.*

Theo stared at Jacob for a few seconds before saying, "If I let you up, will you act in good faith?"

The young man nodded. "I…I promise. I didn't—he was going to kill you all, but Grace…I just…I couldn't let her die."

This perspective left Theo speechless. Was it possible that Grace lived because of what Jacob had done? *Alive.* Grace had been taken before Galena was killed. It was possible, but then, it was also possible that Jacob had learned another lesson from his father. He could have learned how to lie just as easily as Deacon.

Leaning closer, Masajiro offered, "As much as I am loath to say it, they were talking quietly when I found them. Grace was not afraid."

Jacob had called her Gracie, a name Theo himself used. She wouldn't let anyone she didn't trust call her that. Theo sighed and reached out, offering his hand to Jacob, and helped him to his feet. As Jacob stood, Theo pressed him back against the wall so the next barrage of bullets wouldn't riddle him with holes.

"I learned a long time ago just to let him do his thing," Jacob said slowly as he rubbed his eyes with the palms of his hands. "If you play along, he's happy."

"And you're sure they don't know the truth?" Theo asked, throwing his hands out to encompass the ships beyond the police cruiser.

Jacob nodded. "They won't. He doesn't know how to be normal anymore. When he has an audience, even if it's small, he won't show the animal. It's…it's better that way."

Jacob had a clear vision of his father, recognizing that Deacon had been a monster when he'd killed Galena and a snake when he'd salvaged Theo's ship and killed that police captain. That officer hadn't seen what was coming. She'd believed Deacon was on the level until the last possible second, when she'd died.

"*Is* it true, sir? *Is* Gracie…Grace safe?" Jacob whispered.

Taking a deep breath, Theo said, "Yes, Jacob. She's okay."

The young man sighed, a smile growing on his face. "I know how to get them to stop. Let me talk to them. Please let me try."

Theo felt Masajiro's hand on his shoulder as he was about to refuse. Letting Jacob live was one thing, but relying on him to save them was something entirely different. Jacob was a Lovett, a family that had proven their aptitude for deceit. *Are you different from your father and grandfather? I certainly hope so.* Theo exhaled and stepped back from the wall. He stared at Jacob a few more seconds before saying, "Fine, do it."

Jacob nodded and stepped past Theo. About to step around the corner, he stopped and turned to Masajiro, a look of anguish on his face. "Are…are you going to kill him?"

Masajiro's face was emotionless as he replied, "If I must."

Jacob nodded, then moved to the corner, his steps tentative, his hands leading the way so the shooters would stop firing. He cupped his hands around his mouth to yell, "Hey! Stop firing."

"Jacob?" Theo recognized the voice as belonging to the third officer in his welcoming guard.

"Yes, it's Jacob," the young man said. "I'm coming out." Jacob lifted his hands and stepped around the corner.

Half expecting the rattle of weapons fire, Theo was surprised when the young man wasn't killed. He stood trembling, sweat pouring down his temples. Slowly, like a robot, Jacob placed one foot in front of the other and moved down the hall toward the shooters at the other end. *Don't cross us,* Theo thought to him. He was sure that if Jacob had lied and was fleeing his custody, Masajiro would kill him before he reached safety.

Theo's heart pounded. He couldn't move even to see what Masajiro was doing, but when the message finally came, Theo felt a chill run through his spine. Through the silence, Jacob yelled, "It's okay. You can come out." *Go out and get shot?*

Theo felt his legs go weak as Masajiro slipped up behind him. He'd put all his faith in the young man, but was that enough? If Jacob wanted to, he could have walked down that hall to now call Theo and Masajiro to their death.

Masajiro spoke, almost too quiet to hear. "If there is something I've learned since meeting you, Theo, it is that you know your people. If you trust him, then I trust him."

"I...I..." Theo fell silent. Could he trust Jacob? This boy now knew Masajiro was likely going to kill his father. He had every reason not to help them. *Do I still know my people?*

Theo had been able to look at a person and tell their nature and in turn, lead them across the universe. He'd formed bonds of friendship with the crew of *Galena,* not just because he'd trusted them, but because they had trusted him. The decision to go into business with Edward Lovett had changed all that. When Theo had had to hire enough crew for a fleet of ships, he'd compromised that gift. *And we paid dearly for it,* he thought. It wasn't just his wife Galena who'd died, but at least a dozen others. The loss had extended to Theo's daughter, Grace, as she languished in Deacon's captivity, and also to Theo himself, when he'd been trapped by the alcohol in Deacon's bar. *Am I qualified to pass judgement on a person's character anymore?* he wondered as he thought of the angry red welt he'd left on Giselle's face.

Theo closed his eyes and pressed his palms against his temples. "How I wish you were here, Galena. You were always my counsel. You'd have kept Gracie safe."

Masajiro grunted as he shifted his oozing shoulder against the wall. When he was able to speak, he whispered, "Jacob did that, Theo. He kept her safe."

Safe, Theo thought as he took a deep breath and stepped out into the cross corridor. The hair on his arms stood on end as he forced himself to breathe. *In and out. In and out.*

The corridor was designed for combat, with several baffles built into the wall where a defending army could take cover while they fired down the hall. When they were forced to retreat, another set of baffles would open farther down the hall and they would abandon the first. It was behind one of those three-foot half doors that their attackers knelt, their weapons still trained on Theo and his companion.

The acrid smell of burning plastic made Theo glance to the walls where the energy weapons had burned as they hit. *They've carved a groove in the wall,* Theo thought as he looked at the baffle door that should have swung out beside him. Instead of a shield door, there was a puddle of goo on the floor, melted in the heat of the blasters.

The man Theo recognized from his trio of guards was gone. The other two officers kept their rifles on Theo as he inched forward until he came up beside them, close enough to see their fingers twitching slightly. When Theo reached their position, Jacob turned to the officers. "Go to the shuttle room and secure it. Don't let anyone come through. Not even me. Do you understand?"

They're leaving, Theo thought as the two men nodded and jogged off to their new duty. *What did you tell them, Jacob?*

The young man met his gaze and nodded, then motioned for Theo to follow. "Come on. We have to stop my father."

When Jacob turned away, Theo realized why he was helping them. *You've felt that pain yourself, haven't you?* Theo thought as he saw the dark scar that ran down Jacob's neck and disappeared under his neckline.

Though Masajiro had staunched the blood pouring from his wounds, he was obviously weakened, his steps slower and his voice quieter as he said, "Deacon will be convincing the ship's captain that the pirates are on your ship. He will likely be trying to tell him that he needs to send an assault team."

"Then we have to stop him," Theo said.

Deacon was trapped on the bridge, hoping to carve out his new empire from the ashes of his old one. It was going to come down to how well Theo and Deacon could sway a crowd. Theo smiled. *Now we're playing* my *game.*

When they reached the bridge, Deacon was in mid-conversation, his arms gesturing wildly as he said, "Captain Kai, you have to understand, you have been boarded by pirates."

Walking onto the bridge, Theo instantly recognized the captain. "There are no coincidences."

"What?" Masajiro asked quietly.

Turning his head, Theo repeated, "There are no coincidences." The question was whether Captain Kai was a captain who'd saved Theo as she patrolled the skies above Earth, making it a good chance that he would win this war of words, or whether she had been in Deacon Lovett's pocket from the beginning and was now stationed closer. Either option would make for a short conversation. "I know Captain Kai," he said to Masajiro. "We've met before. What are the chances that she was randomly assigned to this detail?"

Masajiro sighed before saying, "Next to zero."

Overhearing their conversation, Jacob said, "She was assigned to us recently after…after Deacon said you killed the last captain," Jacob said softly. "I promise that my father didn't know her before she showed up. But then…"

"Then what?" Theo pressed. He furrowed his brows, trying to piece together the last bit of the puzzle.

Deacon had led two lives—one as the supposed saviour of the system, bringing all of the stations orbiting Jupiter together under one rule. Thousands of ship captains had flocked to his banner in hopes that he would keep them safe from crooked police or diabolical pirates. Deacon pretended to be a messiah, keeping them safe by all means. Those means, however, were the very things that kept those people up at night. The monster that Deacon truly was surpassed any of their worst nightmares. He pillaged and raped, killing anything that was good and whole in the universe.

All to get back at your father for sending you out here, Theo thought as he stared at the pirate. Deacon Lovett was no different from his father. Both were trying to carve out an empire—the elder Lovett with money, the younger with devotion. *Absolute power corrupts absolutely,* Theo thought as he took his first step onto the bridge.

Theo knew that Captain Kai was somehow mixed up in Deacon's dirty dealings, but the question he had to ask was, how? Was she a willing participant or an unlucky bystander? Was her commendation for saving Theo on the *Galena* an exile? But then, how could they communicate? Out here, Deacon was a hero, but the military knew otherwise. They wouldn't have sent Kai to be his liaison. She must have volunteered. *No, she couldn't have just volunteered. She had to have help.*

"My father didn't recognize her when they met," Jacob insisted.

"This is another play," Theo said to Masajiro as they left Jacob against the wall. "Take Deacon."

The bridge of the police cruiser was similar in design to Theo's own ship, with the captain's seat at the centre of the room and the operations seats fanning out around it. A dozen long-range communications technicians were focused on their own terminals. *Likely looking for my shuttle.* The room was blindingly bright. Theo squinted as he looked around at the officers, gauging their reaction to his presence. *You and you, gone. You, a maybe.* Several began to look at each other, silent questions passing between them. *Good. Keeping talking.* Confusion meant they didn't know what was happening. They were as curious about the man and his demands as Kai wasn't.

Stepping into the centre of the bridge, Theo said, "Captain Kai."

The woman spun so fast that Theo heard her foot stomp down heavily to stop her. "Captain Stinson? I—I heard you went to Alpha Centauri."

"Oh?" Theo said with a quick glance to Deacon. Masajiro inched closer, looking more alert. The stims that he'd injected into his thigh were beginning to take effect. Theo focused on Captain Kai. "I guess you didn't hear that I was waylaid in my travels."

"Oh. No, I didn't," Kai said slowly. *Build a house of lies and you won't know where the door is, my dear.* They'd called Theo by name when they'd invited him aboard.

"I'm sure," Theo whispered. The woman sitting at the communications station had heard. Her eyes went wide and she snapped her head up to look at Kai. She began furiously typing something at her terminal. He had his own audience now.

"Captain Kai, this is your pirate, right here," Deacon said, pointing at Theo.

"Captain Stinson? A pirate?" Kai asked, playing into Deacon's oration. They were well acquainted. *You weren't helping waylaid travellers, were you? You were cleaning up the mess.* Theo shook his head. He'd thought he'd found a person with honour when she'd brought her small shuttle to their rescue.

Looking around quickly to the officers, Deacon said, "Things happen, I know. But after Mr. Stinson lost his wife and his second ship, his life...well, I can appreciate his position, just not his actions. Look up his file. He was arrested a few months ago for piracy on my ship. Don't take my word for it, check your files."

Do you think them fools? Theo wondered as he looked around at the officers. None of them feigned disinterest now; they all stared at him, their work forgotten. They had to know the circumstances of that situation. They weren't naive recruits.

"You were all there when you towed his ship back to Jupiter. A ship he'd abandoned, I might add," Deacon said.

Theo glanced at the communications officer as she continued to type at her computer terminal. The screen flashed to a picture of him when he was younger. *No grey hairs back then,* Theo thought.

"Captain Kai, do you know Captain Masajiro?" Theo asked. He had to move quickly. Deacon had said Masajiro had been on the ship before. Masajiro had captained the station before. *Please be who you say you are.*

Kai turned toward the assassin, the colour draining from her face. She recognized Masajiro and immediately looked to Deacon, her eyes flashing. *Is that a message to attack or flee?*

Determined to bring Deacon down, Theo knew he had to deal with Captain Kai first. He had no false hopes that Kai would prove to be an asset. *Perhaps I can pit your crew against you?* Theo wondered as he stared at the woman. The communications officer would soon know that Theo was deputized, something Deacon couldn't boast. *But I can't assume all these people are clean, even if Masajiro thinks it.*

Deacon was adept at telling lies. In his darkest hour he would be his strongest, as desperation fueled him. *A charade it is, then,* Theo thought. He would perform for the people and determine whether Masajiro's faith was warranted.

Smiling Theo took several steps toward the captain. He could see that Deacon was shifting his weight from foot to foot, as if readying to spring for the door. He scratched his arms as if something were crawling on his skin.

Theo nodded to Masajiro as he drew breath to speak. "Oh, Captain Kai, Deacon has lied to you all. He is the pirate. Think about it. If you've been here long enough, you've heard the rumours. You know that I didn't arrive until well after the piracy began. Did I purposely blow up my own ship?"

Captain Kai was silent as she seethed, her nostrils flaring as she stared at Deacon. *You're hoping that he just shoots us,* Theo thought as he noticed the glint of a weapon tucked into the back of the man's belt.

Theo knew he couldn't beat Deacon in a fight, and Masajiro was bleeding again, weakened to the point that he had to lean against the communications officer's console. One of the other bridge officers left his post to administer assistance with a medical kit he'd pulled from the wall. *I have to finish this quickly,* Theo realized. If he didn't surround himself with Captain Kai's crew, Deacon would win.

"Lieutenant Davies, please call security," Captain Kai called out. *Going for the kill a little early, aren't we?* Theo thought. If he'd learned anything during his time as a ship's captain, it was timing. Asking for trust from a crew before they were willing to offer it themselves was asking for a mutiny.

"So, what did Deacon ask for?" Theo pressed. "Did he demand you fire on a ship that hasn't done anything yet? Wound her, I suppose? Tell me, are those the actions of an honourable man? Go ahead, look at the crew manifest." Manifests weren't an exact science, Theo knew. They could be tampered with and they could be delayed. As far as the official manifest noted, Theo's own son Petr still occupied his room, as did two dozen family members of others. *You don't need to know that, though,* Theo silently said to the crew as they raced to confirm his words.

With his moment of opportunity closing, Theo turned to the lieutenant at the communications terminal and said, "Let me tell you all a story—and by all means, I do suggest that you verify it by any means." He knew those means were a quantum radio, designed to have a constant connection to the main datanet on Jupiter Station, where Lieutenant Hollingsworth presided.

Theo turned so his chest was fully exposed to Deacon's weapon. *Go ahead, prove to me you're civilized.* "It's been so long that I can't remember... My ship was attacked by pirates when we were on our way to Earth. Now, how many of you believe in coincidences? I surely don't."

Kai stepped toward Theo, a look of horror on her face. He could see by her quick glances that she was looking to the officers she knew she could trust. *Ah, I was right about you, and you, but not you,* Theo thought as he followed her gaze. Kai was weighing her options for when she had to bolt from the room. She stopped and said, "Lieutenant Davies, where are the security officers?"

The woman was silent long enough for Theo to interject, "You know what the officer's name was that miraculously appeared to ferry my people back to Earth after I'd lost my ship? It was Captain Kai. Now, what a coincidence, that she is the captain of a ship sent out to deal with salvage operations."

Focused on Kai, Theo didn't realize that Masajiro and Deacon had started exchanging blows, the former in a defensive position, fending off the latter's powerful swings.

"Oh, one question, Captain Kai," Theo said. "Who paid you off if it wasn't Deacon?" The accusation was enough to elicit a gasp and even a few whistles. *You're impressed with my audacity. Good.*

"How dare you?" Kai asked immediately. "I am a military officer. Above reproach. My career has been exemplary since I joined. You—"

Theo knew the communication officer would have taken the initiative to call up the captain's file just as she had pulled his. The lieutenant would already know that he was deputized. *But what are you going to do with that information? Will you share it?* In seconds, she would see the information that Theo could only guess at.

There had to be a connection between Kai and Deacon, but that connection had to come from somewhere on Earth. That connection had to be high and long-standing, having occurred long before Kai had rescued Theo. What connection could occur between a ship's captain and a pirate? A pirate whose family was in the business of transportation. And building ships.

There were no coincidences. *Do you have it?* Theo silently asked the communications officer as he slowly turned his gaze on her. The woman swallowed hard as she looked from Deacon to Kai, her mouth hanging open. *I've got you now.*

Glancing at Masajiro, Theo realized the man was starting to waver. Sweat poured down to mingle with the blood and his step was slower as he limped toward Deacon. *Not this time. You're not getting the luxury of a fight.*

Focusing on Kai, Theo said, "So when did you cross paths with Edward Lovett?"

"I-I—" the woman sputtered as she tried to respond, but it was too late for her to dig herself out of the hole she'd created. She was caught; what mattered was whether her people cared. What mattered was whether they remembered why they'd joined the police in the first place. Did they still have the fire to achieve greatness, or were they jaded or worse, corrupted?

Theo still couldn't understand why Kai had protected him so long ago if he was only a pawn in a greater game of chess. *Chess.* Theo envisioned the game piece that Lovett's grandson had fidgeted with the first time they'd offered him the opportunity to leave Earth. *More like set the trap,* Theo thought, and that suddenly slapped his hands together.

"That's it isn't it? It isn't Deacon."

It wasn't Deacon Lovett who Kai worked for, but Edward. It was his great game of chess, not his son's. *You sad fool. You're only another piece,* Theo thought as he looked at the silent monster at the centre of the bridge.

Theo knew now that his first ship hadn't fallen to pirates, but to a much greater threat. Edward Lovett had destroyed his ship, not even caring that Theo's son had been on board. Like a ping-pong ball, Theo had bounced from one obstacle to another, all placed meticulously by Edward Lovett, transportation magnate. Theo had been given an opportunity to leave Earth only as a veiled attempt to get him to take the ships beyond Mars to Jupiter. *It wasn't Deacon I was hiding my ships from,* Theo thought as he looked to the wounded Masajiro. *Edward Lovett didn't want the military to know he'd rebuilt his machine. A machine capable of controlling two star-systems.* Deacon was Edward Lovett's queen, moving from one side of the board to the other.

As if with an afterthought, Theo slapped his forehead, his smile widening. *The jump.* The message embedded in Mykaela's ship had demanded they jump back to Earth. *It wasn't Earth, but the new machine's location.* Theo would have ended up in Deacon's hands even if four decades had gone by.

"Where are those security officers?" Kai said slowly. Her face had gone several shades darker and her breathing was laboured as she continued to glance around the room.

"Does it matter?" Theo asked. "Your ruse has been discovered. These officers know you're connected to those pirates. Your only chance is to give it up. Tell the truth."

I have you now, Theo thought as he watched the crew. They were turning his way as Captain Kai edged close to the silent Deacon.

As if on cue, Deacon stepped forward and began to speak, using his customary drawl. "Do you think these people believe you, Theodore? You are a desperate man with nothing left to lose."

"Nothing?" Theo replied immediately. "I only today recovered my daughter, whom you've held captive for over a year. Want proof? Why don't you ask your son? He sits against that wall, ready to explain."

"Surely you don't think you could threaten my son enough that he would repeat your lies," Deacon said as he stared at his son, his gaze like a dagger piercing the young man's heart.

"No," Theo said. "I don't think I could threaten him. Look yourself. I brought him here to ensure he lived, because you left him to die. That's the difference between you and me, Deacon. You destroy everything you touch, dismissing anyone who doesn't share your vision, killing those who oppose it. I, however, have faith."

"Faith?" Deacon began to laugh. "What do you have faith in, Mr. Stinson?"

Theo offered Deacon the biggest smile he could, even the corners of his eyes lifting. "I have faith in the system."

It had been a long time since Theo had given one of his faith speeches, especially to a crowd so large. *I can do this,* he thought as he soaked in their attention, watching them all until he knew every gaze was locked on him. "I have faith that these officers are going to do the right thing, Deacon. I have faith that they understand that you are an evil man. I have faith that Kai will get her comeuppance and I have faith that the universe will punish vice and reward merit. Do you know what that means? Do you understand faith?"

Theo had faith that the universe was behind him as he took two steps closer to Deacon. He could see that the man was inching his hand toward the weapon secreted in his belt. There would be no fight if the man gave up his pretenses and fired into the crowd. *Is it ballistic or energy-based, Deacon? Are you still civilized?*

Theo was surprised that it wasn't Deacon who responded to the silent taunt by pulling his weapon, but Captain Kai. Before he could respond, Theo was faced with an energy weapon poised inches from his face. The weapon wove and danced long enough to distract Theo. In a flash, Kai kicked out and slammed her boot against Theo's knee, sending him crashing to the floor, howling in pain.

"Your lies aren't welcome here, Captain Stinson," Kai began slowly as she scanned the room. "At first, I didn't believe Mr. Lovett, but now I see the error of my ways. You incite my crew even now, trying to turn them against me."

Rolling on the floor with pain lancing through his leg, Theo only heard half of what the woman was saying. *Can't you all just leave me the hell alone?* Theo silently screamed as he tried to shove the pain away and focus on what the woman said.

When Theo was able to push himself from the floor, it was only to lean against the captain's chair. Inch by inch he dragged himself up, until he stared down at the woman, his face awash in sweat. When she lifted her weapon to strike him again, he was prepared. He boxed her hand with his fist, sending the weapon skidding across the metal floor until it stopped under one of the terminals.

With the weapon out of reach, Theo looked at Deacon, realizing too late that the man had pulled his own weapon. The weapon cracked against his temple, sending him sprawling back to the floor, sliding in the same direction as Kai's weapon.

"Father, please," Jacob said, close by. He'd pushed off the wall and dragged himself to the inner circle of the bridge. He held his hand out to his father like a little child would after having a nightmare.

From his vantage on the floor, Theo could see that Masajiro had taken more injuries. Blood soaked his clothing and his back was arched as he slipped to his left knee, his head lolling to the side to reveal another gash on his temple.

"Mr. Stinson." The words sounded like a proclamation, coming from Deacon Lovett's mouth. "I have to thank you for the wonderful challenge you have offered. You have been a great adversary. To you I bow my head."

"Father, no," Jacob implored as he stepped forward and sank to his knees.

Deacon looked to Jacob, his face devoid of emotion as he said, "You're no son of mine."

The room was beginning to spin as Theo watched Deacon lift his leg and kick Jacob twice in the stomach. The young man retched. As if he'd planned the moment, Deacon danced forward until he reached Masajiro's side and gave him the same treatment, leaving the assassin lying on the floor, moaning. He danced around the man for a second, kicking him twice in the chest and again in the face, until blood spouted from Masajiro's mouth. When Deacon was finished, he turned his weapon back to Theo and smiled. "Now, where were we?"

Theodore Stinson didn't believe in coincidences. He hated the fact that his wife had been killed and his daughter taken. He hated the fact that he'd been forced to send his son away with one of the few people left he could trust. However, he didn't question that there was a reason greater than himself for the terrible events happening around him. He also didn't question the cool touch of Captain Kai's pistol when it was pressed into his hand by the officer seated behind him. *I win,* he thought. Not because he had a weapon to defend himself, but because the communications officer gave him the only thing he'd asked for: faith.

As Captain Kai stepped closer to Deacon, she crossed Theo's path. It wasn't much, but Theo had little left to draw upon. His strength was waning, and the pain in his knee was overwhelming his senses. Theo knew that if he didn't end the fight soon, it wouldn't matter. *Was the safety on or off?* Theo wondered as he tightened his grip on the weapon and lifted his arm.

Theo's world slowed to a snail's pace, as if he hung on the event horizon of a black hole. His arm moved too slowly as Deacon recognized the danger and pulled the trigger on his weapon, spraying the room with energy blasts. *Energy,* Theo thought as he started to laugh.

Theo didn't want to stoop to Deacon's level, but he didn't know what setting Kai had placed on her weapon. When he pulled it forward he only had time to fire a few short bursts before he was engulfed in energy. The reason for his laughter proved warranted, as the energy was just as quickly dissipated through the environmental suit he wore. It wasn't a pleasant sensation and Theo was sure he could smell the acrid stench of his own hair burning, but the suit absorbed most of the energy pulse.

Deacon couldn't say the same. He hit the deck, his chest gushing blood. Mouth agape, he looked at Theo, then at his wounds, then back to Theo. When he was able to muster the energy to speak, Theo could see it was the end. With his last breath, Deacon whispered, "You've killed me. I…I didn't… You've killed me." The man pitched forward, and silence overtook the room.

"Sir," a voice called out from what seemed a thousand miles away. "Sir, what are your orders?"

Theo stood, swooning, then moved to the closest seat, where he emptied the contents of his stomach. Deacon was dead. Kai was being physically restrained by a security officer who'd arrived too late to stop the carnage. Though conscious, neither Jacob nor Masajiro could stand.

"Sir," the communications officer said. "Captain Stinson, what would you have us do?"

"How should I know? You should have a chain of command to follow, don't you?" Theo asked as he sat heavily in Kai's seat, his suit crinkling deafeningly in his ears. *I am not your captain,* Theo thought as he looked at the lieutenant addressing him.

"Sir, I am following chain of command," the woman said. She pressed several buttons on her screen, then ran her thumb along the edge to push the information to the main screen at the front of the room.

As if to taunt him, Theo read in large red letters under his identification, *Deputized by Terran Military Police: Captain Theodore Alexander Stinson.*

Son of a bitch, Theo thought as he realized he'd just become the pawn of another chess player—Masajiro. Theo put his head between his knees for several seconds as he tasted bile in his mouth. *Police captain? What the hell have I done?*

Chapter 17

Finding Loyalty

T heo Stinson's heart was pounding as he marched through the corridor, his retinue close behind. *This is the only way,* he thought as he approached the hold. *They'll understand.* He knew his children would understand the decision he'd made. Petr would be enthralled, Grace would accept. Theo just wished he didn't have to show them in the plant-hold.

Theo had visited the plant-hold several times after Galena's death, but this time somehow held importance. *A true goodbye.* As far as he was concerned, his destination was the hold where his two children were waiting for him. *Safe.* Theo couldn't remember the last time his world had been so small. Instead of worrying about how he was going to save his daughter, spiriting her away from Deacon Lovett's clutches, or stopping the diabolical man's plans of domination, Theo's only goal was to see his children and grieve.

It had been weeks since Theo had returned from the police cruiser where he'd shot Deacon. He'd spent day and night, first with Grace, rocking her to sleep and whispering to her that everything would be okay, then with Petr when he returned from the shuttle with Mykaela. Theo had refused to go to the mess, instead having their food sent to his quarters. It had almost seemed real until the knocking began.

Theo sighed as he stopped at the computer terminal outside the hold and stared into the black screen. He wasn't a vain man, but he found himself checking to make sure no folds were out of place and no lint clung to the shoulders. *Just smooth the hair a bit.* He had to be perfect. He opened his mouth and ran his tongue across the mouthpiece that had been crafted for him on the police vessel. *Almost looks real.*

Theo glanced back to the officers trailing behind him and nodded. *No,* he thought. They were more than just officers now. They were family, having lost their own loved ones, having travelled through space at his side as he took on the mission to stop Deacon and his brother. *You'd be proud of them, Lena,* Theo thought as he turned back to the door and pressed the button to slide it open.

The door opened to the smell of his wife, as if she stood at the door herself to give him a hug and a kiss. He closed his eyes to inhale the scent of the flowers, knowing they would be spreading out from the shrine his son Petr had created. *Lavender,* Theo thought as he lifted his hand to gently touch his nose. Fleeting pine in one second, gone in the next. Sweet and heavy. *Lavender and cosmos,* he thought as his memories returned to their house on Earth where Galena would toil away, making sure every flower was set perfectly, scolding Theo when he placed something wrong. To Galena, the placement of the flowers had a twofold meaning. The first was the aroma, greeting her when she entered the path and the second was the beautiful canvas she enjoyed late at night, when most of the scents had been chased away by the city smog.

Theo smelled many scents he could never catalogue, even some he was sure were new to the garden, planted by the crew of Mykaela's newly named ship, *Virtue. HMCIS Virtue,* Theo thought with a smile. The ship, like his crew, had been deputized and was commandeered in the process. Mykaela and Theo were no longer her owners, but her stewards. *HMCIS Virtue* had a greater calling now.

Theo forced one step in front of the other to march into the hold where his wife had died. *No, not this one. That was a different ship,* he thought. That had been a ship without a name, a ship that he'd

personally overseen being stripped for parts, most being sent to the
depot on Mars, but others, placed in the hold of the *Virtue* for their
future endeavours; where they were going was dangerous and they
would need the supplies.

Theo opened his eyes as he entered the room, drinking in the vision
of flowers and other plants that had spread from one wall to the other.
The cook must love this place, Theo thought as he made his way down
the tidy path through the barley and wheat that spread for hundreds of
feet. Flowers dotted the field as if thrown into the air to scatter
haphazardly. *No one knew what they were creating when they added
to the garden,* Theo thought. *But it's perfect.*

Theo and his retinue slowly filled every spare bit of deck space,
taking care not to step on any of the flowers as they moved. Tentative,
Theo stepped over gardenias and asters until he paused to pluck a
sprig of acacia. *Hidden love,* Theo thought as he lifted the sprig to his
lips. Every flower had a meaning. Acacia was used at a funeral. *How
fitting.* They'd come for a funeral. *And a new beginning,* Theo silently
corrected himself.

Theo stopped beside his children as they stared up at the glass
dome and the scene unfolding above. Grace held Jacob's hand. When
he saw Theo, Jacob dropped Grace's hand. He rubbed his leg for a
second and mouthed the words, "I'm sorry."

Theo had blamed Jacob for Grace's kidnapping, but he knew better
now. Jacob had sacrificed just as much as Theo to keep her safe. Theo
nodded to Jacob and bent low enough to grab his daughter's hand so
he could place it in Jacob's. It was the least he could do for Jacob after
the young man had lost his own family.

As Theo straightened, he felt a tiny hand grab his. *Petr,* he thought
and held tight to his son's hand as the boy pulled him down. On his
knees, Theo was closer to the aroma of the flowers, and the memories
flooded his mind water breaching a dike. So close to the flowers, Theo
didn't need to close his eyes to feel Galena's hand on his shoulder or

her kiss on his lips. He was infused with her presence as he turned to his son, tears streaming down his face.

Petr cupped his hands together and lifted them to Theo's ear as he whispered, "Father, can you see it?"

Petr always had more questions than Theo could answer. *Today is no different,* Theo thought. Petr understood they were having a ceremony to celebrate their victory and mourn their dead. He understood that thousands of ships floated in the space above, flying by the dome in either direction. *You even understand what they're about to do,* Theo thought as he glanced up at the ships and the massive machine that glowed with the light of the sun, even through the tinted glass of the dome.

What Petr didn't yet understand, but Theo knew he would eventually come to, was revealed in his next question. "Father," Petr whispered into Theo's ear, "why are you dressed like a police officer?"

Theo smiled as he embraced his son. "Because, buddy, we have a new mission."

Theo didn't have a choice when he'd saved his daughter. He would have gone to the edge of the universe to save her. *In a way, I guess that's what we're going to do,* he thought as he smiled.

"Oh," Petr said matter-of-factly. He glanced up as the rest of Theo's command staff surrounded them, standing at attention, their own dress mirroring Theo's. Even Masajiro pushed himself from his wheelchair and stood at attention, saluting the plaque on the wall where the crew had listed the names of the dead. *It isn't just your room anymore, Lena,* Theo thought as he stood again and glanced around at his crew and the field of plants and flowers. The massive hold on his ship had been hers, but this belonged to his entire crew.

Theo craned his neck to look above him, where the ships were sliding closer to each other, dropping into the machine's embrace. The machine spanned the entire skyline, almost ten miles of steel and composite, all shining an iridescent yellow as electricity arced in rivulets like solar flares. *It's coming,* Theo thought as he nodded, giving the order to turn on the machine. So close to Jupiter, the *HMCIS Virtue* would siphon off enough plasma to open the bridge.

We'll be okay, Theo thought, and glanced down at his son as the boy reached out to grasp Mykaela's hand. Theo squeezed Petr's other hand as the energy coursing through *Virtue* came to a crescendo.

END OF BOOK 1

JOHN KENT

John Kent is an entrepreneur and freelance writer who lives with his family on the north shore of Lake Ontario. He splits his days between saving the world and walking dogs, whichever happens to be more cathartic. His first novel, Orphan Station, was published in 2014.

www.ingramcontent.com/pod-product-compliance
Lightning Source LLC
Chambersburg PA
CBHW020957120726
47905CB00009B/2735